Laughter in the Wind

Laughter in the Wind

A Novel

JOYCE WHEELER
AUTHOR OF MY LADY

WinePressPublishing
Great Books, Defined.

WinePress Publishing (PO Box 428, Enumclaw, WA 98022) functions only as book publisher. As such, the ultimate design, content, editorial accuracy, and views expressed or implied in this work are those of the author.

This is a work of fiction. Names, characters, places, and incidents are products of the author's imagination or are used fictitiously. Any resemblance to actual persons, living or dead, or to events or locales is coincidental.

Unless otherwise noted, Scriptures quotes are taken from the *New King James Version*, © 1979, 1980, 1982 by Thomas Nelson, Inc., Publishers. Used by permission.

Scripture references marked NIV are taken from the *Holy Bible, New International Version*®, NIV®. Copyright © 1973, 1978, 1984 by Biblica, Inc.™ Used by permission of Zondervan. All rights reserved worldwide. www.zondervan.com

Scripture references marked The Living Bible are taken from *The Living Bible*, © 1971 owned by assignment by Illinois Regional Bank N.A. (as trustee). Used by permission of Tyndale House Publishers, Inc., Wheaton, Illinois 60189. All rights reserved.

ISBN 13: 978-1-4141-1921-2
ISBN 10: 1-4141-1921-6
Library of Congress Catalog Card Number: 2010912942

Contents

THE JACKSON
RANCH HOME

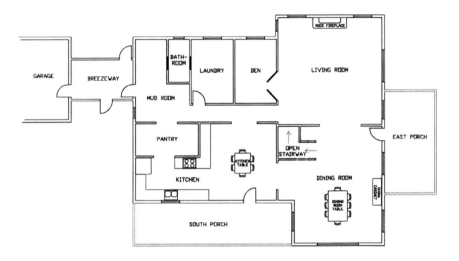

MAIN LEVEL

UPPER LEVEL

CHAPTER 1

Abbie in Somerset County, England (2001)

"DAD?" ABBIE'S VOICE was subdued in the gloom of the barn where she and her father were silently pitching out forkfuls of straw.

When he didn't answer right away, Abbie looked over at him. Ben Miller's broad shoulders were slumped, and he gave a tired grunt.

"Dad," she started again, "how was Clover when you last looked at her?"

Abbie's father glanced at her. "The same as when you looked at her twenty minutes ago."

Abbie thought for a moment as she continued to fork straw. "If she was going to catch anything, it looks like she would be showing symptoms by now, wouldn't she?"

"I'd think so, Abbie, but I've been wrong before." He leaned on his pitchfork and watched her continue to work. "You know the signs as well as I do. If she has a temp or starts slobbering or has blisters in her mouth—"

"I know the signs, Dad," Abbie said, interrupting him. The barn grew silent again as they continued cleaning Clover's stall. Trying to keep foot and mouth disease—a highly contagious virus that emaciated its victims—off the Miller farm was a consuming job in the summer of 2001. The animal epidemic had swept through England, and already there were hauntingly empty paddocks and pastures where once-healthy sheep and cattle had grazed.

It was Abbie's obsession to guard and protect her own herd, which consisted of one cow and one calf: Clover and her mischievous baby, Misfit. Six years earlier, when Abbie had been an awkward ten-year-old, her neighbor Randall Hudson had dared her to walk the narrow sides of the old stone bridge that separated their two farms. When she stumbled and fell onto the rocks below he was both disgusted and mortified. That evening, in his gruff sixteen-year-old manner, he gave her his own orphan calf. Abbie never knew if it was because he had a guilty conscience or if he didn't want the responsibility of caring for it. It didn't matter—she developed a special bond with the scraggly little calf, and Clover grew into a gentle Hereford cow, willing to follow Abbie anywhere if there was some treat involved.

Her dad broke the silence. "I'll finish here. You better go to the lab and get those disinfectant supplies ready in case we get another call," he said, motioning toward the barn door.

Abbie hung her pitchfork on the hook and with a nod toward her dad made her way over the cobblestone path to where a faded wooden rectangle sign hung over the doorway that led to her father's office. Ben Miller, DVM, it read, and it was as unpretentious as the man himself.

In the rural hills of Somerset County, where hedgerows and rock walls separated the farms that dotted the area, Ben Miller was considered both friend and family vet. His family had lived in the area for several generations, and it was the populace's opinion that there was none more dedicated to his profession than gentle Ben—unless it was young Tyler Miller, Abbie's brother, who would be joining his father as soon as he finished his veterinary studies.

Abbie could hear the voice of her great-aunt, Lena Talley, as she neared the office. Lena was her dad's aunt, a thin woman in her seventies who always wore slacks and a long-sleeved blouse. Her permed gray hair hosted a cotton beret in warm weather and a wool beret in cold weather. She had the habit of peering at people over her glasses, and her sharp blue eyes seldom seemed to miss anything. Abbie was always impressed that her mom, Lois Miller, was able to continue her bookwork while apparently listening to Lena's monologue.

"Well, now, there's that Abbie." Aunt Lena's deep, rather nasal voice announced the obvious fact to Lois as Abbie entered the office. "I was just telling your mother that I remember so well the FMD of the 'sixties. My dad wouldn't go to the barn for weeks after his herd had to be put down. Just sat in the house and moped until my mother wanted to cry—or scream, I don't know which." She permitted herself a grim smile. "You know, of course, that a lot of people are saying it's bioterrorists who've caused this whole bloody mess. And it just could be—who knows anymore?"

Before Abbie could reply, Aunt Lena, who had no children of her own but was a self-proclaimed expert on the subject, zeroed in on Abbie's recent school test scores.

"So you passed all the goose exams. You know, of course, that they aren't nearly as hard as they used to be."

Abbie and her mom exchanged knowing glances. Lena was notorious for renaming things to suit herself. She was referring to the General Certificate of Secondary Education, abbreviated GSCE, and which Abbie, at age sixteen, had just completed and passed.

"I hear you'll be joining that Clair Hudson and doing that darn-fool study of being a housekeeper to kids this fall." Lena pushed her errant glasses back to their proper place on her nose and then lowered her head so she could peer over them again. "Clair has more fool ideas than her coxy pilot brother, Randall, but I thought you had more sense than that!"

Abbie wanted to say she was going to take training to be a nanny but Aunt Lena was off on another subject.

"But zingers! Will you ever outgrow that red hair?" She gave Abbie another grim smile. "You look like your dad, Abbie. You know, of course, that isn't a bad thing, except for that hair." She turned back to Lois and shook her head. "I don't mean to be unkind, but it's a good thing she has brains, because with that red hair…"

Aunt Lena trailed off in midsentence.

Lois Miller said forcefully, "In my eyes, and in her father's eyes, she's beautiful!"

Abbie shook her head at both of them, and then went into the next room where supplies lined the small lab's shelves. Aunt Lena and her mother had argued for years over Abbie's looks. After several tearful sessions as a little girl on her mother's lap, Abbie was persuaded that Aunt Lena wasn't aware her remarks were outrageously rude. In fact, her mother often reminded her that Aunt Lena was actually very fond of her grand-niece—in her own strange way.

Abbie began to gather the disinfectants, tubs, stiff-bristled brushes, and sponges that would be needed to do a scrub-down on anyone who would enter a farm where there was a suspected outbreak. Her father had made several visits to worried farmers lately, and government procedures dictated thorough disinfecting measures be taken before entering or leaving a premise.

She was rechecking the supplies when Aunt Lena's next comment made her eyes widen in shocked agitation.

"You know, of course, Lois, the Queen's beauty contest is coming up. Why don't you have Abbie enter?" Lena's voice carried amazingly well into the lab.

"Well…" Abbie thought she heard a trace of indecision in her mother's voice.

"Absolutely not! No and no and no!" Abbie hollered from the small room. She was not beauty candidate material—even thinking of such an idea gave her an unnamed fear.

The shrill ring of the phone broke the quiet that descended in the next room. Lois quickly assured the caller that she would give the message to Ben immediately. Abbie knew by the sound of her mother's voice that she and her dad would be making a quick trip to someone's farm because the farmer suspected one of his animals was infected with foot and mouth virus.

In a very short time supplies were loaded into the vehicle and Ben and Abbie were traveling down the narrow country lane. To Abbie's mind, even the leaves on the trees hung dismally in the summer's heat.

"I'm glad you're through with school for a while, Abbie," Ben said. "With all this extra rigmarole, I need a nurse to help me."

"It'll be really nice when Tyler gets back from vet school," Abbie said, wishing her brother were there already. "Aunt Lena is always going on about 'the joys of having a son work with you'—she claims I upset all the animals with my red hair." She glanced over at her dad and grinned.

"Ah, Aunt Lena's wisdom." Ben smiled for the first time that day. His feisty aunt and her unending pearls of advice were either a source of irritation or amusement depending on the mood of the recipient.

Joe Laughten was waiting for them by the gate to his farm. The worried look on his face caused a feeling of anxiety to settle over Abbie, and she wasted no time getting out the disinfectant bucket and scrubbing every item her dad would be taking onto Joe's place.

"A rather nasty affair," Joe told Abbie's dad as she helped the vet into his paper coveralls and then his rubber suit. "I shouldn't be surprised at anything."

Finally the scrubbed Wellingtons were on Ben's feet, and he and Joe set off to inspect and examine Joe's herd of dairy cows. Abbie willed herself to wait patiently by the gate, but several times she found herself pacing back and forth, craning her neck to see where the men were.

Within thirty minutes they had returned. Both men looked upset. "Get the sign out, Abbie," her dad said heavily, shooting a dismayed look in Joe's direction.

Abbie found the dreaded poster and slowly stapled it on the gate. It was a warning to visitors that foot and mouth disease had been suspected on the premises—and it effectively sealed off Joe's place.

Ben stood just inside the gate and used his cell phone to call another vet to inspect the herd and give a second opinion. When that vet arrived, the same precautionary disinfecting took place before he went onto Joe's farm. Once again Abbie paced the road while she waited for the results. When the men returned again, that vet made the call to the Department of Environment, Food, and Rural Affairs (DEFRA) in London to confirm the diagnosis.

Joe's herd would have to be killed to keep the disease from spreading.

By late afternoon a slaughter team, a bio-security team, leak-proof lorries, and an escort vehicle were swarming over Joe's place. Abbie stood beside the silent dairyman with tears in her eyes. A lifetime of work poured into improving his herd was going to be demolished within hours. Abbie knew Joe Laughten loved his animals and had taken excellent care of them. He was the epitome of a good and faithful steward of his land and cattle.

With an unflinching voice, he gave consent to the slaughter team to kill all cloven-hoofed animals on his farm to avoid the spread of foot and mouth to surrounding farms.

Her dad slowly walked over to the gate to join the two of them. "Joe," he said with a catch in his voice, "I'm sure sorry."

"A nasty business. I guess they'll completely disinfect my place, and there'll be no livestock allowed here for six weeks. A nasty business." A slight smile crept over his homely features. "The missus says we'll take a little vacation now."

"Ah yup. You might as well." Ben tried to smile, but Abbie thought it was a failed attempt.

After she helped her dad shed the paper coveralls, and everything was double bagged to suit the bio-security team, they were allowed to leave. The twilight was deepening as they neared home.

Ben cleared his throat several times. "Abbie, I suppose you realize that our farm is right next to Joe's."

Abbie couldn't answer. The lump in her throat that had been increasing all day had become a monstrous affair, and hot tears cascaded down her cheeks.

"You know what this means now, don't you, Abbie?" he said in an unusually gruff voice.

She nodded mutely, and her dad reached over to pat her trembling shoulder affectionately.

"Ah yup. I thought you did." Ben sighed.

"Can't we take Clover and Misfit someplace else?" The words came out in heartbroken sobs.

"No, no, of course we can't." Her dad shook his head sadly. "They're probably already infected—we'd be guilty of spreading this bloody epidemic even more. The rule is that the adjacent farms have to put their animals down too."

Her dad drove into their quiet yard and shut off the car's engine. "I'm sorry, honey."

Abbie found every conceivable treat that Clover had ever liked and walked out to the small paddock where the brown and white cow and calf were. She waited by the rock wall until the gentle creature was beside her, and slowly fed her all the choice morsels.

She thought of crawling on Clover's broad back like she used to, but instead wrapped her arms around Clover's neck and buried her face into the familiar smelling cowhide and cried—again. Misfit bucked around playfully. When she didn't hear the usual laugh from Abbie, she came over and bunted her as if to say she wanted playtime, not cry time.

Until the evening shadows were long and she could barely see their outlines anymore, Abbie raced around Clover, chasing Misfit, and in turn was chased by Misfit until they were both worn out. Finally the calf plopped down beside her grazing mother and Abbie did the same. She scratched Misfit's soft ears, gazed into the liquid brown eyes, and knew it was time to leave.

"And I'm not going to say any prayers tonight, either," she sniffed, looking at the night sky. "I've prayed and prayed—every night on my knees, even—for a miracle to save Clover and Misfit." She looked in disgust at the evening stars. "For Someone who creates all things, it seems pretty pathetic that You can't save one cow and calf."

Abbie thought she never had been so relieved to see her brother's solid frame as when he strode through the kitchen door the next morning. She didn't mean to snivel, but when he hugged their mom and squeezed Abbie's arm, her tears spilled onto her cheeks.

"Chin up, old girl," he told her softly. His brown eyes so much like her own were filled with worry and compassion.

"How's Dad doing?" Tyler directed his question to Lois.

"He's exhausted. But it'll be better now that you're home for a while." Abbie's mom usually tried to find the bright side of situations.

"All of the government workers are here to… well, you know," Abbie gulped out. She looked out the kitchen window at the convergence of personnel in coveralls, and she didn't know if she wanted to chin up or run and hide under her bed.

"Yooo! Where is everybody?" Aunt Lena's brisk tone startled the three of them as she jerked open the kitchen door. "I see you finally got here, Tyler. And just in time. The road is swarming with those blasted blokes. Killing fine cattle—if I ever get my hands on the terrorist that planted all this bloody misery…"

She broke off in mid-sentence as Ben came up the path behind her. Abbie thought her dad looked years older than his normal self, and even his voice sounded older.

He ushered Aunt Lena through the door before he greeted his son. "Tyler, glad you're here. Lois, you and the others stay in the house until this business is over with."

He left abruptly with Tyler at his heels, and Lois quietly shut the kitchen door.

"And do you know that some bloody Yankee was hollering at me to get disinfected?" Aunt Lena sputtered. "As if he thought I had lice or something. I guess I gave him a piece of my mind. I've been through more of these blasted things than I care to count." She continued to grumble while Abbie and her mother ushered her into the living room, far from the activities that were taking place outside.

"There are a lot of American veterinarians helping out," Lois murmured soothingly. "Ben says he's glad they're here. It's all just more than the local vets can handle." She turned to Abbie. "Why don't you turn on the telly and we'll catch up on some news?"

"I can tell you there's nothing good on the telly. Just some blithering newsman rattling on about Tony Blair," Aunt Lena snorted. "That, and the fact that some bad egg seems to think all the farmers are getting rich from the government because they're being compensated. Those coxy nitwits should be in our shoes before they prattle on. And I do hope you'll remember we always keep our composure, Abbie. We keep a stiff upper lip. These things happen. God knows why. I'm sure I don't see a hair's worth of sense to it, but there you 'ave it."

Abbie stood by the TV screen and looked at her mother. "Should I turn it on or not?"

"Leave it off. And I'll tell you something else," Aunt Lena hardly paused for breath, "why in tarnation are we importing meat when we have good healthy beef right here in this country?" She plopped into the nearest chair and crossed one skinny leg over the other before she continued on. "That's what the news says. Get this! Somebody imported illegal meat that was infected. The scraps were fed to hogs, and the hogs caught this bloody disease, and before you can say 'horsefeathers' the whole blasted country is infected with it. Now I say let's tar and feather the importers of illegal infected meat! That's what I say!"

Abbie nodded in agreement. Her beautiful cow and calf were dead, and it was somebody's fault. Tar and feathers would be too good for the culprit!

Abbie discovered that being in the house when all the action was outside was stifling. Her mother seemed to think the same thing, and before long they wandered out the front door, leaving Aunt Lena in the living room, watching the telly after all.

When they saw Ben and Tyler talking to a tall young man, they joined them. Ben reached out to her mother and quickly drew her to his side.

"This is my wife," he said, and included Abbie by saying, "and my daughter."

"I'm sure sorry, folks. I had no idea how bad this is for you all." The young man shook his head and added, "I'm from Oklahoma, USA, and we came over to help. But there just is no way to compensate for losing your herd."

"No there's not!" Abbie burst out. "I could just shoot the bloody jerk who's responsible for all this!"

The younger man grinned and nodded his head. "I hope you realize that I'm an American and I'm on your side."

Tyler looked at Abbie and shook his head. "My sister lost her entire herd. One cow. One calf."

"They were a very special cow and calf, Tyler," Ben said softly. Reaching over to shake the American's hand, he said, "Thank you for caring. We appreciate it. Tell your government to be careful of importing food from countries with FMD or they'll be in the same fix we're in right now. It's cost our country over two billion dollars. It would cost the States many times that."

More comments were exchanged before Tyler and the American walked over to the escort car. Before long the last of the government teams was leaving and an eerie silence seemed to settle over the farm.

Abbie sat with her parents and Tyler on the terraced area in front of the farmhouse and thought she had never experienced such quiet before.

"I've been thinking," Lois finally said, "since you two are going to be working here together, we need to enlarge the lab." She looked from

Tyler to Ben. "We've talked about it before; now we have time to get it done."

"I don't want to even think about that now," Ben countered flatly. "We'd have to go into Clover's stall and I don't think Abbie could handle that."

Abbie saw Tyler look at his mother and nod an affirmation to Ben's words. She was surprised to see sparks of determination flash from her mother's eyes.

"You know, Ben, you might be surprised at what we women can and cannot handle. Anyway, this farm has always been too small to handle many animals, which is why you became a vet in the first place. With Tyler joining you, we could take our barn and make it into a larger clinic and surgery. We could start by enlarging the lab. Instead of using the compensation check to buy more cattle, we should use it to redo our vet facility."

Abbie looked at her mother and nodded. Lois was always coming up with ideas, and this one was more ambitious than most of them. "I like it, Mom. It would give us something to do—give me something to do until I leave this fall."

"Where are you planning on going this fall, Miss Abbie?" Tyler teased.

"Where Clair is, and we're both going to be nannies and get rich taking care of rich people's children!" Abbie smiled at her brother and added, "Even if Aunt Lena thinks all we're doing is housekeeping for kids!"

"Well, Clair is kind, and she's a natural with kids, but you have a temper and I can't see my little sister taking orders from a doting mama," Tyler said with a hint of humor in his voice. "I have this mental picture of my red-haired sibling bopping an overzealous parent on the head."

That remark brought light chuckles from everyone.

"Ah yup. Say, did Aunt Lena go home?" Ben asked.

"Yes! Thank God!" Lois exploded. "I've heard enough about bioterrorists to last me a lifetime."

Tyler shook his head. "She came charging up to me and declared that God rewarded the wicked rather than the good, and she for one was going to do a lot of complaining in church this Sunday."

Abbie looked away. *Aunt Lena isn't the only one who's going to complain. There's no good reason why Clover and Misfit aren't here enjoying the sun and grass. God didn't reward that good cow and her calf—no how.*

She looked over at the empty paddock and felt the lonesomeness steal into her heart all over again.

Sunday dinner at the Millers was a subdued affair. Abbie was grateful that Clair Hudson had joined the family after church, but even her light comments seemed to fall heavily on the assembled company.

The minister at their local church had prayed for the families affected by the disease, and everyone said that was appreciated. They also said they appreciated Ben Miller. Abbie knew her dad felt responsible for preventing more outbreaks of FMD in the neighborhood. He seemed to be redoubling his efforts to keep the disease away from everyone else.

After dinner dishes had been cleared away, Abbie helped her mother carry in the peach pie for dessert. To everyone's surprise, Randall Hudson walked briskly into the dining room.

"I say, is that some of your delicious pie?" he asked, and gave Lois Miller a hug.

"Hey, Randall, you old bum!" Tyler bounded out of his chair and Abbie winced at the bone-crushing handshake he gave Randall. The two young men were good friends as well as neighbors. More than once Abbie had heard Tyler say he appreciated his friend's keen observance of situations and equally astute solutions.

Within moments, Randall was seated beside his sister, Clair. Extra tea had been poured and a plate with peach pie topped with whipped cream sat before him.

"So you're home for a couple of days, Randall," Ben said. He seemed to be toying with an idea. "And Tyler is home for a couple of days." He picked up his cup of tea and looked speculatively at the two young men. "You know, I've been thinking of expanding the lab. Maybe the three of us could start by tearing out some walls."

Abbie looked at her mother and shook her head in bemusement.

Lois raised a well-defined eyebrow. "What a wonderful idea, Ben," she countered dryly.

The talk quickly drifted to other topics. Randall was an airline pilot, and he often amused both families with tales of travel. He and Clair were both tall and slender with light-colored hair and gray eyes—definitely a Hudson characteristic, Aunt Lena often declared. But where Clair was the epitome of tact and kindness, Randall could be blunt and often abrasive.

Maybe Randall is conceited, or as Aunt Lena says, coxy. Or maybe he's just too darn confident of himself. Either way, he's sort of a pain. Abbie felt a twinge of guilt for thinking it. After all, Randall was the one who gave her Clover, and at the very least she should be grateful to him that she had the happy memories of her gentle Hereford.

It was soon decided to make a tour of the lab and barn and figure out their plan of action. All six of them trailed out to the barn, discussing ideas and suggestions.

Tyler and Abbie were in Clover's stall when Randall walked in and began to knuckle-tap the wall between the lab and stall. "I think we could take this wall out in no time—it doesn't seem to be a load-bearing one," Randall observed. "You're not saying anything, Abbie. I say, that's pretty unusual for you."

"This was Clover's stall." Abbie thought she shouldn't have to say anymore than that.

"Clover? Oh, yes. Clover, the goofy calf I gave you." Randall shrugged his shoulders dismissively.

"She was not goofy!" Abbie bristled, and instantly decided he was completely tactless.

"This must be a picture of her." Randall took down a framed picture of Abbie riding on the back of her pet and handed it to her rather cheekily.

"Look, kid, she was a cow, just a cow. Get over it." He gave no indication that he noticed her flushed cheeks and moist eyes. "And one more thing," he continued. "If you're going to college, get that blasted red hair out of those braids and get it cut." He turned on his heels and walked smartly out the door.

Abbie thought her brother was strangely silent. She gave him a quick glance before doing what she felt any respectable and outraged English girl would do in like circumstances.

Abbie squinted her eyes and stuck out her tongue at Randall's departing back.

"Bravo, old girl. Bravo," was her brother's quiet response.

CHAPTER 2

Four Years Later (2005)

$\mathcal{T}$HE VILLAGE FOLKS said it was a whirlwind romance, but Aunt Lena said anyone with half a brain could tell that Tyler Miller and Clair Hudson had eyes for each other for a long time. The couple had decided on a fall wedding, and they often were seen walking hand in hand with a smitten look prone to young lovers.

When Abbie walked into her father's vet office a week before her brother's wedding, she knew her Aunt Lena would be there. She had seen the bike Lena used propped against the wall of the converted barn. Aunt Lena had two forms of transportation: her trusty bike with its flowered white basket, and her CBV, as Aunt Lena herself had dubbed it. The surrounding community agreed she had aptly named her old jeep the "Citizens Beware Vehicle"—her driving was atrocious.

Lena was sitting on one of the high stools in front of the customer counter.

"Well, there's that Abbie," she said. "I hardly see you anymore since you started taking nanny jobs and traveling all over the country. You know, of course, that I also heard you've had boyfriends. Now you just be careful with the men, young lady."

Lena peered with knowing eyes over her glasses at Abbie and then quickly turned to Lois.

"She's turned into a nice-looking young woman." Lena cleared her throat and leaned conspiratorially toward Lois. "I don't mean to be unkind, but I wonder if she knows anything—"

Abbie's mom interjected forcefully. "Her father and I think she has both brains and beauty."

Abbie grinned at both of them and walked over to give her great aunt a hug. It always amused her that Aunt Lena acted miffed over that display of affection.

"You know, of course, what you should do, Lois," Lena continued as she squirmed away from Abbie. "You should have her enter the Queen's beauty contest."

"Well…" Lois was hesitant.

"Absolutely not! No and no and no!" Abbie stated firmly. The three women went through this same scenario every year.

"I hear you're the bridesmaid and Randall is the groomsman at this big wedding coming up," Lena said, pulling her cotton beret more firmly onto her permed hair. "You know, of course, the old saying, 'Always the bridesmaid and never the bride.' I remember when my mother thought I'd never catch a man and then after I caught Floyd she thought she'd never see me again. She cried the whole time before the wedding. That's when Floyd said as long as she felt that bad we may as well move in with her and Daddy." Lena peered over her glasses at Abbie. "That was a great idea, I might add. Floyd helped Daddy, and Daddy gained another cribbage player."

She tilted her head and actually looked through her lenses at Abbie.

"You know, of course, that I was able to stay with my parents all my life, and you would do well to consider a young man who would live close by…Lois, why aren't you answering that phone?"

"I guess I thought it was my head ringing," Lois muttered as she picked up the receiver.

While her mother was on the phone, Abbie turned to gaze at the remodeled office with her usual feeling of satisfaction. The family had spent a lot of time working on the old barn, and when they were finished they were proud of the large surgery room, expanded lab, and most of all—for Lois's sake, who worked there daily—the bright and cheerful office. Abbie's family's practice had increased. In the past year, her dad had finally restocked his small farm with some select Hereford cattle.

Her father asked Abbie if she wanted to invest in any more livestock, but she was quick to say no. She was a young lady now with other interests. Deep in her heart, however, she knew the reason she abandoned the idea was her fear of losing more cattle to FMD. Over the years she had put away her childish pout at God, but she often thought He didn't listen to her any more now than when she had prayed for Clover and Misfit four years earlier.

Abbie's mom carefully replaced the receiver and looked at her. "That was Clair and she wondered if you would join her and Tyler at the pub for lunch."

When Abbie started to say no, her mother interrupted her. "I guess that American vet that was here a few years ago is there and wants us all to come, but Ben and I need to close up shop early and run some errands for the wedding." She looked at Abbie and smiled. "He said he wondered if you had killed any bioterrorists yet."

"You know, of course, if there were any around, Abbie could shoot 'em and I'd bury 'em," Aunt Lena said emphatically.

She and her grandniece exchanged high-fives on that one.

Abbie decided to ride her own bike to the pub. It was a short distance, and the September day begged enjoyment. She pedaled slowly and savored the early fall sights, and she thought if only she could have gracefully gotten out of this lunch, she would have gone fishing in the stream between the Miller and Hudson farms.

The lunch proved to be what Abbie had thought it would be. The American and his wife were friendly and talkative—indeed, he kept them entertained for more than an hour with stories about his vet work in the southwestern United States, relating story after story about the cowboys and their broncs and cattle herds.

Typical pub stories, Abbie decided, and instantly could hear Aunt Lena say the same, sniffing in disdain.

However, to Abbie's surprise, both Clair and Tyler seemed fascinated with all the tales. They kept asking questions, which fueled both the Americans to even greater heights of storytelling, and left Abbie with a keen desire to find an excuse to politely leave.

Throughout the following days, Abbie noticed Clair and Tyler were talking more about the United States than they were about their own wedding. At any given time they would burst out with some tidbit they thought others would enjoy hearing about the American west. They brought out maps and pored over places with strange sounding names, such as "Oklahoma," "Timbuktu," and "Albuquerque."

Meanwhile, Abbie fretted about the many details of Clair and Tyler's wedding—which they seemed oblivious to—and decided she was ready to see them married and off on a honeymoon.

It was an emotion she was shocked to find she shared with Randall Hudson.

After the wedding rehearsal she had stayed at the church to tweak some flower arrangements. As the rest of the wedding party trailed out the sanctuary's old wooden doors to the hall where lunch would be served, she became absorbed in her task and was startled to hear Randall's voice close behind her.

"Are you able to discuss something other than your cow?" he asked her.

She turned to look at him with questioning eyes. Randall usually caught her off guard with his strange remarks, but throughout the years she had formed an odd attachment toward him. He seemed to appear in her life when she had problems he assured her only he could solve, and afterward he would disappear for months at a time. She was his best friend's pain-in-the-neck little sister, he would remind her, and she would retort that he was her brother's pain-in-the-neck best friend.

Now he seemed genuinely annoyed. "All the Millers and soon-to-be Millers want to talk about is vet stuff and America. Why doesn't anyone want to hear about pilots and England?"

"Or nannies and England?" Abbie rejoined

"Or Bristol and England?"

"Or Somerset County and England?"

"Or cider and England?"

"Or—in fact," Abbie shook her head, "why in the heck can't they talk about their wedding? I never thought I'd be so relieved to have them married and gone." She felt guilty the moment she had said it.

"Randall," Abbie implored, putting her hand on his arm, "I didn't mean that at all. I think the world of Clair and Tyler. I just have wedding jitters. As Aunt Lena keeps pointing out to me, I'm more uptight than the bride."

For a brief moment he covered her hand with his own and smiled down at her. Even in comfortable trousers and a short-sleeved shirt, he looked the professional pilot. "Well, Miss Uptight, let's head over to the hall and get this lunch over with."

"Do you know how many luncheons I've been to this week?" Abbie asked as they walked slowly out of the stone church. He shook his head as she answered, "More than I want to count."

"That's what you get for being the bridesmaid," he said, not totally unsympathetic. "Do you want to know how many bachelor parties I've had to go to?"

She looked at him disgustedly. While she had painstakingly recorded hundreds of gifts in a lovely bound book for Clair and Tyler, Randall had managed to absent himself until the previous night's one and only bachelor party. She shook her index finger at him and groused, "One bloody party, Randall Hudson. And I bet all you did at that one was drink like a sop!"

His gray eyes twinkled at her. They were at the bottom of the stone steps, and he stopped and turned to look at the old church behind them. Its walls were covered with ivy, and the old hewn rocks had slight cracks and depressions in them.

"How old do you think this church is?" he asked.

Abbie frowned and tried to remember her history. "Probably a couple of hundred years old. Why?"

He was silent for a while before he finally turned and resumed their walk toward the fellowship hall next door. "I was thinking how disappointed those folks who built it would be if they knew England was considered secular now."

Abbie could feel her frown deepen. "That's a bunch of rubbish. There's Christian people all over the country."

"How many young people go to this church?"

"Well…quite a few. However," she launched into her best Aunt Lena impersonation, "there is one young man I know of that hardly ever comes."

"Could you possibly mean me?" When she nodded he was quick to defend himself. "I'm hardly ever here on Sundays."

"Even when you are here, you don't come."

He stopped abruptly and looked down at her. "Why, Miss Abigail, I didn't know you kept track of me!"

"I don't!" she protested hotly. "But Aunt Lena does."

He gave a derisive snort and resumed walking. "Lena goes to church for the sole purpose of seeing who is and isn't there."

"That's not exactly true, Randall; she does have her faith." Abbie lapsed into silence as they walked into the hall. If she wanted to be honest, she'd have to admit Randall had a valid point about Aunt Lena.

The wedding day dawned clear and beautiful and it occurred to Abbie as she tore from one place to another on her pointed high heels that she ought to feel grateful at least for the weather. The Miller-Hudson union flowed along without any major problems, to her great relief. As usual, the mothers cried, the fathers shook hands, and the young people in the wedding party were lively and handsome.

The day that had caused her so much trepidation flew by, and she mentally clicked off each event until at last it was time for the bride to throw her bouquet and the happy couple left for their honeymoon.

It seemed to Abbie as she headed down to the stream to fish the next afternoon that she should give some profound thought to the whole matter of life's changes. Weddings were important events, she reasoned. Dads giving away daughters, young men accepting new responsibilities, and, of course, mothers facing the empty nest challenge. However, after all the preparations and wedding worries the only thing she wanted to think about was enjoying some time alone. She found her favorite spot and threw the line in rather absent-mindedly.

Abbie sat on the mossy bank and yawned. She almost hoped she didn't catch anything to save the work of cleaning fish. She watched the lure with increasingly sleepy eyes. The water gurgled under the stone bridge and made its way through several little cascades until it once again joined together and headed its cheerful way to the ocean. It was like a lullaby, she reflected, lulling her to sleep.

More than once she found herself nodding off until finally she stretched out on the ground, still holding her pole. It wasn't long before her fingers relaxed their hold, and the pole slipped unnoticed out of her hand.

Much later, when she was suspended between sleep and partial wakefulness, she noticed irritating tickles on her nose. She wrinkled it several times, and rubbed her hand over her whole face, lapsing back into her half-formed dream.

What could be on her forehead? Same irritating tickle. Without opening her eyes, she raised her hand slowly and swatted herself. As she lay there collecting her thoughts from sleepdom, a feather seemed to be jumping from one spot of her face to another. She heard a muffled chuckle, and opened her eyes quickly. Randall was leaning over her with an innocent blade of grass.

"You have ten freckles on your nose," he informed her. "Also, there are three on your left cheek and five on your right cheek."

"Did you count any on my chin?" Her voice was croaky.

"None there."

"What about my forehead?"

"I couldn't tell without pushing aside your hair."

"I see."

"Also," he said as he straightened up, "you have lost your fishing pole."

She sat up so suddenly she felt dizzy. "What?"

"I was fishing downstream when this unmanned pole, excuse me—unwomaned pole—came floating along quite nicely."

"Was there a fish on it?"

"No, worst luck."

"I hope you rescued it for me?" One never knew if Randall was in a rescue mode.

He patted the ground beside him, and she gave a sigh of relief to see her pole resting on the grass.

"I must have dozed a bit." She yawned slowly, remembering to cover her mouth.

"Yes, well, you have grass in your hair, and probably all manner of little creatures on your body." He pulled several blades of grass off her hair to prove his point. "Why didn't you nap like a normal person—in the house on a bed?"

She gave him a perplexed look. "I didn't think I was sleepy until I sat down here."

"You stayed up way too late last night at the wedding dance."

"I didn't stay up any later than you did—in fact, you brought me home, remember?"

He laughed softly. "Of course I remember. I wasn't that foxed."

Abbie looked at him with a raised eyebrow. "You were a little foxed—you insisted on taking all three of the bridesmaids home and had to ask directions to get to our place."

He raised his own eyebrows at that information, and they sat side by side without saying anything for a while.

"Clair and Tyler make a good couple," he finally murmured offhandedly.

Abbie nodded. "I've always followed Clair; she studied child care and became a nanny and so did I—we both worked at some of the same places. I'll miss her when I go back to my present job."

"So are you going to follow her now and get married like she did?"

Abbie gave him a withering look. "I think not."

He smiled at her and slowly stood. Reaching down for her hand, he pulled her effortlessly to her feet.

"Well, young lady," he paused while he reached down to fetch the wayward pole, "you better head home even though you haven't caught anything to brag about."

She brushed bits of earth and grass off her jeans before she reached for her pole. "Thanks, Randall. Dad gave this to me—I wouldn't have wanted to lose it." She gave him a grateful smile and turned to leave.

And then as an afterthought, she turned back. "When are you going back to Bristol?"

"This evening. When are you leaving?"

"Tomorrow morning. I wonder if our folks will be glad to have everyone gone and their peace and quiet back?"

He was standing straight and tall with his arms folded across his chest and an amused twinkle in his eye. "I would imagine there's a certain relief to have the chicks gone from the nest."

She shook her head at him, and with a wave she turned toward home. She hadn't gone very far when she heard him shout her name. She stopped and turned around. He was holding up a fine line of fish and grinning like a Cheshire cat.

For some reason, the months that followed became a source of frustration to Abbie. She supposed she was trying to do too much; at least that's what everyone kept telling her. She was taking extra university courses along with being employed as a nanny, and there was always some test to study for or some major crisis with the children whom she was caring for or some family member at home who needed a listening ear. And then there were the sunsets.

Or, rather, there was the lack of sunsets. She didn't know why it became an issue in her life that she could never see a sunset. There were too many trees around the farm, too many buildings where she was working, and too many hours inside houses where there was no view. She was becoming far too cranky and sometimes her little charges told her that very fact.

If all of that wasn't enough to rankle her, Clair and Tyler's news of heading to the United States in August put the frosting on the cake. They were excited about Clair receiving a childcare job on a ranch—a very rare opportunity, Clair enthused. Tyler had the privilege of working with a local vet plus the opportunity to study at an agricultural university. They'd be gone nine months, so Tyler was looking for someone to help his dad. Abbie had to force enthusiasm in her voice when they talked with her about the move, and afterward she felt petty that she couldn't rise to their same excited level.

But it was when she was in church that she became the most agitated. She either felt the sermons were abysmally bland or blatantly forward. Surely a preacher could talk about what Christians need to do without all this "personal walk with God" stuff…this "ask the Lord what He wants you to do" stuff…this "give your heart to God" stuff. All that stuff was a source of war in Abbie's soul. Why wasn't it enough just to be a common, ordinary Christian trying to do what a Christian should do? In the back of Abbie's mind was a picture of what she thought doing what the Lord wanted her to do would look like—putting her red hair in a bun and being a missionary in Africa.

Absolutely not. No and no and no!

Such were Abbie's thoughts as she drove home on a drizzling Sunday morning in April. Her mood was as gray as the day. She was meeting her folks at church, and because it was Mr. and Mrs. Hudson's wedding anniversary, the two families were having a small celebration at the Millers' afterward.

Abbie could hear the first hymn being sung as she walked up the old stone steps, and the door gave its usual creak as she slowly pulled it open. Not finding any easily available spot in the back pews, Abbie walked on tiptoe so her heels wouldn't clatter on the wood floor. She finally reached a partially empty pew halfway up the aisle.

"The Old Rugged Cross" droned on to the third verse, and she debated whether to bother to find the correct page or just hum along until they reached the chorus. She could see her parents several pews ahead of her, and she began a systematic search for other people she knew. Suddenly she gave a small start, and then a halfhearted wave. She had discovered Randall with his folks directly across from her.

He had caught her eye and was discreetly pointing behind him. When she followed his intended direction, she gave another halfhearted wave to Aunt Lena.

By this time the quavering soprano behind her had geared up for the chorus and was cherishing that old rugged cross. Abbie decided she could cherish it just as well as the next person and joined in with great gusto to exchange it some day for a crown.

It seemed cold and damp in the church. It seemed like the sermon took forever. It seemed that no matter how hard Abbie tried, she couldn't keep her mind on the minister's message.

It seemed like a very long hour.

The light lunch Abbie's mom had promised turned into a bountiful buffet. Once everyone was warm and their stomachs pleasantly full, there was a companionable lull in the conversation around the huge dining room table.

Tyler cleared his throat several times, and Abbie noticed he looked at Clair with increasing nervousness.

"Well, everyone," he said, breaking the silence, "Clair and I have some news to share with you." He put his hand on Clair's shoulder, and she placed her hand over his and beamed.

"In about six months, there is going to be the sound of two"—he held up two fingers—"little babies. Clair and I are expecting twins in October!"

The group's complacency completely evaporated. Everyone started talking at once and congratulations rolled around and around the table. It was an exciting event for both families—the first grandchild or, in this case, grandchildren, to grace the families. Clair and Tyler admitted they'd had trouble keeping the secret to themselves, but they wanted to make the announcement when all the family was together.

When there was some semblance of quiet, Aunt Lena, who had remained strangely silent, peered over her glasses at Clair. "You know, of course, I suspected this. You looked a little pudgy to me. I don't mean to be unkind, but what are you going to do about this darn fool trip to the States?"

Tyler answered with a slight edge to his voice. "It's been canceled, of course."

Aunt Lena wasn't through. "Canceled? What about the deposit Clair made to her agency? Are you going to get that back?"

When they both shook their heads, she scanned the whole assembled group before her eyes rested on Abbie.

"You know, of course, Abbie, that you must go in their place. It's perfectly obvious that the money wouldn't be wasted that way, and you could see a little of the world and get your good humor back before you come home and settle down."

"Absolutely not!" Abbie said flatly. "No and no and no!" She glared at Lena before adding, "Is there any part of this no that you don't understand?"

Aunt Lena clucked and looked away. "There's really no use being mule-headed like your father is prone to be at times."

Abbie's dad sat up straighter and shook his head, only slightly amused.

"You know, of course, that this nanny business is also nonsense, about as silly as going to the United States, but young people nowadays don't often use their common sense. You may as well make a little money and come back here and try to catch a man who would be good enough to marry you and then you could start a fam—"

She was interrupted by both Lois and Abbie talking at once. If flashing eyes and flushed cheeks were any indication of extreme irritation, Aunt Lena was in danger of being annihilated on the spot.

"Ladies, ladies. Please." Ben was standing behind his wife and daughter, a restraining hand on each of their shoulders. "This is bad for Clair's babies—all this rabble—they'll think we're at war."

Lois took a deep breath and said very quietly, "Abbie, will you help me clear off the table, and we'll bring in dessert?"

Everyone immediately began stacking plates and silverware, all trying to talk at once to erase the awkwardness of the moment. Abbie, without a glance at Aunt Lena, gathered up as many plates as she could carry and tried to make a dignified exit to the kitchen.

"That woman has gone too far this time," her mother sputtered as she slammed into the kitchen after Abbie. "Don't pay her any mind, honey. She's just a silly old busybody that can't seem to ever keep her mouth shut."

Before Abbie could answer, Randall wandered into the kitchen with his hands in his pockets. "Delightful lunch, Lois. Absolutely delightful." He patted Lois's shoulder. "I'm quite sorry that Abbie and I have to leave right now—we'll be back later."

He put his hand on Abbie's back and propelled her out the kitchen door.

Abbie would have liked to protest, but there was an amazingly huge lump in her throat. Her mother's immediate defense of her had brought tears to her eyes, coupled with the embarrassment of Lena's words in front of the Hudsons. Or if she was extremely honest with herself, in front of Randall Hudson. She blinked several times and let him lead her to his car.

When he had gotten her settled in the passenger side, he quickly got in. In a moment the car had purred to life, and they were driving down the narrow country lane.

She looked away from him and tried to keep the snivel that was building up inside her from erupting. She found herself sniffing and wished he had at least given her time to grab her purse so she would have some tissues.

Reaching in front of her, he opened the glove box and produced the very item she desired. He smiled, ruffled her hair, and said in a mild voice, "Get over it, kid."

In just a few minutes he had found a spot to park the car off the road. Before shutting off the motor, he adjusted his seat for more legroom, and then he reached over and lightly clasped her shoulder.

"You've never let Lena bother you before. What's happening, Abbie?"

She leaned back into the warmth of the cushions and shook her head. "Nothing." Flashing him a watery look she added, "Everything."

"It can't be both, you see; it has to be one or the other. Either nothing is happening in your life, and you feel bored, or everything is happening and you feel overwhelmed. Which is it?"

She shook her head in bafflement.

"Is that bloke you've been dating giving you trouble?"

She looked at him startled. "How did you know I was dating anyone? And no, there's no trouble because there's no bloke anymore. And," she informed him, seeing another question forming, "he was only a mild fling. Nobody serious."

He took his hand off her shoulder and put it on the steering wheel. With a sideways glance at her he seemed to be carefully considering his next choice of words.

"You know, you might think about this trip to the States." He held up his hand as she started to sputter. "Listen carefully, Abbie. Not because of any of the silly reasons Lena gave, but just because it is an opportunity to travel, see the world a little, and give yourself a little space from everyone." He paused and reached over to pat her knee. "Families are good and wonderful, Abbie, but sometimes we just have to branch out and make our own mistakes."

"But—"

"You've been in a dark mood for several months now. Everyone has noticed it."

"I—"

"Don't dismiss this out of hand without thinking carefully about it."

"You—"

"Listen to me. I gave you good advice once before. Remember when you were all shook up over that stupid cow?"

"Randall Hudson! Clover was not a stupid cow and you know it!" Abbie's tears dissipated in a flash over his outrageous statement. Once again her brown eyes flashed fire and her cheeks were slightly flushed. "And you might give me a chance to actually finish a sentence!"

He folded both arms across his chest and looked at her. "Yes, right. I'm waiting."

"Yes, well." She pressed her hands together and looked out the window. "You see—actually there are a number of things that bother me, and they just can't be swept away by saying 'get over it.' You see—"

"I once told you two things: get over the cow and get your hair cut. And you listened—the next time I saw you that ugly braid was gone, your hair was short and fluffy and you looked better. Now I'm giving you more good advice: get over Lena, and take this opportunity to do something different."

She glared at him. "Fluffy? How could hair be 'fluffy'?"

He gave careful study of her hair and finally shrugged his shoulders. "Short and curly. Does that sound better than 'fluffy'?"

"I suppose I could be grateful you didn't say 'red and fluffy.'"

29

"I suppose you could be grateful that once again I'm giving you good advice."

Abbie looked straight ahead and simmered. Finally she said very slowly, "I feel like doing just what I did the first time you gave me your gems of wisdom."

"And what would that be?"

She turned to look at him, having decided she was going to act just as childishly as she had when she was younger. She squinted her eyes and stuck out her tongue at him.

Randall's shocked expression soon gave way to suppressed laughter. He reached over and turned the key to start the motor. Glancing at her, he shook his head and reached over to tug a little tendril of her hair.

"Now that we have that all settled, Miss Abigail—and we do have something settled, don't we?" At her reluctant nod, he continued briskly, "Yes, rightly so. Let's go back and enjoy some cake and ice cream."

Abbie leaned back into the rich upholstery of Randall's car. She gave an exasperated sigh and thought to herself that she didn't appreciate people telling her what to do with her life…especially Randall, who always seemed to be rushing her from one situation to another.

However, she supposed she could think about what he had suggested. She could also talk to Clair and Tyler and her parents. But when the decision was made, it would be hers and hers alone.

She looked out the window at the tree-lined road and her mind held a silent debate. It was really a most stupid idea, yet maybe it wasn't quite as outrageous as she had first believed it to be. But to leave England for some unknown spot with no family around would be agonizing. No, it was totally out of the question.

Yet maybe there would be sunsets she could actually see—sunsets over a western prairie. But then again, surely there was a spot in England where there were beautiful sunsets.

CHAPTER 3

Heading West, Summer (2006)

*I*T WAS TRULY the most agonizing and difficult decision Abbie had ever had to make. She was completely torn—one minute wanting to leave, the next moment thinking it was the most ridiculous idea anyone could ever have.

Clair and Tyler had volumes of information for her. She learned the ranch was in a place called South Dakota (directly below North Dakota, Tyler informed her, tongue in cheek) and that there would be three children under the age of five to care for while the mother attended a university. Abbie learned about the climate, the ranching business, and the state of South Dakota, and wondered as she was poring over it all why she was listening to Aunt Lena and Randall Hudson, of all people.

Her parents were careful to let the decision be hers, and more than once Abbie's mother trounced on Aunt Lena for offering too much unwanted advice. But finally Abbie came to realize she wanted to go more than she wanted to stay. After that, time seemed to evaporate as a visa and work permit were obtained and final preparations were made. When the last good-byes were said at the airport, Abbie took a deep breath and marched resolutely onto the plane.

Abbie was delighted her seatmates were an American couple returning to the States after their British vacation. As the jet roared into the air and settled into its flight pattern, they exchanged tidbits of information with each other.

When Abbie said she was going to South Dakota, they reacted with surprise.

"I was born and raised in western South Dakota," the woman said, her dark eyes alert and interested. "Although we live in Kansas now. What's the name of the place you're going to?"

"I'm supposed to end up in Pierre."

"Correction," the lady said immediately. "It's not prounounced pee-air. It's the state capitol, and it's pronounced as one syllable, like the word *peer*."

The husband leaned over his wife and gave Abbie a knowing smile. "Merrill is a walking encyclopedia and she loves to instruct. She can tell you everything you need to know."

Within moments Abbie had her notebook out and was learning the dos and don'ts of western South Dakota. "Don't," Merrill said, holding up her hand with a mischievous twinkle in her eye, "ever ask a rancher how much land he has. It's like asking a person how much money he has in the bank." She added with emphasis, "In the same line of thought, don't ask how many cattle they have—same reason."

Merrill tilted her head to one side and said, "It seems to be all right to ask those questions when you are east of the Missouri River, but not when you are in what they call West River country."

Abbie wrote that down dutifully.

"When they talk about caking their cows, they don't mean chocolate cake in a pan." Merrill grinned. "They mean they are giving their cattle cubes of mineral supplement that adds dietary necessity."

More writing.

"*Outfit* has several different meanings," Merrill continued. "For example, 'let's take my outfit' means 'let's take my vehicle to wherever we're going.' Or it could mean the person's ranch. 'On this outfit we raise crossbreds.' Or if two women are shopping they could get excited over an outfit to wear."

"Clear as mud," the husband intoned.

"How upset do these people get if you ask the wrong thing?" Abbie asked a little timidly.

Merrill laughed and her dark eyes danced with delight. "You'll find the people to be big-hearted and mostly friendly. I'm sure they won't be offended at what you say."

"Just don't mention gun control and you'll do fine," her husband added.

"Oh, yes, gun control. Good thing you mentioned that." Merrill's demeanor became even more scholarly. "People in the area where you are going like their guns. Rifles, pistols—in fact, most outfits have gun racks in them—"

Abbie interrupted. "Outfits, meaning a vehicle?"

"Correct. You're a fast learner!"

Abbie liked this intense woman, and time passed quickly while they visited across the miles of the Atlantic. When they landed in the United States, the couple stayed with her until they were sure she had the right plane to go to Minneapolis. She felt a bit forlorn when they waved good-bye and scurried off to their own connecting flight.

When she was settled in the jet that would take her on the next leg of her journey, Abbie gave a sigh of relief. Minneapolis, then Pierre. *Peer,* she corrected herself, and nodded at the middle-aged gentleman who took the seat next to her.

There are some men, she decided as she looked at him, that you know immediately are gentlemen. From his clear, intelligent eyes behind rimless glasses, to his pleasant smiling face, all indications were that she was blessed with another interesting fellow traveler.

Before long she learned he was a minister traveling to a conference, and he learned she was an English nanny traveling to a new job. They might have made small talk for the rest of the flight if Abbie hadn't blurted out a question that had been bothering her for months.

"How do you know if you're really saved?"

He looked at her kindly. "Do you go to church?"

She nodded.

"Do you tithe?"

She raised an eyebrow and nodded slowly.

"Do you do good works?"

"Sometimes."

He smiled at her again. "None of these things mean you are saved. Have you asked our Lord Jesus to come into your life to guide and direct your ways, and do you rely completely on His wisdom? I believe that's what being saved means. It's a heart matter, Abbie, not an outward show."

After a short pause he continued. "It's my opinion that people are afraid of asking God's will because they think God wants them to immediately become missionaries in some far corner of the world."

Abbie looked at him in amazement. "Exactly!" She lowered her voice slightly. "That's exactly the way I feel."

"You're not alone in that thought. But I believe God will use us no matter where we are. We can serve Him wherever He places us, with whatever people He surrounds us with, and in every circumstance He allows us to be in."

Abbie thought about that. Finally she said rather slowly, "It's surrendering my will to God's will. But," she mused aloud, "how do we ever know what it is that God really wants us to do?"

"That's a very good question. This has been my experience: the more I read and study the Bible, the more I know what the Lord expects of me. The Bible is His instruction to us. Do you have a good study Bible?"

She shook her head.

"Let me jot down several that I like and use quite a bit," he said, taking out a notepad and pen from his pocket. "I should add," he said as he finished writing and handed the note to her, "that I believe God uses the talents and gifts and interests He gave us to serve Him. In other words, the things you probably enjoy doing now are most likely the things He would have you continue doing." He gave her a wry grin.

"Presuming, of course, they are within the framework of what God allows."

She glanced at him and smiled back. "You know, I have been in turmoil for months." She was trying to collect her thoughts to present them intelligently. "I've been unsettled in church, sporadic with my prayers—actually, quite defensive about my faith. I would guess this has been the Holy Spirit trying to make me realize I was lacking a very important step."

"You are a very astute young lady. I would agree with you that the Holy Spirit has been calling you. And I also believe that is another way God speaks to us. He—"

"Drinks, anyone? We have coffee, water, or juice." The flight attendant's interrupting voice was slightly bored but she was efficient, and soon Abbie and the minister each had a bottle of water. Their intense discussion had been interrupted, however, and they lapsed into mundane visiting before the long descent into Minneapolis.

As they parted company, Abbie reached out to shake the minister's hand.

"Thank you so much for talking to me. You've answered a lot of questions that have been bothering me."

"Well," he answered with a smile and gave her a firm handshake, "praise the Lord. Perhaps this is why there was a mix-up back in New York and I was given an earlier flight."

Abbie was grateful for the longer layover in Minneapolis. After she had eaten the all-American hamburger and fries, she wandered over to a secluded set of chairs. Easing herself into a comfortable position in one of them, she settled her tote close beside her. For a while she watched the people coming and going, but when she allowed her mind to wander, it took a definite course of its own and replayed all the minister had told her.

To really do the Lord's will and not want her own way was going to take a while to get used to. She liked being in control of her own life. But she didn't like being tied up in knots over her future—as she had been in making the decision to come to America. Leaving her family had been hard. Even leaving Randall was a little bit upsetting. Darn him—she would miss his advice even if she thought it was wrong most of the time.

She glanced idly out the windows and watched another plane settle onto the runway.

As soon as she could, she wanted to get a study Bible. Even though she had memorized scripture and read parts of the Bible, she never had seriously buckled down and read it from cover to cover.

She sighed. There just never seemed to be any time for that.

But I must make time. If I want the peace of mind that comes with surrendering my will to Your will, I better find the time to know what You want me to do.

Amid the hustle and bustle of the airport, with loudspeakers announcing incoming and departing flights, Abbie made a decision. No bells or whistles or flashing red lights, no applause, no television cameras—only a heartfelt prayer that changed her forever.

I've fought this for a long time, Lord. Maybe ever since Clover died—I don't know. I just know that I want and need Your direction and guidance in my life. I want to walk with You wherever You would have me go. I didn't ask You about coming to this country. I was too stubborn and proud. I wanted the decision to be all mine. I ask forgiveness for being mule-headed. If I made the right choice, it was only because of Your grace and mercy.

After her prayer, the airport was as it had been before. There was the same animated movement all around her. But she knew immediately she was different. One would think, she mused, watching the people come and go, that a person who was committed to the Lord's will would feel shackled and bound to God and His laws. Instead, she felt wondrously free. She took a deep breath and could almost feel her spirit soar.

I like this feeling, Lord. It's like You and I are riding a tandem bike, and You're in front deciding where we're going. I'll just stay on the back seat and pedal. Life with You in control could be quite an adventure!

If Abbie could have heard the excitement in heaven over her repentant soul, she would have been astounded. If she could have seen what the future held for her... but then again, it's best to take one day at a time.

CHAPTER 4

South Dakota

*T*HE WIND THAT tore at Abbie's hair and body as she walked across the tarmac at the Pierre airport seemed to come from hell's furnace. It was hot and vicious, determined to take every ounce of moisture out of the land and the people.

Like the rest of the passengers from the small commuter plane, she was grateful for the building's coolness, but unlike most of them, no one was there to meet her.

She gathered her luggage and waited for Mrs. Davis, the coordinator of the nanny program. It soon became apparent that she was practically the only passenger left. Just as she decided to ask the information desk if there was a message for her, a tall and attractive blonde woman with two children in tow and one in her arms came blowing through the main doors.

"Wowser!" the woman announced to no one in particular. "What a beautiful day this is." She stopped and scanned the nearly empty room. When she saw Abbie she immediately came over with her children trailing behind her.

"Abbie Miller?" she asked, and when Abbie nodded, she introduced herself. "Kada Jackson. Mrs. Davis called and said her mother was taken to the hospital this morning—sounds bad—so we decided that I could pick you up. Sorry I'm late. Had to get the rug rats all ready to go—wasn't expecting to come back to town today." This was all delivered in a rather raspy voice accompanied by a huge smile.

"I see…and this must be Sage?" Abbie asked, looking at the listless baby in Mrs. Jackson's arms.

"Yup, Sage here, he's nine months. Skyler, the typical two-year-old, is laying on the floor bawling, and Scilla is pouting about something. Yup, we're all making a darn good impression, I can tell." She laughed a hoarse raspy laugh, and started coughing slightly.

"I would suspect we could blame it all on the wind?" Abbie asked with a smile. She had met prospective families in all sorts of circumstances.

"You got that right. Is this all your luggage? If it is, let's brave the wind and head outta Dodge."

Abbie decided 'head outta Dodge' must mean Mrs. Jackson was ready to leave. Outside, it seemed like the wind had picked up even more. She wondered if it could pick up thin little Scilla and blow her away.

Fortunately, the Jackson van was parked close, and after the children were buckled into their car seats, Mrs. Jackson zipped out of the parking lot and headed toward a Wal-Mart store.

"I just gotta pick up a few things," Mrs. Jackson spoke loudly over Skyler's whimpering. "How about I leave the outfit running with the A/C on, and you can wait here with the kids?"

"Is there something Skyler wants?" Abbie thought it could be a long wait if the little boy didn't stop crying.

"Aw, Skyler, what are you bawling about now?"

"Go you!" His tears seem to cascade down the dirty little cheeks in volumes.

"Aw, you spoiled little rat. You just want to hit the candy aisle," Mrs. Jackson responded, shaking her head. She pulled the van into a parking space. "Abbie, is there anything you need? Because if there is I better get it for you—we won't be coming back to town for a while. I was going to pick up a bunch of bottled water for you, OK?"

"Sounds perfect."

After Mrs. Jackson and Skyler left, a quiet settled over the van. Abbie noticed the pale baby was drifting off to sleep. His wispy blond hair stood on end from the effects of the wind, and with every breath it seemed to wave back and forth. She also noted that Scilla was eyeing her hair with interest from the backseat.

"Is that your real hair color?" Scilla finally asked.

Abbie laughed slightly and shifted in her seat to face the brown-haired girl. "I'm afraid so."

Scilla looked dubious. "Mom colors her hair from a box."

Suspicion confirmed. She smiled. "How old are you, Scilla?"

"Five. Daddy don't know you're coming."

"I suppose not. The original plan was for me to stay in Pierre tonight and go to your house tomorrow."

"Daddy don't know nothing about you at all."

"I see." What Abbie saw was trouble. If Mr. Jackson didn't know she was coming, it could be quite a hullabaloo.

She turned back to look out the window. The wind gusts seemed to rock the van, and swirls of dust circled around and through the air. She wondered how hot it actually was. For a second, a cool and peaceful vision of the old stone bridge and the gurgling stream in Somerset County flashed through her mind.

When Mrs. Jackson and Skyler returned, she had a hard time holding the door open for the little boy to jump in. When she got into the van herself, her tangled blonde hair was practically standing on end.

"I don't know when I've seen wind like this!" she exclaimed. "Well, at least not since the day before yesterday!" She flashed Abbie a grin.

They left the parking lot and soon crossed the Missouri River. As they headed west on Highway 14, Mrs. Jackson settled back in the driver's seat and lit a cigarette. At Abbie's astonished look, she muttered a little under her breath and gave Abbie a sheepish look.

"I know, I know. Wade barks at me all the time for smoking in the van with the kids. I'm trying to quit, but it ain't easy, honey."

"I hear it's not."

"Do you like country music?" Putting her cigarette in her mouth, Mrs. Jackson reached over with her free hand and punched in a CD. Soon the sound of guitars and drums filled the air, and a female singer with a husky voice began a heartbroken lament of lost love.

Abbie frowned slightly and glanced at Mrs. Jackson. The willowy blonde was listening to the music with intense concentration. When the song ended, she expelled a pent-up sigh.

"What did you think of that?" she asked Abbie with what seemed to be undue urgency.

"I just had a silly thought; for some reason it crossed my mind that it could be you singing."

"Hey! You're good! It was me—how did you figure that out?" Abbie was spared from answering when Mrs. Jackson started sputtering and coughing.

"Dang cigarettes, I gotta quit 'em."

"I should think they'd be quite a hindrance to your singing voice."

"Yeah." Mrs. Jackson laughed softly. "You and Bill are right in tune about that."

"Bill?"

"The band leader. Plays lead guitar."

"I see."

The road headed straight west for miles and miles. For a great part of those miles, Abbie saw fields of wheat that had been harvested. The sheer size of each field was beyond anything she could have ever imagined. When she asked Mrs. Jackson about the equipment used to handle such a volume, she was disappointed she didn't seem to have a clue.

When Abbie asked about the breed of cattle on the Jackson ranch, she was surprised that Mrs. Jackson was unable to give her any concrete answers about that either. Thinking perhaps that she had unwittingly blundered by asking wrong questions, Abbie decided to ask about her singing. Finally, she had hit upon a subject that was near and dear to

Mrs. Jackson's heart. For many miles Abbie listened to the plight of a seemingly frustrated singer who had found a band to sing in but who couldn't find enough time to pursue her career. She wrote songs, she informed Abbie, and she knew she had a bent toward songwriting and singing. She loved being on stage with her band, and since the band was located in the same university town where she would be attending classes, it would be so much easier to practice with them.

As Mrs. Jackson rambled on about her singing, her studies, and her new job as a waitress, her children gradually fell asleep and finally there was complete quiet in the back seats. Abbie stifled several yawns and glanced again at her new employer.

"So, now you have the job of taking care of the rug rats!" Mrs. Jackson met her glance with a grin. "And I'm one step closer to my dream. It's a good trade-off, don't you think?" She gave a raspy laugh and lit another cigarette. The highway ahead seemed to stretch out to eternity.

Finally they turned off the paved road onto a gravel road. Almost at once the blonde woman's demeanor seemed to change. Abbie was aware of the whiteness of Mrs. Jackson's knuckles as she clenched the steering wheel. There was a tenseness in her attitude that hadn't been there before.

The children were waking up, one by one, and Abbie glanced over the seat to check on the three of them again. She felt a twinge of alarm at the baby's hollow cough and reached back to feel his face.

She was reassured by his forehead's coolness, but her nanny radar was kicking in. For one thing, the mother had never so much as glanced back at her children the entire drive home. She hadn't talked about them nor had she mentioned how she expected Abbie to care for them while she was gone.

Mrs. Jackson's raspy voice broke into Abbie's thoughts. "Ah, about the house…it might seem strange to you. For one thing, I just haven't had time to clean, and for another…" she left her sentence dangling in mid air as they drove over the auto gate into the yard.

The ranch seemed like a well-planned place to Abbie. The barn looked to be well constructed, with ample corrals. Several other buildings were arranged in symmetrical order, and the house in front of them was a two-storied home with a big southern-facing porch. Abbie noticed there was a smaller porch that graced the east side of the house.

"And here is *the ranch*." Abbie was surprised at the bitterness in Mrs. Jackson's voice. "The pride and joy of the Jackson family. If you don't love every little board and brick on this place, there's something wrong with you." She gave a mirthful laugh and turned to Abbie. "I'm from the city; I can't get excited over this godforsaken place."

The wind was still gusting, but its full fury seemed to have passed, leaving in its wake a hot and parched land. The heat boiled up around them as they unloaded the van and quickly carried everything into a breezeway.

"This is the only door we use," Mrs. Jackson informed her as they hustled into a long and narrow space. She led the way through a door that admitted them to the house, and Abbie knew at once that it was indeed a strange place.

By the time they had gotten the children settled, Abbie had seen enough to understand that Mrs. Jackson probably hadn't had time to clean for a very long time. The clutter wasn't as forbidding, however, as the black carpet throughout the house. Black curtains shrouded every window, and the result was a grim and dark interior. It seemed dank and musky smelling, as if it had been closed up for a long time. The air conditioner belched out cold air continually; in contrast to the heat outside, it was chilly in the house.

"Your room is upstairs—turn left when you get to the top." There seemed to be a tightness in Mrs. Jackson's voice. Suddenly she called out, "Scilla! Show Abbie where her room is!"

Picking up her luggage, Abbie followed her little guide up the stairs. The black carpet ended at the first landing and oak steps continued to the top. As they proceeded up the steps, more light seemed to come into the house, and as they reached the hallway, the air became fresher.

Her room was at the end of the hall. It was bright and cheery with a queen-sized bed that was heaped with inviting pillows and boasted crisp white sheets. Sheer curtains with half-closed blinds were on the south and west windows. Best of all in Abbie's eyes was the clean and sparkling private bathroom.

"My room is just across the hall. Wanna see it?" Scilla asked. Without waiting for an answer she darted across the hall and opened her door. When Abbie peered in, it was as clean and inviting as her room.

"Very nice—both rooms are very nice," Abbie said, but she was puzzled. Why were these rooms so different from the downstairs?

Scilla was watching her closely, rocking from one foot to another. Her scrutiny almost made Abbie uncomfortable, but suddenly the little girl blurted out, "Your hair is like a brand-new copper penny. I like it."

Abbie crouched down beside her and gave the thin little body a hug. "That's about the nicest thing anyone has ever said about my hair. Thanks."

When she joined Mrs. Jackson downstairs, the other woman was setting an assortment of store-prepared food on the table for the kids. None of it was nourishing, but Skyler seemed enthused about the doughnuts and Sage was in the high chair chasing some Cheerios around the tray with his little hand.

Mrs. Jackson seemed preoccupied and distant, but when she heard Abbie yawn she quickly glanced up. "Hey, kid, you look bushed! Maybe you better grab something here and head up to bed."

Abbie yawned again. "I think it just hit me that seven in the evening here is about," she counted ahead seven time zones on her fingers, "two in the morning in England."

She put together a sandwich and munched on some potato chips while Mrs. Jackson groused at the kids. Stifling another yawn, Abbie patted Sage's little fuzzy head and leaned over to kiss his forehead.

Skyler watched this with wary eyes. When she reached over to pat the top of his head, he told her bluntly, "No!"

Moving on, she gave Scilla a hug, told Mrs. Jackson good night, and made her way through the gloom of the downstairs toward the stairway. She noticed again the better light and air as she climbed up the steps.

Her room seemed like a haven. After a quick shower she snuggled into the luxury of a down pillow and light comforter. Yawning once more, she mumbled tiredly, "Good night, Lord. I crossed over the bridge today and took Your hand. Probably just in time. I need help in this strange and windy prairie."

CHAPTER 5

Wade Jackson

*B*EING A GOOD steward of the land was an inherited duty of the Jackson family. As Wade made the turn in his field and set the chisel back into the soil, he realized again how much he enjoyed the challenge of good stewardship. It revolved around timing, he had decided—the right time to work the field, the right time to plant, the right time to fertilize and to harvest, and in today's world, the right time to market.

With all the wind, the right time to work his field that day had come later in the afternoon. By the time he had gotten his equipment ready and climbed into the tractor cab, the gale had been reduced to merely a gusty wind.

He knew he would be working late into the night. Wade Jackson liked to work. With his powerful frame and his ability to stay focused on any given task, he accomplished a lot with his days.

Yet he was a worried man. The land didn't cause his worries—he knew and understood the ways of the seasons. It was his wife who caused him to make round after round in the fields with a worried pucker on his forehead and exclamations of disgust to the air-conditioned cab.

He knew she was getting ready to leave him. If seeing her little car fill up with odds and ends of packed objects wasn't clue enough, her change of disposition was a complete giveaway.

She acted, he reflected while checking his machinery in both mirrors, as a person who had been under a heavy weight of indecision and had finally come up with a solution. Right or wrong, something had been settled in her mind, and he knew from past experience she wouldn't be swayed from her intended objective.

The question before him was how to react. One time he had exploded in rage at her. He had been savage and loud and came close to slapping her. Too close—he saw the fear in her eyes. But whatever had prompted her to act the way she did that time was an even more fearful force, and he knew she wouldn't back down.

That time he had stormed out of the house and saddled up his horse. While he furiously rode through the pastures checking his cattle, he spurred Jake until they were on a high ridge and he felt the tremor in the horse's body.

He would never forget the remorse that surged through him when he realized what he had done. It was not his habit to abuse his animals. As he dismounted with trembling legs, he begged forgiveness from both God and horse.

Wade made a vow that day: his temper was not going to control him again.

When do you say to yourself your marriage is over? How many times do you go through the motions of reconciliation only to know deep in your heart there is no healing, only more wounds? What is best for the kids? Which parent should keep them? What settlement is adequate? What will people think?

The biggest question in his mind revolved around the spiritual consequences of separation and divorce. The Jackson family had strong feelings on families staying together.

There were no answers for him that evening, and as he drove his tractor and equipment into the yard, he wondered if there ever would be.

When he entered the house, Kada was sleeping on the sofa in front of the TV. He quickly checked the two boys in the downstairs room and made his way silently up the stairs, turning right to the empty master bedroom. She refused to sleep upstairs; he refused to sleep downstairs. A ridiculous situation that proved, he knew, the mule-headedness of both of them.

Even though the sun had been up for an hour, the interior of the downstairs the next morning was gloomy, and Wade had to be careful walking into the clutter of the room where Sage's crib was.

This was the morning ritual between him and his youngest son. He smiled at Sage's eagerness to be picked up. Holding the damp little body close, he glanced over and saw Kada's inert frame wrapped in blankets on the bed. As usual, after waking up in front of the TV, she had crawled into bed beside Skyler.

Wade walked quietly out of the room with Sage in his arms and headed down the hall to the utility room. Sorting through the laundry, he finally found clean clothes for the baby.

"There you go, fellow. Clean diaper, clean clothes—do you feel like a new man?" Sage's answer was a toothless grin as Wade finished pulling the little shirt over his tummy.

Before he started his morning coffee, he settled his son in the high chair and they began their usual one-sided conversation.

"Cheerios or crackers?"

"EEEhhh."

"Milk or water?"

Sputtered spit rolled down Sage's dry shirt.

Wade put morsels of bananas on the tray and waited for the coffee to brew. When he heard light footsteps coming down the steps he was puzzled. Scilla rarely got up that early.

He was totally unprepared for the slender form in capri pants and tan sleeveless shirt that materialized in the kitchen. He was even more surprised when she came forward with her hand outstretched.

"Mr. Jackson?" Her voice had a clipped British accent. "I'm Abbie Miller."

He shook her hand solemnly. "Hello, Abbie Miller." He paused, and then with a raised eyebrow inquired, "Am I supposed to know an Abbie Miller?"

She laughed lightly and withdrew her hand. "I believe you should know who I am, but I also believe you probably have not been told about me." She tilted her head and her brown eyes twinkled. "I'm your children's nanny."

Wade folded his arms across his chest and gazed at her. Nannies with accents and red hair did not often appear on the Dakota prairies.

"Miss…is it *Miss* Miller?" At her nod he continued. "Miss Miller, uh, does my wife know you're here?"

Again her eyes twinkled. "Yes, I didn't appear out of a genie lamp. Your wife picked me up at the Pierre airport yesterday afternoon."

"Really." He suddenly remembered his manners, and quickly poured two cups of coffee. Handing her one, he motioned for her to sit at the overflowing table where the previous night's meal still remained.

Before she sat down she ran her fingers over Sage's downy hair. "And how are you, Mr. Sage?" He gave her a toothless smile and continued chasing down banana pieces.

Wade brushed some crumbs off a chair and sat down. He eyed a box of doughnuts skeptically and finally decided they would at least be filling. He quickly opened the box and offered Miss Miller one. He thought she must have had the same doubts about them because she hesitated slightly before reaching in with her slender hand and pulling one out.

"Did my wife happen to mention why she hired you?" he asked, breaking a doughnut in half and taking a bite.

"She said she was going to college."

"Fascinating. Did she mention what college?"

"Not that I recall, except to say it's close to her band."

"Ah, the band. They call themselves The Wild Boys Plus One. They're located in Spearfish." At her blank look he pointed west. "That direction."

"I see."

"Did she say when she starts?" He was slightly puzzled at how calm he felt, considering the obvious implications of what this little gal was saying.

"She talked about tomorrow. I guess I'm really not sure. Mr. Jackson, this is very good coffee." He watched her get up and refill her cup, and he appreciated the fact that she also refilled his.

"Mrs. Jackson and I have a very obvious communication gap," he said, aware that he needed to explain his ignorance. He absently watched her tickle Sage's bare foot.

She sat back into her chair and looked at him with serious brown eyes. "Would it be possible to open up some windows and doors downstairs?"

"Yes, but let's wait until Mrs. Jackson leaves. She has issues with fresh air." He would clarify that later, he decided, but at that moment he was thinking of some riding he needed to do. Usually he hung around the house until he was sure Kada was awake and functioning and capable of watching the kids. But since this Abbie woman was there, she could watch them and he could get started on his day's work.

Abbie agreed readily, and when he left the corral with Jake and his dog, Shy, he noticed she was outside holding Sage on her lap and swinging on the homemade swing set his grandfather had built years ago.

All during his early morning ride to check the cattle, Wade wondered what Kada would tell him.

This must be how it happens, he thought. *You worry and worry about something, and when it stares you in the face for a showdown, you just do the best you can do.*

Lord, help me to stay calm.

He wasn't surprised to see Kada waiting for him at the barn when he came slowly riding in. She looked worried, pacing in front of the hitching rail.

He willed his voice to be pleasant. "Good morning," he greeted her as he swung off the saddle.

"We need to talk." Her voice sounded strained.

He wrapped the reins around the rail and turned to look at her. She was an attractive woman with long and shapely legs. He always enjoyed the way she looked in short shorts or, for that matter, tight fitting jeans.

"You need to talk, Kada. You must have forgotten to tell me a few things." He decided he had better keep his hands busy, and stepped over to his horse's side to loosen the cinch.

"I've paid this woman to stay here until June to watch the kids," Kada began. "When I say I paid, that's exactly what I mean—I used Dad's money."

"Your inheritance money," Wade said as he pulled off the saddle and blanket. She stepped aside to let him pass into the saddle room and nodded when their eyes met.

"I want to go to college, Wade. I want a degree." She had followed him into the small room.

"A degree in what? What interests you, Kada, besides singing in the band?" He smacked the blanket and saddle down onto their proper rack and turned to look at her. Her face was pale, and he noticed her hands were clenched.

When she answered, her voice was low and full of anger. "I know what you think. You think I'm a dumb blonde floozy that doesn't have brainpower to turn a page. You think—"

"Let me tell you what I think." He hoped his voice wasn't as harsh on her ears as it was in his mind.

Wade walked over to a barrel and grabbed a can of oats to take to Jake. Kada followed him outside and watched while he poured it into the pan. He thought her breathing seemed labored, or maybe it was his own heart pounding that made it seem that way.

"I think I almost killed this horse once because of you," he stated flatly as he took off Jake's bridle and watched his tall gelding nuzzle the grain.

"Not because of me, Wade Jackson." Kada's voice cracked suddenly. "You wouldn't have that much emotion over me. It was because of your grandparents' stupid house!"

"Because of what you done to the house, Kada. Because I came back and you and the Wild Boys had tacked voodoo wall hangings everywhere. Because all the floors were covered in ugly black carpet, and because the windows were covered with black drapes, and because for some unknown stupid reason we can't open any windows without you going berserk."

He was glaring at her and his voice was raised, but he was totally unprepared for her reaction. She looked horrified. Her eyes seemed to glaze over and her hands shook uncontrollably.

"It's not voodoo! Shut up about that! Shut up about it! It's the house—it's the house!"

"Kada." He spoke softly, and then said her name again even more gently. "Kada, what happened with you and the house?" He wanted to reach out and hold her, but she was so overwrought he hesitated.

"It tried—it wants—" She struggled to regain her composure, and after a short pause she said flatly, "Nothing. Nothing happened."

Wade leaned against the hitching rail and studied her carefully. It was the same response he always heard. He shook his head and sighed. "OK, we hit a blank wall there. Let's go on to some other issues we have."

She seemed relieved to change the subject. "I've taken out a student loan, and I have a job to help with expenses. I'm staying in the dorm to cut costs."

"When are you leaving and when are you coming back?"

"I'm leaving tomorrow, and, and...I don't really know when I'll be able to come back. The band has a lot of bookings."

"Why not leave today, and why bother to ever come back?" He stared straight ahead with his hat pulled low over his eyes, and his voice was very quiet.

"What are you saying, Wade?"

He turned his head to see her reaction. She was clearly astonished at his suggestion.

"We haven't shared a bed for a long time," he replied. "We don't talk to each other. Obviously you planned this for months without sharing any of it with me. Let's end it. I want full custody of the kids. What do you want?"

She seemed momentarily caught off guard. Several times she opened her mouth to say something and then closed it again. Finally, she looked at him and said coldly, "I want four years of college."

"I'll get the papers drawn up."

"I'll sign them."

They looked at each other without either saying another word. Suddenly she turned and with hurried steps headed toward the house.

He watched her go, not sure what emotion was raging in his chest.

CHAPTER 6

The Jackson Ranch

ISTRAUGHT. THAT WAS the word Abbie would have used to describe Kada Jackson the morning after Abbie arrived. When she discovered Abbie had visited with her husband, she seemed unable to concentrate on anything, and she finally headed out to the barn.

It was a strange morning even for Abbie, who was used to many difficult mornings with new families. Mrs. Jackson only had two people listed to call in case of an emergency: the children's doctor and a neighbor lady by the name of Marilyn. Other than that, she seemed to have very little input on her children.

Abbie had taken the three children outside, and when they saw Mrs. Jackson return from the barn, Skyler made a happy dash toward his mother. She picked him up absently and just as absently put him down by the porch.

"Mama, up!" Skyler insisted, but Mrs. Jackson gently swatted him on the behind and told Scilla to entertain him. There was quite a skirmish as Scilla tried to lead him away. Eventually Skyler broke into a tantrum and threw himself on the ground kicking and screaming.

Abbie hesitated to intervene, feeling it was the mother's duty, but Mrs. Jackson only shook her head and disappeared into the house.

"Scilla, leave him alone," Abbie said quietly. "You and I and Sage are going to swing. When Skyler gets up, he can swing too."

"He's always bawling," Scilla said plaintively.

They were only on the swings a few minutes before Mr. Jackson and a huge German shepherd dog appeared. The dog gently nosed the crying Skyler and sat down with a baffled look.

"You don't know what to do with him either, do you, Shy?" Mr. Jackson said to his dog. He shook his head as he looked down at his unhappy son. "Skyler." Something in his tone caught Abbie's attention.

Skyler turned his volume down immediately, as if he also sensed there was a force he didn't care to tangle with.

"Skyler, either turn it off, or I'll give you something to bawl about."

"Want Mama!"

With one swoop, Skyler was in his dad's arms. He quit crying, and he had a surprised look as he and Mr. Jackson disappeared into the house.

Shortly afterward, Mr. Jackson came out alone and backed the van to a gas tank. From there he drove to the shop, where even from a distance Abbie could see he found things to fix and take care of. Finally he backed the van to the breezeway door.

Soon he was loading a number of musical items into the back, and Mrs. Jackson was taking things out of her car and putting them into the van. Abbie noted there was very little conversation between the two.

By that time Sage was sleeping in Abbie's arms and she could feel the heat of the sun's rays beating on her back. She was loath to return to the house, but Scilla and she were both ready to quit swinging.

After Abbie entered the house, she was unsure where to lay Sage. Scilla guided her into a back room where his crib was. The smell of dust and stale cigarette smoke was so heavy in the air that Abbie cringed inwardly.

Abbie took note of the situation. Skyler was absorbed in a video, Sage was asleep, and Scilla, for the first time all morning, had left Abbie's side and disappeared. Since she had no children to care for at the moment, Abbie decided to see if the Jackson adults needed her help.

She found them in the kitchen, each with a cup of coffee in their hands and having a quiet, intense conversation.

"There's been a change in plans," Mrs. Jackson announced briskly when she saw Abbie. "I'm leaving today. I want to show you how to run the washer and dryer—you may not be familiar with American models."

Her manner was completely different from the day before. No slang talk. She seemed cold and distant, and when she showed Abbie how the different appliances worked, she was brief and to the point. Abbie almost wished the former Mrs. Jackson would appear.

Mrs. Jackson gave a quick and half-hearted tour of the kitchen. Abruptly, without a glance at her husband, she said she needed to take care of some other things and made a quick exit into the hallway.

"Coffee, Abbie?" Mr. Jackson asked, and at her nod, poured a steaming brew into a cup and handed it to her.

"You've probably noticed that Skyler is a complete mama's boy. He's going to miss her a lot." Mr. Jackson was looking at the dark curtains on the window while he spoke.

"Little boys often have a great attachment to their mothers," Abbie said. She paused to take a drink of coffee and then asked, "Should I make lunch for everyone?"

"Great idea." He walked into the next room where Skyler was watching TV, and Abbie heard him ask Skyler with a trace of irony in his voice if there was room on the sofa for any more toys.

It was always hard to find things in a different kitchen, but this one proved more challenging than most. There was no rhyme or reason to the placement of things, Abbie noticed, as she opened cupboard doors and found a mishmash of items sprawled in disarray. It was going to be a bit of a tussle to prepare food! She was in a small debate with herself about what an American family would usually fix for lunch when Mrs. Jackson reappeared.

She looked gorgeous. Her blonde hair was pulled back into a loose twist, her slim figure was encased in white slacks and an apricot colored top, and she wore sandals on her feet. Abbie saw that her toenails were painted the same color as her top. It was a silly thing to notice, she thought absently.

"You look very nice," Abbie told her.

Mrs. Jackson granted her a tight smile. "I'm ready for the road."

"Don't you want to eat a bite first?"

"No, Abbie, I'm ready to go. I've already said good-bye to the kids and Wade." She looked uncertainly at Abbie. "I... probably won't be back for quite a while, so whatever you want to do in here, go ahead. I really don't care."

Two questions flashed through Abbie's mind. Usually children were upset when their mother planned to be gone—why weren't these children? Even though Sage was asleep, she would have thought both Scilla and Skyler would be close at hand when their mother left. Instead, Skyler was absorbed in a movie, and Scilla had disappeared upstairs. And how long was "quite a while"?

"I've never been told to do whatever I wanted to do in a home. You might regret those words," Abbie answered, with an attempt at some light humor. She would have said more, but Mrs. Jackson's grim expression silenced her.

"Listen, I hate good-byes, so I'm outta here." She gave Abbie a snappy salute and within seconds was out the door.

It was the most unusual leave taking Abbie had ever witnessed.

She hadn't realized that Mr. Jackson was also outside. Through a slit in the dark curtains she saw him open the van door for his wife. They exchanged a few words, and when she drove away he abruptly turned and walked into the house.

"Let's get rid of these curtains," he said as he brought in a huge cardboard box and plopped it in the middle of the kitchen floor.

Abbie gave him a startled look. He meant business and was already whipping the ugly dark shrouds off the window with his strong hands. He reached out to hand them to her, and she deposited them into the box. In a very short time the kitchen had light.

"Well done, Mr. Jackson."

He looked very pleased with himself and gave her a brief nod. "On to the rest of the house, Miss Miller."

Abbie was slightly amused that Skyler never quit watching TV while his father took down the curtains in that room. From there they moved into the back room where Sage was sleeping, and when the light began to filter in, she was shocked to see a fireplace.

"This was my grandmother's living room—her pride and joy," Mr. Jackson informed her. "It's going to be that again."

He almost savagely ripped away the ugly mass that hung on two French doors that separated the living room from another room. "This, Miss Miller, is the office. Kada had made it into a studio, but since we moved all her equipment out this morning, it will be a studio no more."

Abbie had an eerie feeling looking at the heavy black drapes that were hung all around the former studio. "This almost gives me the creeps," she said. "I wonder if we should move Sage out of your grandmother's living room before we take all these dusty things out."

"Yes, you're right. I'll close the doors again, and we'll leave it to later."

By now the carton was heavy, and they both manhandled it into the hallway. The utility room and mudroom were quickly taken care of. Abbie hadn't noticed the small bathroom tucked away in the utility room, and even in there Kada had hung the same thick black curtains.

"Did Mrs. Jackson get a discount with these?" she asked, wondering if that was the reason the ugly things were hanging on every window.

"I have no idea," he said, taking down the final pair that covered the hallway door. "Help me push this box into the breezeway, and we'll get the lot of them out of the house."

"That was accomplished very quickly, Mr. Jackson," Abbie said as they walked back into the kitchen.

"Yes," he murmured absently, looking at the curtainless windows. "I've actually accomplished quite a bit this morning, Miss Miller." He turned to her and smiled. "But we have only just begun. Before tonight we are going to have this carpet out of here."

"Wonderful!"

By evening, Abbie was far less enthusiastic. Mr. Jackson had kept her on a fast pace the entire day. It was as if he couldn't wait to eradicate every trace of his wife's decorating folly.

They relocated the bedroom furniture for the boys to a sunny and light upstairs bedroom, rolled up the carpet throughout the entire downstairs and carted it outside, removed the strange wall coverings, and reverted the office back to its original purpose.

As the evening brought slightly lower temperatures, Mr. Jackson opened the doors and windows, and while Abbie tiredly put supper on the table, he scrubbed Sage's high chair tray with gusto.

Scilla had kept busy with them most of the day. She coughed from the dust they stirred up but refused to leave. Even Skyler tried to help, but soon found the work tiring and didn't complain when his dad put him in his new room for a nap. If it worried Wade that Sage slept most of the day, he gave no indication of it.

"I believe I worked you too hard today," he said as she yawned for the fourth time during their meal.

She laughed a little embarrassedly. "I'm getting used to a different time zone."

"Oh, of course you are. I forgot about that. Listen, when we're done eating, you quit for the day. I'll finish up."

For the first time in her nanny career, Abbie left supper dishes and three bedraggled little kids for someone else to take care of. She was asleep seconds after her head hit the pillow.

In the days that followed, Abbie came to understand that while Mrs. Jackson was vague and unsure of what a nanny should do, Mr. Jackson had no problems with laying out a schedule. He was energetic and focused, and when he started a job he meant to finish it. He also expected her to keep his same pace.

As far as Abbie could tell, he didn't seem overly upset that he had become the sole parent in the house while his wife was gone, or even that she had left.

The house needed to be thoroughly cleaned, he told her, and he was willing to take time away from his ranch work to get it that way. Between the two of them, they washed the windows, took out garbage bags full of trash, emptied cabinets and the pantry, and cleaned and reorganized everything else. The vacuum cleaner, little used for several months, found itself running almost continually on the carpet that lay dusty and forgotten under the monstrous black carpet.

"Paint," Mr. Jackson stated simply one afternoon while the two were taking a momentary break at the cleaned kitchen table.

She looked at him warily. "Paint?"

"I've always wanted to repaint the hallway and kitchen."

"You have?"

"Do you paint, Abbie?"

She answered slowly. "I have been known to paint." Visions floated before her—red braids splattered with white paint, a sprinkling of white freckles on her face. Aunt Lena had declared Abbie had more paint on herself than the walls. "You realize, of course, Mr. Jackson," she informed him, "that my main job is to care for the children. Actually, I haven't really seen them enough to get acquainted very well."

He leaned back in his chair and studied her with a noticeable twitch in the corner of his mouth. "You've seen them constantly for the last couple of days."

"That's quantity time, sir, not quality." She looked down at Sage, who was patting the cleaned floor with his beloved teddy bear. She actually leaned forward to take a closer look. There was something decidedly different about him.

"What are you seeing?" There was a sharpness in Mr. Jackson's voice.

"Is it my imagination, or does there seem to be more color in his cheeks?"

"I thought this morning he wasn't as pale as usual. He coughs less."

"So does Scilla. Good heavens, all that dust and dirt was probably doing them in."

"From the way you sounded the morning after we cleared all that junk out, it almost did you in." He pushed back his chair and grinned at her.

"We all were a bit croaky from it, I would say." Abbie slowly stood and surveyed the bright and airy kitchen. "What a wonderful transformation in three long days. But—" she looked at Mr. Jackson with a troubled gaze, "what is Mrs. Jackson going to say about all of this? I worry about her reaction."

"I wouldn't worry at all about such matters if I were you," he replied shortly. "Kada will be so engrossed in her singing that she won't give it a second thought."

CHAPTER 7

Sunsets Apart

"*B*ILL."

He always answered his phone that way.

"Hey, this is Kada. Is the band practicing tonight?"

"We practice every night, with or without you."

"At seven?"

"Right." There was a brief pause. "I thought you weren't going to be here until tomorrow."

"Change of plans."

"Did he kick you out?"

"That's tacky, Bill. I'm hanging up."

Kada snapped her cell phone shut and laid it on the console between the seats. She had left the gravel road behind, and now her cruise control was set at sixty-five as she headed down Highway 34. Even in August, the road wasn't crowded.

She was treating herself to a Coke and a cigarette. Her CD player was cranking out sad tunes but Kada wasn't sure what emotion she felt as she headed west. She had both dreaded and looked forward to this day. Now that she was actually closer to her dreams, she wondered if she had made the right choice.

Maybe I should write a song about that, she thought, *a sad song about achieving one dream and watching another one go up in smoke.*

She had planned her getaway for months. While Wade hustled around his ranch and zeroed in on every detail, she schemed her own tactics. She felt justified in walking out of his life, but when she was honest with herself, she knew there was no justification for walking out on three kids.

If the miserable place wasn't so far away from everything, I would have tried a little harder to keep it all together, she reasoned. But deep down she knew that even if that house had been near the college she would never stay within its frightening walls. Goosebumps popped out on Kada's arms. She was so scared of that house that she hadn't been upstairs for two years. When Mrs. Davis from the agency had phoned to say she actually had a gal coming, Kada knew she had to get a room ready for the nanny. After several failed attempts at trying to force herself up the stairway, she had finally hired a neighbor to come and clean the room.

Kada blew smoke rings into the air and shook her head. Torrie McGovern was not her favorite person, but she was willing to come and clean and keep her mouth shut. She thought if Torrie knew Wade had wanted a divorce she would have done the work for nothing. Torrie was always talking to him about the ranch and asking him for all sorts of advice. When Wade talked to her, Torrie acted like a god had spoken.

"Honey, he'll be up for grabs pretty soon. Sink your sweet little claws in deep." Kada said the words aloud and tried to find a tune that would go with the thought. Failing at that she scrunched more comfortably into the van seat and thought about the little rug rats.

Scilla was such a tattletale—she told Wade everything. Sometimes Kada thought her daughter liked getting her in trouble. Kada had never bonded with Scilla; for that matter, she hadn't bonded with Sage either. Skyler was another story. He had Wade's dark eyes, and sometimes when she saw him watching her with those big peepers she had almost lost her resolve about leaving.

"Almost persuaded…" She sang the whole song while the miles rolled away.

Kada knew many songs—knew them, crooned them, and put her heart into every word. That's what Bill said made her good. Bill was one of the best band managers, lead guitar players, and backup singers in the area. He was a strange fellow, she thought. He had his graying thick hair in a braid down his back, he always wore Lee jeans and a white shirt, and he usually laced his tennis shoes with bright orange shoelaces.

She asked him once about the goofy bright shoelaces. He told her that was his way of telling the world he was a rebel and then laughed quietly. She often thought with his beaked nose and dull beady eyes that people should have been repulsed by him. Instead, his mesmerizing quiet confidence drew people to him.

She inhaled the last of her cigarette and stamped out the ashes in the empty ashtray. *Wade must have cleaned it out when he was getting the van ready for me. I wonder if it made him happy to think he won't have that job anymore.*

He had surprised her this morning. She had thought he would blow up and try to make her change her mind. She'd had all her arguments ready, and then he slapped her with the "let's end it" thing. She had been prepared for anything but that. When he'd said he wanted full custody of the kids, she didn't know if she wanted to laugh or cry.

She still didn't know. But he made the offer and she was going to hold him to it. She wanted to walk out. However, she hadn't planned on being pushed out. Still, if it was freedom she wanted, she guessed it was freedom and a free college ride she would get.

It would help a huge amount if she were positive she still didn't love him. Darn Wade anyhow. He had told her from the beginning they weren't right for each other. Maybe if she had tended to her babies and her business at home instead of singing with the Wild Boys…

She punched the cruise control to seventy-five. There was a limit to how much time she wanted to think about all that. Besides, it made no difference now anyway. She couldn't stay with Wade and the kids as long as the house hated her.

By Thursday of that week, Kada was settled in her dorm room and had quickly adjusted to her new routine. She was a good waitress and she collected above-average tips, but best of all, she decided that evening as she raced from the café to where the band was practicing, she felt a wonderful freedom from the kids—and her husband.

The sun setting over the Black Hills gave out a lustrous beauty. Kada looked up at the majestic mountains shrouded in gold, took a last puff of her cigarette before grinding the stub under her foot, and quickly opened the door to join the Wild Boys.

The porch screen door on the Jackson house banged shut as Abbie carried Sage outside. It was Thursday evening, and it was the first night she hadn't gone to bed early, she realized. She finally was acclimating to the time change.

The August day's heat had given way to a gentle warmth, and now with the supper dishes done and the two older kids out at the barn with Mr. Jackson, Abbie was ready to enjoy a few minutes of peace and quiet with this little guy who was rapidly stealing her heart.

She nuzzled the top of his head and felt the soft downiness of his fine hair. He made a contented little sound and seemed to snuggle deeper into her arms.

Sitting on the porch steps, Abbie gazed upward at the evening sky. Bands of clouds had appeared, and as the setting sun's rays hit them, they seemed to glow with hues of pinks and purples.

"This is beautiful Sage, enjoy it," she murmured into his soft little ear.

As the sun slowly descended behind the hill, a dazzling spectrum of colors gleamed with a rare and wild beauty that filled the entire western sky. The clouds deepened into darker violet shades shadowed by bands of gold in a display that left Abbie wondering if she had left Earth and entered heaven.

"Wow, wow," she breathed as the entire sight slowly began to fade away and a lonesome cricket started chirping.

This is what I'd call a sunset, Lord! No, no, wait a minute. I'd call it a glimpse of Your glory. This is Your awesome, incredibly beautiful creation!

She sat contentedly as the shadows began to lengthen, and she could hear Mr. Jackson's and the kids' voices as they shut the cubbyhole door to the chicken house. She heard Skyler start to cry because he had taken a tumble and Mr. Jackson's low rumble as he comforted him. She watched as a whole parade of cats followed the little procession from the chicken house to the front porch, and in the back of her mind the question of why any woman would give this up to sing in a smoky bar niggled at her.

"Why are you sitting here in the dark?" Scilla asked her as she bounded up the porch steps ahead of her dad and Skyler.

"I thought Sage and I would watch this beautiful sunset," Abbie replied, wondering anew at the little girl's energy.

"Don't you have sunsets where you come from?"

"Actually, yes, but for some reason I never seemed to be in the right place at the right time to see them." *Amazing,* she thought. *Now I step out the kitchen door and the whole sky looks like paradise.*

Scilla plopped down beside her and gazed at the deepening twilight. "Do you watch these things, Daddy?" She was looking at her dad as he came slowly up the walk with Skyler.

"Probably not often enough. Why don't you get ready for bed, Scilla? It's been a long day." Wade picked up the whimpering Skyler and carried him as he walked up the porch steps past Abbie. "You're up way past your bedtime, Miss Miller," he said, grinning at her good-naturedly.

Abbie slowly rose with Sage and turned to follow them through the door. "I think I'm getting used to your time zone," she said. "By the time I go back home in June, I'll be on Yankee time and will have to readjust to waking up to tea and crumpets."

He was holding the door for her and she saw the look of surprise that came over his face. "You're leaving in June?"

"Oh, but I thought you knew that." She stopped to look at him.

"I must have forgotten." He let the screen door slam behind him.

It was the first night she helped her boss put his kids to bed. Sage was easy—he was already in his pajamas, and with his teddy bear and thumb for comfort, dreamland wasn't far away.

Scilla jumped into some ragged pajamas and dove into her bed, muttering a "God bless" as she burrowed under the sheet.

But Skyler had problems. He had misplaced his blanket, and Abbie searched the whole house before she finally found it wadded up in a corner in the pantry. He wanted his mother, he wanted a drink, he wanted crackers. Finally at the end of his patience, Mr. Jackson said if Skyler wanted one more thing he was going to get a spanking. Skyler seemed to know he had pushed the household to its limit, and with muted whimpering lay back in his bed, refusing to close his big dark eyes while Abbie was in the room.

When she finally crawled into her own bed, Abbie thought of Tyler and Clair. *I wonder how Clair would have handled living way out here? Personally, I think she would have flown back home on the next plane, with or without Tyler. I haven't even had time to e-mail anyone—better do that tomorrow, since the boss has the computer up and running now.*

Lord, I'm too tired to even be homesick.

CHAPTER 8

Summer Ends—School Begins

*T*HE NEXT MORNING Abbie made the JELL-O squares she had promised Scilla and Skyler. She was setting the rest of their lunch on the table while absently listening to Mr. Jackson's side of a phone conversation and thought he sounded slightly ruffled and annoyed. She heard him say, "No, Torrie, I didn't know that. Thanks for telling me." There was a slight pause and then he added, "Right. I'll see you then."

When he set the phone in its cradle on the kitchen counter he turned to the ever-hopping Scilla.

"Scilla, did your mother tell you school starts next week?"

"What?" Scilla almost shrieked the word. "I don't have any clothes!"

Mr. Jackson looked at her with a raised eyebrow and turned to Abbie with a slight frown. "Not quite six and already she thinks she doesn't have a thing to wear."

"With good reason, Mr. Jackson. She's outgrown everything." In fact, that very morning Abbie and Scilla had made a thorough check of Scilla's closet to see what she did have for school clothes and the findings were very meager.

Mr. Jackson sat down at the kitchen table and spooned some beans on Skyler's plate.

"No! No want." Skyler's limited vocabulary usually conveyed his wishes. If it didn't, Abbie had discovered Scilla was a great interpreter.

"Why not?" Mr. Jackson asked.

"No good."

"I guess that's plain enough," Abbie said, and watched Skyler pick up two beans and put them on the table. He had gotten into trouble with his dad the previous day for throwing what he didn't want to eat on the floor.

Father and son exchanged glances, and Abbie noted that Skyler soon looked her way with his dark eyes. She couldn't decide if he was embarrassed to be scolded in front of her, or if he thought she was responsible for his trouble in the first place.

Abbie looked away from him and studied Scilla's long and tangled brown hair. "I could probably take care of Scilla's hair, but the clothes are another matter," she mused aloud.

"I think we will get these kids ready and go to Pierre this afternoon," Mr. Jackson informed her. "There's a number of things I need—plus what Scilla needs. Important things, Scilla, like paper, crayons, pencils—"

Scilla interrupted with one word. "Clothes!"

"Apparently the children don't wear uniforms here?" Abbie asked.

"Not unless you call jeans and T-shirts uniforms."

"Well, at least those items won't be hard to find," Abbie shrugged. "Will Scilla be going to school all five days?"

"No, actually, our district has a four day week. There is no school on Friday, and Scilla, being a kindergarten kid, only goes Monday, Wednesday, and Thursday." Mr. Jackson was drumming his fingers on the table, and Abbie decided that might mean he wanted to finish lunch so they could get started on this shopping excursion.

Within the hour they were heading east and, unlike Mrs. Jackson's limited knowledge of cattle and field equipment, Mr. Jackson gave a running commentary on both, plus which neighbors lived where, and where the school was located.

"Clive Barrows lives down this road with his folks—Clive and I are about the same age."

"Daddy, what's Clive gonna say when he sees Abbie?" Scilla asked.

Abbie turned to look behind the seat at Scilla and noted a genuine look of concern on the little girl's face.

"Knowing Clive, he'll have something to say." Mr. Jackson seemed to be suppressing a smile.

"Clive always says he don't like redheads," Scilla informed Abbie solemnly.

"I wonder why not?" Abbie felt compelled to ask.

Scilla waited for her dad to answer.

"I think it's because when he was a little boy in school, a red-haired girl wanted to kiss him," he said rather slowly.

"I suppose that could be traumatizing." Abbie didn't mean to sound so tart.

"Instead of kissing him like he was expecting, she bit him on the lip."

"Oh… I see." Abbie noted her boss was quite amused at his story.

Time seemed to fly that afternoon as Abbie and Scilla shopped for clothes and school supplies. Mr. Jackson took the two boys on his errands, and when he returned to the mall a couple of hours later he seemed in unusually good spirits.

Abbie inwardly groaned when she saw several paint cans on the floor of Mrs. Jackson's little car. By the time everyone was buckled in and packages were stashed there was hardly any room to even breathe.

"I bought a used Tahoe," Mr. Jackson announced as they headed downtown. "This car smells too much like cigarettes, it's too small, and I want something with four-wheel drive to go back and forth to school with." He looked over at Abbie. "Plus, I understand that employers generally provide some sort of transportation for their nannies."

"Sometimes they do," Abbie said slowly. "Who told you that?"

"I called Mrs. Davis. She said she would get in touch with you soon. Her mother seems to be doing well and is home from the hospital."

"That's good. It is unusual not to have any contact with the coordinator when a new job begins."

"Well, I guess I wouldn't know anything about that." He was obviously still thinking about his new vehicle. "We'll have to get this car unloaded. I'll drop you off at the grocery store, and while you're getting everything on that long list you have, the rest of us will get resettled in the other outfit."

He whipped around the grocery store parking lot and stopped by the front door. "See you in a little while." She barely had time to get out before he was heading back down the street.

It would be so nice to sit down and have a cup of tea and catch my breath. Being Mr. Jackson's employee is a little like being on the edge of a whirlwind.

By the time she had made all her purchases, he was back, exuding a great deal of enthusiasm over the SUV he was driving.

"How did you get this deal done so fast?" she wondered as groceries disappeared with amazing ease into the back of the Tahoe.

"I have friends in high places." He shut the back door and showed her how it latched. "Do you want to drive home?"

"Absolutely not! No. I mean no and no and no."

"Some day, Miss No and No, you'll have to take it to drive Scilla to school."

"You do realize, Mr. Jackson, that everyone in this country drives on the wrong side of the road."

He laughed and guided her to the passenger side. "You can practice on our country road where there isn't much traffic. You'll do fine."

"But I'm horrified I might have an accident with your children." Abbie was serious as she got into the shiny black Tahoe.

He shut the door for her and left to put the grocery cart away. When he returned and they started for home, he said, "I'll take care of it next week because her teacher said for the first week only she'll have the kindergarten kids go only two days. After that, you'll have a little experience driving on the right side of the road. You can take her in the morning, and Torrie, her teacher, will bring her home in the afternoon."

"I see." Abbie turned to check the children in the cavernous back seats. Sage had his thumb and teddy bear and was already drifting off to sleep. There was plenty of room for the three kids, all their packages, and the groceries.

She sniffed the air. No cigarette smoke. "Well, it is a very nice 'outfit.' I hope I don't wreck it."

He glanced at her and said wryly, "Think American. Not British."

"It's rather difficult to change nationalities in the space of four days."

They were quiet for a few minutes.

"What do you think of our prairie and sky, Abbie?" Wade asked suddenly.

"I've never seen the sky dome over the entire horizon like it does here." She paused to look out both side windows. "Do you ever feel like you're in the desert with all this brown?"

He gave her another fleeting glance before turning his attention back to the road. "August is always brown in western South Dakota. We usually don't have a lot of rain then. It's always pretty and green in the spring—sort of takes us by surprise after months of brown, and then months of white."

"But I see cattle grazing and I wonder how there's any nourishment in the dry grass."

Mr. Jackson nodded. "I've seen calves come off these pastures and weigh good in the fall. There's more good stuff there than what you might think."

"Do you sell your calves in the fall?"

"No, I run 'em until they're yearlings."

"So do you still have your yearlings on pasture now?"

"I sell them a week from today."

She looked at him with concern. "I hope I haven't asked too many questions. My Aunt Lena tells me I'm like a dog with a bone when I want to know something."

He laughed at that. "Well, my grandmother says you'll never learn unless you ask questions."

Shy's tail wagged slowly as Abbie eased down beside the big German shepherd lying on the porch. She let out a tired sigh and rubbed her aching muscles.

It was her first Sunday in America, and when given the choice either to go to church with Mr. Jackson and the children or stay at the ranch, she quickly had decided to stay at the ranch.

"Your boss is crazy," she flatly informed Shy, and was rewarded with a raised dog eyebrow and indelicate grunt.

She idly tried peeling layers of paint off her arm, but they seemed to have a strange unwillingness to let go of her.

"You're lucky you didn't get painted along with the hallway and kitchen," she added, patting his noble head and getting rewarded with a slurp across her paint-splattered cheek.

Abbie's ability to paint had not improved significantly since she was a young girl, and her enthusiasm for the project was limited when they began. However, the afternoon they returned home from town, Mr. Jackson had decided to get started. By late Saturday the walls boasted fresh paint, and the atmosphere in the entire downstairs was a sharp contrast to the way it had looked when Abbie first stepped into the house.

Lord, I don't believe I've ever been so tired. It's all I can do to care for these three kids and keep up with what the boss has in mind. I can't understand why he has felt so driven to clean the house up. What will Mrs. Jackson think when she comes home?

Abbie yawned and leaned back on the porch step. She enjoyed the view of the little creek winding its way from the hills toward the house, and this August morning was proving a little cooler than the temperatures earlier in the week.

Abbie's thoughts drifted to her three little charges. *I believe since the house is cleaner, Sage looks better. He's still too pale and somewhat listless, but Lord, I know You'll be with him and lay Your healing hands on him. Skyler misses his mother. Help me to know how to fill the gap without taking his mother's place. Scilla—she sometimes acts like she's relieved her mother is gone. I can't quite put my finger on it. It's easy to see she adores her dad. Thank You for Your help and guidance caring for these children. I should have asked for this when I was home in England taking care of kids—I would have done a better job.*

"Shy, do I dare have a cup of tea, or shall I take a nap like you're getting ready to do?"

The big dog raised himself slowly, breathed hot heavy air in her face, and walked down the porch steps to the shade of the big cottonwood tree. He made himself comfortable before looking her way again.

They blinked at each other across the yard, and Abbie decided man's best friend had the right idea. She slowly walked back into the house. The sun beamed its light into the dining room. With its fern-splashed wallpaper and oak wainscoting, it was a cozy area. She decided to take a tour of the whole house.

When Abbie had finished her inspection of the light and airy rooms, detailed wood trim, and tasteful carpets, she marveled that Mrs. Jackson had such a dislike for it.

Mr. Jackson had insisted on arranging the living room the same way his grandmother had. It was a comfortable and homey room. In fact, Abbie decided as she stretched out on the sofa, with the breeze gently blowing the curtains and a robin chirping softly outside, it was almost perfect.

But why did Mrs. Jackson leave in such a hurry? Abbie sighed sleepily. And why hadn't she called this first week to see how the children were faring under a stranger's care? And why was the downstairs covered in mourning crepe?

Abbie drifted to sleep, the questions remaining unanswered. For over an hour she slept without being disturbed. It was while she was between sleep and wakefulness that she heard the laughter. She frowned before she drifted into sleep again.

She dreamed Mr. Jackson was watching her paint. With every brushstroke he became amused and would burst forth with a hearty chuckle. It began to annoy her until finally she threw the bucket of paint at him. There was a loud thud when it hit him and he immediately stopped laughing. Suddenly she was back in England, fishing with her dad…

CHAPTER 9

Torrie McGovern

*A*S HE WAS driving the children to church and contemplating his new situation, Wade decided there was no point in breaking the news to his neighbors that he and Kada were divorcing. He hoped he wasn't committing a sin by what he didn't say. For all practical purposes he intended to explain Abbie's appearance as the gal Kada hired to watch the kids while she took a few college classes.

He didn't know what the little British nanny would say if she knew Kada wasn't coming back at all. She seemed to have high morals, and the appearance of being a divorced fellow's hired help could be quite controversial, he figured.

That morning he had realized Abbie was one tired redhead. He wasn't surprised she wanted to stay at the ranch rather than go to church, but he hoped he didn't come back to find her terrified and ready to go back to England.

He had never understood Kada's fear of his house. For that matter, his own mother had seemed reluctant to stay there alone. It was foolishness to him. His grandmother loved the place and he wondered why in the world Kada couldn't have been more like her.

He glanced in the rearview mirror and cringed. Skyler was looking at him, and he could tell by the expression on his son's face that he had something on his mind.

"Where Mama?" Skyler had asked the same question repeatedly since Kada left.

"Your mother is in Spearfish, and she's going to school," he repeated the same information again. He knew already what the next question would be.

"When Mama come?"

Wade paused, and wished he could give his son the complete truth. "She'll be back as soon as she can." Maybe she would be back—at least to pick up the rest of her things. He didn't know if Skyler would be as willing to let Kada go the next time as he had been the previous week.

He crested the top of the hill and Valley Community Church came into view. He and his family had attended the white country church for several generations. In fact, his great grandfather had been one of the founders—when the countryside was just beginning to be settled, a group of men decided to build one big church in a central location for the entire community. They had located the elementary school nearby. Both had served families well for many years. Several houses clustered together on the prairie's edge before the breaks of the Cheyenne River changed the landscape.

The congregation never asked anymore where Kada was. They seemed to know when she sang late on Saturday nights she wouldn't be awake for early Sunday church service.

As Wade made his way into the sanctuary, Torrie McGovern waved at him, and soon he had the kids settled in a pew behind her and her parents.

Wade, Torrie, and Clive Barrows had grown up in the area and had gone to the local school together. They had attended Fort Pierre for their high school years, and while Wade and Clive served a stint in the military, Torrie had attended college to become a teacher.

Torrie was tall and dark, with thick wavy hair and a gorgeous figure. More than one young fellow had eyed the McGovern ranch and Torrie with appreciation. Not only was she one of the valley school teachers, she was also considered quite a ranch hand and made a striking picture on her horse.

After the service, the usual rolls and coffee were served, and the small congregation spilled outside to visit with one another.

David McGovern, Torrie's dad, had helped Wade's family gather and sell their yearlings for years. In turn, Wade helped the McGoverns gather and sell their calf crop the following month. There was an easy camaraderie between the families that years of working together had developed.

"What time are your truckers getting there Friday?" David wanted to know as the two men stood together under the elm trees.

"About nine. I guess if you want to come about seven that should be early enough."

"Need any help getting 'em out of the big pasture the day before?"

"Don't think so, David. Clive and his folks usually help, and I hired a couple of high school boys this year."

Torrie was walking toward them with Scilla and Skyler on either side of her, each holding one of her hands. Wade noticed the sunshine made auburn highlights on her dark hair. She flashed a brilliant smile at him as she came closer. "Guess what? With our four-day school week, I get to come and help on Friday!"

The hills and draws of Wade's steer pasture were steep, and unless a rider rode through each one, a bunch of yearlings could easily be overlooked. Wade was grateful Clive and his parents were willing to help him every year when he sold the cattle at auction.

Amazingly, even thought she was slightly hefty, Clive's mother, Marilyn, loved to ride her black mare at these events. When she scouted a pasture, you could bet she checked every hiding place. Wade returned her waved greeting and grinned as she ducked her head to keep her hat from spiraling off her head from the strong gusts of wind.

It was very warm and very windy that Thursday afternoon, but in spite of that, the high school boys seemed to relish the roundup. Wade himself felt the surge of excitement working cattle always brought.

The six riders fanned out over the pasture, and soon their yips and hollers could be heard above the wind as they routed the steers from their grazing.

Shy always traveled with Wade, but he had never learned the secrets of a cow dog. Most of the time Wade held his breath and worried that the big dog might cause a wreck and scatter yearlings in every direction.

Once the steers realized they were moving out of the pasture, they began a steady walk toward the gate, and as each bunch joined the others, the walk became faster, until those in the lead snorted and broke into a run.

The riders likewise quickened their pace, and soon all of them were in a fast trot—some behind, some on the sides. Wade always checked to see if Shy was staying out of trouble. Knowing yearlings' habits, he pushed Jake into a fast canter so he could turn the lead steers in the right direction. Once the steers were headed down the correct draw to the gate, they again kicked up their heels like school kids enjoying a holiday.

The mile they traveled after they went through the gate became much slower. As usual, once the joy of leaving the main pasture had dimmed, the steers became balky, and the ride settled down to grim determination.

Clive and the boys took down their ropes and used them to flick the plodding animals' broad backs. Shy took the opportunity to bite some beefy legs and, to everyone's amazement, never endured a direct kick.

Suddenly Marilyn's horse made a side leap, and it spoke of her horsemanship that she stayed on board.

"Rattlesnake!" she hollered as Wade rode up to her. She pointed to the coiled and aggravated reptile. With its fangs showing and forked tongue darting in and out, plus the constant rattle of its tail, the snake was a repulsive sight.

Rattlesnakes had always put a cold chill down Wade's back, and he wasn't slow in getting off his horse with his lariat rope. Marilyn quickly reached for his horse's reins while he swung at the ugly head with the end of the rope. With the first hit the snake was slightly stunned, but before Wade could hit it again, the snake made a strike and he heard Marilyn call out, "Watch him!"

The next hit was more successful, and Wade made several more whacks until the life was beaten out of the snake. Still, the body kept moving as if loath to give up the battle, and when Wade planted one foot on its head, it writhed in vengeance around his boot.

With his knife he quickly cut off the rattlers, handed them to Marilyn and grinned. "You can add this to your collection."

"Good grief—thirteen buttons. What a moose!" She was in good humor as she pocketed them. Since the rest of the crew had the yearlings going through the last gate, Wade and Marilyn rode leisurely to join them.

"How is everyone, Wade?" Marilyn asked, tilting her head so she could hear his answer above the wind.

"Good. Did you know Kada was going to college?" He figured she had heard.

"Torrie was telling Clive that. Who's watching the kids?"

"She hired a gal—Abbie Miller—to take care of them when she's gone."

Marilyn rode a short distance with a frown on her face. "Who is Abbie Miller?"

"When you all come up to the house for something to drink, you can meet her."

"But is she local?" Marilyn turned to look at Wade.

Wade replied with as much of an accent as he could muster. "No, quite British I would say."

They had joined the others and were riding through the herd on their way to the house. The steers would settle down and graze in the evening, and the well water filling the rubber tire tanks would satisfy their enormous thirst.

Soon they had all dismounted and tied their horses to the corral posts. The high schoolers were still full of energy and chased each other with their ropes. Wade noticed Clive's parents moved with studied slowness. He also noticed Clive wanted time alone with him. They walked a measured distance behind the rest of the crew, and Clive's quiet words were no surprise to him.

"Kada's gone?"

Wade turned to look at his blue-eyed friend. "She's taking college courses."

Clive was studying him intently. "Any more to the story?"

"When there is, I'll let you know." He gave a wry smile to soften his remark.

Wade headed up the porch steps, and he noticed everyone's hesitation to follow him.

"Since Kada left, we've been using the kitchen door," he explained and held the door open for them to enter.

"Wow! Wow!" Marilyn exclaimed as she stepped into the clean and bright kitchen. "Am I in the right house?" She seemed a little embarrassed at this outburst and looked at Wade apologetically.

"Yes, ma'am, you are at the right house. Let me introduce you to the British painter who made all this possible."

Abbie was presented to everyone and soon a pitcher of iced tea was being poured into glasses and chocolate chip cookies were passed around while the crew settled comfortably around the big kitchen table.

When there was a lull in the conversation, Marilyn looked at Abbie and asked, "So you're the one who instigated all this painting?"

"Actually, Mrs. Barrows—"

"Oh, call me Marilyn."

"Actually, Marilyn, Mr. Jackson was the instigator, and I was the slave labor."

Wade grinned at her. "I don't believe the British ever won a war by their painting abilities," he said.

"When Winston Churchill said we would never give up, he wasn't talking about painting the queen's kitchen." Abbie's brown eyes seemed to twinkle at everyone.

There was a lot of good-humored teasing, and when it was time for everyone to leave, Wade heard Marilyn invite Abbie over for coffee in the near future.

Wade, Clive, David, and Torrie quickly gathered the steers out of the horse pasture the next morning. Before the semis pulled into the yard, the yearlings had been penned and were ready to load.

"I sure wish someone would tell me how they back those outfits up like that," Clive said, admiring the driver's skill at putting the semi trailer snug against the loading chute on the first attempt.

"I wish they would too," Torrie replied. "I still have to look at that gate you bent backing the horse trailer up to our chute."

"I wouldn't have hit it if you'd hollered 'whoa' instead of 'go.'" Clive had a mischievous look on his face.

Torrie batted Clive with a small fist. "I hollered 'whoa' until I was blue in the face. You just can't hear."

Clive cupped his hand behind his ear. "What?"

Wade shook his head at the two of them. For as long as he could remember, they were usually arguing about something in good-natured fun.

When the semi driver rolled up the gate to his trailer, they waited to hear how many critters he wanted in the first compartment. When he hollered twelve, they quickly separated twelve head and chased them up the loading chute into the trailer. As usual, the sound of hoofs on metal made a clanging noise, and that, along with the ceaseless wind and muted bellowing, created a din. The next compartment could hold twenty, and so it went until the first trailer was completely full.

The driver rolled down the gate and latched it, and then quickly drove his semi out of the yard and stopped it along the road. He parked and came back to help the other drivers and crew load their trucks. In short time, the semis held Wade Jackson's main source of revenue for the year, and they started down the road to the Ft. Pierre livestock auction.

"Your steers sure look good," David told Wade. "Hope they bring a good price."

"Yeah, who knows?" Wade answered. If there are a lot of buyers, if the futures in the cattle market are good, if, if, if…his profit margin hinged on all the many "ifs."

"Torrie, you better go up to the house and meet Abbie," Clive said. He looked at her quizzically. "Or have you already seen her?"

"I met her when I brought Scilla home from school the first day," Torrie answered, twisting to unsnap the buckles on her chinks.

"Oh, I just met her yesterday. She's darn purty for a redhead. I wonder if she likes to dance," Clive mused, looking in the direction of the house.

Torrie whipped her chinks around and threw them into the cab of the McGovern pickup. "You'll have to ask her, Clive." She and her dad had their horses loaded in the horse trailer and were getting ready to go home. "Good luck at the sale, Wade. Is she going with you?"

"Who, Abbie?" Wade shook his head. He wondered why Torrie would even ask that question. "Thanks for helping, David, Torrie. I always appreciate it."

Torrie's white teeth flashed in the sunlight as she gave him a winsome smile. "See you later," she said out the passenger window as her dad started the pickup and eased it into gear.

"Daddy!" Scilla was running toward him with excitement in her eyes. "Can I go with you and Clive to the sale?"

Wade tousled her brown hair and on impulse picked her up and gave her a toss in the air. She giggled with wild abandon when he caught her and hugged her before setting her firmly on the ground again. "Sure—just hurry up and be ready because I want to leave right away."

In a short time, Wade, Clive, and Scilla were heading to the Ft. Pierre sale barn and the auction. When Wade's steers were brought in the arena, there was the usual quick bidding, and within half an hour over a year's worth of work had been sold.

Wade looked at the sale ticket with a raised eyebrow. Sale expense, beef check-off expense, trucking expense. *Whattya know?* he thought grimly. *Even a little left for me.*

He was pocketing the check when Torrie appeared. "I didn't know you guys were coming," Wade said as she walked up to him.

"I came by myself. Thought I'd see how the market went." She was in tight fitting jeans and when she patted Wade's arm he caught a whiff of her perfume. "I thought you might like to take your help out to lunch now that you're a rich man."

"Clive and Scilla are getting a head start on that," Wade told her as he guided her to the sale barn café. "We better hurry or they'll be eating the last piece of pie."

They found the pair sitting at a table. Clive was in the middle of a story, and when Wade and Torrie sat down, Clive merely raised his hand while he continued in detail until the end. Wade knew Scilla was enthralled with all of Clive's tales—even if she had heard them before.

He wished Torrie wouldn't sit so close to him. Every time he moved his arm he would brush hers, until finally he tried to unobtrusively move his chair slightly away from hers.

While they were ordering lunch and discussing the sale, Wade's mind was busy subtracting and dividing the check he had just received. There were a lot of expenses, and usually outlay was greater than income. With Kada's college tuition added on, he realized bleakly that he would have to stretch every dollar even further.

Every year since he was asked to buy his grandparents' place, they had sat with him and discussed the amount he could afford to pay them. His grandparents were more than fair, he knew, but as always, money was incredibly tight.

"Don't you think so, Wade?" Clive was asking him. At Wade's obviously blank look, Clive glanced at Torrie and said, "He's thinking of where to spend all that money."

"Yeah," Wade snorted. "Cake, corn, taxes—and now Scilla is into clothes—and that's the way the money goes."

"Daddy! You made a—a—what's that word when things sound alike?" She looked at Torrie for help.

"Your dad made a rhyme," Torrie answered. "Wade the poet." Once again she patted his arm.

"A man of many talents," Clive added, "including painting."

"Abbie tried to paint too, didn't she, Daddy?" Scilla giggled.

Wade grinned. "Abbie muttered a lot, and painted a little." He glanced over at Scilla with her brown hair combed neatly into two pigtails. "But she also cut and fixed your hair, put your school clothes in order, took care of your brothers, cooked meals, and kept the rest of the house clean. So we won't give her too bad a time about her painting."

He was a little surprised at the annoyed look on Torrie's face.

CHAPTER 10

Toads and Kangaroos

THAT SAME AFTERNOON, Abbie was entertaining company. Mrs. Davis, the nanny coordinator, had come from Pierre to make sure all was well and to personally hand Abbie her first check.

"I suppose Mrs. Jackson plans to be back over the weekends," Mrs. Davis said while she and Abbie were having a cup of tea.

"I'm looking for her, although she never came last weekend, and as far as I know, never has called."

Mrs. Davis looked surprised. "Oh, surely she has, and you just aren't aware of it."

"Well," Abbie replied slowly, "I suppose I should say she has never called me, and I have never heard Mr. Jackson say he heard from her either."

"I never met her husband. It's so unusual for people in our ranching area to hire nannies—has that been working out satisfactorily?"

"For someone who didn't know I was coming, he seems to have adjusted quite well."

Mrs. Davis frowned and set down her cup. "He did not know you were hired as a nanny for his children?"

"No," Abbie replied, wishing she had kept that information to herself. "More tea, Mrs. Davis?"

"I never heard of the spouse not knowing, especially since there has been quite a large sum of money deposited to pay you." She shook her head at Abbie's offer of more tea and drummed the table with plump fingers for several seconds. "Keep me informed on matters, Abbie, and if you are uncomfortable being here alone with Mr. Jackson, call me. We'll work something out."

She pushed back her chair and looked intently at Abbie. "Are you sure he didn't know? Did he specifically say that?"

"Yes, Mrs. Davis, he specifically said that." Abbie answered more sharply than she intended. She hastened to vindicate her boss. "He's a good parent to his children, and other than insisting that I help paint the kitchen and hallway, he treats his hired help very well." She hoped her attempt at humor would pacify the overly sensitive woman.

"I don't believe helping paint is in the agreement, Abbie. You seem to have to do a lot more work than what the contract says you have to." Mrs. Davis frowned again as she stood.

Abbie stood also and tried her best to give a reassuring smile. "I really don't mind. I'm sure when Mrs. Jackson comes back I'll have some days off."

"Absolutely. It very specifically states in your contract that you have the weekends off. Oh, by the way, I understand you have a vehicle to drive. I suppose you've had quite a challenge learning to drive on the opposite side of the road. Many of the nannies from England have a hard time adjusting."

"The first several times I got in on the wrong side. I'm getting used to it now." She lifted Mrs. Davis's huge purse off the floor and handed it to her.

"Yes, well, be sure and call me if there are any problems."

Abbie promised she would. When she opened the front door, the warm wind swept over the two women, and Mrs. Davis quickly looked toward the western sky. "I always check for rain clouds. Even if we do need a rain, I don't want to get caught out here in a storm."

Before she got into her small car, Mrs. Davis reminded Abbie once again to call her if there were any problems. Abbie nodded. After the car headed down the gravel road, Abbie sighed and turned back toward the house.

She hated to admit to herself that she was disappointed with Mrs. Davis's first visit. Abbie had thought they would discuss the children more, but instead had spent a great deal of time discussing Mrs. Davis's mother. She wondered if Mrs. Davis would be much help if there were any potential problems, and she realized she had very little confidence in the woman.

But it wasn't just Mrs. Davis who irritated her. Torrie McGovern had eyed her with derision the first time they met. When the shapely teacher brought Scilla home from school, she barely acknowledged Abbie and immediately rolled her eyes when Abbie started speaking, which Abbie assumed was some slight due to her British accent. She told Scilla the same words Mrs. Davis had used: "Call me if there are any problems." Abbie's good humor had been severely tested after that remark.

"I suppose both of them think I can't handle three little kids and a household," Abbie grumbled aloud as she mounted the porch steps. "No doubt only a great American cowgirl is so gifted." Abbie was already tired of Clive Barrows's unending praise of Torrie's riding skills.

She had known at once she would like Marilyn Barrows. Her compliments and wit—plus the fact that she invited Abbie over for coffee—had been a ray of sunshine. "But I daresay even that good lady must get tired of hearing about Terrific Torrie," Abbie grumbled again.

When Abbie entered the clean kitchen, she looked at it with satisfaction. She was grateful her boss had spent the first week getting the house in order, even if he had commanded her about like a drill sergeant. She had seen little of him the past week, but had used the time to become better acquainted with the children.

Abbie was concerned about Scilla's thinness and persistent cough. It was a hollow, rasping bark that would erupt suddenly and last far too long. Sage's cough was almost the same, and on top of that he was still too pale and listless. Skyler was the healthiest of the three, but he followed her around with sad, dark eyes, and most of his talk centered on wondering when his mother would come home.

"At least," she said aloud to no one, "Sage is beginning to have a little more color—I'm quite sure of that." She knew the removal of dust and cigarette smoke would improve both Scilla's and Sage's coughs, but Skyler's lonesomeness bothered her. Those were the things for which she would have appreciated some guidance from Mrs. Davis.

She wished her mother were there. At home in England she could always give her mom a call, and their visit would set the world to rights. If not her mom, then Clair would give her the answers and reassurances she needed. Suddenly, family and beautiful England seemed very far away.

Please, Lord, I don't dare give in to homesickness right now. I need that proverbial stiff upper lip Aunt Lena always talks about.

Abbie had just finished putting away the washed teacups when she saw Skyler standing in the kitchen doorway with his blanket.

"Where Mama?"

"Did you have a good nap, Skyler?" she asked, quickly walking toward him. She picked him up and, as usual, he stiffened in her arms and wanted down.

"Do you know," she continued as she ignored his actions, "that I love rocking little boys and telling them stories?"

She gathered his blanket and snuggled him in her arms while settling in the rocking chair by the dining room's sunny windows.

He was unresponsive, but at least he didn't wriggle away as he usually did.

"Once upon a time there was a wonderful little boy named Sky."

He looked at her and scowled. "No, I Skyler."

"Once upon a time there was a wonderful little boy named Skyler. He had a favorite blanket that was covered with galloping horses and cowboys in red bandannas."

"No! No horses!" He quite indignantly pointed out the dogs on his blanket.

"But the blanket that he loved the most had pictures of dogs, and every time he looked at them he was reminded of his dog, Fido."

Skyler's eyes showed a small spark of humor. "No! No! Shy! Not Fido, Shy!"

"Shy was a little tiny dog that could do tricks."

There was the tiniest of smiles on Skyler's face. "No! Shy big. Shy not little." He was waiting expectantly for her to bobble up more of his life.

"One time Shy found a kangaroo in his water dish."

"Nooo," he began uncertainly.

"Or was it a frog? I get them mixed up."

Skyler had put his hand on Abbie's shoulder and was studying her hair. "Frog—no—toad."

"Ah, yes, it was a toad. Shy was so busy drinking water that he drank the toad, and it hopped right down into his big belly."

Skyler was speechless.

"No one would have ever known about it except whenever Shy wanted to walk, he hopped instead."

"Hopped?" Skyler asked, and then slipped off her lap to start hopping on his knees.

"No, like this," Abbie told him, and she crouched down on her haunches and started making wild leaps. "Ribbit! Ribbit!" she croaked out, and soon she and Skyler were hopping all around the dining room floor making toad and frog noises.

They both were laughing and hopping when Skyler shouted, "You funny!"

He was still hopping and croaking when she heard Sage's cry from upstairs. She left her game with Skyler and ran upstairs. Sage was sitting in his crib with drool wetting the front of his shirt, but when he saw her coming he grinned and bounced while he waited for her to pick him up.

Soon she had a dry shirt and diaper on Sage, and both boys were eating a light snack she had prepared. They looked at her expectantly as they finished eating, and she decided what they needed was some good summer sun.

As the late afternoon gave way to early evening, Abbie and the boys puttered around the yard. They investigated an old sand pile and made roads and sputtering sounds. They moseyed over to the swing set and she sang songs with them as she slowly moved back and forth with Sage and gave Skyler light pushes. They wandered out to the barn, petted each and every cat, and tried to remember all their names. They and the parade of cats strolled down a trail that led to the creek and stopped to watch some deer leap gracefully over the barbed-wire fence. Finally, they ended up at the chicken house and waited while the slowpoke chickens cawed their way carefully to the little trap door. When the last hen dawdled, Skyler shooed her into the coop and closed the door with great importance.

They were ambling toward the house when Mr. Jackson and Scilla drove into the yard. Scilla was full of sale details and rambled on at great length about being with Torrie and Clive.

Abbie was puzzled. "Where is Clive? I thought he left with you."

"Daddy told him to ride home with Torrie—they both had things to get, and Daddy wanted to get on home." Scilla was flushed with pleasure to be the one in the know.

"How did your afternoon go, Abbie?" Mr. Jackson wondered.

Abbie smelled the fresh evening air, saw the beginnings of another sunset, and was aware of a curious happiness that seemed to radiate from within her being.

"We had an absolutely wonderful afternoon," she said, smiling.

CHAPTER 11

This Little Pig

"THIS LITTLE PIG went to market," Abbie crooned to Sage, holding his soft, fat, little foot and tweaking his big toe. He enjoyed the game as much as she did and was already squirming in his high chair.

"This little pig stayed home." She lightly pulled the second toe.

"This little pig had roast beef, and this little pig had none." She quickly passed over toes three and four.

"And this little pig," Abbie paused dramatically while Sage began giggling, "went wee, wee, wee, all the way home!" He broke out into baby guffaws as she lightly tickled him from his little toe to his soft little ear.

"I don't know who enjoys that more, you or Sage," Mr. Jackson said as he handed a cup of morning coffee to her in the sunlit kitchen.

"Probably me," Abbie laughed, taking the offered cup and settling onto a kitchen chair. "Well, Mr. Jackson, what is on the schedule for this week?"

"First of all, since you've been here well over a month, you can drop the Mr. Jackson bit and call me Wade."

"I suppose I could," Abbie agreed. "It's just that we are taught to call our employers 'Mr.' or 'Mrs.' to ensure a certain professionalism."

"I have great admiration for your professionalism, young lady, but being called Mr. Jackson is wearing a little thin with me." His eyes crinkled at the corners and he grinned at her to soften his remark.

"Good heavens, if that's the case, 'Wade' it will be." She took a long, slow drink of coffee and thought again that he made the best brew she had ever drunk.

"OK, moving right along to the next item of business. There will be cattle work, which means extra people for meals. I'll have to see who can come when, but I would imagine that Wednesday will work the best."

Abbie nodded and rejoiced that he had picked a day when Torrie couldn't help because she would be teaching at school. "Did I tell you that your grandmother Marie called yesterday and said they would like to come when you had the cattle in?"

"Really?" Wade poured milk into a child's cup, snapped the lid on, and watched Sage try to aim it into his mouth. "They haven't wanted to come out for a couple of years. Guess they must have heard the house was in better shape…either that or Scilla told them about the redhead that could hop like a toad."

"Oh, very funny. I had no idea Skyler could communicate so well about our toad game."

"You probably had no idea he would make you tell his Sky and Fido story to him every night either," Wade answered, and gave a little hoot of laughter before he took another drink of coffee.

She grinned at him and shook her head. Skyler had shown everyone who would take time to watch how he and "Bee"—his name for Abbie—played their new game. He even had the ribbit down perfect, although, as Wade had pointed out, it was a British sounding ribbit. The one consolation from all the harassing she had received was Skyler gradually had quit asking for his mother.

"Wade," Abbie said, deciding to broach a topic that had been bothering her, "do you want to tell me why Kada has never come home?"

He set down his coffee cup and looked at her. When he finally spoke his voice was clipped. "Kada and I are getting a divorce. The papers have been drawn up, and I have full custody of the kids."

He looked away before he added, "She won't be coming back, Abbie. Especially since Skyler has finally quit asking about her. I'll take the rest of her things to her, but we both thought it best for her to not upset Skyler's life anymore."

"I see."

"I doubt that you do. I think you find it unimaginable that a mother could leave her children."

"I find it heartbreaking. Not only for the children, but for the mother." Abbie shook her head and put down her empty cup. "She's missing so much and she won't realize it until it's too late."

Wade didn't speak until he had filled both cups again. When he was resettled in his chair he said, "When Kada knew she was pregnant with Sage, she wanted an abortion. Her so-called singing career was taking off. She had things to do, places to go, and it didn't include a baby. We had a long discussion, and the gist of it was this child was going to be born."

When Abbie started to speak he held up his hand and shook his head. "I don't know if you've ever worked with a child who has fetal alcohol syndrome, Abbie. The poor little kid has to go through a lifetime of disability because his mother couldn't leave the booze alone while she was pregnant."

Once again she started to speak and he stopped her. "I told Kada that while she was carrying this child, she would give up her drinking and her singing and do whatever she had to do to give the baby a good start in life. After he was born, she could do whatever she wanted to. I thought we owed our baby every chance we could give him to have a normal life."

He took a deep breath and put some more Cheerios on Sage's tray. "I figured she would leave eventually, but she did keep her end of the bargain. She quit both her drinking and her band, and she basically stayed home and brooded. Now I have to keep my part and let her go."

Abbie was silent. When she looked over at Sage he bobbed his head and gave her a toothless grin. She reached over and tousled his downy hair and said a silent prayer of gratitude that he was even allowed to be born.

"I would imagine," she finally said slowly as she twirled her coffee cup around, "that those months were pretty tough. I would suspect you prayed a lot."

He nodded his head. "Yeah."

"I appreciate you telling me."

He smiled at her. "I would appreciate it if you could keep it to yourself."

"Whatever is said will come from you—not me. It's that professionalism I was talking about."

"Does that mean we're right back to 'Mr. Jackson'?"

She laughed and shook her head. "I think we can go with Wade."

Fall was definitely in the air that afternoon. With Scilla at school and Skyler and his dad checking fences, Abbie decided it was too beautiful a day to stay inside. She had been waiting for a chance to clear some neglected flowerbeds, so while Sage napped, Abbie armed herself with a rake and hoe and inflicted serious damage on the weed crop.

For some reason, Shy had decided to stay with her. Usually he was Wade's best friend, but he had declined Wade's invitation to jump in the back of the pickup. Instead, he had flattened his ears to his head and whined, looking at Abbie for support. "Must be feeling a little hoppy this afternoon," Wade groused, casting her an accusing look.

Hoppy feeling or not, Shy followed her every footstep, sometimes so closely that she would almost trip over him. He would look so apologetic that she didn't have the heart to scold him. Finally, after she took a tumble because of his hovering, she gave him a little woman-to-dog lecture.

"Shy, did you notice that I was on the ground?"

He whined and licked her face, and she decided he needed mint-flavored dog food.

"Is there some reason for this behavior?"

He plopped down beside her and with a woebegone expression expelled a huge sigh.

For a while they studied each other in silence. His dog eyebrows seemed to move up and down with consternation, and his tail moved along with the eyebrows.

"I really expected different behavior from a German shepherd of your size."

He licked her hand delicately.

"It's so hard to get mad at someone who's licking your hand," Abbie muttered as she stood and brushed the grass off her jeans.

There was a swift movement along the east bank of the creek as a group of deer sprinted to the top of the hill and quickly disappeared. Abbie watched the flight in puzzlement, wondering what had scared them.

She wondered even more as Shy practically knocked her through the door as she entered the house. "Good grief, Shy, what is it with you anyhow?" She was totally exasperated with him.

That evening she recounted Shy's actions at the supper table. Wade shook his head. "The cattle were acting goofy today too. They were all bunched in a corner of the pasture."

"So were the deer—they acted like they were spooked."

Wade looked thoughtful. "Maybe—maybe you better not let the kids outside tomorrow."

"Why not, Daddy?" Scilla looked intrigued.

"Well," Wade hesitated before he said more, "sometimes a mountain lion goes through these parts."

Abbie's heart began to pick up speed. "I didn't realize they were in this area."

"They're everywhere," Wade said flatly, "even if the game and fish department say they aren't."

Wade changed the subject, but Abbie found herself wanting to shut and lock the doors after the children were put to bed, and there was no discussion of putting Shy back outside.

Abbie slept fitfully that night, waking from strange dreams and tossing and turning until she would doze again, only to repeat the cycle all over.

Suddenly a harsh scream echoed through the darkness, causing her to bolt upright in her bed. It was followed by an eerie silence, only to be broken again by an agonizing cry that grew louder and louder in painful intensity until the night was filled with the horror of the sound.

Abbie thought her heart was going to beat right out of her chest. Quickly, in trembling haste, she hurried to check the children and saw Wade running down the stairway with his rifle in hand.

Amazingly, the kids were still sleeping. She quietly left their rooms and wrestled with the indecision of whether to stay upstairs with them or wait for Wade downstairs. There were no more noises. Instead, the very air seemed permeated with quiet fear.

Abbie found her knees were shaking as she went down the steps, and when she reached the foot of the stairs, she was undecided if she should turn on a light or not.

"Better not," she mumbled to herself. "I might make myself a target. It's probably those stupid terrorists Aunt Lena is always talking about." She felt no comfort from her grim humor.

Not wanting to chance running into things with her bare feet and stubbing her toes, she dropped down to her knees and started crawling toward the porch door. In the night's blackness, she imagined all sorts of scenarios, and each picture made her grow more fearful. When she finally found the open door, she slowly inched herself to a standing position, and pressed against the screen to peer into the haunted night. To her horror, something stealthily pressed against the backs of her legs. At the same time, a presence pushed against her through the screen from the outside.

"Help!" she burst out, and there was instant bedlam with a cacophony of cursing and barking. She found herself being thrown to the floor, and a great weight crushing on top of her.

She started a frenzy of kicking to dislodge whatever it was, but was stopped in mid-kick by a slurpy tongue rolling across her face.

"Shy?" she yelped, and instantly heard Wade's voice over her.

"Abbie?"

"Wade?"

"What in the—what are you doing down here?" he asked, and she momentarily felt his hand pass over her shoulder.

"I came to see where you were. Where are you? I can't see you!" His weight was smothering her and she began kicking to free herself.

"Watch the feet, Abbie. Your feet are a lethal weapon!"

"Oh, sorry. Is this your hair?" After a short pause, she muttered, "Oh, I've got a hold of Shy's leg."

Wade had jumped to his feet and reached down to pull her up beside him.

"I think a cat just went through and killed something along the creek," he said. "I'll have to wait until morning to check it out."

She gasped and thought of all sorts of critters that might have met such a terrible death. "Do you think it was a horse?"

"No, not making that noise. More likely a deer."

"That's awful! I've never heard such a horrible sound."

"I've never heard anyone shout that close to me," his voice held a trace of annoyance. "What was your problem?"

Abbie was slowly recovering her common sense and also a little of her bravery. She took a deep breath. "Were you standing just outside the screen door?"

"Yeah, I came back to the porch because I was more than a little spooked and I couldn't see anything. I guess I was standing there just waiting—just trying to see out into the darkness." His hand found her arm. "What did you think it was, Abbie?"

"I had no idea—but you weren't the only one that was spooked. I about jumped out of my skin between Shy behind me and you in front of me. How did you get the door open so fast?"

He gave a slight chuckle. "Adrenaline. I had two thoughts: get in the house, and put the rifle down before I accidentally shoot somebody. Abbie, don't ever scare me like that again when I'm holding a gun."

They were shuffling their way to the stairway where a glimmer of light was coming from the nightlight in the upstairs hallway. Suddenly, Abbie saw a movement in the darkness beyond the dining room window and let out another shriek.

"Something's moving out there!"

"Abbie," Wade's voice held a trace of exasperation, "you are seeing a tree branch blowing in the wind."

"Let's turn on a blasted light!"

By this point they were at the foot of the stairs, and Wade flicked on the light to the stairway. She noticed he looked quite grim, and with each step he took he looked even more so.

"Are you hurt?" she wondered aloud.

"I'm in excruciating pain," he moaned. Looking a little sheepish, he added, "I was so rattled when I heard all the noise I slipped my pants on and shoved my feet into my boots without socks."

She looked down in dismay at his feet. "Oh boy."

He sat down on the steps and began to try to pull off the left boot. It wasn't budging.

"Would the boot jack help?" she asked. When he nodded, she hurried upstairs to his room. Within seconds she returned, and he stood to put the boot in the slot and tried to work his foot out. It wasn't budging.

"Maybe if I pulled on your boot it would help," she offered.

He sat back down on the bottom step and she grabbed hold of his boot to begin a seesaw movement. Finally, after a lot of maneuvering, his foot began to slowly inch out of its prison.

"Wowsers," he said, using Kada's expression. His foot slid out of the neck of the boot, and Abbie set it down beside him. They both studied the effects of a sockless boot experience.

"I think the pig that went to market must have met a terrorist," Abbie observed.

"Ha! If you think that one is bad you should take a gander at the one that had roast beef."

Abbie shook her head in sympathy over that one's obvious dilemma. Suddenly another thought struck her. "Wade, what about the other boot?"

"Yeah. I'll try the boot jack first."

She watched him for several agonizing moments as he tried to extract his foot. He slumped back down on the steps in defeat.

"Maybe some baby powder would help," she suggested, and scurried back upstairs to Sage's room. She was back in a flash and liberally sprinkled powder on his leg, hoping it would work down into his boot.

"I doubt that'll work," he informed her flatly.

Once again they began to work together. She pulled, he pulled, nothing happened.

"I can't get any leverage," he grumbled. "I need something to brace against because you're darn near pulling me off the step."

She scowled at him before turning around and straddling his foot. "Fine. I know what you're thinking. Just don't get smart about it."

"Well," he replied indignantly, "where else but your backside can I put one foot against to get some push power?"

"I said just don't get smart about it."

There was a moment of silence, and when he spoke again his voice sounded muffled. "Abbie, do you always wear these moose pajamas to bed?"

She turned her head around to glare at him. "They are a present from the last people I worked for, and they are extremely comfortable. So there."

"I see."

There was nothing more said as they began anew to work off his boot. Just at the point where Abbie was thinking he might as well live with one boot on his foot forever, there was a sudden loosening and the next instant both boot and Abbie were tumbling to the floor.

"Awww," she heard him moan, and she hurriedly crawled over to him to assess the damage.

They both were silent as they observed the final battleground. Finally, Abbie cleared her throat and asked if he would like a bandage.

"For which one?" he replied mournfully.

"Ah, well, my concern is still on the one that went to market."

"That coward? It's the poor little devil that cried all the way home who really took the beating."

"Wow." Abbie was impressed that it was indeed the little one that was rapidly turning black and blue.

"Do you want me to help you upstairs?" she asked and tried to stifle a yawn.

He leaned against the steps and looked her up and down. "You just want to take all those moose and go to bed, while me and the pigs stay up and suffer."

"You know what I think?" she said as she stood and reached down to help him stand. "I think from now on you better sleep with your socks on."

CHAPTER 12

Kada's Confession

THE WILD BOYS Plus One usually packed in a good crowd, and the dance at the Watering Hole in Ft. Pierre was no exception.

Kada was blasting out a torchy love song while behind her Bill was filling in all the gaps with his own unique harmony. The electric guitars were winding up to a crescendo and the crowd was noisy and amused as they watched her stage antics.

When the band broke for intermission, Kada saw Clive Barrows heading in her direction.

"Hey, old man Clive! Come here and talk to me!" She waved at him and watched his blue eyes take in her appearance with an appreciative smile.

"You're hot tonight, Kada. You sound great!" he greeted her and grinned even wider when she gave him a hug. "Can you come over to the table with Torrie and me and have a drink?"

"You and Torrie? Hey! Is something happening in the old neighborhood I need to know about?"

Clive shook his head. "Naw, she was just bored and suggested we come here tonight to hear you sing."

And that has got to be the lie of the century, Kada thought. Torrie McGovern couldn't care less how Kada sang, she was sure of that. She must want to gloat because she heard about the divorce.

Kada took Clive's arm and made a slow, sultry sashay over to the corner table where Torrie was waiting. She gushed at Torrie, flirted with Clive, and made any type of conversation impossible with her barrage of jokes and raspy laughter. She noticed Torrie's smile was becoming strained and saw relief in the other woman's eyes when the band started filing back on stage.

"Say, Kada, when you have another break, come over here and we'll catch up on neighborhood news," Clive said as she started to leave.

"Sure thing!" *Over my dead body.*

The next set was considerably longer, and Kada was sure Torrie would convince Clive to leave. However, they seemed to be dancing quite a bit and every time Kada saw them, they were acting as if they were having a wonderful time.

"Your friends are waiting for you," Bill pointed out as they put down their guitars for another intermission. "But you'd better quit talking and laughing so loud with them or your voice is gonna give out before we're ready to quit."

Kada gave a scathing look in Torrie's direction and turned to Bill with narrowed eyes. "She can't wait to give me all sorts of cozy little details about her and the ex."

"So what?" Bill looked down his beaked nose at her. "You made the choice to leave the guy. He's fair game, so don't let her get under your skin."

With her head held high, Kada sashayed through the crowd yet again, stopping when someone would compliment her, laughing and hugging this one or that one. Finally she reached the table where Torrie and Clive were sitting. She permitted herself a cold beer and waited expectantly for Torrie's claws to come out.

"Scilla is having fun at school, but I suppose she tells you all about that," Torrie said with a sly smile.

"Nope, she never said anything at all about school. How many kids do you have this year?"

Clive began a detailed history of attending students and who their parents were and rambled back to when he and Wade and Torrie were kids at school. He even asked Kada if she heard the story of the little redheaded girl in school who wanted to kiss him.

It was a new story to Kada, and she laughed uproariously when he told how the girl had bitten him instead.

"Speaking of redheads," Torrie interrupted, "that nanny you brought here is something else." From the tone of her voice, Kada gathered Torrie wasn't giving Abbie Miller a compliment.

"She sure has a way with kids." Clive seemed eager to smooth over Torrie's remark.

"Hey, Clive, you old son of a gun! How didcha end up with two pretty girls?" A boisterous newcomer pulled up a chair and sat beside Kada. He'd had several beers too many and was in a talkative mood. Kada recognized him as one of Wade's acquaintances.

"Did ya hear about the mountain lion at Wade's last week?" he asked, putting a beefy arm around Kada's shoulders.

Whether he was drunk or not, Kada welcomed his interruption and smiled at him encouragingly. She also noted with smug satisfaction that Torrie was not happy to have him join them.

"It tried to kill a horse right by the house but that li'l redhead got it chased away before it done any damage. She got all the kids inside and Wade went after it with his rifle. But what was the deal about the moose, Clive?"

Clive was momentarily at a loss for words, but Torrie was quick to speak.

"That's a bunch of bull! She never chased anything away. She was scared to death, screaming all over the place. Good night, where do you guys come up with all this stuff?"

"Well," the guy gave Kada's shoulder a little squeeze and shrugged, "you couldn't have found a better gal to stay with Wade and the kids.

She's got your li'l guy bouncing all around happy as a clam—told him some kangaroo story—Wade gets a big kick out of telling it." He seemed oblivious to Torrie's outburst.

"But what about the moose?" Kada wanted to know. She could tell by the look on Clive's face there was some sort of story there.

"Yeah, what about the moose, Clive? I jus' can't remember the deal about the moose. I heard you talking about it the other day at the card room, but I jus' can't remember whatcha said." The drunk's words were slightly slurred.

"There was no moose, for Pete's sake," Torrie sputtered. "You guys get everything twisted."

Clive was strangely silent.

"Well, old Wade is a-lookin' good, kids are a-lookin' good, and by golly, you're lookin' pretty hot yourself." The man gave Kada a low appreciative whistle. "I like ta hear ya sing. Now get back up there and croon me a love song!" He laughed with gusto at his own remark and, giving her another hug, pushed back his chair and left.

"If that isn't the most absurd story I've ever heard," Torrie groused to his back. Kada didn't know if she meant the mountain lion, the moose, or Kada looking good.

Kada finished her beer and rose also. "Hey, nice seeing you guys," she said brightly. "I better do as the man says and get back on stage and croon him a love song!" She laughed her raspy laugh and made her way back to the stage.

"You must have lived through whatever she dished out," Bill noted as he handed Kada her guitar.

"Yeah." But it wasn't what Torrie had said that bothered her; it was the big guy's remark that Skyler was happy as a clam. She realized her little rug rat must have gotten over her, and part of her heart was breaking from hearing that news. *But that's what you wanted—you wanted to be free and you didn't want Skyler hurt. You got what you thought would make you happy.*

She still wondered where the moose fit in.

It was on the long stretch of road back to Spearfish in the early morning hours after the dance when Bill cleared his throat and asked Kada what was wrong.

"You've been too quiet, girl. You sang good, you looked good, but that last hour before we quit, your mind was a million miles away." He asked her again what was wrong.

She shook her head and pushed back into the passenger seat of the van. "Bill, sometimes you ask too many questions." She gave a hollow laugh.

"If it's a problem with the band, it's my business. If it's personal, I'll stay out of it."

She quickly glanced over at him. The light from the dash illuminated his face. His eyes shifted from the road to her, and back to the road again, and a thought raced through her mind that the only time he showed emotion was during a song.

"No problems with the band. I just—I guess life moves on, people move on, and even my little rug rat has moved on and isn't crying for me anymore." She looked out on the moonlit prairie they were skimming by. "I know. I know what you're gonna say. I made the choice—family or fame."

Neither spoke for several miles. Kada reached down to the Thermos and poured herself another cup of coffee. At Bill's nod, she refilled his cup on the console between them.

"I'm listening if you want to talk," he said softly, drinking from his warmed up coffee cup.

"I suppose I need to talk to somebody," she said. "I know what I say won't go any further."

He nodded in confirmation and waited for her to continue.

"Wade is going full steam ahead on the divorce. He's made it fair. We talk occasionally. I never call the house because we felt it would be better for the rug rats—better if they just relied on Abbie Miller. I get the feeling Torrie has no use for the redhead."

"Because why?"

"I don't know—maybe she's wanting to jump into my spot, and this gal is already there."

"She's jealous of the hired help?"

"Sounds like it." Kada drank the bar coffee and made a face. She had definitely tasted better. Wade had always been able to brew up delicious coffee. She shuddered and looked straight ahead.

"Do you believe in haunted houses, Bill?"

"No."

She felt the shivering go all through her body. "Wade's house is haunted."

"Is that a known fact, or just your supposition?"

"That house tried to kill me, Bill—I know it did! You can shake your head and make all the remarks you want to—just ask Ace Olson!"

Bill's voice was sarcastic. "Ace Olson, the whacky weed-smoking drummer I fired when I took over the band? I would really respect his opinion."

Kada ran a shaking hand through her blonde hair. Again there was silence for several miles.

"Look, girl," Bill finally said gruffly, "I know you and Ace had this affair going for several months. He kissed and told. Everyone in the band knew."

"Oh, that's just great!" she said vehemently. She felt the overwhelming shame she always had when she thought of her behavior with Ace. He was cute and naughty and for some reason he brought out all the wildness in her. But after what happened at the house, he vowed he never would come near the place again. She in turn vowed he never would come near *her* again.

What happened at the house—this time, she was going to tell it all. She was going to tell Bill everything that happened that terrible night. Maybe he could make some sense of it.

When she started talking, her voice was trembling. She admitted her affair with Ace. The Wild Boys Plus One had been booked for a dance the same night Wade and Clive wanted to go cat fishing on the Cheyenne River. There was quite an argument between her and Wade and she knew he was right when he said she had no time to raise her kids because she was always with the band. But she had persevered, and when the dust settled, she had left with her guitar, and he and Clive left with Skyler, who was just a baby at the time, and little Scilla to spend the night fishing at their camp.

Kada had drunk too much during the dance, and by closing time she was in no shape to drive home alone. Ace quickly volunteered to get her home in one piece, and with a lot of catcalling and hooting from the band, they left with another six-pack of beer to drink on the way to the ranch.

She was too drunk to care that she was bringing another man home to her marriage bed. The house was dark and silent when they opened the door to the kitchen. They fumbled with an embrace and started to head upstairs, whispering and laughing. But just when they were at the first landing, a strange and low rumbling began, and it quickly picked up volume until the house seemed filled with maniacal laughter. Kada remembered screaming and turning in fright to go back down. Ace hurried down the steps as fast as he could.

Suddenly something pushed her and she became enveloped in a suffocating softness. In her drunken haze she fell, bumping against Ace as she tumbled downstairs. She screamed in terror but her voice was lost in the house's roaring. Kada didn't know how they escaped, but Ace dragged her to his car, and they sped away into the night, both of them too scared to even look back.

Kada's hands were clenched into fists in her lap. She was breathing hard and beads of sweat broke out on her forehead. "In my worst nightmares I still hear that diabolical laugh," she said hoarsely.

Bill glanced at her with a trace of compassion in his eyes. "Maybe it seemed worse because you were apparently very drunk."

She shook her head. "There's more, Bill. Let me tell all of it to you."

He reached over with one hand and patted her arm. "Maybe you should leave the rest until another time."

"No!" her voice was harsh. "I want to tell all of it—then you'll know why I say the house hates me and wants to kill me!"

He put his hand back on the steering wheel. "There's a logical explanation for this, Kada. Maybe Wade could help you figure it out."

She covered her face with her hands and shook her head. Her voice wasn't steady as she began the second part of her story.

When she came back to the ranch late in the morning, Clive's pickup was by the door. She had decided to admit to the two men she had drunk far too much. There would have been no other way to explain her hangover and the dark circles under her eyes. Wade was disgusted, but it wasn't until Clive left that he expressed complete outrage and said if she couldn't handle her booze any better than that, she had better quit drinking and quit the band.

Kada was contrite and adamant it wouldn't happen again, but she flatly informed him quitting the band wasn't an option.

As the days went on, Kada tried praying but there was no release from her fear. She continued singing whenever she could, always ready to leave that horrible house and never ready to return. Ace had decided the house was cursed, and he wondered if anyone had died on the stairway. When he suggested that, Kada remembered Wade telling of his uncle falling to his death on those very steps, and she became even more terrified.

Ace thought it would be a hoot to avenge the dead uncle's spirit, telling Kada to place the house in mourning. Why she went along with his foolishness was beyond her, but he seemed to be able to talk her into anything.

When Wade and the kids left to visit his parent in the Badlands of North Dakota, she and Ace and a dour-faced man who seemed to be nameless brought in carpets and curtains, and soon the floors in the downstairs were covered with a black and purple carpeting the nameless man had bought for a song from a motel renovation. They draped the windows in black curtains from the same source. The man's pride and joy was the weird wall covering he had tacked onto stiff cardboard, which they stapled to the walls in short order. Kada asked him what the strange lettering on the walls meant, and he gave a short bleat of a laugh and told her it was black magic to chase away evil spirits. He told her since her prayers didn't work, she may as well call on another power.

She decided she needed the power of whiskey to calm herself and found the bottle she had stashed in the pantry.

The day had been hot for late September, and they had all the doors and windows open. When evening came and darkness settled over the land, they lit a candle. While Ace smoked pot, she drank more whiskey, and lost in their eerie world of self-induced hallucinations they began to giggle and recite all the silly incantations they could think of.

The candle had just sputtered out when a blood-curdling scream echoed over the hills and seemed to engulf the house. It was shrill and horrid, and evil seemed to fill the room like a dark avenger until it seemed to Kada's numbed mind the whole ranch was permeated with a force of darkness. She started screaming back until she lost consciousness.

When she came to, dawn was breaking and she saw Ace sprawled on the floor by the stairway. She was crying as she called his name, and to her great relief, his eyes opened and focused on her wildly before he sat up.

He didn't stay long. He told her he was sure all was well now with the house. But he said he was never supposed to come back, and he vowed there and then that their relationship was over, and he made her say the same vow.

She was left to face Wade alone. He was furious about the decorating, as she had known he would be. She shut up the house for the winter and made another vow to herself that never again would the doors or windows be opened to let in the forces of evil power she thought were hovering over the ranch.

Kada felt drained as she ended her story to Bill. There had been so much fear in her life the past two years. Now that she was away from the house and the ranch, she could look back and wonder how much of it had come from her guilty conscience. She let out a shaky breath and looked over at Bill.

He shook his head at her glance. "Quite a story. There's a logical explanation for all of it, of course, but whenever people start thinking of forces of good and evil, they become scared." He gave a snort of derision. "There is no such thing, Kada. There are no supernatural forces of any kind. There's one life for us, and we can make it whatever we want to by our choices. When life is over, it's over. No heaven, no hell—just nothing."

Kada looked at him in surprise. "You don't believe in God?" she asked incredulously.

"Do you?"

"Of course I do! Even if I don't sometimes act like I should, I still believe there's God and heaven and hell." She added with a touch of self-pity, "And I've been living in hell for a couple of years."

"You believe and you're miserable. I don't believe. I do what I think is best and leave it at that."

Kada turned away from him and watched the lights of Spearfish glow in the early morning dawn. She pondered his words, but one thought became dominant in her mind.

I'd rather have a weak faith and my problems instead of no faith and no emotions.

CHAPTER 13

Early October

"IT'S MY TURN, Skyler. You put the last bulb in." Scilla's voice was loud with authority.

Abbie was conscious of a power play between the two siblings as the three of them knelt in the flowerbed's dirt. Skyler frowned and gave his sister a shove.

"Skyler," Abbie said firmly, "this time it's Scilla's turn. Next time it's yours."

Scilla carefully put the tulip bulb in the hole and pushed in dirt until it was covered. To Abbie's chagrin, she took a very long time. Instead of moving over so Skyler could take his place beside Abbie, Scilla obstinately squatted in the dirt, patting, patting, patting the ground.

"You! Move!" Skyler lost his patience and shoved his dawdling sister.

"Ack! See what you did, you brat? You made me fall!" Before Abbie could stop her, Scilla flung a handful of dirt at her brother.

Both kids began yelling and hitting until Abbie had each one by the shoulder, pulling them apart.

"That is enough!" Abbie scolded both of them. "Scilla, you sit on the porch until I tell you to leave, and Skyler, you sit over on the other porch until I tell you to leave. I don't want to hear one more word out of either one of you!"

With a great deal of protesting from her young charges, Abbie plopped both of them down where they were to stay. She returned to the flowerbed and soon was aware of sniffling from both kids. It wasn't long before sniffling gave way to crying, and Abbie's tender heart could only endure that for a short time. Laying her garden spade on the ground, she brushed the dirt off her jeans and gazed at their abject little bodies.

"All right," Abbie finally informed them, "we are going to take a break, and I want both of you to come into the house, have a drink of milk, and go to your rooms for a nap. When you wake up, we'll do something else."

They were still sniffling as she helped each one get settled in bed. She kissed the tops of their heads and rather grumpily returned to the flowerbed.

What should have been an enjoyable afternoon project with the kids had evaporated into a dismal cloud of petty fighting. It had been building up for several days. Both Scilla and Skyler seemed to have a chip on their little shoulders. According to Torrie, the kids at school had peppered Scilla with questions about Wade and Kada's divorce. Some of the childish taunting even seemed to be directed at Abbie. Scilla had said that when Abbie came, her mother had left, and the look she directed at Abbie seemed to indicate she had doubts about Abbie's role in the whole matter.

According to Torrie, Abbie fumed as she flung another bulb in a hole and pounded the dirt around it. If Scilla's and Skyler's behavior wasn't enough to raise her hackles, Torrie's actions the past couple of weeks were the proverbial straw that broke the camel's back.

When that woman brought Scilla home after school, she stayed and stayed—stayed for supper, stayed to put the children to bed. Stayed and insinuated she needed to help because, as she would sigh and cast furtive little glances in Abbie's direction, it was apparent that her help was so needed.

Even worse was the blasted weekly Friday night pitch game that Clive had instigated. Thirteen point pitch, the card game of bidding and setting—so easy, they had said, and had given her a list of rules that would make a grown man cry.

Torrie had immediately made it into a personal competition against Abbie and relished every game Abbie lost. The third week, Abbie changed into Aunt Lena and bid recklessly. When Torrie announced she would bid 10 and both guys passed, Abbie jutted out her chin and bid 11.

Wade had raised his eyebrows and leaned toward her. "Go for it, kid." He proceeded to set her.

The next hand Torrie bid 11. Both men passed. Abbie bid 12.

"You don't learn, do you?" Torrie had scoffed. Abbie squeaked by with 12 points and won the game.

Maybe that was why the previous night Torrie had come armed with new rules. They would play partners, she said—she and Wade against Clive and Abbie.

Clive, Abbie soon learned, was a very cautious bidder. They lost the first game, and Torrie crooned to Wade about being a great partner.

It's just a game, Abbie, it's just a game. Sit back and enjoy yourself—and bid.

Abbie dealt, and when Torrie bid 10, Clive shook his head.

"I don't have a thing," he said warningly to Abbie.

Wade passed.

Abbie smiled sweetly at Clive. "Eleven—in clubs."

Wade laughed. "In clubs, Abbie? You're set, Miss Brit."

Clive moaned. "I said I didn't have a thing." Both he and Torrie threw down their cards after the first play.

Wade hummed a little tune under his breath and grinned at Abbie. She threw down a non-counter, and his grin faded a notch.

"Now, why did you play that way?" he scowled at her. He studied his cards intently before putting down the off jack to take the trick.

It was his lead. After spending considerable time mulling over what card to play, he finally slapped the king of clubs on the table.

"Oh, dear, dear, dear." Abbie gave another sweet smile, and laid down the very safe point of a deuce.

Wade's eyes began to twinkle. He put his arms on the table and leaned forward. "Abbie, you bid eleven points and you didn't have the king or queen. Where did you learn to play cards?"

She tilted her head and flashed him a demure and dimpled smile. "Aunt Lena."

"Aunt Lena. And did she usually win?"

"I don't recall, but she always had fun. Your play, Wade."

"You know I'm going to set you, don't you?" he teased.

"For heaven's sake, set her and get it over with," Torrie groused, fiddling with her downed cards. "Anybody that bids that much without a king and queen has no card sense whatsoever."

"Well," Clive countered with a tiny glimmer of hope on his face, "she just might be able to pull it off."

"Thank you for your confidence, Clive—and your joker," Abbie said sweetly. "Your play, Wade."

"Mm-hmmm." He held a silent debate with himself, and then laid down the queen of clubs.

She gave him a non-pointer.

"Abbie," he said softly, and leaned even closer toward her, "did Aunt Lena mention it was a mistake to win at cards when you're playing with the boss?"

"Not that I recall. Are you going to throw down your off three?"

Clive burst out in a loud guffaw as Wade slammed the innocent off three down. Abbie pounced with her three of clubs. When she played the jack of clubs, he had no other card to play and she had won the hand.

"That was sheer luck." Torrie's voice could be heard over Clive's jubilation.

Abbie and Clive won the last two games. When they had finished and were snacking on chips, Clive, as was his habit, went over most of the plays again. Torrie argued incessantly with him over the accuracy of what he remembered. Wade just shook his head at Abbie and refilled all their glasses.

"We'll win next time, Wade," Torrie said as she and Clive were leaving. Clive was several steps behind her, and he impulsively reached over to give Abbie a bear hug.

"By golly, if I wasn't scared a redhead would bite me, I'd give you a kiss," he laughed as he was heading out the door.

Wade had followed, and it wasn't long before Abbie heard Clive's older pickup start and saw his headlights turn east on the cut-across road.

It was considerably longer before she heard Torrie's car start. She had put away the cards and food items, and there was no reason for her to stay downstairs any longer. She was in her room when she saw Torrie's lights head west.

It was the memory of that evening plus Torrie's attitude toward her that caused Abbie to slam another tulip bulb into the ground. She had a feeling she would be replaced quite quickly when the final divorce papers were signed, and she wondered what the folks in England would say when she returned so soon.

She also wondered why the very thought of leaving bothered her so much.

CHAPTER 14

October Sunday

SUNDAY MORNING'S PEACEFULNESS after Wade and the children had left for church was like a balm for Abbie. This was the one day of the week that was exclusively hers, and she relished the quietness of it.

She liked Valley Community Church, and she was getting acquainted with the congregation. What she didn't enjoy was enduring Torrie's possessive behavior toward Wade and his children. After several Sundays of Torrie treating her like a ninny of a nanny, Abbie chose to stay home and worship in peace.

She had ordered a study Bible and was reading the New Testament. She read slowly and carefully and gained a lot of insight from the comments written below the scripture text.

"This is really something, Shy," she said to the German shepherd as she sat reading on the porch steps. "It speaks to me. It must be because for the first time I'm reading it with the feeling these words were meant for me."

But after a few more pages, she found herself looking up to gaze wistfully at the prairie before her. The leaves on the trees along the creek were hues of golden splendor and the cobalt blue of the sky made a perfect backdrop for the lazy puffs of clouds that ambled slowly through the atmosphere. Abbie took a deep breath. "It's like air from heaven," she informed Shy, who looked at her as if he might understand. "This prairie air is so fresh—I love it."

She closed her Bible and stood. Either today was the day she was going to take the plunge and do what she had wanted to do ever since she arrived—or else she might as well forget it and spend the winter wishing she'd had the courage to go through with her desire.

"Lord, if I'm not supposed to go, then please let Mrs. Barrows have other plans," she said aloud.

Abbie stalked into the house and made a phone call. When she returned to the porch several minutes later, she was grinning from ear to ear and had changed from her tennis shoes to boots. A short time later she had saddled up Jake with the smaller saddle she had found in the barn and they were heading down the cut-across road between the Jackson ranch and the Barrows ranch.

"I hope I'm not making a terrible mistake taking the boss's horse without his permission," she told Shy as he trotted along beside her. He looked up with raised eyebrows and swallowed several times before letting his tongue slip to one side of his open mouth.

The previous week when she and the kids had trailed into the barn behind Wade, Abbie had noticed this saddle and commented on it. Wade had told her it was Kada's and said if Abbie ever wanted to ride, he would saddle up Jake for her. She hoped that meant she had his permission to go riding without specifically asking him.

It was a perfect autumn day. The sounds seemed to carry through the air with unusual clarity. She could hear the pheasant rooster's crow across the hills, and high in the western sky southward-traveling geese were making their melancholy calls to one another.

Jake settled into an easy rhythm. The clopping noise of his hoofs against the hard-packed dirt road added another harmonious sound to nature's orchestra.

I love the quiet when I can hear Your world, Lord. It's so perfect—everything You create is so perfect. This day is a blessing, and I'm grateful that I can have this time to enjoy it.

Abbie knew she wasn't a great rider, but she had always enjoyed the times she had been allowed to take a horse and go for little jaunts across the English countryside. This open space with its endless hills had been calling to her ever since she had arrived, and it begged to be seen from the back of a horse.

Much too soon she was riding into the Barrows ranch, and when Jake saw Marilyn standing by the corral waiting for them, he began to whinny. It caused the other horses in the corral to answer back. Marilyn shook her head over the din.

"Did you see the geese, Abbie?" Marilyn wanted to know as Abbie dismounted.

"I saw and heard them. Quite a sight." Abbie felt slightly bowlegged as she took Jake's reins and tied him to a corral plank.

"Isn't that Torrie's saddle?" Marilyn asked abruptly, peering intently at the leather carving on the fenders.

"Torrie's? I thought Wade said it belonged to Kada."

"Well, he bought this saddle from Torrie when she had a new one made for herself. Kada rode about half a dozen times and then seemed to lose all interest in it." Marilyn fed Jake a cake cube, and his head bobbed up and down in appreciation.

Marilyn continued. "Now if Clive were here today, he would bore both of us to death by telling all the details of Torrie's new saddle, and he would point out the differences between your English saddles and our Western ones—and on and on and on. I love my son, but he's a talker!"

The two women and Shy made their way to the yard gate, and Abbie was instantly fascinated with the volume of flowers lining the sidewalk to the house's door. Mums of every size and color were flourishing and seemed oblivious to the slight frosts the area had received.

"These are beautiful! I didn't realize you were such a gardener!" Abbie exclaimed.

Marilyn smiled. "I love flowers; I'm not so crazy about vegetables and canning, though."

Once inside the house, the smell of freshly perked coffee added a welcoming aroma, and soon Marilyn was placing a large homemade cinnamon roll on Abbie's plate. They sat at a big round table that had seen years of wear and tear. In what Abbie interpreted as defiance of her male-dominated household, Marilyn had a vase of fresh cut mums standing bravely in the center of the table—next to several decks of cards.

"This is such a treat, Abbie," Marilyn enthused as she poured coffee. "Both Clive and his dad are at the old prairie dog town trying to kill rattlesnakes. They'll be disappointed they missed you, but I'm glad to have a little one-on-one woman talk."

Abbie exchanged knowing smiles with her. "Hen talk is most definitely needed once in a while," she said. "Did I hear someone say that the snakes are denning up now?"

"Yup. That's why the men are out at the old dog town. Snakes give me the creeps, and I've been around them all my life," Marilyn declared. "When I see one, I want it dead."

"What about the prairie dogs? Do they move out when the snakes move in?" Abbie bit into the soft texture of her roll and gave an involuntary sigh. "These are delicious, Marilyn!"

"I can give you the recipe if you want it. They're pretty easy to make." Marilyn took a bite of her roll and continued. "Prairie dogs will leave that part of the dog town, I guess. With all the bureaucrats and environmentalists trying to ruin grassland with miles and miles of prairie dog towns, rattlesnakes are almost preferable."

Abbie grinned at her. "I think people everywhere have issues with governments and misguided people. My Aunt Lena blames almost everything on terrorists."

Marilyn laughed lightly. "Tell me about your family, Abbie, and England. I want to know all about it."

For the next half hour, Abbie and her congenial hostess shared thoughts about their countries. Then Marilyn abruptly changed the subject.

"How is Scilla since her mother left?" she asked.

"Scilla? Most people ask about Skyler." Abbie paused thoughtfully. "He was so attached to Kada."

"Yes, I know, but after Wade adopted Scilla, she seemed to hardly even want to be around her mother. I've just wondered how she is now."

Abbie looked at Marilyn intently. "Isn't Scilla both Kada and Wade's daughter?"

Marilyn shook her head and answered slowly. "No. I hope I'm not telling tales I shouldn't be. Scilla was about two years old when they were married. Wade adopted her. I don't know who her real father is."

The older woman looked so dismayed that Abbie tried to reassure her. "Actually, I wondered about her aloofness to her mother myself. I believe the divorce has upset her some—either that or Torrie McGovern trying to take her mother's place bothers her." Abbie laughed a little self-consciously about that unintended revelation.

"Aw, yes. Torrie. I used to think she and Clive would get hitched." Marilyn tilted her head back and gazed at the ceiling. "I actually hoped they would. I don't know what happened there." Marilyn shook her head and looked at Abbie. "She seems to be after Wade now. Do you think he's interested?"

Abbie grinned at Marilyn and slowly stood. It was past time to take Jake back home. "I think any man is interested in a pretty girl who likes him," she said, taking her coffee cup and plate to the sink.

"I think you're right." Marilyn chuckled as she and Abbie left the house. Shy was waiting rather impatiently by the yard gate. He pressed close to Abbie as they walked to the corrals.

"I'm surprised Shy came with you," Marilyn said as she reached down and scratched his ears. "He always sticks pretty close to Wade."

"He has a thing about protecting me. But I'm not sure if he'd be any help—except to trip somebody."

Both women laughed, and Abbie reached down to give Shy a guilty rub.

Untying the reins, Abbie led Jake to a feed bunk. He stood patiently while she stepped into the bunk, and with that added height, stepped easily into the stirrup.

"Hey, you get on like I do!" Marilyn hooted. She opened the corral gate so Abbie could ride out.

"We who are short do what we have to do, right? Thanks for the visit and goodies!" Abbie said and gave Marilyn a thumbs-up before she headed down the road.

She urged Jake into a slow trot and began to replay the visit with Marilyn in her mind as she rode home. She had never realized that Scilla wasn't Wade's daughter. Why would she? It was definitely unexpected information. And she also hadn't known Clive and Torrie had dated. So many revelations for one afternoon!

"A triangle, Jake, yes indeed," Abbie said as she smoothed the horse's mane. "Wade, Torrie, and Clive—aren't you glad you aren't in that situation?"

Jake tossed his head impatiently.

"Oh, for goodness sakes. Just because you want to go home to some oats is no sign you can't visit about this," Abbie scolded.

Some grouse flew up as the trio started down the cut-across road. Jake tossed his head again and made a slight jump to the side.

"Now listen, horse," she said, "don't be trying any tricks like that on me. Some fine mess it would be if I fell off and you went tearing home alone. Good grief, I can just hear Torrie add that to all the other imbecile remarks she likes to make about me."

Abbie relaxed the reins slightly and decided to let him run a short distance. After he had puffed up a hill, he settled down to a comfortable trot and, gradually, to a fast walk.

She savored the smell of gum weed. When a whimsical breeze began to rattle the tall grass in the road ditch, she caught a whiff of pungent wildflowers that had weathered the first light frost.

All too soon she was heading up the last hill before home. Jake began to walk faster and broke into a trot, and suddenly both rider and horse were ready for a last crazy dash. Abbie relaxed the reins again and Jake began to thunder up the hill. Abbie felt like they were flying as they crested the top and went galloping toward the gate.

She gave a quick look down at Shy, who was racing as fast as they were with his ears pinned close to his head. "Yes!" she yelled with exuberance as Jake turned into the open gate and began slowing down.

"Aw, no!" she said in the next breath. Standing with her hands on her hips and looking like Godzilla herself was Torrie, and beside her with no welcoming smile whatsoever was Abbie's boss.

Abbie was slightly out of breath as she rode closer to them. Before she could even say hello, Torrie reached out to grab the reins.

"Get off and let me take him to the barn. Don't you know you don't ride other people's horses?"

When Jake jerked his head back and made a backward lunge, Wade quickly stepped up and grabbed the bridle. The horse settled down to Wade's quiet "whoa."

"Pretty good when you can't even stop a horse from running away." Torrie was standing back now and shaking her head. "Screaming all the way down the road." She was winding up to say more when Abbie's bottled-up resentment uncorked and spewed out.

"Would you just shut up? Would you just once shut that big honking mouth of yours and mind your own business? This horse was not running away and I was not screaming and don't you ever yell at me and grab my horse's reins again." Abbie was almost out of breath, but she yelled one more thing. "Is there any part of this you don't understand?" She felt like every red hair on her head was standing on end.

Torrie opened her mouth but quickly closed it again when Wade shook his head at her. He released the bridle and looked up at Abbie.

"You better take Jake to the barn, Abbie. I'll be there in a minute."

Abbie nodded. As she was riding away she heard him speak to Torrie, and by the time she got to the barn she could hear Torrie's car driving over the auto gate.

When Abbie slid off Jake, her legs were trembling. Never in her life, not even to Aunt Lena, had she exploded like that to another person.

Oh, dear God. What have I done—how much did I say? What if the children heard me?

She felt like burying her face in Jake's warm neck and crying in frustration. Somehow the thought of Torrie making her cry was comparable to hearing Randall say, "Get over it, kid."

"I should have stuck my tongue out at her," Abbie muttered as she loosened the cinch to take the saddle off. She realized belatedly that Wade was standing behind her. She also realized her hand was shaking.

Wade finished the job for her. He put the saddle on its rack while Abbie found the oats and poured the grain into a pan. Neither said anything as he slipped off the bridle and slapped Jake's rump as the horse walked out of the barn and into the corral to find his oats.

Abbie looked at him with serious brown eyes. "I shouldn't have ridden your horse without asking for your permission. I'm truly sorry about that," she said quietly.

"I didn't even know you could ride." Wade took a deep breath and pulled his hat down a little lower on his forehead. "When I suggested you ride Jake, I meant in the corral while I watched."

"Yes, well—I'm not good, but I enjoy it."

He looked away and let out another deep breath. "Did you ever consider that Jake might be more horse than what you could handle?"

She frowned slightly before she shook her head. "No, not for a second. Why do you say that?"

"Because last spring when Torrie was riding him to rope at a branding he bucked with her."

Abbie absolutely couldn't help it—she started grinning. "Really? How very delightful!" She quickly ran her hand over her mouth to erase her smile. "But of course she stayed on and made a wonderful ride."

The corners of Wade's mouth were twitching as he put his hand lightly on Abbie's back to guide her toward the house. "Actually, she fell off at the first leap and landed in a cowpie."

"You're joking! Surely you're joking with me?"

"I would guess you might enjoy seeing a sight like that." He stopped and looked at her quizzically.

Abbie smiled as she considered the consequences of such a tumble. Then she shook her head and continued to walk toward the house. "Wade, we need to talk about Torrie. I truly think she stirs up a hornets' nest when she comes and stays for supper and tries to put the children to bed. Why don't you take the woman on a date so she doesn't have to go to all that work just to be around you?"

Wade seemed to be caught off guard by her last remark. Finally, he said, "I know she gets out of line. I think she's trying to be helpful." He glanced down at Abbie. "I don't want to date anyone, Abbie. I'm not in the mood."

They walked up the porch steps together before he added, "But if it'll keep the peace, I suppose I could pick her up and take her over to Clive's once in a while."

CHAPTER 15

Wade's Women

THE WEATHER WAS changing, Wade decided as he and Jake rode along the ridge toward the ranch. The sun had been shining when he left home to check the cattle in their fresh pasture, but now the clouds were forming in the west, and the wind had a bite to it.

He would barely have time to unsaddle Jake before he had to leave to pick up Scilla. For the past two weeks he had been running up to the school three afternoons a week to get her. It was a measure to keep Torrie from bringing Scilla to the ranch so he could keep the teacher and the nanny apart.

A gust of wind tore at his hat, and he pulled it even farther down on his forehead. He saw the deer bunched on the lee of the hill, but as soon as they caught his scent they bounded through the draw and up the other side. As always, he tried to see if there were any bucks with big racks—one he had seen another day was a beauty, but everyone around probably had their eye on him.

Wade ran a mental checklist of fall work he could click off: *winter wheat planted, cows preg tested, hay hauled home, cake ordered, corn ordered, heifer calves weaned, fall shots given, wood cut for the fireplace, propane tank filled...wait. Where in the heck is Shy?* He tried to remember when he had last seen the dog during the ride.

Glancing back, he made a quick search before his eyes started to tear up from the sharpness of the wind. Shy could usually find his way back home, but Wade always felt better if he and the dog got there at the same time.

Back at the barn he quickly unsaddled Jake, but instead of turning him out, Wade left him in a stall to cool down. Outside, he scanned the ridge from where he had just come, hoping to see the big dog returning, but all he could see were tumbleweeds blowing.

Once in the SUV and on the way to the school, Wade saw even more tumbleweeds dancing in the wind. Some of them had blown into the barbed wire fences, and that was the end of their dance.

End of the dance. End of the marriage. The thought reminded him he had taken the rest of Kada's belongings to Spearfish the previous week, and they had signed the divorce papers in front of her lawyer. Wade was surprised when the guy said he wanted to compliment them for settling their affairs in a reasonable manner.

He was also surprised when Kada gave him three envelopes addressed to each one of the kids. She wanted Wade to keep them for her. She said when the kids were older she wanted each to read what she had written.

Kada had moved from a dorm room to a small apartment. When Wade carried in the boxes, he shook his head in mild amusement. One huge table dominated the room, and it was piled high with both college books and music. Mostly music, he noted.

It was hard on both of them, he decided. The final good-bye to a marriage is gut wrenching.

That thought led him to Torrie.

He wished she would give him some space. Abbie was right when she said Torrie shouldn't come over after school anymore. He had called Torrie that Sunday night and told her that he would be getting Scilla at school from then on. Torrie was still fuming over Abbie's outburst and put a lot of blame on "that redheaded shrew."

He had almost lost his own temper. When he trusted himself to speak quietly, he reminded her of her own shrew-like words. She must have sensed he was angry at her because she backed down immediately and said she would see him after school.

He had even taken Abbie's advice and picked up Torrie to go to Clive's for a Friday night pitch game. But Clive was quite mournful that he had lost Abbie as a card partner, and somehow the whole evening felt flat. He hadn't taken Torrie anyplace since. He just was not, as he had told Abbie before, in the mood for another relationship.

When he pulled into the schoolyard he realized he was the last one to get there. Scilla came running out of the building to get into the outfit, and he leaned across the seat to help her with the door.

"Torrie wants to see you, Daddy, but it's not because of anything I did. She just wants to see you about something." Scilla was out of breath and started coughing.

He waited until the spasm was over before he spoke. "How are you feeling?"

"Tired! But I have lots of papers to show you and Abbie, and I colored something green for Skyler and something blue for Sage."

"I'll just be a minute. By the way, Abbie was making some gingersnap cookies this afternoon."

"Did she already roll 'em in sugar? That's supposed to be my job."

He pulled a strand of brown hair back from her forehead. "I have no idea, but when we get home we'll find out."

"Make it quick, Daddy!"

When Wade strode through the school door, he wasn't surprised to see Torrie waiting by the window. He wondered if she was standing there purposefully to show off her figure against the light. Torrie had a shape worth looking at twice, or maybe even three times.

After a few pleasantries, she came right to the point.

"I wondered if you'd like to come over for supper tomorrow night. The folks are going to be gone and I thought it would be nice if we could have some time to talk, seeing as I'm not to come to your house anymore."

"I don't know if I can, Torrie. I'm going to the sale at Philip tomorrow, and I don't know when I'll be back."

Her demeanor stiffened perceptively.

He thought he'd better try again. "Thanks, though. I appreciate you asking me. Look, about coming to the house—it wasn't Abbie's idea that you never come. But two women trying to get supper and put kids to bed does not work, Torrie. She's paid darn good to take care of the kids. That's her job, and she does it just fine. Leave it alone." He smiled to soften his words. "About supper—maybe another time if you still want to have me."

Torrie tossed her thick mane of dark hair and smiled at him beguilingly. "I want to have you. The question is, do you want to come?"

"Torrie, you and I and Clive have been friends for a long time. You know he still carries a torch for you. I can't step into his territory."

They held each other's steady gaze for several seconds before she slapped him.

"Guess what," Abbie greeted Wade and Scilla as they came through the door. "I'm an aunt—twice over! I have a niece and a nephew and their names are Sheryl and Steven and they are absolutely adorable!"

She helped Scilla take off her coat and beamed at Wade. "I'm so excited!"

"Hey, Dad! Two!" Skyler held up two fingers.

Wade picked up Skyler and gave him a bear hug before he set him back down. "When did you find that out?" he asked Abbie.

"This afternoon. I got an e-mail and then about an hour ago Tyler called and I got to talk to everyone. Did I tell you I was excited?" She laughed happily and swung Scilla around in an impromptu dance.

"I take it mother and babies are doing fine?" Wade asked.

"Indeed they are. Clair sounded amazingly chipper for just delivering two babies."

Wade saw cookies on a plate and helped himself. "I have to finish up chores, but you can give me the rest of the details when I come back in."

Abbie waved him out the door with smiles and had already turned to Sage in the high chair before he had left the house. Wade almost tripped over Shy, who was sprawled out by the porch steps with mud caked on his legs. He growled several choice epithets at the dog and started walking toward the barn.

While he was backing the horse trailer to the chute, he mumbled. When he forked some hay over to the horses, he grumbled. When he started the tractor to put hay in the bale feeder for the five old cows he was taking to the sale tomorrow, he stewed.

He slammed the cubby door shut for the hens and chewed them all out for not laying enough eggs.

Because he knew he didn't dare go back to the house in that frame of mind, Wade walked down the trail to the creek. The wind was even colder than before, and the sun was slipping behind the western hills.

He didn't take kindly to being slapped. He had laughed at the school and walked out the door, but as far as he was concerned, that was the end of his relationship with Torrie. Besides, Clive was his best friend, and until Torrie had started her campaign for Wade, everyone had supposed Clive and Torrie would get married some day.

Wade took a deep breath of chilly air. *I think I'd better stay away from the women, Lord. They are sure a confusing and frustrating lot.*

He turned and started retracing his steps back to the house, but when he saw the big buck deer fade into a side draw, he froze in his tracks. Now THAT was a big rack.

Thinking of the deer made him think of the night the mountain lion killed the deer to the east of the house. He had mixed emotions about that night. Every time he thought of Abbie and her silly moose pajamas he wanted to laugh. She looked cute as a button wearing them, but then she generally looked good wearing anything. Abbie was an amusement to him…unlike the other women in his life.

When he had seen Jake racing over the crest of the hill with Abbie on his back, he had visions of her being thrown or, worse yet, being dragged. It wasn't until they zipped through the gate that he realized she was in control. She was in control until Torrie made a fool of herself, and suddenly the temper he always associated with redheads exploded.

He thought Abbie had had good reason to pin Torrie to the wall. After the slapping episode, he thought so even more.

Maybe I should be grateful for that slap. It gives me the perfect excuse to stay far away from Torrie. It will be a joy to just think of the ranch and the kids and not worry about women.

Several days later Wade turned the calendar over to November. Several snow flurries had blown through, and the skies were metal gray with short bursts of sunshine.

He and Abbie had finished their midday meal, and Abbie had poured them both one last cup of coffee before they went their separate work ways.

"What do you know about Thanksgiving, Abbie?" he asked, watching the two boys as they finished eating.

"An American celebration—turkey, dressing, mashed potatoes." She smiled as she took a drink. "I've been looking at magazines."

He smiled back. "I'd like to invite my family over for Thanksgiving dinner. The folks used to come down from North Dakota for Thanksgiving. Grandma Marie always cooked a big meal." He looked out the window. "That was before Kada and I were married."

"When did your parents move to the North Dakota Badlands?"

"When I came back from the service. Mom grew up in that area, and when there was a ranch next to her folks that came up for sale, she really wanted Dad to buy it." He handed Skyler one more apple slice.

"It must have been quite a change for your family."

He noted the compassion in her brown eyes. "Yeah. It took Granddad quite a while to get over that. Mom, though—Mom just never liked this place. Grandma and she got along OK, but for some reason Mom always wanted to head back to where she grew up. Her family is scattered all over those Badlands."

"I believe anyone could get along with your grandmother. She's totally delightful. We share a fascination for this house and she told me quite a few things about it when they came out last month. But what about your dad—has he adjusted to the move?"

Wade stared at her thoughtfully. Finally he took a swallow of coffee and set down his cup. "I think so. I guess he wasn't as upset as I was that everyone was leaving. You might say my granddad and I share a fascination for this ranch. It's...very important to us. When the folks left, I stayed here at the house with them. We had good times together, but his health sort of took a nose dive, and they decided they should move to town to be closer to a doctor and hospital."

"But anyway," Wade said, wondering how he had gotten off on that subject, "to get back to Thanksgiving, there would be about eight extra people. Think you could handle that?"

Her eyes twinkled at him with good humor. "I think I can handle that, Mr. Jackson. It'll be fun to have company!"

Sage started banging on his tray, which meant he was ready to be put down. He rarely coughed anymore. In fact, looking at him, Wade found it hard to remember how listless Sage used to be.

When Skyler saw Sage crawling across the floor, he wanted down from the booster chair. Soon both boys were crawling and babbling talk only the two of them could understand.

"Did I tell you that I got more pictures of the twins on e-mail today?" Abbie asked.

He shook his head.

"This time they're of the folks, Clair's family, and even Aunt Lena."

"Aunt Lena was holding a baby?"

Abbie laughed at that. "Absolutely not. Aunt Lena standing behind two infant seats with babies."

Wade stood with his coffee cup. "You'd better show me that."

They headed into the den where his computer was set up, and she quickly brought the pictures onto the screen. He knew her father immediately. One glance at Ben Miller's brown eyes and red curly hair was an affirmation that he was Abbie's dad.

They laughed at Aunt Lena's unsmiling face as she stood behind the babies. He would have known without being told she was British—she had the blue eyes and delicate skin and, more notably, a tart and reserved manner that even a picture reflected.

"Who's this guy?" He pointed to a good-looking slender young man in uniform. He was holding a baby and smiling confidently into the camera.

Wade glanced at her, waiting for her reply. She was gazing at the screen with a tender expression and a little smile played around her lips.

"That's Randall. I believe I've told you about him."

"Clair's brother."

She straightened and said briskly, "Yes, Clair's brother. The one who agreed with Aunt Lena and decided I should come here." She turned to Wade, her brown eyes twinkling again. "I believe I told you there was quite a row about the whole matter. He has a way of bossing me around."

Wade decided from the look on her face that she wasn't at all averse to being bossed around by this Randall guy. And for some reason, it didn't set well with Wade.

That evening after Wade had gone through the usual nighttime routine of giving his children hugs, listening to prayers, and covering them up for the night, he headed downstairs for some quiet time of his own.

He was surprised to see an outfit drive in, and when he switched on the yard light and saw Torrie hurrying up the steps, he was even more surprised.

He opened the door before she could knock. For a moment she seemed uncertain, but when he invited her in, she entered swiftly. He had barely shut the door and turned around before she began speaking.

"Wade, I've got to talk to you. I'm so sorry about last week. I've been so ashamed of myself." He noticed there were tears in her eyes. "Please, we've been friends for so long." She reached out imploringly to him, and the next moment she was sobbing on his chest.

Of course, he put his arms around her. What else could he do? He smelled the richness of her hair, felt the softness of her.

"Aw, Torrie," he whispered, closing his eyes while he held her close.

"Wade," she said, raising her tear-stained face, "we need to talk. My car is running. Come with me."

"Let me tell Abbie I'll be gone for a while." He released her and made his way upstairs.

When he knocked on Abbie's door, it seemed to take her forever to open it. She looked at him questioningly while he told her he was going out for a while and if she needed him he'd have his cell phone. He had already turned and started walking down the hall before she asked him if there was an emergency somewhere.

"No, Torrie just came and we're going for a drive."

"I see."

CHAPTER 16

Thanksgiving (2006)

ABBIE QUIETLY SLIPPED out of Scilla's bed and headed into the big upstairs bathroom. Wade's parents had been persuaded to take her room with its private bath, and the evening before she had indulged herself in a long bubble bath in the old claw foot tub that had graced the bigger bathroom since Wade's great grandparents' day.

When her makeup was on and jeans and a light cotton sweater had replaced her beloved moose-patterned pajamas, she headed downstairs. Already she could smell the coffee. As usual, when she came through the archway to the kitchen, Wade was standing with his arms folded across his chest, waiting for the coffee to finish its last sputter that signaled it was ready.

"You're up early too," he told her and poured them each a cup.

"Turkey and dressing time." She gave him her morning smile, which, he had informed her several days earlier, was a slightly sleepy looking affair, not at all as bright as her noon smile.

Soon the kitchen was filled with the aroma of onions and celery simmering in melted butter. Toast was popping out of the toaster at an alarming rate, and the turkey was sprawled in an undignified manner waiting for the atrocity of being trussed and stuffed and baked.

They ate their toast standing up, and Wade quickly left to start his morning chores. Abbie wondered what time Wayne and Shelly Jackson would be up. They had told her not to worry about their breakfast, so she puttered away the next hour and prepared more of the dinner menu.

She enjoyed Wade's family. They were comfortable to be around and in many ways reminded her of her own family. Wade's brother, Wyatt, his wife, Karen, and their daughters had stayed with Wade's grandparents the previous night but were all coming to the ranch for dinner.

The morning flew by and soon the rest of the family arrived. There was a general hubbub of people talking, children playing, and everyone taking sample bites as they waited for the meal to overflow the large dining room table.

Wade's grandmother Marie remarked how she loved seeing the homestead looking so nice. She gave Abbie a hug and said she thought the table set with the older dishes from the china cupboard made a wonderful celebration.

Turkey, dressing, mashed potatoes, gravy, sweet potatoes, salads, rolls, relish trays, pie, and ice cream—by the time they reached the pie stage, they groaned and said they would all need naps to sleep off their gluttony.

While the family was visiting around the dining room table after the meal, Wade's grandfather Art looked toward the top of the stairway.

"It seems like a long time ago that Blaine fell down those steps," he said sadly. "He would have enjoyed this get together. He liked for the family to be here."

Abbie threw Wade a questioning look. "I guess I never told you about that," he said to her. She noticed the muscle in his jaw tighten. "Blaine was Dad's brother. He—somehow stumbled at the top of the stairs and fell to the bottom."

She involuntarily glanced at the top step before she scanned the faces in front of her. From their somber looks, she realized it had been a family heartbreak that still had repercussions. She almost could hear Aunt Lena scold her for the questions she wanted to ask.

"That's—it's always such a tragedy when we lose family." Abbie was fumbling for adequate words. "It must have been a very hard time for all of you."

Grandfather Art turned to her. "He broke his neck and died instantly. It was quick." He said the words as if he wished he hadn't brought up the matter at all.

Wayne cleared his throat. "Well, it's in the past, I guess. We all miss him, Dad."

There was an uncomfortable silence. Abbie decided to brave a question. "When did this happen?"

"Twenty years ago this fall," Wade's grandmother said, and she added quickly, as if she wanted to change the subject, "Abbie, have you ever heard this house laugh?"

"Grandma, I've been living here for a long time and I've never heard this house so much as snicker," Wade said, smiling fondly at his grandmother.

"Oh, fiddle faddle. You and your grandfather both scoff at this, but it's true. Sometimes when both porch doors are open and the wind is from the northeast, this house gives a little chuckle."

Wade's mother leaned forward. "A little chuckle? If I heard a house chuckling I would probably jump out of my skin!"

Scilla was sitting beside Shelly and looked at her in bewilderment. "Can you really jump in and out of your skin?"

Everyone laughed over that remark, and it seemed to restore the good humor of the day.

Abbie would have liked to contemplate all that had been said on Thanksgiving Day. In fact, there were many issues to ponder, but time moved quickly, and she only found brief moments to mull over the past days.

There was Wade and Torrie. After the night Torrie came to visit, they had seemed to resume their relationship, and yet Torrie seldom came to the house. When she did, she was quite civil to Abbie and rarely interfered with the children. Abbie was puzzled over the attitudes between her boss and the schoolteacher. They seemed to be genuinely fond of one another, yet neither made any effort to actually have a date.

Wade himself had seemed more relaxed. There had been talk of more Friday night card games with Clive and Torrie, but the weeks before Thanksgiving had been so busy that they decided to postpone the games until later. Abbie was relieved. As much as she enjoyed Clive's storytelling and his humor, she found his constant talk a bit wearing. He loved history, and he loved details. When he told about some incident that happened to someone, Abbie generally got a complete rundown on all the family relationships for three generations past. She was always surprised when Torrie would listen intently and pounce on him if he made any historical errors.

There was also the Jackson family. She found herself wondering what made the uncle stumble and why there was a reluctance to talk about him. Wade never offered any more explanation, and she thought it odd he had never mentioned it to her before.

Her family in England seemed to be doing well, according to the e-mails she received with regularity. But there was a concern about Aunt Lena.

Abbie's mother had written that since the twins had arrived, Aunt Lena had spent fewer days with the family. In fact, she had seemed unusually interested in the Internet as of late, and she even went so far as to purchase a laptop. This was unheard of! She wanted to read the e-mails Abbie wrote to the family, and when she found out Wade and Kada had divorced, she was quite agitated for several days. In fact, Abbie's mother wrote, Aunt Lena seemed unduly worried about Abbie living alone with her boss "way out in the middle of nowhere," and even railed at Randall for letting Abbie go to such a place.

The latest e-mail her mother had sent was dated Sunday, November 26. She wrote of the twins and other newsworthy events, but the last sentence read:

So very strange. Aunt Lena has decided quite out of the blue to visit a distant relative for a week. Quite unlike her to leave home for that long.

CHAPTER 17

Aunt Lena's Visit

I'LL SIT BY the window, Randall. That way you can keep any terrorists away from me."

Randall stowed both his and Lena's carry-on bags in the upper compartment along the aisle, and with a shake of his head, he settled down beside her.

"You know, of course, that my husband and I traveled a great deal," Lena said, peering past Randall to check for suspicious characters. "He was a good man; lazy but good. Sometimes I swore I had to drive a post beside him to see if he moved, but he was good to me and we saw lots of new places together. We never traveled first class like this, but like I said, you have all these connections because you're a pilot, so we might as well take advantage of them."

She rapped Randall's arm with her knuckles. "It's a good thing you and I at least have the common sense to check out this situation of Abbie's. I call it her awammon situation. Abbie always has some sort of situation in her life. I will be so glad when she finds a man and settles down. You know, of course, that whoever marries Abbie will have his hands full. She can be as stubborn as her father."

"Yes, right," Randall replied absently, and it didn't escape Lena that he winked at the stewardess as she made her way to the back of the plane.

"I can't believe her folks couldn't see the danger in awammon. It's as plain as the nose on your face—"

She abruptly stopped talking as the roar of the plane engines became deafening as they got ready for takeoff.

Soon the big jet had taxied down the runway and like a giant bird lifted into the air. They were on their way to the United States.

Lena quietly looked out the window at England getting smaller and smaller. When she couldn't see her native land anymore, she peered over her glasses at Randall.

"How soon till we get there?" she asked.

"You'll have plenty of time to take a nap, Lena," he replied.

"You know, of course, that I will do no such thing. As I was saying before we took off, what on earth were her folks thinking of to send that child away into that situation—"

"Lena," Randall interrupted her, "you and I sent Abbie away. She would still be home if you hadn't had the crazy idea she should take Clair's place, and at the time I agreed. It's probably one of the few times, dear lady, that you and I have agreed on anything. If you hadn't been so worried about her and claimed that I was responsible for her leaving, I would not be chasing across the globe with you to check up on her."

Lena again rapped his arm with her knuckles. "We're not checking up on Abbie." She lowered her voice to a conspiring whisper, "it's the awammon situation we're checking out."

Randall frowned. "What on earth is the 'awammon situation,' anyway?"

Lena peered over her glasses disgustedly at him. "I would have thought someone with your experience would know." She leaned closer and said quietly, "Awammon stands for 'Alone With A Man in the Middle Of Nowhere.'"

Randall burst out laughing and leaned back in his seat. "Yes, right. Well, on that note, I think I'll take a long snooze. We want to be our best when we're out in the middle of nowhere trying to find Abbie." He seemed to purposefully slam both eyelids shut.

"I thought you had one of those gadgets—those SPOG things."

Randall opened one eye. "GPS, Lena—Global Positioning System."

"Well, if you're going to be boring and sleep, I may as well lean back and close my eyes. You know, of course, that I won't sleep a wink."

Lena needed time to reflect. She had sat in her rocking chair at home for a long time concocting her latest scheme to bring Randall and Abbie together. That they were perfect for each other didn't seem to be obvious to anyone but her.

She had thought if they were apart from each other for a while, they would come to their senses. But how was she to know the silly Americans would get a divorce and Abbie would be in that situation? When she had first approached Randall about the two of them going to the States, he had acted like she was demented. She had to use all her wiles, including the one she hated most: the crying scene. Finally he had come around. Of course, part of it was because she finally offered to pay for everything. With her money and his connections, they had gotten great travel arrangements at a low price. Randall really was a tightwad, she had decided.

I'm sure once Abbie and Randall are together they'll realize what I've known all along—they are a nice English girl and a nice English boy who will marry and live close to our family. I simply cannot understand why no one else can figure this out. Here I am a poor old woman and I have to get everyone on the right track! Traipsing all over the world at my age.

Well, it will all be worth it to get those two married. Brother and sister marrying sister and brother. Everyone will be close together that way.

Lena yawned and momentarily lost track of what she wanted to think about.

Let's see now. I'll have to make sure there are plenty of opportunities for Randall and Abbie to be alone together.

I'll have to…

She yawned once again and thought sleepily that Randall must be snoring. That dreadful racket certainly wasn't coming from her side of the seats.

When the loud knocking at the porch door began that Monday afternoon, Abbie had no idea her world was going to be turned upside down. She couldn't imagine who would be rapping like that, and when she opened the door and Aunt Lena came striding past her, she wondered for a brief second if she was seeing things.

"Aunt Lena?" She turned slowly to stare at the tweed-covered apparition that stood before her.

"Of course it's me. I've come to stay."

Abbie stuttered and repeated, "You've come to stay?"

"For a week." The droll voice behind her was instantly recognizable and Abbie spun around to see Randall standing in the kitchen with a confident smile on his face.

"Randall!" she whooped, and the next second she was in his arms and enjoying a very long and satisfying hug.

"You have company, Abbie?" She heard Wade's voice from a distance.

"Who are you?" Aunt Lena asked Wade sharply as he strode into the room.

If he was annoyed at her tactlessness, he gave no indication, and with a smile said pleasantly, "I'm Wade Jackson, and I just have a hunch you're Abbie's Aunt Lena."

"I was sure she would have told you about me. Now perhaps you would be good enough to show me where I'm to stay, and then you can carry my bags in," Lena said frostily.

Abbie was embarrassed at her aunt's tone, and she rolled her eyes and shook her head as she caught Wade's eye. She was unaware that she was gripping Randall's hand in both of hers until the two men introduced themselves to each other and tried to shake hands. She blushed and released her hold.

"Of course you know you are so in the middle of nowhere that the SPOG thing could hardly find you," Lena reported, her wool beret slightly askew on her freshly permed gray hair.

"GPS," Randall clarified.

"And what is this?" Lena asked as Sage padded into the kitchen on all fours.

Abbie scooped him up and hugged his solid little body. "Not 'what,' Aunt Lena," she scolded lightly. "'Who.' This is Sage, our baby. I mean… I mean… Wade's baby." Abbie knew from the heat on her face she was going to blush all over again.

"You know, of course, that your face is as red as your hair," Lena retorted, causing Scilla, who had been standing in the hallway, to dart over to observe Abbie's discomfort.

"This is Scilla, and Skyler is watching TV." Wade came to Abbie's rescue. "And I think, Abbie, that your aunt will want your room, with the attached bathroom, and we can put Randall in the extra bedroom by the boys."

"And where will Abigail sleep?" Lena demanded.

"With me, of course. In her moose pajamas. She'll be quite safe," Wade said with only a hint of a smile.

Both Lena and Abbie's mouths dropped open, but Randall exploded into loud guffaws while Wade grinned mischievously at all of them.

"And that was just the first ten minutes," Abbie e-mailed to her mother that evening. "Please pray continuously for me!"

Aunt Lena slept almost all of the following day, retiring even earlier than the children that evening.

Wade and Randall visited at the kitchen table while Abbie cleaned up the kitchen. It was an enjoyable time and the conversation drifted easily from one topic to another. When she had finished, they decided to enjoy the warmth of the fireplace.

"I'm still totally shocked to see you," Abbie told Randall. He had patted the spot on the sofa beside him when she had entered the room and had given her a light hug when she sat down beside him.

"Lena wanted to come. You can't believe all the wiles she used on me. She even cried."

Abbie was aghast. "Aunt Lena cried? I can hardly believe it."

"Oh, yes." He sighed and stretched out his long legs on the coffee table, and then took his arm away from her shoulders to collect the cup of coffee Wade brought in. "I decided if she wanted to come so badly as to resort to tears, it must be serious." He took a sip of coffee. "Thank you, old man, you make great coffee."

Wade smiled slightly and handed Abbie her cup.

They made some plans for the rest of the week, deciding the visitors should see the tree-decorated capitol building in Pierre, and as Wade pointed out, Abbie should see it too. He also suggested that Clive go with them.

"No one knows South Dakota history any better than Clive," he said. "He can tell you all sorts of interesting little tidbits about the building and the grounds."

And so on a brisk, sharp day in late November, Randall drove his rented car onto the lot behind the capitol, and Clive began his official duty as tour guide.

He started with the Flaming Fountain Memorial on the grounds. In the middle of his remarks that it was a veterans' memorial, one of the many geese that inhabited the pond took an instant dislike to Aunt Lena. It began by waddling straight toward her and honking quite disrespectfully.

"Shoo! I say shoo!" Aunt Lena waved her purse at it. The rather fat goose was thwarted momentarily, but as they began the walk toward the Fighting Stallion Memorial, it began to follow, honking loud, insistent honks. When Aunt Lena stopped and turned to peer at the goose over her glasses, it flapped its wings and stopped as well. When she turned around and began walking, the goose followed and honked. The whole scene made quite an interesting procession. Every time Clive started to explain the significance of the memorial, the goose became even louder.

Finally, Randall gave the unwanted bird a kick in the tail feathers, and with an indignant hiss and honk, it waddled off, muttering in goose talk all the way back to the pond.

"Now then," Clive said, "the reason for this memorial is because the governor of South Dakota was killed in a plane crash along with seven other people. It was a sad day for our state."

"A plane crash?" Randall was immediately interested. He had all sorts of questions to ask Clive as they began to walk toward the capitol building.

"Who would have thought such a lovely building would be out here in the sticks?" Aunt Lena asked no one in particular. She stopped to gaze up at the copper dome. "You know, of course, that this is modified Greek Ionic structure and it looks like it's made out of limestone."

"No, Aunt Lena, I didn't know that," Abbie answered.

Lena sniffed importantly. "I suppose the interior is some horrid remodel."

Clive overheard her remark and winked at Abbie. "It'll be hard to see a lot of the interior because every year after Thanksgiving, Christmas trees are brought in and decorated from organizations across the state."

Once they were inside, even Aunt Lena was awestruck at the grandeur of the capitol rotunda. Beyond all the greenery that festooned every railing and stairwell was the splendor of the wide marble stairway, the terrazzo tiles on the floor, and the marble wainscoting. Of special interest to Aunt Lena were the marble-appearing columns.

She strode over to one of them and peered intently over her glasses at it. She even tilted her head to look through her glasses and walked around the column, clacking her tongue all the while.

"These are called scagliola columns," Clive informed her.

"Of course you know I thought that very thing." Aunt Lena actually smiled at Clive. "It's considered a lost art, but of course you knew that, I'm sure. This is manmade marble, and I don't know when I've seen any better. You know, of course, Abbie, that it's made out of milk, ink, and marble dust."

"Don't forget the yarn," Clive added.

"Yes of course, Clipe. I forgot to mention the yarn."

"Uh, my name is Clive, ma'am, not Clipe."

Randall and Abbie exchanged looks and decided not to mention that in Aunt Lena's world, "clipe" meant to tell tales.

But Aunt Lena was on to other finds. Tilting her head way back she looked up at the dome and gave a startled gasp. "I say there, what are those Greek goddesses doing in South Dakota?"

Abbie and Randall both followed her gaze and saw murals painted high above them. Clive pointed out all four of them, and said they represented agriculture, livestock, industry and mining, and love of family and state.

He added, "I love to share this tidbit. They were painted in 1910 by a guy named Edward Simons." He grinned at them with blue eyes sparkling. "Now to relieve your necks, come over here and look down at this blue stone set in the tile."

As they rubbed their aching necks and looked down, there was indeed a blue stone.

"Well, Clipe, what's the story on that?" Aunt Lena demanded.

Clive gave Abbie a puzzled look and then launched into the story. He said the floor had been laid more than a hundred years earlier by sixty-six Italian artists, and each one of them was given a blue stone to lay in the floor.

"Have all sixty-six stones been found?" Abbie wanted to know.

"No, but fifty-five have been counted. Probably the others are under some carpet or walls."

"And the reason why they were given the stones?" Aunt Lena asked

"Oh, I think it was because it was a way for them to leave their signatures without actually writing anyplace," Clive told her.

They started a tour of the Christmas trees. Each one was decorated differently, and they were all shapes and sizes. Abbie felt like she was in a fairyland, and she and Randall wandered from tree to tree, admiring each one of them. Somehow they became separated from Clive and Lena, so they decided to explore on their own and walked up the marble stairway to the second floor. After admiring the dome and murals at a closer vantage point, they walked up the third stairway.

Abbie leaned against the rail and watched the people down below, trying to see if she could spot Clive and Aunt Lena.

"Well, now that we are alone, Abbie, tell me how South Dakota and this family treats you." Randall was studying her with raised eyebrows.

"I hate to say this, Randall," she flashed him a smile, "but you were right. I did need to get away. Distance has a way of making us fonder of our families."

"But I think something more has changed you than just distance from your family."

She reached up and stroked his firm jaw. "You are one perceptive friend. Yes. Something wonderful happened to me at the Minneapolis Airport." She took her hand away and looked down. "I've not told this to anyone else, Randall. I had quite a visit with a minister on that flight. He helped me so much. He answered the questions I was too self-conscious to ask anyone else."

Randall raised an eyebrow. "And?"

"And I asked the Lord—right in the middle of the airport—to lead me. You might call it being saved, or you might say I gave my life and heart to the Lord."

She paused before she added, "I have peace of mind now. Do you remember that verse we learned as kids?"

"Something about the peace that passes understanding," Randall answered her. "Quite right. You look contented."

"I am contented most of the time. Unless Torrie McGovern is around—for some reason she brings out the worst in me. Sometimes I think Aunt Lena is right about red hair and hot tempers."

Randall gave one of Abbie's curls a gentle pull. "I believe Clive mentioned that particular young lady several times while we were on the road."

Abbie thought Clive did far more than just mention Torrie. But for now she wanted to hear about Randall. "Tell me about your life—how is everything going for you?"

"Aside from your Aunt Lena, very well." He frowned as he peered down to the main floor. "How can that woman see so well? She's waving at us."

"That must mean she's ready to leave," Abbie said, and both of them headed to the stairway.

The next afternoon found both Aunt Lena and the children napping. Wade had invited Randall to come with him to the school to pick up Scilla, but Randall declined, and instead he ushered Abbie to the comfortable chairs flanking the cheery fireplace.

After several minutes of pleasantries, Randall hunched forward in his chair. "So what is your opinion of your boss?"

The question surprised Abbie but she decided, knowing Randall, that he was gathering information to report back to the family.

"He's very thoughtful of his children, and he's easy to work for," she said. "Probably one of the better bosses I've had."

"It must have been awkward when you learned they were divorcing."

149

Abbie nodded and wondered where Randall was going with his line of questioning.

He sat back in the chair and eyed her coolly. "Lena says you are in a situation. She calls it 'Abbie's awammon situation.'"

"My awammon situation? Good grief, what does that mean?"

"Alone With A Man in the Middle Of Nowhere." Randall cocked an eyebrow and gave a suppressed snicker. He held up his hand when Abbie started sputtering indignantly. "Actually, Abbie, she has a point—I would think working here with only the husband at home has put you and Wade in an awkward position."

Abbie stared into the flames before she replied slowly, "I'm just doing my job, Randall. I was hired to take care of three children. That's what I'm doing." She looked at him and smiled briefly. "He and the neighbor lady, Torrie McGovern, are, uh, are… well, they like each other."

Randall studied her closely before replying. "You and Wade like each other also."

She frowned and stated flatly, "We have a good working relationship. He's the boss; I'm the hired nanny. That's all, Randall. Aunt Lena is stirring a pot that has no fire under it."

"Oh?" he said with doubt in his voice.

They locked eyes in the silence that followed until finally Abbie scowled and shook her head. "You and Aunt Lena have devilish imaginations."

He laughed at that and stretched his long legs out in front of him. Putting both hands behind his head, he smiled at her. "Abbie, you're always so cute when you get riled up. I suppose ever since you were the little sister tagalong, I've ruffled your feathers."

"That's true. But I'm still very fond of you," Abbie acknowledged, giving him her dimpled smile.

On Friday morning Lena uncharacteristically followed Wade into the mudroom.

"I've been here four days now, Mr. Jackson. Today I will go with you to get Scilla from her school." She rapped his arm with her knuckle. "You haven't as yet showed me your ranch or cattle. How many cattle do you have anyway?"

"Well, not enough, Mrs. Talley. I will be happy to show you around, but I can't take you to the school because Scilla is home for the day."

Lena looked around sharply. "Home?"

"Yes, Scilla has Friday, Saturday, and Sunday off from school. She's home those days, and also on Tuesdays."

"That's good! More time for her to be a supervisor—of the other children. Yes, that's good. You know, of course, that the children and I could help you chop wood out in the back forty or wherever you go." She frowned and pulled her sweater tighter over her blouse. "There aren't any rattlesnakes out, are there?"

"Oh, yeah. They're terrible in the wintertime."

"Mr. Jackson," she replied frostily, "it is not nice to fool an old lady."

Wade met her cold stare with a smile. "Mrs. Talley, I would imagine you are not easily fooled."

"You are correct in that assumption. I must also tell you that you have placed my niece in a situation that I find intolerable."

Wade folded both arms across his chest. "And that situation would be—what?" he asked testily.

"I'm not surprised I have to spell it out for you. She's alone with a man in the middle of nowhere. Need I say any more?"

He studied her carefully before replying. "No...no, I understand what you're saying. I've thought the same thing myself, and I'm planning on taking steps to... uh... rectify the—"

"I call it the awammon situation, Mr. Jackson," Lena said crisply.

"I see. And you came all the way from England because you were worried about Abbie and this...this situation?"

"That, and to try and convince two rather dithering young people that they need to get married and settled down close to family."

"You mean Abbie and Randall."

"You know of course that I mean Abbie and Randall."

"Well, well. Fascinating, Mrs. Talley. Very fascinating."

"Where is Randall? I thought he would be here with you," Aunt Lena huffed as she came into the kitchen that evening.

Abbie was preparing supper and had been enjoying a rare moment alone with the children. She was getting weary of invaders in her domain, and as much as she appreciated this surprise visit, she knew she would be relieved when the normal routine resumed.

"Wade took Randall for a look around the ranch, and they aren't back yet," Abbie informed Aunt Lena. She thought her aunt looked tired and offered to make her a cup of tea.

"That sounds very nice, Abbie. Thank you."

Aunt Lena eased herself into a chair and focused on Scilla.

"You know, of course, little girl, that you have a very unusual name."

Scilla looked uncertainly at Abbie.

"Do you know what it means?" Aunt Lena questioned.

At Scilla's blank look she softened her voice. "'Scilla' is actually a very pretty flower. It is bell shaped, and it can be either blue or white—I have many of them in my yard at home. They come up in the early spring. I'm surprised Abbie didn't think to tell you that."

Abbie thought of all the spring flowers that would be cropping up in England in a couple of months, and a tiny wave of homesickness washed over her.

"I thought of it when I first arrived, but we were so busy cleaning house I forgot." Abbie stepped around Skyler to get two cups.

"Have you forgotten anything else while you've been nanny, cook, and housekeeper for this family?" Aunt Lena retorted.

Abbie's defenses began to rally, but she carefully set down two cups of hot tea before she replied. "I don't think so, but why do you ask?"

Aunt Lena took a sip and seemed to grit her teeth. "Even the tea tastes different here in the middle of nowhere."

Sage crawled under the table and attempted to stand, only to bonk his head on the underside.

"Ouch!" Abbie smiled at him as she rubbed his downy head and pulled him from underneath the table and onto her lap. She smiled again and rubbed his head. "Ouch-ouch-ouch!"

He studied her with great seriousness, torn between crying and laughing, but when Skyler stood beside her and said, "Owse!" laughter won, and soon it was a game for the two boys, with Skyler hitting his own head with his hand and hollering "Owse!" and Sage laughing his happy baby laugh.

Abbie and Scilla joined in the merriment. These were the moments Abbie loved—the unexpected happy times when the children were laughing, supper was cooking, and the evening was beginning to settle over them like a cozy blanket.

She glanced over at Aunt Lena and was dismayed at her aunt's grim demeanor. Giving Sage one last hug, she lowered him to the floor and immediately all three kids were crawling into the dining room hollering "Owse!"

"You should have children of your own," Lena said stiffly.

Abbie took a drink of her own tea before replying. "I thought it prudent to be married first," she said tartly.

"You know, of course, what I mean," Aunt Lena was equally tart. "You have no business being out here with an unmarried man."

"He was married when I came, Aunt Lena. And you better remember that it was you and Randall who thought I should be here in the first place."

"The situation has changed. You better tell the agency to get someone else and come home with Randall and me. It would be a nice Christmas present for your parents."

Abbie slowly pushed her chair away from the table and walked over to the oven to check the casserole she had made for supper. She mentally counted to ten and then twenty. She also sent an urgent prayer for control over her temper, which seemed to be boiling in frustration over such a suggestion.

Finally she took a deep breath and turned to look at Lena. "Absolutely not, Aunt Lena. No and no and no." She said it very softly—yet very firmly.

Aunt Lena stared at her in silence before pushing her own chair back and walking out of the kitchen.

"I say, Abbie, this is quite a ranch," Randall enthused after he and Wade had shed their coats in the mudroom. "The size is unbelievable compared to what we have at home."

He put his cold hands on Abbie's neck and laughed at her shrieks of protest. "Wade said it was only a normal-sized place in this area, but it looks big to me." He opened the oven door and took a whiff of the cooking casserole. "Wonderful, I say, wonderful."

Abbie gave him a distracted smile and asked Wade if he would gather up the kids and get them settled at the table.

By the time Aunt Lena put in her appearance again, the meal was almost ready to be enjoyed. She peered over her glasses at both Randall and Wade, listening to Randall's impression of South Dakota and the ranches with very little expression on her face.

"I pray," Skyler announced and folded his small hands. They hardly had time to bow their heads before he began. "Gawds bess food, Gawds bess Shy, Gawds bess—" he struggled to remember who else he wanted God to bless, and finally giving up, shouted, "Men!"

"Do you mean 'amen,' Skyler?" Wade asked him quietly.

They took note of his emphatic nod, and began to pass the food around.

"I remember Abbie asking God to bless her cow Clover one time," Randall mused as he heaped his plate full.

"She deserved to be blessed," Abbie retorted. "She was a good cow."

"Your father helped you raise several good calves with that cow," Aunt Lena remarked, taking small amounts of everything.

"I'm puzzled about something, Abbie," Randall said, buttering a roll. "You used to have ten of the most delightful freckles on your nose. What happened to them?"

Wade looked at her sharply. "There's six—she never had ten when she came here."

Abbie finished putting some peas on Sage's tray and had to sit still while Scilla came over and counted out loud the freckles in question.

"Six!" Scilla announced triumphantly and laughed when Abbie crossed her eyes in an attempt to see her own nose.

Aunt Lena was chewing very slowly and looking from one to the other with a puzzled look.

Abbie herself was puzzled as to what difference it made how many of the blasted things were sprinkled across her nose. She was also slightly surprised Wade had bothered to count them.

"I know I had a good count, because she was sleeping at the time," Randall persisted.

Abbie didn't know why she glanced at Wade, but when she saw his eyes sweep over her face with a distinct frown, she quickly turned to put more peas on Sage's tray. "I fell asleep when I was fishing," she offered lamely to no one in particular.

"How can you fish and sleep at the same time?" Scilla wondered.

"Well, you see, it's very obvious you can either do one or the other, but not both. In Abbie's case, Scilla, I had to rescue her fishing pole down stream because she…ah…she became sidetracked and fell asleep." Randall seemed quite proud of his explanation.

"You know, of course," Aunt Lena offered rather vaguely, "that the English climate is so much better for the complexion than here, whether one has freckles or not."

"Guess what we are having for dessert?" Abbie said, not caring that she was completely changing the subject. "Aunt Lena suggested we have bread pudding." She looked at Wade. "I hope you don't mind an English dessert."

"You know, of course, that he should be grateful that you fix any kind of dessert," Lena snapped.

Abbie caught Wade's eye across the table and shook her head while she rolled her eyes. She appreciated his courtesy to her uninvited guests, but she had a feeling his patience, as well as hers, was wearing a little thin.

Saturday was the last full day Randall and Lena would be there. Their plans were to leave early on Sunday morning and take a scenic route to Sioux Falls. They would return to Minneapolis on a different flight that would still allow them to make their connection to London. It was Randall's idea, Aunt Lena informed Abbie. He said they might as well see more of the country while they were there.

Everyone seemed in a conciliatory mood, and when Clive came over in the late afternoon to play a promised game of cribbage with Aunt Lena, all met him with warm greetings. Randall and Abbie had a pleasant visit by the fireplace while the cribbage players were in the sunny dining room.

Wade had worked outside most of the day, and when darkness settled in early, Abbie watched him walk slowly toward the house. It was not his custom to walk at a slow pace, and she wondered if he was hurt. She met him at the door in the mudroom and was relieved when he shook his head at her inquiry.

He had only been in the house a short time when Torrie drove up. Abbie thought all three men went overboard with enthusiasm when Torrie walked in.

It became a cribbage tournament, and Abbie was grateful that Aunt Lena was enjoying herself. Aunt Lena and Clive became partners against Randall and Torrie. All were good players, and good-natured arguing appeared to suit the four of them.

Wade watched in silence for a while and then carried Sage into the kitchen where Abbie was fixing a platter full of cold meats, cheeses, and crackers. He leaned against the counter to watch her and then suggested they use paper plates.

While he rummaged in the pantry to find them, Abbie asked him if he would look for the jug of apple cider.

He found that also, and soon they had found chips and dip, and put together a relish tray. Together they brought the prepared lunch into the dining room, and their guests gratefully acknowledged the service and continued their game. Aunt Lena and Clive were ahead, and Aunt Lena meant to keep it that way.

Abbie divided the rest of the evening between keeping the snack tray filled and taking care of the children. When it was past all three kids' bedtimes, she gave the little boys their baths. Wade came upstairs as she finished and together they tucked them into bed.

When they had heard the last prayer, Abbie found herself yawning. She looked wistfully into her bedroom and thought with a guilty pang that she would be so happy to be in her own room the next night.

Wade was waiting for her in the hallway. "You look tired, Abbie. Are you ready to see your guests leave?"

She had the ridiculous urge to lean against his solid frame and put her head on his chest. "I must be," she murmured, looking up at him. She thought if he knew what she was thinking he would make a dash for the safety of the downstairs.

He smiled at her and the unruly piece of dark hair that always brushed over his forehead moved slightly. "You can sleep tomorrow after they're gone." For a brief moment their eyes locked, and she wished she knew what thoughts were going through his mind.

"I feel like I could sleep for a week," she said as they walked down the hallway to the stairs. She wondered what their guests thought when the two of them came slowly downstairs with Wade's hand resting lightly on the small of her back. She also wondered why her heart was acting weird and, most of all, she wondered if anyone could see she was blushing.

Was it my imagination or did the cribbage game end rather suddenly?
Abbie had gone into the kitchen to get more apple cider while Wade wandered over to check the game's progress. She hardly had a platter of cookies ready before Torrie was in the kitchen asking if she could help.

"Who won?" Abbie asked.

Torrie and Abbie had exchanged very few words since the horse incident and were awkward around each other.

"Clipe and Lena." The two young women looked at each other and started chuckling.

"This is embarrassing, Torrie. 'Clipe' is an English word that means 'tells tales.'" Abbie shook her head. "I think he would be a little mortified if he knew what she meant."

"I think we'd all be mortified if we knew what Lena really was thinking," Torrie said in a quiet voice. "She claimed she was too tired to play anymore, but I think there were other reasons she wanted to quit."

Abbie couldn't quite meet the other woman's knowing look so she hastily thrust the platter of cookies at Torrie.

"If you take these in, I'll bring the cider." Abbie quickly turned to get a tray for the cups.

As soon as Abbie made her appearance, Aunt Lena directed, "Sit here," and vacated her own chair next to Randall.

After everyone was served, Abbie found herself cozily close to Randall with his arm resting on the back of her chair. Clive and Torrie were having a long and heated discussion about the cribbage game, and Aunt Lena seemed to find an urgency to quiz Wade about the shortest route to Sioux Falls.

"You make delicious goodies, Abbie." Randall munched on a gingersnap, his gray eyes taking in her slightly flushed cheeks.

She leaned back in the chair, only to spring forward as his hand started to massage her shoulder.

"I think, though, you've been entertaining too much—you look tired."

"I'm not tired," she said, "I just need a little hot cider to perk me up." She gave him a bright look.

Randall threw back his head and laughed loudly. "I know that look. It's the 'crabby Abbie leave-me-alone-I'm-not-tired look.'" He now had everyone's attention and shook his head at Wade. "She's so cute when she gets mad and prickly at everyone. Ever since we were kids and she'd wear out following us older ones around, she wouldn't listen when we told her she should stop and go to the house."

"That's because you guys always saved the fun stuff until last and didn't want me in on it," Abbie said with a slight laugh, and backhanded him lightly on the chest.

He raised his arm off the back of the chair and ruffled her hair slightly. "Let me tell you, folks, in case you don't already know it, Abbie has a temper."

"I do not!"

"Yes, you do." He gave her a hug that threatened to spill her uplifted cup of cider. "I should know. I lived around this gal for a long time. Brought her home from dances when she couldn't see straight—"

"Randall Hudson!" Abbie interrupted and set her cup down with a thud. "You're the one who couldn't see straight, for crying out loud. It took all three of us girls to get you headed down the right road."

Aunt Lena was instantly intrigued with this story, as were Clive and Torrie. Abbie noticed Wade was looking down at his cup, neither smiling nor joining in.

"Abbie was wearing this gossamer dress and had all the young lads swooning after her—"

"Wrong again. I was wearing Clair's chosen color of yellow and everyone agreed I looked terrible in it."

"Red and yellow, catch a fellow—but in Abbie's case, I think it scared them all away," Aunt Lena said dryly.

"You ladies are so wrong," Randall protested. "Abbie looked sensational. She had her hair all piled up in cute little curls, all of her freckles were powdered and subdued—"

"Wrong, wrong, wrong. My freckles are never subdued and you know it, smarty pants Randall." She looked at Randall crossly. "Your memory isn't what it should be. Are you sure you can get Aunt Lena back to England?"

"You know, of course, that he probably can't. You better pack your bags and come with us." Aunt Lena smiled at her clever remark.

Abbie didn't miss the look Torrie gave Wade. For once she was grateful to Clive for his ability to fill in awkward pauses with an unending stream of talk. It reminded him, he said, of a story he had heard, and for the next several minutes he had almost everyone's attention.

Abbie herself quietly murmured that she would bring in more cider. Once in the kitchen she let out a soft sigh. Something was wrong with this picture, and she couldn't put her finger on the problem. She only knew there was a silent war going on in her heart.

She shook her head sadly. *There is a war and I don't even know what the battle is about. Am I homesick? I don't think so. Do I have more than a fondness for Randall? Well...*

I must be tired. Tomorrow will be better—tomorrow will see the old routine back in place. But after this week, will anything be the same as it was before Randall and Aunt Lena came?

CHAPTER 18

The Redhead and the Redneck

SCILLA WAS A rowdy sleeper. She tossed and turned, muttered and kicked, and after several direct hits from her little pajama-clad arm, Abbie decided she might as well get up and let the day start.

She could hear Aunt Lena's snoring through the closed bedroom door as she made her way to the bathroom. *I'm embarrassed to say this, Lord, but I'm so glad they're leaving today. I'm ready to have my house back, my family back.* She dwelt on that thought for several seconds while the warm water from the shower cascaded over her.

What am I saying? These kids aren't really my family. Maybe I've been living in a dream world, Lord, pretending this is my home and family. Maybe I don't belong here. It's so obvious Torrie would be perfect in this spot.

That thought certainly didn't help the battle in her heart.

Abbie smelled the coffee as she headed downstairs, and when she turned the corner he was leaning against the counter looking at her with his gray eyes. She was slightly surprised at her disappointment to see Randall instead of Wade.

"I say, Abbie, you used enough water in that shower to cover half the territory here."

"And good morning to you, too, Randall," she said, giving him a slight tap on the arm as she reached for cups.

"Is Lena up yet? We planned on getting an early start."

"I heard her talking to herself in the bedroom when I came downstairs. Did you make the coffee or did Wade?"

"Why do I get the feeling if I made it you would dump it down the drain?" His right eyebrow had the usual lift he used when he was slightly annoyed.

She gave him her morning smile. "Because you make absolutely terribly brews, and Wade makes absolutely delicious ones."

"Are you comparing the two of us?" He seemed rather testy.

"Did you wake up on the wrong side of the bed this morning, Mr. Hudson?"

Abbie was shocked when he reached for her and buried his face in her hair. "You're so feisty in the morning, Abbie. I've always quite adored that about you."

His voice seemed loud in the morning stillness. When she finally disentangled herself from his arms, she discovered Wade was standing in the hallway door, and he wasn't smiling.

To make matters worse, Aunt Lena was peering at them over her glasses from the dining room archway. She took her time looking from Abbie and Randall and finally to Wade, her blue eyes seemingly taking in every detail. Whatever she thought she saw seemed to give her a great deal of satisfaction.

"You know, of course, that one of you big brutes will have to carry my suitcase down these steps. Abbie, I don't know how you stand to run up and down them all day caring for those children." She stepped smartly into the kitchen. "Who made the coffee?"

Since they had said their good-byes to the children the night before and had decided to eat breakfast down the road, Aunt Lena and Randall took only enough time to have a quick cup of coffee before they said their final farewells to Abbie and Wade.

"You know, of course, that I'll give a full report to your parents," Aunt Lena said. "If you decide to come home early, that will be good. I hope I didn't leave anything. Well, if I did you can bring it with you when you come home."

It was obvious she didn't want any endearing hug from her niece. She slapped her hands together as if to dust off any Out-in-the-Middle-of-Nowhere nonsense from her hands. Her wool beret was jammed on her gray curls. Lena Talley was clearly ready to go home to England.

Randall shook hands with Wade, but when he came to Abbie he caught her up in a bear hug that nearly took her breath away. He brushed his lips against her cheek and said he would see her in June.

Abbie didn't miss the speculating look Aunt Lena bestowed on the two of them. Her aunt merely tapped Wade's arm as she breezed by him.

"Nice to have met you, Mr. Jackson," she said on her way to the door.

"Have a safe trip home, Mrs. Talley," Wade answered.

Soon they were out the door, more last-minute niceties were uttered, and finally Abbie stood alone on the cold porch waving as they turned at the auto gate and headed down the road.

Wade was leaning against the kitchen counter when she walked back in. She shivered slightly from the brisk outside air and noticed immediately he wasn't smiling.

"Well," she said, looking at him uncertainly.

"Well." It was flatly said.

"This has been quite a week."

"Yeah." He folded his arms across his chest and kept his eyes on her face.

"It'll be nice to be back in a normal routine."

"Will it? I imagine you'll miss all that hugging stuff."

She frowned at him. "Hugging stuff?" she asked, an edge to her voice.

"You and Randall seem pretty chummy."

She gave an exasperated sigh. "Randall is an old neighbor. We've known each other since we were kids." She picked the empty cups off the table and headed to the sink.

He unfolded his arms and looked out the window before turning back to her. "Has he always been so cozy with you?"

"Cozy? What does that mean, Wade?" She opened the dishwasher and realized it was full of dirty dishes. *Fiddle, I must have forgotten to turn it on last night. Maybe I can squeeze four more cups in.* She started rattling around cups and plates to fit the extras.

He waited until she had poured soap into the holder and shut the door before he answered.

"That means, Abbie, that I come into my kitchen and see you and the guy all close-like, and he's telling you how he likes you in the morning. I call that cozy." Now the edge was in his voice.

She pushed the button on the dishwasher and it began its usual grumble. "This kitchen must bring out the cozy for both of us," she said as she headed toward the refrigerator.

"What? What does that mean?"

Abbie had the fridge door open and had completely forgotten what she was looking for. Finally she slammed it shut and turned around to face him. "That means that I'm coming from the laundry room one evening and see you and your old neighbor here in this kitchen and *you're* all close-like ...hugging-like ...real cozy-like."

Their eyes locked in silent warfare before he looked away. "That's different, Abbie. There wasn't anything to that." He looked back at her defensively. "Not that I should have to explain anything to you anyhow."

"Do you fancy cereal for your breakfast?"

"Why do you ask me that with your annoyed British accent? You almost sound like your Aunt Lena."

Abbie put her hands on her hips and glared at him. "Annoyed or annoying? And I may sound like my Aunt Lena but don't you ever dare tell me I act like her!"

He turned abruptly and jerked open the cabinet door. "Cereal is fine—here's the bowls. I meant that you sounded annoyed, not that your accent irritated me. For crying out loud, Abbie, let's just drop the whole matter."

Abbie was simmering. She knew she was getting into hot water bringing up Torrie, and as he said, he shouldn't have to explain anything to her. On the other hand, he brought up the subject of her and Randall, and she shouldn't have to explain anything to him either.

Wade put cereal bowls on the table and started rummaging in the drawer for spoons. Abbie slammed down a couple of juice glasses and once again opened the fridge door.

She heard him breathe out a long sigh. "Abbie, you and I have never argued about anything. We've lived together for almost four months, and for a redhead and a redneck, we've done pretty good." He paused momentarily. "Why don't you turn around and look at me instead of staring into the fridge?"

She didn't want to look at him. For some silly reason she felt like crying, and if she turned around he would know that.

Abbie straightened up and slowly closed the refrigerator door. Taking a deep breath, she looked up at the ceiling as she struggled for composure. He was directly behind her and he put his hands on her shoulders, turning her to face him.

Wade looked at her steadily until she dropped her eyes and mumbled, "Don't look at me that way. Darn it all, Wade, I don't know what you're thinking."

His hands slid to her back and he pulled her close to him. When she buried her face in his chest he let out a ragged sigh and with a half-laugh said, "I don't know what either of us are thinking. We almost sound jealous of each other."

She closed her eyes and thought of how solid and wonderfully warm he felt. The image of Randall floated lazily through her mind—cool and slender. Another thought drifted through her mind and she stifled an embarrassed laugh as she pulled away from Wade.

"I think I'm going to be hysterical," she informed him. "I haven't had any man hold me for months. Now you're the second one in less than an hour." She smiled at him and added, "I think I hear the kids waking up."

Peace and quiet. Wonderful peace and quiet, Abbie decided as Wade and the kids left for Sunday school and church later that morning. He always asked her if she wanted to go with them, and sometimes she did. The congregation was a friendly group and the minister preached from the heart. She had enjoyed the times she had gone; however, on this turbulent Sunday morning she needed time to herself. She finished putting the remnants of breakfast away before she took the food scraps and set them on the porch for Shy to eat.

Just You and me, Lord. I need help this morning fitting the pieces into this puzzle of life.

I've committed a nanny no-no, Lord. I like my boss too much. He mentioned being jealous. That puzzle piece sure fits what I've been feeling about him and Torrie. I wonder what I would do if he looked at me with the same expression on his face that he had when he held her?

I better not think of when he was holding her. It makes me…jealous.

Abbie looked at the clouds moving in from the west. The sun that had graced the early morning hours was losing its punch, and she thought for the hundredth time how grateful she was that Randall and Aunt Lena had left as soon as they did before the unsettled weather blew in.

She returned to the house and slowly started up the stairs to her room. She wanted to get the bedding changed and her personal items back where they belonged. Seeing the sheets and pillowcases stripped off the bed and folded neatly on a chair gave her a belated appreciation for her feisty aunt.

I know she's Your child, Lord. But You know, of course, how she irritates me…always has. Some of Your children are harder to love than others. And then there's Randall. I've always liked him with a perverse kind of fondness. In his own odd way, he's been there for me. But I'm pretty sure he's not the one for me. I was getting tired of all his hugging. What was he trying to prove this morning anyway?

She shook her head at that episode as she found fresh bedding in the linen closet. *It was like a staged event, Lord. How many people can we shock by making it sound like we've been together lots of mornings?*

Suddenly a very unappealing thought began to form in her mind and once the thought took root it flourished and grew until she burst out with a swear word.

"Oh, that dirty rat! He did that purposely so Wade would see it! Of course, that's it! That cad! That conniving Brit! When I get my hands on him he'll wish he'd never been born!" Abbie was shouting to an empty house. To show the world how mad she really was, she slammed the linen door shut.

Abbie muttered and mumbled the entire time it took her to remake her bed. To think Randall would be such a hypocrite as to make Wade believe there was something between them when there was nothing! Absolutely nothing! And Wade believed it. Wade really thought she had feelings for Randall.

I don't like this, Lord, not one bit. I don't like Randall manipulating things in my life. Even if it did make Wade a little jealous and he… we… and… well, it was just a little tiny hug… didn't mean a thing, I'm sure. Well… it meant something to me, but I doubt it did for him. I wish it could have meant that he likes me. I mean, I know we like each other, 'a redhead and a redneck,' he said.

Sometimes, Abbie decided, examining your feelings too much can be a tiring occupation. With that in mind, she bustled from room to room straightening up the clutter and bringing a semblance of order.

She added carrots and potatoes to the roast beef she had put in the oven earlier, and when all her busy work was done, she settled close to the fireplace with her study Bible. Reading the Word was always balm to a troubled soul, she reflected. She hadn't taken time all week to study. While the fireplace crackled and the wind began to make its own music, she lost herself in the pages of wisdom.

"Bee, I cold!" Abbie could hear little running feet coming down the back hallway that led straight to the living room. Before she could put her bookmark in place, Skyler came in sight and quickly crawled up beside her. "I cold!" he repeated, his dark eyes full of expression. He snuggled close to her.

"How come you're so cold?" she wondered and put her arm around him to gather him even closer.

"No heat." His tone was solemn.

"No heat at church?"

"No! No heat in—"

"In the Tahoe," Scilla helped explain as she came in. Wade, carrying Sage, was close behind her.

Sage's little nose looked quite pink, and she noticed all four of them seemed chilled.

"Oh boy, what happened?" she directed at Wade.

"I don't know. We had heat when we left, but coming home all I could get out of it was cold air." He placed the bundled Sage on Abbie's lap. "I have to make a quick run out to the calf pasture to make sure the float on the tank is working. Do I have time before dinner?"

At her nod he hurried upstairs to change clothes. Before she had Sage unbundled Wade had already returned and was putting on his heavy Carhartt coat. Sage seemed unaware that it was a cold ride home from church. He smiled at her as she pulled off his snowsuit. One shining tooth decorated his little gums, and another was struggling to make it two.

"Are you cold too, Sage?" she crooned to his happy face. He looked at her with delight and gurgled a word that sounded like, "Mum, mum, mum."

"Is he saying 'Mom'?" Scilla wondered. She had slid off her coat and was standing close to the fireplace.

"I think it's just an easy sound to make," Abbie told her. "Are you all hungry or did they have some rolls at church?" She attempted to rise, but Skyler grabbed her arm with a determined grip.

"Bee! I cried."

"Because you were so cold?"

"No! Daddy left!"

Abbie looked at Scilla for an explanation. "Daddy thought Skyler would be all right in the Sunday school room with Torrie, but when he left, Baby cried." Scilla was obviously disgusted with that performance.

"No baby!" Skyler hollered indignantly. "Scilla baby!"

"Let's go into the kitchen so I can finish dinner. Do you smell the roast beef and potatoes and carrots cooking?" Abbie carried Sage and ushered Skyler into the aroma-laden room. Scilla bounced in behind them and suddenly decided she was starved.

"Scilla baby. I no baby." Skyler muttered several times to Sage as Abbie settled the younger child into his high chair.

"Skyler, it's OK to miss your dad when he leaves. You're not a baby, and neither is Scilla, but I bet you both are hungry, right?"

"Right!" Scilla agreed enthusiastically. She rocked back and forth on her feet and tilted her head to one side. "Lena said you really miss your dad, and that he really misses you. She said he really, really wants you back in England."

"No! Bee here." Skyler's eyes began to cloud and his forehead puckered into a promise of a cloudburst.

Abbie picked him up and hugged him close to her. "I'm glad you think I should stay, Mr. Skyler." She kissed the softness below his little ear and then twirled them around to the cabinets. "Is it going to be your Winnie the Pooh plate, or the big boy blue plate?"

He thought for several seconds while he patted her cheek with his warm hand. "Big boy boo."

"He means blue," Scilla informed Abbie as she skipped around the table.

Abbie put Scilla's energy to work setting the table, and she listened with good humor to all the bits of news Scilla seemed to know. It was good to have the relaxed atmosphere of just family again. Odd how quickly the extra guests seemed to disrupt the flow of familiarity.

When Wade returned, their late noon meal was ready. Amid the usual chatter of children and the passing of food, the almost spilled water, and the dropped spoons, came a poignant atmosphere that caused Abbie to stifle an uncharacteristic surge of emotion. She would miss times like this when she had to return to England.

"That was good, Abbie." Wade leaned back in his chair and wiped some gravy off Sage's cheek. "Lena informed me that you are cook, housemaid, childcare giver, and chauffer here, which is much more than what a nanny job is supposed to be. She suggested I give you a raise."

Abbie raised her eyebrow. "What did you say to that?"

He grinned across the table at her. "I said it was probably a good idea. With Lena, it's better to give her the idea that she's right."

"Sometimes in her own weird way she has a point." Abbie quickly added, "Not that I think I need a raise. I enjoy what I do."

Sage yawned and leaned over to Wade with his arms outstretched. It was a signal that he was ready to get out of the confines of the high chair. After Wade untangled him from bib and tray, he set him on the floor and they watched with amusement as he tried to decide if he wanted some cuddle time on Wade's or Abbie's lap, or toy time with Skyler. However, this time, even with Skyler's enticement with his favorite red car, he wanted Wade's lap.

Wise choice. Abbie blinked with surprise when that thought skimmed through her mind. She quickly rose and began clearing off the table. Scilla bounced around her with dirty plates and glasses. She chattered nonstop, but Abbie only half-listened.

It was after the kitchen was clean once again and the boys and Scilla were napping that Wade found Abbie sitting in the wing chair in the living room in front of the fireplace. She had her feet propped up on the coffee table, a fresh cup of coffee in her hands, and was gazing out the east window at the increasingly heavy clouds. Occasionally a flake or two of snow would flutter through the air.

He moseyed over to the fireplace and took the poker to stir up the fire. When he had accomplished that she asked him if he had examined the heater in the Tahoe.

"Yup. Found the problem. Fixed it." He put his hands in his pockets and looked at her. Finally, he settled himself across from her on the sofa.

"Abbie, I think we have a conversation that we need to finish."

"Would you like me to get you a cup of coffee before we start?"

"I'll get one after a while."

She nodded. For some reason she was having trouble getting a deep breath. He seemed to be having the same problem because he let out a huge sigh before folding his arms across his chest.

"I want to explain about Torrie." He held up his hand as she started to speak. "Just let me tell you what the deal is here." He paused as if unsure how to begin, then cleared his throat and looked over at the fire.

"Torrie and Clive have liked each other since they were kids. Everyone always thought they'd get married. After he got back from the service and she started teaching school, we all figured it was only a matter of time before a wedding happened. Except nothing ever happened, and all of a sudden she was here quite a bit, and—" he glanced over at Abbie, "and Kada and I were divorcing, and you came."

Abbie took a drink of coffee and felt her insides tighten. This was going to be the grand declaration of his and Torrie's affair.

"Torrie asked me to have supper with her one night. I don't know...I just wasn't ready for that. She was supposed to be Clive's gal, not mine. When I told her that, she got mad." He grinned a little lopsided at Abbie. "She slapped me and that made me mad."

Abbie raised her eyebrows at him.

"We didn't speak for quite a while, and when she came here that night and you saw her, she was feeling pretty bad about all that had happened."

"And you were comforting her, of course." Abbie thought her voice sounded strained. Wade looked at her and frowned.

"Yes, Abbie, I was comforting her and that's what you saw." He studied her before he continued.

"She finally realized that it was Clive she really wanted. He had asked her to marry him a couple of years ago, and instead of telling her he loved her, he told her how their ranches could be joined together. She told him to get lost."

Abbie wasn't sure she had heard correctly. "Did you say Torrie wants Clive instead of you?" She shook her head in amazement.

Wade gave her a disgruntled look. "Why does that surprise you?"

"I—uh, I just wouldn't have ever guessed that. That's what she told you for a couple of hours that night while you were with her?"

"We were only gone about an hour, Abbie." He gave her a roguish smile. "I didn't know you were keeping track of the time."

"I was thinking of the children."

"Fascinating. Did you think I would leave them and never come back?"

"I thought when you came back you would say you'd found a new mother for them. I was also thinking that my time here in South Dakota would most likely be coming to a screeching halt."

He smiled at her and stood. "You have more of an imagination than I gave you credit for, Miss Miller." When he left to get himself a cup of coffee, she blushed. If he could have read her mind at the moment, he probably would have been very surprised at her imagination.

She herself was shocked!

CHAPTER 19

You Are My Sunshine

*A*BBIE ROLLED OVER in bed, stretched as far as she could, lay kitty cornered, and then rolled back into the middle. Having her own bed and room to herself was a little like heaven, she decided, before springing up and heading to her own bathroom.

She started singing during her shower. When she was finished, dressed, and ready to head downstairs, the same little song was still playing in her mind. That, of course, explained why she was smiling and humming "You Are My Sunshine" as she bounced into the kitchen.

Wade was leaning against the counter as usual. She decided immediately that Wade leaning against the counter made a much better picture than Randall leaning against the counter.

She beamed at him and he shook his head at her.

"You've got a lot of wattage in your smile this morning, Abbie. You must have slept good in your own room."

"I slept like a top! How about you?"

"I didn't sleep worth a plugged nickel and it's all your fault."

She studied him closely and decided the fine lines around his eyes were a little more pronounced than usual.

"Did I feed you something that didn't agree with you?"

"No."

"A tired redneck—this could be serious."

He laughed at her and without warning put his arms around her waist to pull her close to him. "I didn't sleep because I kept thinking of a certain redhead with six freckles on her nose."

"Was it a nightmare?" She melted against him, enjoying the strength of his arms around her.

"It was a challenge."

She looked up at him in surprise. "Thinking of me is a challenge? I don't recall that ever being said before."

"That's probably because no one has ever accused any of your admirers of putting you in an awammon situation before."

"Oh, I see." She reluctantly left the warmth of his arms to start their breakfast. "Aunt Lena must have been talking to you."

"Yeah. And she has a point." He poured orange juice into two glasses and set them on the table. "Abbie, I had more to say yesterday before Scilla came downstairs and interrupted us. And part of it was this... situation we find ourselves in."

Abbie gave a little laugh. "I wonder if Aunt Lena told Scilla to supervise us. She seemed pretty determined we needed to watch a movie together."

"I'm glad she's going to be in school today," Wade said flatly.

"Ah—before we talk about that, I need to tell you something." Abbie put the skillet on the stove and then turned around to face him. "There really is nothing between Randall and me. No matter what it may have looked like, or what Aunt Lena might have said to you."

That unruly piece of hair was over his forehead again. His eyes were twinkling and the look he gave her produced goosebumps on her arm.

"Fascinating. You mean when he was holding you—like this—it meant nothing?"

Abbie could only shake her head mutely as he ran his hands slowly down her back and drew her close to him.

"What about when he kissed you?"

"He never kissed me," she gulped breathlessly.

"The fool."

Her arms were twining themselves shamelessly around his neck.

Even Abbie's imagination couldn't have done justice to the way she felt when Wade Jackson kissed her.

The rest of Abbie's day was spent redoing most of what she tried to do with her head in the clouds. *Lord, this is the craziest thing that's ever happened to me. I've bumbled along this whole day and it's a wonder I haven't put Sage in the dryer and a load of clothes on the highchair.*

But now what? she asked herself in the middle of the afternoon. *Now what?*

Think of this logically, she scolded herself after she found the toaster in the refrigerator. *Think, Abbie. Would you leave England and your family to marry a man with a ranch and three kids in South Dakota?*

Lord, if this is Your will, I would marry Wade in a heartbeat. I can't believe I'm saying that before he even tells me he loves me. This is serious, Lord. The man kisses me once and I'm ready to say, "I do."

"Abbie?"

She let out a small yelp and turned around to see the source of her daydreams standing behind her.

He laughed at her befuddlement. "What are you doing standing in the dining room looking at the china cupboard?"

"I, uh, was checking your grandmother's china."

"Is something broken?"

His face was tinged with color from the cold wind, and his hair was unruly from the black cap he had just taken off. She absently reached up to smooth his hair and was embarrassed when she realized what she was doing.

"Your hair is, uh, broken," she mumbled.

At his surprised look she put her hands together in front of her and shook her head. "You shouldn't kiss me like that in the morning, Wade. I haven't been myself all day."

"Well," he said, drawing her close to him, "I locked Shy in the barn twice this morning. He's pretty put out at me."

"What are we going to do about each other?"

He laughed softly and ran his hand over her shoulder and down her back. "I've been wondering that ever since I saw you in your moose pajamas."

She looked up at him and beamed. "They're really something, aren't they? What about the slippers that go with them?"

"Yeah, the whole outfit is a doozy."

"Wade, I thought you had feelings for Torrie."

"I have feelings for one little redhead—who, I might add, has kept me on a roller coaster for the past week with her old neighbor."

"Old neighbors are for the birds." She hugged him. "Both of them can fly south for all I care."

He gripped her shoulders in both his strong hands and moved her slightly away from him. "Are you going to want to fly back to England this spring, Abbie?" His face reflected his seriousness.

Her heart began to race and she took a deep breath. "At this moment it's the furthest thing from my mind."

"Which means?" he asked her softly.

"Which means that I've absolutely tumbled headfirst in love with you, Wade Jackson."

The expression on his face went far beyond the look he'd had the night she saw him and Torrie together.

She caught her breath and blurted out, "What are you going to do about that?"

CHAPTER 20

Common Sense Decision

*W*ADE BELIEVED IN being responsible and using common sense. He told Abbie that several mornings later while they were waiting for their first cup of coffee. He discovered after he made that announcement that he had forgotten to put coffee grounds in the coffee maker, and he didn't miss the expression on Abbie's face when he had to start the whole process all over again.

They needed time, he told her, to be sure of their feelings. She needed to make sure she wanted to live away from her family and her country. She also needed to be sure she wanted to be a rancher's wife and live, as Lena had mentioned many times, in the middle of nowhere. She needed to realize she would be raising three children that weren't hers and figure out how she would juggle her feelings about stepchildren with the children she and Wade might have.

She had listened quietly to all he said, and when he paused, she reached up and ran her slender fingers across his whiskered chin. It was then he realized he had forgotten to shave that morning.

"What do you need to be sure of in the way of feelings?" she asked softly.

He hadn't meant to put his arms around her slender waist or give her a whisker rub, but she just had that effect on him. He also kissed her several times, and even though he was standing in front of the coffee maker, he never heard its gurgle that indicated the coffee was done.

It wasn't until she moved out of his arms and poured their coffee that he collected himself to answer her question.

"Yes. I need to be sure—" He stopped mid-sentence, his mind blank. There had been a whole host of reasons and issues that he had thought of during the night, and now he couldn't remember a single one of them.

"Is Kada an issue?" Abbie asked.

"Well, maybe. I need to be darn sure I don't make another mistake like Kada."

When Abbie's brown eyes flared up at that remark, he quickly reassured her that she wasn't anything at all like Kada.

"What I meant was that the divorce papers were only signed a little over a month ago, and I just wonder what people will think if I jump into another marriage so soon."

She nodded. "What other issues do you have, Wade?"

"Well," he cleared his throat, "maybe the children might need a little more time to adjust to you." When he said the words aloud, he thought they sounded ridiculous; his children adored Abbie. "You know, Abbie, we just shouldn't rush into anything. Time is always needed to make important decisions, and besides, we need to be sure of our feelings."

She had looked at him a little sadly and nodded again.

Suddenly common sense seemed utterly stupid, and he made sure she understood how much he loved her.

And he did love her. When he thought Randall had come all the way across the pond to make a play for her, he was furiously jealous, and it had surprised him. He didn't know when he had come to think of her as his, or when he had started visualizing her in his home forever.

All he did know for sure that morning was that he was having trouble doing chores. He left the house with his mind muddled, and when he came back to the place from feeding his cattle, he realized he had forgotten to shut a couple of gates. By the time he retraced his steps, he was out of sorts with himself.

Clive was waiting for him by the time he finished. The two of them were headed to Ft. Pierre for a bull sale. He hoped he wouldn't absentmindedly bid and buy a bull he didn't want. He also hoped he could talk to Clive without seeming like an old busybody.

After they were several miles down the road in Wade's pickup, Wade cleared his throat and without looking at his friend said, "Clive, there's somebody who thinks the world of you."

Clive looked at him with startled blue eyes. "Oh, no. I just can't get serious about a redhead. I still have bad memories about getting bit on the lip."

"I don't mean Abbie!" Wade retorted. "She's my redhead, and I sure don't have any trouble kissing her."

Clive was astounded. "When did all this happen?" He immediately blurted a second thought. "Does Torrie know?"

Wade squirmed a little self-consciously while he was driving. "I've always liked Abbie—I guess I didn't realize how much until that neighbor of hers showed up." He glanced over at his friend and couldn't read the expression on his face.

"Clive, Torrie is the one who thinks the world of you. I would imagine you feel the same about her."

"You know, of course," Clive began, mimicking Lena Talley, "that she told me to get lost when I asked to marry her. She sure as thunder started chasing you after that." Clive's tone was bitter.

Wade took a deep breath. He had no desire to play cupid, but Torrie and Clive were his friends, and between the two of them being proud and stubborn, they had managed to make each other miserable.

By the time they reached the sale barn, Wade had related Torrie's broken-hearted confession about her feelings for Clive and her reason for refusing his marriage proposal. He told how she slapped him, and how she acted toward Abbie. In fact, one of the reasons she tore into

Abbie the day of the horse incident was because she realized Wade was terrified for Abbie's safety. "Beyond common concern for hired help," was the way Torrie had said it to Wade.

"Clive, Torrie has always carried a torch for you, but you really hurt her feelings when you said your folks' ranch and her folks' ranch could be joined together to make one big place if the two of you got married." Wade shut off the pickup and looked at his friend. "She thought she'd get even by chasing me but she finally realized I wasn't who she wanted. Now she just doesn't know what your feelings are for her."

"But she should have known that I've always loved her. She's always been my girl. She should have known I'm not ambitious enough to care about working that big of a place." Clive slowly got out of the outfit and shut the door.

Both men were silent as they walked into the sale barn. Not to hear Clive talk was a new experience for Wade. Even when Torrie had started flirting with him in front of Clive, the man had always been able to maintain a constant flow of stories.

When they entered the sale barn café they headed over to a corner booth. It wasn't long before the room was crowded, and a couple of fellows they knew needed a place to sit and asked if they could join them. They hashed over the weather, the government and politics, cattle prices, and a little local gossip.

There was a slight pause in the conversation and Wade absently added cream and sugar to his coffee before he remembered he hated sweetened coffee. He saw Clive raise his eyebrows at him and shake his head.

"Are you guys after some bulls?" Clive asked their friends.

They both shook their heads.

"Well, I'm sort of planning on it," Wade said, "unless they go too high."

The talk drifted to which bull sellers sold what genetics, when they sold, and at what prices.

They paid for their lunch and made their way to the bleachers around the sale ring. It was after they sat down that it dawned on Wade that not only had he forgotten to bring the seller's catalog, he hadn't even gone to the pens before the sale to check over the bulls. He was thoroughly disgusted with himself.

This being in love business is going to ruin the ranch.

"Do you need anything downtown?" Wade asked Clive as they left the sale barn to go home.

"Well, maybe I do, and maybe I don't." Clive grinned and his capped gold tooth sparkled in the late afternoon sun.

Wade waited for him to explain that remark and fervently hoped he had remembered to take his keys out of the pickup before he locked it.

"You know, even if you had bid on those bulls, you never brought your horse trailer to take 'em home." Clive raised an eyebrow at Wade.

"Well," Wade floundered, grateful to feel his keys in his front pocket, "I wasn't sure I would get any. No sense pulling the trailer if I didn't need it."

"Uh-huh." Clive waited patiently for Wade to unlock the door. "I think you've got problems, Wade."

"How's that?"

Both men had gotten into the cold pickup and Clive shivered.

"Start 'er up, man, and let's get some heat in here," he groused as Wade had given no indication that he himself was cold.

Soon the outfit had purred to life, and the exhaust was sending out puffs of smoke into the cold December air. Wade turned to look at Clive and was clearly nonplussed to see his friend shaking his head and grinning at him.

"What? What's that all about?" he asked testily.

"I was just kinda watching you today."

"Oh, boy."

Clive grinned even wider. "It's kinda funny, Wade. You seem to be… uh… forgetful like. I guess you sort of forgot you don't ever use cream 'n sugar in your coffee."

Wade stared out the windshield and couldn't think of anything to say.

"You know, when Torrie started her case on you, I was pretty hurt. You'n me have been friends for a long time. I knew you and Kada were having trouble—everyone knew that—and I could see that you were trying not to let Torrie get too close, but she's a persuasive gal, and I just figured it would only be a matter of time before you divorced Kada and Torrie moved in."

Clive's words rolled out like a well-rehearsed play. He barely stopped for a breath before continuing.

"And then along came Abbie. She changed everything. Torrie knew it and was mad as hops. I knew it and wondered if I might have a chance with Torrie again. You even knew it, I think, but didn't want to admit it to yourself. You talked about her all the time. You'd get this little smile on your mug and tell about her hopping around with Skyler, or imitate her accent—all those things. She changed the picture for all of us. I don't think she meant to, she just came and done her job. Actually, she done above and beyond her job, and never complained."

Wade gave him a sheepish smile. "Lena thought I should give her a raise."

"I think you should give her a diamond ring, Wade. She's a keeper. You give Abbie one, and I'll try again with Torrie. Maybe this time I can say the right words."

Wade looked out the windshield again. "It's so soon after the divorce. I don't know what people will think of that," he finally said.

"They're gonna talk about it, doofus. People always talk about everything." Clive gave a happy chuckle. "You and I talk about people all the time. It's human nature and this is a love story—makes the women all happy to think their hero Wade met the girl of his dreams."

Wade put the pickup in gear. "Clive, you are so full of it. No wonder Lena Talley called you Clipe."

The middle of December had arrived with wind and spitting snow. Abbie had taken Scilla to school and headed to Pierre for Christmas shopping, and Wade had been pacing the floor for the last hour worrying about her.

Even though it was only 3:30 in the afternoon, the sun's dim light was edging closer to the western hills, and the last place he wanted Abbie to be was on their gravel roads after dark. She had assured him she would be back in time to pick up Scilla. The last time he called her on her cell phone, she said she was ready to leave Pierre.

He had done chores in the early morning light so he could stay in the house with the two boys during the day. But after their noon meal he had decided to bundle them up so he could get the evening chores done early. Even though they were in the warm tractor cab, their cheeks looked a healthy pink by the time they were back in the house. The fresh air had made them sleepy, and they were both snoozing on the sofa.

Wade was getting ready to call Abbie's cell again when he saw the Tahoe coming down the road. She drove into the garage after he had opened the door, and Scilla flew out of the vehicle like a flash.

"Daddy! Guess what? Torrie has a diamond ring, and she says she's—what's that word, Abbie?"

"Engaged." Abbie was slowly opening her door.

"Engaged! To Clive! And they're having a huge, huge wedding in June and all us schoolkids are invited!"

"Well, well," Wade said, and raised an eyebrow at Abbie. She flashed him a smile and handed over some sacks before getting out of the Tahoe. "He didn't waste any time."

"You knew about this?" Abbie asked as she opened another door and gathered more sacks and packages.

"Yeah."

It took several trips into the house for both of them but finally the groceries and packages were put away, supper was in the oven, and three kids were racing their new wind-up teddy bears on the dining room's wood floors.

"You're a little quiet tonight, Abbie," Wade observed as he leaned against the counter and watched her putter around the kitchen.

"I know. I was worried about the weather while I was shopping, and driving home seemed a bit scary. Guess I'm a total coward about these long distances and iffy weather."

"I don't think you should be going alone during the winter," Wade said. "From now on I'll go with you."

She leaned against him and murmured, "That would be wonderful."

He wrapped his arms around her and kissed her, completely forgetting that he might have an audience.

"Daddy! What are you doing?" Scilla was shocked.

"I'm kissing Abbie." There were times when only the truth would do.

"Doing!" Skyler scolded and tried to push his way between them.

Abbie laughed and backed away. "'Doing' indeed, Mr. Skyler." Wade noticed a light blush on her face as she bent down to pick up the indignant little boy.

"Don't you kiss my Abbie, Skyler," Wade teased.

Skyler's dark eyes flashed as he realized this might be a new game, and soon he was planting slobbery kisses on her cheek.

Wade pulled him away from her and after setting him on the floor he told him not to kiss his Scilla. Immediately Skyler made a dash for Scilla, but she would have none of it and ran shrieking into the living room.

"It's a good thing it's Thursday, Wade," Abbie told him. "Maybe she'll forget what she saw by next Monday. It could be embarrassing if she told the kids at school that she saw her dad kissing the nanny."

"I think tonight her dad and the nanny better have a little cuddle time after the kids are in bed." Wade smiled. "The nanny seems to be making herself scarce every evening and the dad is getting tired of sitting by the fireplace alone."

"The nanny wants to give the dad time to think."

"The dad wants to know what the nanny thinks."

"The nanny thinks… oh, that's Sage crying!" Abbie walked swiftly into the dining room to take care of Sage, and Wade was left to mull over what it might be that the nanny thought.

"Daddy, are you and Abbie engaged too?" Scilla asked as Wade tucked her in to bed that evening.

Wade sat on the edge of her bed and ran his hand over her brown hair. "I haven't given her a diamond ring yet, but we are talking about getting married."

"What would I call her if you were?"

"What would you want to call her?"

Scilla looked at him with gray-green eyes—Kada's eyes—and suddenly they filled with tears and she flung herself into Wade's arms.

He held her until she had quit crying, and when she was tucked back in again, he asked what was wrong.

"I don't wanna be bad, Daddy, but I want Abbie to be my mom so much. She don't always tell me good-bye and leave. She don't say 'rug rat.' I hate that rug rat stuff—it sounds ugly. But I already got a mom so how can I call Abbie that if you and her get married?"

"You're allowed two mothers, Scilla," Wade said, attempting to soothe her. "One who is here taking care of you, and the other who loves you very much but has left because she has an ambition to sing." He smiled at her woebegone face. "You can consider yourself lucky because you have two mothers who are trying to do their best for you."

"What if she wants me back and I gotta go with her? What if my real dad wants me and I gotta go with him?"

"Have you been worried about that, Scilla?"

At her tearful nod he pulled her to him and gave her a bear hug.

"The first time I saw you, and you looked at me with those frightened little eyes, I wanted to protect you from all the things in your world that were bothering you," he told her softly. "I adopted you right after your mother and I were married. You're my legal daughter, and unless you decide to make a different choice of dads, I'm the one who'll raise you. No one can take you away from me unless you want them to."

She pulled away to look at him. "Never, promise God?"

"Never, promise God."

She eased back under the covers and gave him a watery smile. "When are you and Abbie getting married?"

Wade tucked her in again and kissed her forehead. "We're going to decide that tonight."

"You seem lost in thought," Abbie said a few minutes later, walking toward him while he stood by the fireplace. "Are you OK?"

"I am now," he murmured, pulling her close. He enjoyed the fragrance of her hair and the soft warmth of her, and he almost forgot what he had intended to talk to her about.

"What would you think of a June wedding for us, Abbie?" he asked finally, trying to rally common sense.

"Absolutely not. No and no and no." She leaned back to look into his startled face. "Do you want to wait clear 'til June to get married?"

"I just thought you might want to think about this for a while," he said, shrugging.

"Mr. Jackson, you are the one who seems to have to do a lot of thinking. I've made my decision."

He smiled at her, enjoying the feisty flash of temper in her eyes. "What did you decide, Abbie?"

"Either we get married soon, or I'll have to leave soon."

His smile faded. "What the—what are you talking about?"

She sighed and slipped away from him until she was standing at the other side of the fireplace. She hesitated before she answered, and her voice sounded uncertain. "I'm trying to remain a virtuous woman, Wade. But I have to be honest with you. Whenever we're together like this, the most immoral thoughts are dashing into my mind." She clasped her hands in front of her and graced him with an Aunt Lena imitation. "You know, of course, this is a situation I pray a lot about."

He watched the way the light from the fireplace danced over her face and hair. Those brown eyes that had delighted him the first time he met her now looked troubled. She was without a doubt the most intriguing and honest woman he had ever met. He loved her beyond a shadow of doubt.

He walked over to her and ran his hand over her copper-colored tendrils. "In that case, Miss Miller, in order to protect you from yourself, and because I love you more than life itself, will you marry me very soon?"

She gave him one of her high wattage smiles. "How soon is very soon?"

When he told her, the brown eyes flew open in surprise. "That's—only about a week away."

"Is that soon enough for you?"

"If you don't stop looking at me that way it's not going to be soon enough." She seemed to be having trouble catching her breath.

"Then I better stop looking and start kissing."

CHAPTER 21

Lena's Lament

LENA TALLEY SAT in front of the small gas fireplace in her parents' old home and concluded it had been a perfect day for her. She had dusted and shined all her mother's old furniture and lovingly cleaned the knickknacks and china settings.

Lena had been in a mellow mood ever since she had returned home from the States. It had been so much fun to surprise the Millers with her announcement that she had visited Abbie. She was a trifle disappointed, though, that they hadn't really acted extremely surprised. Nevertheless, she was able to inform them about her lecture to both Abbie and that man she worked for.

Miss Pepper, the crotchety cat Lena adored, jumped onto her lap and began her usual kneading and purring. "You know, of course, Miss Pepper, that unless I had dragged Randall there with me, Abbie might have been getting ideas about that man. The way it was, she soon realized that Randall was the right one for her."

Lena smiled as she patted Miss Pepper's head. "In fact, as we were driving away I asked Randall if he didn't agree with me that there might be a marriage soon, and he gave that little quirky smile of his and said he definitely would agree to that."

Lena rocked and self-righteously added, "I suppose I should go to Christmas Eve service tonight, but with the snow and all, I'm going to call Ben and tell him I'll just stay put. Tomorrow he can get me for Christmas Day, although it might make more sense to go tonight than tomorrow. All that fuss over those twin babies wears me out."

Lena rocked in her chair for several minutes trying to decide which place she wanted to go to the most. Finally she made her call to Ben to say he could pick her up Christmas Day.

She wondered as she rocked when Randall and Abbie would get married. Fall weddings were nice and that would give them time to find a house nearby and get settled in. Funny about Abbie, she seemed so content out there in that godforsaken country. In fact, Lena couldn't quite put her finger on it, but there was something different about Abbie. Maybe she was just growing up.

That must be it.

Miss Pepper jumped off her lap and ran into the kitchen. That meant her cat food dish was empty. Lena got up to take care of that duty and decided to turn in early. Tomorrow would be a big day.

Lena hadn't seen Randall since they had returned, and she thought he seemed in unusually good humor at the Millers' Christmas Day dinner. Lois had done her customary job of beautifully decorating their home, and everyone was waiting with their mouths watering for the turkey and trimmings.

Lena never bothered with gifts, but usually the Millers gave her a present. She was a little miffed this year that they seemed to have forgotten that. In fact, Lois seemed quite preoccupied, but it was probably because of all the racket and fuss over those twins.

Ben said the holiday grace, and Lena thought his voice cracked a trifle when he asked for a special blessing for Abbie. Well, he needn't think it was all her fault that Abbie wasn't there. Randall was a little to blame. Of course, next year all would be different.

It wasn't until dessert was served that Ben stood up and cleared his throat.

"I have an announcement to make," he said. "A marriage announcement."

Why, that sly fox of a Randall! He must have asked for Abbie's hand and now Ben is going to tell them all about how Randall and I went to the States and what a wonderful idea that was. Lena started smiling like the cat that swallowed the canary.

She even caught Randall's eye and nodded in a sage way. She thought he fidgeted in a manner most unlike himself, but of course a young fellow like that who seemed to wink at all the airline stewardesses in the country might be a little remorseful about settling down. When he and Abbie had little ones, those redheaded little kids running around would be worse than these twins they all fussed about so much.

Lena shuddered at the thought. Maybe they should live a little farther away from her than what she first planned.

Ben stood a little straighter and took a deep breath. Before he began, he reached for Lois's hand and pulled her up so she was standing beside him.

"Good night nurse, man," Lena muttered impatiently under her breath.

Is it that hard to say your daughter is going to marry an old family friend? What if the silly girl had decided to marry that western person? With Abbie's temperament she would not have let a little thing like living millions of miles away from England stop her for a second. It was such a good thing I intervened and took Randall out there. I didn't care at all for the way that man looked at Abbie. And the things he said—"moose pajamas" of all things! The pagan.

"Well, Lois, I guess we have everyone's attention," Ben said, looking around at the smiling group. "We have a surprise for you all and we wanted to save it for when we were all together."

He and Lois exchanged glances.

"Last night in South Dakota, at a little country church's Christmas Eve service, our Abbie and her boss, Wade Jackson, were married. His three children stood up with them."

Everyone began talking at once and the hubbub grew louder and louder as each one wanted more details.

Lena sat immobile in her chair. *I must have heard wrong.*

"What did you just say, Ben?" she rasped out sharply, and everyone quieted immediately.

"I said our Abbie and Wade Jackson got married last night. And I want to also say that he called us to properly ask for permission to marry our daughter."

Ben gave the Hudsons a smile. "Randall has told us that he is a fine young man and that Abbie seems to be happy in her new home on the prairies of Dakota. He was pretty sure they were serious about each other. He told us that as soon as he and Aunt Lena returned from their visit. He and Wade have had several phone conversations since then."

Lena turned to glare at Randall. He in turn grinned like a vampire and gave her a thumbs-up.

"Aunt Lena," Ben added, "you must be quite proud of yourself that you were the one to suggest Abbie head out west."

She opened her mouth several times but nothing came out. Everyone was so busy talking again that she knew she wouldn't be heard anyhow.

When Lena could decently excuse herself, she walked home. The chilly damp wind seemed to cut right through her cloth coat and she felt every day of her seventy-two years.

The usual tea ritual with her mother's fine Bavarian tea set gave her little comfort as she sat in her scheming chair and fumed over the outcome of all her hard work.

A trip clear out to that miserable barren land had been a complete waste of time and money. She had endured all of Clipe's talk and spent a week in a strange bed for nothing. All the while that miserable Randall knew it was for nothing. She could have met her end with a terrorist bomb on the plane and it would have been absolutely for nothing.

Miss Pepper jumped onto Lena's lap and started kneading her claws on her wool slacks. "You're the only one that has any sense, cat. Stay home and be grouchy, and let the darn fools take care of their own life."

Lena gave a disgruntled sigh and sat in the fading afternoon light with her cat on her lap and her mother's tea service beside her. She felt like crawling into bed, pulling the covers over her head, and disowning the whole lot them. Then they'd be sorry. Where was that copy of her will anyhow?

As soon as Miss Pepper jumps off my lap I'll look in Daddy's antique desk. Come to think of it, it has been well over a year since I last changed the blasted thing.

CHAPTER 22

Kada and Bill's Christmas

CHRISTMAS CAROLS WERE playing in Kada's apartment as she was getting ready to go to Bill's place. They had decided several nights earlier that they might as well spend Christmas day together since they were both alone.

Bill claimed it was just another day for him—he worked at his job; he came home. But she wanted more than that, and finally he agreed to have a mid-afternoon meal—which he said he would cook. She was to bring the dessert.

No problem, Kada thought, and she went to the bakery for a chocolate cake. She hadn't bought any gifts except to pick up a box of candy for Bill. She had always had trouble with Christmas gifts, cards, and holiday decorations. The only sign of Christmas in her apartment was a small nativity scene she'd had since she was a little girl.

The oyster stew supper the band members had the other night had been fun. Last year she had missed out on that. Last year when she was carrying Sage she had missed out on everything. It was a long nine months, that pregnancy. She wrote a lot of music, but most of it was depressing to sing.

But that was over. She had been working on several new songs, however with her college courses she'd had very little time to perfect them.

The wonderful smell of chili greeted Kada as she opened the door to Bill's small house. She was always amazed at the starkness and cleanness of his place. Everything had a place, and everything was in its place. There were peg hangers at the door, where he expected his guests to hang their coats, and she had learned the first time she visited him that he expected her to hang her purse under her coat.

"Smells good in here. Have you been cooking all day?" she asked as she followed him to the kitchen.

"The joys of a Crock Pot, Kada. You should get yourself one." He took the cake from Kada and put it on the counter. "What did you do this morning?"

"I slept. I stayed up so many nights studying that I'm a million years behind on sleep."

"Did the ex put down the money for your next tuition bill?" he asked ambiguously.

"Well, not yet, but he will. Wade usually does what he says he's going to. Hey, did I tell you the news from the old neighborhood? At the dance last week one of Wade's friends beat a hot trail over to me and said that Torrie and Clive were engaged." Kada gave her raspy laugh. "Torrie must have decided Clive was better than nobody."

"Did she think Wade was out of reach?" Bill asked.

"Oh, who knows or even cares. I'm not even thinking about any of that." She quickly changed the subject to one that concerned her more. "Bill, do you think we could try singing 'Blue Eyes Crying in the Rain' in a different key? I think it needs to be lower for me."

"Last time we played it lower, and you thought it should be higher."

"Yeah, that sounded like it was in the basement."

They took their time over the chili and garlic bread. The sun was just going down when Bill brewed a pot of coffee and they savored the cake along with the coffee.

It was while they were in a mellow mood that Kada asked him if that was the way he usually spent Christmas.

"I've spent this day many ways," he replied solemnly.

"What did your family usually do?"

For a while, Kada thought he wasn't going to answer her. When he did, his voice seemed far away, as if the memories had brought unwanted thoughts into focus.

"I was raised here and there, but mostly on the reservation. My family was whoever I was able to live with at the time." He gave a derisive laugh. "My mother had about a thimble full of Sioux blood, but she liked all the traditions. She drank herself to death."

"Is that why you don't drink?" Kada asked quietly.

"That's why I don't drink," he answered flatly. "I've seen too many drunk old men wet their pants and too many drunk women passed out in their own vomit."

Kada gave a shudder. "That's a pretty gross description."

"It's also a pretty accurate one."

She gave a raspy laugh. "My mother was death on drinking. I was raised on the fourth pew back from the front of the Methodist church. We went every Sunday."

"So much for environment producing like behavior," Bill said. "My mother was an alcoholic and I don't touch the stuff. Your mother was the opposite and you drink a lot of booze."

"Bill," she protested, "I don't drink that much!"

He tilted his head back and gave a mirthful chuckle before he said, "When you were pregnant with Sage, the best thing your ex done was to keep you out of the band and at home." He gave her a hard look. "Fetal Alcohol Syndrome babies are a sad lot, Kada. They suffer for life from disabilities their mothers imposed on them. I wish the women who can't stop drinking for the nine months they're pregnant would be forced to take care of the kids they've handicapped."

"Have you been talking to Wade?" Kada was annoyed. "That's the lecture he gave me. He told me to shape up and stay away from booze and the band until Sage was born, and after that I could do what I wanted. I tell you, that was the longest nine months I've ever spent."

"But you did it, Kada, and now that little boy has a chance of good health because his ma did the right thing." Bill gave her a fleeting smile.

"Yeah." She smiled at him. "Yeah, I guess that's right. He didn't deserve any less. It wasn't his fault he came along when I didn't want another baby." She became thoughtful, and finally said, "I wasn't a good mother to any of the rug rats, Bill. Both Scilla and Sage had this terrible cough and Sage was pale and didn't seem to have any energy. I doted on Skyler, but he was getting so spoiled. Wade would spank and I would spoil. Not a good combination." She gave a wry smile. "That's what my parents did in reverse. Dad spoiled and Ma spanked."

"I never knew my father. I still don't have any idea who he is."

"What about siblings?" Kada was finding out more about Bill Rissix in this conversation than she had in all the years she'd known him.

"There were several. Two died in infancy, one died at about age ten after living on a feeding tube for most of her life. A foster family took care of her." His face was grim. "I have a half brother on the reservation that can barely tie his shoes because of alcohol. I haven't seen him for years."

Kada shook her head and decided maybe Bill had a reason for his expressionless eyes. "How did you ever turn out the way you did—how did you become a band manager?"

"I had two goals when I was a kid: grow up and get out." Bill abruptly stood and took his cup over to the coffee maker. He filled his cup, then hers, and sat back down.

"I joined the army at seventeen. Stayed in for twenty years. I thought of staying longer but, well, I didn't." He granted her a small smile. "End of story. I usually don't tell as much as I have. You must have asked all the right questions."

"Once in a while I do something right." She had more questions, but from the look on his face it seemed evident that he was through talking about himself.

"How come," he asked her after the dishes were done and they were sitting in the living room, "you don't ever attend any services if you were raised in church?"

Kada felt the familiar unsettledness that always descended on her when she thought of church. "I promised myself when I was growing up that as soon as I was out from under my mother's thumb I would do just exactly what I wanted to do." She paused reflectively for a moment. "She was one of these churchgoers that thought every sermon was for someone else. She was super-critical of everyone, including me. Whenever I do go I seem to see her sitting beside me making sure I know how sinful me and the rest of the congregation are."

She suppressed a shudder. "I was an only child. There were hardly any other relatives around. It was sorta lonely."

"What about your dad?"

Kada laughed. "Dad wore his little bolo tie and his suit coat and scrunched down on the other side of me. Ma dominated the family. The only thing he ever done on his own was to put a CD in my name and Wade's. When he died, the bank notified me. Ma never did know about it."

Bill rocked in his Lazy Boy and looked at her with hooded eyes. "Tell me about this faith of yours."

She gave a short laugh. "That's kind of a hard question. I guess I've not ever been asked that one." She was at a loss for words and sat silently while she thought about her answer. Bill waited patiently.

"I...I believe God created the world. I believe Jesus died for our sins. I think that when we do wrong things He forgives us. I... I think He is a loving God and doesn't want us to be lost and in hell." Kada squirmed a bit at the last part.

"I have a serious problem with that," Bill said. "If this Jesus went through the agony of the crucifixion, He wouldn't just pat you on the head when you sin and say, 'That's all right.' Why even bother with the cross if everyone keeps right on doing what they've always done? It looks like you should have to change your ways and quit this sinning stuff—it doesn't make sense to me, and that's another reason I don't believe any of it."

"Great Scott, Bill, I don't know." Kada threw up her hands. "I never thought of all that. I just say my little, 'Thank You, God,' prayer at night and let it go at that."

"I'd call that a pretty watered-down faith," he said flatly.

"You can call it whatever you want," Kada said, now more than a little annoyed. "At least I believe something."

Later that evening when she was back at her apartment, Kada rummaged through the boxes of things Wade had dropped off. She was searching for the Bible she had growing up. She had dutifully marked in it all the verses the Sunday school teachers told her to. She thought maybe she could find something in it that would answer the questions Bill had raised.

Finally finding it at the bottom of a box, she sat cross-legged on the floor and opened it up to the first page, where it said, "The Bible speaks directly to you."

She skimmed through the paragraph—"all-time best-seller," "more than an answer-book," "easiest to understand."

"Where do you begin?" That was the next headline. "If the Bible is fairly new to you, start with the book of Mark."

Another headline: "What about your personal problems?" She flipped through the pages until she came to "Fearful." There were three verses in that part:

"Fear not, for I am with you. Do not be dismayed. I am your God."
—Isaiah 41:10

He does not fear bad news, nor live in dread of what may happen.
—Psalm 112:7

"You are my hiding place from every storm of life; you even keep me from getting into trouble! You surround me with songs of victory."

—Psalm 32:7

"Why didn't I find this when I needed it so bad?" Kada asked out loud. She read the verses over again and again and looked up where they were located in the Bible. It occurred to her that she had never even thought to look in the Bible after the frightening house episodes.

Then she turned to the gospel of Mark. After she read the first seven chapters, her legs were numb and she slowly got up and hobbled over to a comfortable stuffed chair.

She reread the highlighted verses she had found:

Baptized as a public announcement of their decision to turn their backs on sin, so that God could forgive them.

—Mark 1:4

"Turn from your sins and act on this glorious news."

—Mark 1:15

"The delights of wealth, and the search for success and lure of nice things come in and crowd out God's message."

—Mark 4:19

Turn their backs on sin. Kada thought about that for quite a while. It didn't say to continue doing the same sin over and over and expect forgiveness. It said to turn your back on sin. Turn from sin—repent.

Kada read through the rest of Mark, including Christ's crucifixion and agonizing death. *What had Bill said?* "If this Jesus went through the agony of the crucifixion…" *But He* did *go through the agony. The Bible says so.*

She put down her Living Bible. There was a lot to think about. She slowly showered and brushed her teeth, thinking about what it meant to turn her back on sin. What would she have to give up? Did it mean she should go back to Wade and try again, even if they were divorced?

Kada crawled into her unmade bed and plumped her pillows a couple of times. The streetlight cast a dim glow into her bedroom and she watched the tree branches make weird shadows on the wall. Another verse from Mark crossed her mind.

"Without God, it is utterly impossible. But with God everything is possible."

—Mark 10:27

With God it would be possible to sing in the band without drinking too much or being too vulgar. No, wait—that wasn't the way she should say that. With God it would be possible to sing in the band without being vulgar or taking even one drink. Bill would help her on that one. That was rich—did she think God needed Bill's help?

Her heart was troubled and torn. She didn't want to go to church. She didn't want to go back to Wade and the rug rats. She wanted to sing in the band. Maybe if she would start eliminating some of her sins, it would be a step in the right direction.

I'm a major big sinner, Lord. Adultery, leaving the kids and Wade, drinking—my sins have become as comfortable as old shoes. I've gotten used to them.

She was too used to them. She had told so many dirty jokes that the band members told her she was wilder than the wild boys.

I need You to help me. We could start on some of the smaller ones—like the drinking and dirty jokes and stuff like that. Going to hell scares me. I'm worried that I'm headed there.

Ever since she and Ace Olson had stupidly put the black rugs and curtains in Wade's house, Kada had been afraid of going to hell. When Wade had asked her about voodoo, she'd almost become hysterical. Her mother had preached on incantations to Satan all the time and lectured that people who did that were just one step away from the gates to hell.

I know Jesus died on the cross so sinners like me can go to heaven. I just never realized before that I have an obligation to turn away from sin, turn my back on sin. I never really understood that before You can forgive me, I must sincerely want to quit my sinful walk. And tonight I do—please help me have this same repentance tomorrow.

Kada thought it was strange that an unbeliever like Bill asked the question that brought her closer to God. If it weren't for Bill's words, she never would have tried to find her Bible in the first place.

About Bill, Lord. I feel so darn bad he had such a rough time. How come he knew about the cross? I guess as long as I'm asking You impossible things like helping me not to sin, I might as well ask You to help Bill too.

CHAPTER 23

Mrs. Wade Jackson

*A*BBIE WOKE IN the early dawn of Christmas morning and stretched beside her sleeping husband. He mumbled her name and pulled her closer to him, and she snuggled into his warmth.

"Merry Christmas, Mr. Jackson."

"Uh-huh. Same to you, Mrs. Jackson." His voice was croaky, and he smiled without opening his eyes.

"It's snowing a little."

"It must be too dark to see outside. How do you know that?"

"I have my eyes open."

He smiled again, and still without opening his eyes found a very kissable spot on her shoulder.

Abbie grinned as the eastern sky slowly became lighter. She ran her hands through Wade's thick dark hair and stretched against the length of him.

"Wade, our wedding was very nice. You did a good job arranging everything." She could feel his shoulders shake with suppressed mirth.

"You spent most of yesterday afternoon telling me we should have eloped," he said, prying open one eye for emphasis. "When did you decide it was 'very nice'?"

"When we were finally downstairs having wedding cake with everyone."

He laughed out loud and raised his head to look at her. "Your old neighbor warned me that you get pretty uptight about weddings. He said to make it small and simple."

She shook her head and traced her finger against his whiskered chin. "Bossy Randall even tells my husband what kind of wedding we need. He's incorrigible. "

Wade propped his head on his elbow and gazed at her. "Is that some kind of contagious disease?"

"I hope it's nothing you catch—"

Wade raised an eyebrow in perfect imitation of Randall, causing Abbie to dissolve in a fit of giggles.

They enjoyed their early morning coffee in the dining room, admiring the gracious old home in its holiday attire. A nicely formed cedar from the river breaks was decorated and stood in the south bay window. Opened gifts were splayed out in front of it.

When Wade had seen how worried Abbie was about their upcoming wedding and how excited the kids were over their wrapped Christmas gifts, he decided unwrapping presents would be a welcome diversion during the hours before the Christmas Eve service. Abbie was grateful—she was slightly embarrassed over how nervous the thought of standing in front of people made her.

"I like the way you've made the house look, Abbie." Wade sat on one of the dining room chairs and watched her light a candle in its hurricane globe surrounded by Christmas greenery.

"I think the kids had fun decorating," Abbie agreed. "Did you see the snowman Scilla made from cotton balls?"

"His nose seems to be missing."

"It was a candy corn and Skyler ate it," Abbie informed him. That fact amused both of them and they chuckled companionably. Abbie sat beside him and ran her hand lightly over his shirted arm.

"I'm glad it's just us today," she said. "After all the excitement of yesterday this will be a nice quiet time for the kids to get used to you and me being married."

Wade nodded and gave her knee a playful squeeze. "I didn't have any trouble going from boss to husband. Hopefully the kids won't have any trouble adjusting either." Suddenly he was serious as he put both hands around his coffee cup and gave her a quiet look. "This is the first time the kids have had any kind of Christmas—usually it just floated around as another day for Kada. Other than listening to country-western holiday music, there wasn't much else going on at Christmas while we were married."

"Why was that?"

"I'm not sure—when Kada didn't want to talk about something, it was pretty hard to get anything out of her."

Abbie thought for a moment. "Your mother told me Kada's mother is a difficult person. Do you suppose she was the problem?"

Wade nodded and smiled. "Mom was being very kind to say she is a difficult person. Kada's mother is a hard woman to like. I think she made life miserable for both Kada and her dad most of the time." He looked over at Abbie and gave her a slow wink. "I don't want to talk about my ex-wife, Abbie. What I want to do is let you know how much I appreciate all you've done to make this house a home for me and the kids."

It was barely noon when the phone call came from Abbie's family. She hit the speaker button and her mother's soft voice with its pronounced accent rolled into the room. It was evening in England, their company had left, and she and Ben were clearly ready to hear wedding news.

Lois wanted clothing details; Ben wanted weather news. Abbie promised her mother as soon as she could she would e-mail pictures, which caused Ben to laugh. The last time Abbie tried to send pictures ended up in a lengthy exchange between Tyler and her over the nuances of the whole procedure. Tyler had thrown up his hands and said in his best Aunt Lena imitation that it was a good thing she had beauty, because where technology was concerned, she didn't have brains.

Abbie laughed good-naturedly and hardened her resolve to master the whole mess.

When Wade asked about Aunt Lena, there was a studied pause before Ben said that Aunt Lena needed to learn she couldn't manipulate everyone's lives. Lois added that she would be up to her old tricks before long, but on this Christmas Day, she had slunk home like a dog with its tail between its legs, and they hadn't heard from her the rest of the afternoon.

They all exchanged news of the twins as well as information on the three Jackson kids. When it was time to hang up, Lois said she knew it would be hard for Abbie to get back to England, but if Aunt Lena could fly to South Dakota, she didn't know why she and Ben couldn't do the same.

Wade volunteered to pick them up at the airport whenever they could make the trip and added if they wanted to come in May they could see some brandings. Ben sounded enthused about that immediately.

Finally the sliced turkey and dressing, whose mouth-watering aroma had filled the house all morning, was ready to be brought to the dining room table. Abbie had wanted to make their first Christmas together a special occasion, and she and Scilla had carefully set glasses and flatware on the white tablecloth along with the flowered china plates.

When Abbie placed the bowl of mashed potatoes on the table, Scilla was bouncing from foot to foot wondering if she should use the cloth napkins she had found in the china cupboard drawer.

"That's a good idea! We'll be extra fancy today," Abbie told her. But in her haste to put them around the table, Scilla accidentally knocked over a glass and quickly dissolved into tears as it shattered into several pieces.

"Hey, it's just a glass, Scilla," Abbie comforted her. "No big deal. Just let me pick up the pieces so you don't cut yourself."

However, it seemed to be a big deal to Scilla. She threw down the napkins and ran upstairs crying. Abbie and Wade exchanged glances before Abbie carefully picked up the fragmented glass.

While Abbie put the rest of the meal on the table, Wade went upstairs. Skyler thought it was his brotherly duty to wait at the bottom of the steps until Scilla returned, but soon hunger overtook loyalty, and he crawled up on his booster seat and looked mournfully hungry.

It took a while for Wade to convince Scilla that breaking a glass wasn't nearly as bad as delaying a delicious Christmas dinner, but finally Abbie's new family was gathered at the table and she was able to thank the Lord for her many blessings.

"It's a funny thing about blessings," she told Wade later. The kids had finished eating and were playing with their new toys while the two of them enjoyed a slice of chocolate wedding cake. "When I left England, I wanted this trip to South Dakota to be a small blurb in my life; something that I was very nobly doing to help out Clair and Tyler. But later, after God took over, I began to see it as a huge blessing, and I liked God being in control because all of a sudden life was much more exciting."

She looked across the table at Wade and marveled at the many details the Lord had mastered to bring the two of them together. "Isn't God amazing, Wade? When you think of how we fell in love, it's a miracle."

His eyes twinkled as he put down his cup. "I wonder if Aunt Lena will ever realize the Lord was using her to play Cupid?"

They read Randall's e-mail in the afternoon.

Congratulations, Mr. and Mrs. Wade Jackson,

I am justifiably proud of my acting ability. Not that it takes any acting skill to enjoy hugging Abbie, but I'm sure she was getting tired of the whole matter and was wondering what I was up to. In the first place, I wanted Lena to think that I suddenly realized what a gem our little Abbie was, and in the second place, I wanted Wade to be persuaded he had competition.

It didn't take very long to figure out that Abbie thought her boss was a very fine fellow. The boss let the cat out of the bag when he seemed to know just how many freckles the nanny had on her nose. If that wasn't enough evidence, the black look he gave me when I said Abbie was sleeping when I counted those little rascally freckles was a sure conviction.

Lena will, of course, never forgive me and probably at this very moment is writing you out of her will, Abbie. Take heart—she routinely adds or subtracts from that very worn document.

I believe you mentioned, Wade, that our lovely Miss Torrie is engaged to Clive and that a June wedding is planned. My congratulations to them also. I am amazed Abbie consented to even the tiny Christmas Eve nuptials. I was firmly convinced she would insist on a justice of the peace ceremony. What a brave girl you are, Abbie.

I certainly enjoyed my visit to South Dakota, and perhaps one day can fly Ben and Lois across the pond to visit. Tyler and Clair would like to make the jump also, but until the little ones are a tad bit bigger it might be a stretch to say that that would be enjoyable.

A very blessed Christmas to you and your family.

Randall

Abbie read the note a couple of times. She hadn't realized what a dual role Randall had been playing. She shook her head and looked at Wade as he read the whole thing once again.

"I'll bet he enjoyed pulling the wool over everyone's eyes," she groused. "He probably snickered all the way back to England."

The following afternoon, Wade decided to call Kada and tell her he and Abbie had been married. He thought she should hear it from him and not someone else. Abbie agreed, but she felt a twinge of nerves as he began the conversation with his ex-wife. It seemed to go smoothly, and suddenly he handed the phone to her.

"She wants to talk to you," he said. There was no time to read his expression.

"Yes, hello, Kada?" Abbie said.

A raspy laugh came over the line. "Do you think the world can handle two Mrs. Wade Jacksons?"

The remark caught Abbie off guard. "I... I rather think so. How are you?"

"I'm doing good. Look, Abbie, I'm so glad it's you and not Torrie. She wouldn't have been right for Wade, but I just want to say that I wish you and him all the best. He deserves it."

"Well, I... well, thank you, Kada. I appreciate that."

"It's better for the rug rats, too. Listen, is Wade still there? I need to tell him one more thing."

"He's right here—ah, good-bye, Kada. Take care." Abbie felt slightly dumb for adding the last words. She handed the phone over to Wade and gave a sigh of relief that her part of the conversation was over.

The rest of the phone call was short, and Wade hung up with a peculiar expression on his face.

"She thanked me several times for telling her myself," he said, turning to Abbie. He put his hand under her chin and kissed her lightly. "I never thought I'd be telling one wife I married another wife."

"Almost like a soap opera."

CHAPTER 24

New Beginnings

ABBIE WASN'T QUITE sure how the idea of a New Year's Eve party at their house evolved, but the neighbors seemed to think they could have a welcoming party and a wedding shower combined with a New Year's Eve party all at once.

They assured her they would take care of the food, so with Wade beside her that evening she began to greet their friends and neighbors. Marilyn took over the food arrangement, and not only was the kitchen table running over with baked goods, but the dining room table was filled with gifts.

Abbie realized she knew most of the guests, having seen them at the school parties and church, and the ones she didn't know introduced themselves. Children were everywhere, running up and down the stairs making various levels of noise, and Scilla seemed overjoyed to have school chums see her home.

As the evening unfolded, men congregated beside the fireplace and women visited in the kitchen. Torrie decided there needed to be a little more mixing, and she went to drag Wade out of the men's group to help Abbie unwrap presents. The thoughtfulness of the gifts impressed Abbie. Not only had the neighborhood shopped for her, they had also considered Wade.

Abbie was shocked beyond words when she finished unwrapping a large framed picture of the old stone bridge at her parents' place in England. It was a winter scene, and the ice crystals from the trees and the clear running water were stunning.

"Who gave us this?" Wade wondered. "What are we looking at, Abbie?" he added, taking the picture from her and studying it carefully.

"The card says 'Clive and Torrie.' It's a picture from my parents' farm! See the old stone bridge, and the little stream that separates our farm from the Hudsons'? It's absolutely beautiful!" She moved toward Torrie, who was smiling at them. "Thank you so much!" she said and impulsively gave Torrie a hug.

"How did you get this?" Wade asked.

"This is the marvel of the Internet age," Torrie explained proudly. "Abbie's brother, Tyler, took the picture and e-mailed it, and then we printed it and had it framed. He said he was able to go out early in the morning and get this after a foggy night."

Wade looked down at Abbie with his eyebrows raised. "Is this where you go fishing?"

"Yup! I've caught some big trout in that stream. See how it breaks down into some cascades over here," she pointed with her finger, "and then comes together farther down?"

"I suppose this is where the freckle-counting episode took place?"

Abbie glanced at him and her brown eyes flashed with humor. "You may be right." She took the picture from him and said to Torrie, "This will sit in a place of honor. Thank you both so much!"

Wade and Abbie both thanked their guests for the gifts—not just the presents, but also the gift of friendship. There was a short pause afterward, and Abbie was relieved when Clive began to clap and the rest joined in.

"Well," Marilyn said as it grew quiet again, "the food's on the table so you all better come and fill up your plates!"

Abbie watched her new neighbors as they filed into the kitchen. They were of mixed ages—young couples with little children, older ones with high school kids, and those of retirement age. The men wore boots and jeans and buttoned shirts. The women had sweatshirts or sweaters over jeans or slacks. They were of all shapes and sizes, and they shared a common love of the land and their country. Many wives had extra jobs off the place, and there were those who helped their husbands outside, their complexions ruddy from the sun and wind. They had known one another a long while, engaging in the easy banter of people who are comfortable with each other.

"Abbie," Torrie was standing next to her, "some day when we're alone, I'll tell you the whole story of why I acted toward you the way I did."

Abbie smiled. "We'll get together for coffee."

"You girls better get your plates before it's all gone," Clive hollered from across the room, and if his piled-up plate was an indication of how much everyone else was taking, it was definitely time to get in line.

When midnight came, there was a great deal of commotion while everyone wished everyone else a happy new year. Suddenly sleepy children were bundled up, vehicles were started to warm up against the winter chill, and the kitchen was rapidly cleaned until it was hardly noticeable there had even been a party. They had all enjoyed themselves and it had been a break from the usual routine. The next day—no, actually, that day—would start 2007 and bring its own joy.

The days that followed the New Year's Eve party were enjoyable for Abbie. She and Wade found places for their new treasures, they were able to spend time together with the kids, and there were special moments when they shared their hopes and dreams.

The picture of the old stone bridge found its place of honor on the dining room wall, where Abbie would savor the memories of family in England.

School started again, and Scilla hollered, "Good-bye, Mom!" every time she left. Skyler looked at Abbie with dark, troubled eyes, sometimes forgetting and calling her "Mom" in echo of Scilla, and sometimes calling her "Bee." Other times he tried not to call her anything.

Sage was learning a few words—"Da" came easily—and he would bounce with delight when he saw Wade. But when he wasn't feeling well, such as when teething came and caused him misery, he wanted Abbie, and he would hold out his little arms and cry "Mum-ma," which, of course, melted her heart. She would rock him until he was comforted and fell asleep.

She wondered what Kada would think if she knew her children called Abbie their mom. She herself couldn't think of anything worse if she had been in Kada's shoes.

It started snowing in the middle of January, and Wade would leave early in the morning to start feeding his cattle hay and cake. He had a system of wells to water them, and by the time he had finished haying all the different groups, it would be almost noon. He and Abbie always enjoyed another cup of coffee before she finished putting their meal on the table.

Wade would usually have stories about Shy and the big dog's efforts to help. Once the morning chores were done, Shy usually found the porch and napped the rest of the day. There were also stories of deer, coyotes, or cottontails that drove Shy crazy because they burrowed into a protected spot where he couldn't reach them. Abbie, in turn, had children and household stories to tell Wade.

The outside world seemed far removed from the snow-covered hills and peaceful rhythm of the ranch.

CHAPTER 25

Heartbreak

ON THE LAST Saturday in January the wind blew cold and spitting snow made visibility poor. During the night several hard blasts shook the house and Abbie sleepily crawled out of their warm bed to make certain the kids were covered. When she returned and snuggled under the covers close to Wade, she sighed with contentment. She loved the security of her husband. When the wind whistled around the corner of the house there was no comfort comparable to being held in his warm embrace.

It wasn't quite daylight when the phone beside their bed started ringing. Wade groped sleepily to find it. His morning voice sounded hoarse when he croaked hello.

Abbie sat up worried. Phones didn't ring in the early morning hours unless there was trouble.

She saw the sleepy look on his face give way to alarm and he darted a quick glance at her. Her fears for her family's safety began to rise. She heard him ask, "When did it happen?" "Where is she now?" and "How bad is it?" and she felt her heart start to pound with dread.

When he replaced the receiver he gave her a blank look as if the news he had heard was so terrible that he couldn't comprehend it.

"What happened?" she asked, reaching out to him.

He shook his head. "That was one of the guys in Kada's band. Kada and Bill had a wreck early this morning." His voice sounded disbelieving. "Bill is in surgery right now at Rapid City Regional…" He left his sentence dangling.

"And Kada?" Abbie felt cold fingers of trepidation seize her.

"Kada… is just barely hanging on. They don't have much hope for her."

Abbie put her hand on her mouth and felt instant tears spring to her eyes.

He reached over and pulled her close to him. She could feel his heart racing and the unevenness of his breathing.

Suddenly he released her. "I better start getting the cattle fed. We may be making a trip to Rapid." He was already out of bed, pulling on his clothes. Before she had time to reach the bathroom door, he was gone.

As Abbie hurried downstairs to make breakfast she repeated the same plea over and over: *Please, God, please be with the doctors and with us. Please, God.*

While she was setting the table the phone rang again. The voice on the other end was hesitant. He asked for Wade, and when she said she was Wade's wife and Wade was outside doing chores, he seemed unsure if he should give her any information. She said they had gotten the call about Kada that morning, and knew the seriousness of her condition. Finally, he said with sadness touching his voice that he was from the hospital, and that he regretted to tell them Kada Jackson had died at 5:47 that morning. He went on to say that she had an organ donor card in her purse, and there were certain procedures they needed to go through. He wondered if Wade could call him as soon as possible.

"I'll tell him immediately," Abbie answered, trying to keep the quaver out of her voice.

She wondered if Wade would try to feed all his cattle before he came in. If that was the case, she needed to take his cell phone to him so he could make the call. She bemoaned the fact that he'd left in such a hurry that he had forgotten it.

The sound of his tractor sent her flying out the door to flag him down. He got out of the cab and strode toward her in the frigid air, and seemed to know before she got the words out that Kada was gone.

"Oh, man," he said, his voice full of anguish. "I was afraid she might not make it."

Abbie mutely held open the door to the warm kitchen. "She wanted to be an organ donor—there's a number here to call so they can…"

She looked away while she struggled for composure. Taking a deep breath she handed him the paper on which she had written the phone number.

He stared at it blankly, slowly took off his Scotch cap, and went to the phone.

Lord, help. Help us both as we make decisions. Help us tell the children in such a way that they will be at peace. Oh, Lord, be with the kids!

When Wade finished the call, he shook his head and looked at Abbie. Disbelief and ragged emotion were carved on his face.

She quickly set two cups of coffee on the kitchen table and walked over to him. "I'm so sorry, Wade, I'm so sorry." Her voice broke as she wrapped her arms around him. He clung to her tightly and neither of them said anything for a while. Abbie noted the normal sounds of life as the wind blew, the clock ticked, and the tractor's engine rumbled outside. Yet their world had been turned upside down. For a second their eyes locked in mutual grief, and then he absently patted her as he withdrew his arms and reached for his cup of coffee.

"We have to make some plans here, Abbie," he said before he took a drink. "I can go to Rapid alone, or you can come with me, but we can't take the kids."

"Maybe Marilyn?" she looked at him questioningly.

"Yeah." He sighed and slowly walked back over to the phone.

As Abbie buttered the toast she both listened to Wade's brief conversation with Marilyn and thought of things she needed to do before they could leave. She was torn between deciding if she would be more help staying home with the kids or going with Wade, but the matter was settled when he hung up and told her Marilyn would be there as soon as possible. He added that he and Abbie would leave after he had finished the minimum of chores.

Neither noticed the little form standing in the archway to the dining room until Scilla's plaintive voice broke into their thoughts.

"What's going on? Why is the tractor running forever and how come Marilyn is coming?" She was rocking from leg to leg as she was prone to do when agitated, and her eyes darted from one to the other as she waited for an answer.

Wade rubbed the back of his neck and threw Abbie a desperate, unspoken plea. "Uh, Scilla, Abbie and I have to make a quick trip to Rapid this morning. Marilyn is coming to watch you kids until we get back."

Fear began to creep onto Scilla's face. She walked closer to her dad, but her eyes were on Abbie. "Why? Why do you have to go and why do we have to stay?" she asked.

"There's been an accident, Scilla," Abbie said softly, setting down the toast. "Your mom and her friend Bill have been in a serious accident."

Scilla seemed to freeze in her tracks. She looked mutely at both of them, but once again her question was directed at Abbie. "Are they dead?"

Abbie knelt beside the tense little body. After a quick look at Wade, she took a deep breath and put her hands on each side of Scilla's worried face. "Today your mother entered paradise, Scilla. She's with God. She left her old body behind, and God has given her a beautiful new one—like a moth changing into a butterfly."

"But—what happened?" Scilla looked bewildered.

"We don't know for sure." Wade's voice was heavy. "She and Bill were in a car wreck—he's at the hospital now, and the doctors are taking care of him."

"Why couldn't the doctors take care of… her?" Scilla twined a strand of Abbie's hair around her thin little fingers.

Abbie hugged her. "I'm sure the doctors did all they could do. Sometimes God wants His children with Him in heaven."

"How do you know that God wanted her? Maybe she's just dead." Tears were forming in Scilla's gray-green Kada eyes.

Wade threw Abbie a questioning look as if the same thought was on his mind.

Lord, how do I know this is true? I need help on this!

"Well, because, Scilla, I feel certain your mom believed in the Lord." Abbie took a deep breath. "I think God knew that I was to be here for you and Skyler and Sage when He took your mom home to be with Him."

"And Daddy, too? You're here for Daddy, too?" Scilla demanded, brushing at her eyes.

"She's here for all of us." Wade ruffled the brown flyaway hair and reached down to pick up Scilla. He gave her a quick hug and added, "Listen, Scilla, I need Abbie today, so she's going with me, and Marilyn is staying with you kids. I want you to be good—help the boys and don't cause any fights."

"Will you, like, see her today, Daddy?" Scilla's voice quavered.

"Probably. If I do, I'll tell her—" Wade swallowed a few times, "I'll tell her good-bye from all of us."

He swiftly put Scilla down, grabbed his cap and the piece of toast Abbie buttered, and walked out the door.

Abbie felt like she was moving in slow motion. So many things to do, so little time to do them. She woke up Sage—to him it was like any other day. She quickly changed him from pajamas into play clothes and gave him breakfast.

Skyler was the last one up. He wandered downstairs while Sage was eating.

Oh, Lord, help! Help me reach this little boy with the right words.

"What do, Bee?" he asked sleepily, holding his teddy bear and dragging his blanket.

She picked him up and hugged him. "What do? Ah, Skyler. Bee and Daddy have to go clear to Rapid City today."

"Why?" he wrapped his warm little hands around her neck and laid his head on her shoulder.

"Well…," her mind was blank, "because," she finished lamely.

"I go, too."

"No, today you and Sage and Scilla are going to stay here with Marilyn. And your daddy and I want you to be as good as you possibly can be, OK?"

He kicked his feet against her before he answered, "No, go you."

She laughed softly and sat him in his booster seat. "How about, 'Yes, eat breakfast'? I have some toast and milk ready for you."

While Skyler ate she chatted with him about his day. She told him they would be back in the evening, and that it would be a long time for Marilyn to be away from her own home, and she wanted him to be sure and take his nap and not fuss.

He looked at her with mournful dark eyes.

After breakfast when she took both boys back upstairs to help Skyler get dressed, she felt she must tell Skyler about Kada. If she didn't, Scilla would.

Lord, Lord, I need help. Help me to say this so it won't break his heart.

She plopped Sage onto the middle of Skyler's bed and found some toys for him before she turned her attention to Skyler's clothes for the day.

"I go you, Bee." His sad little voice broke the silence.

"Skyler," she sat down on the bed and picked him up, "today is a very different day than what we usually have. Do you know why?"

He shook his head.

"Early this morning, you see, while you were still sleeping, God wrapped His gentle arms around your mother, like this." Abbie encircled Skyler with her own arms and gave him a hug. "He whispered in her ear that it was time to for her to leave and go with Him to her home in Heaven."

Skyler studied her intently.

Abbie took another deep breath. This was the hardest thing she ever had to do.

"I think," she said softly, looking into his dark eyes, "I think before she left, she blew all of you kids a good-bye kiss, like this." She kissed her fingers and blew it in his direction. "Ping!" she exclaimed, and patted his cheek where the imaginary kiss landed.

He frowned at her. "Mama leave?"

"Yes, but she would want you to know there will be a time when you're all together again."

She braced herself for the next question.

"When?" His eyes never left her face.

"I don't know when, Skyler. Only God knows that. But for now He wants you to know your mother loves you very much."

He patted his cheek. "Mama kiss?"

She nodded her head.

He wasn't finished. "But why you go?"

Abbie smiled at him. "Because your mother left so fast she wasn't able to take care of everything, so your dad and I will go and take care of those things for her." She hugged him again and added, "I need to hurry and get myself ready to go, sweetheart. The quicker we leave, the quicker we'll be back home tonight."

Surprisingly, he reached up and patted her cheek. "I blow you kiss all day, OK?"

Abbie wanted to bury her face in his soft brown hair and cry. Instead she said that would be wonderful, and eased him off her lap.

She heard Wade's footsteps on the stairs and knew he would be ready and waiting for her if she didn't hurry. Her mind seemed to be going in all directions at once, and it was with great difficulty that she fielded questions from Scilla and Skyler, changed to a warmer sweater, popped some needed items into her purse, and tried to think of what else she should do.

When Abbie realized Clive and Marilyn were downstairs, she quickly grabbed her coat and purse and headed down to greet them. She told them some last-minute instructions about naps and teddy bears and blankets, and thanked them several times for coming.

Wade had his coat on and was carrying Sage down the steps moments later. Both Scilla and Skyler were trailing after him and Abbie heard Marilyn breathe a quick intake of air when she saw the kids.

"I'm so sorry, you guys. I'm just so sorry to hear this," she said, and gave Wade and Sage both a tearful hug.

Clive shook his head. "Torrie is coming later on this morning. She thought she could help Mom a bit. Boy, we just never know when these things are gonna happen, do we?" He put a hand on Wade's shoulder. "Tell me what needs to be done and I'll do your chores tonight."

Wade was quiet on the long drive to Rapid. After they hit I-90 he punched the accelerator to 80 mph and concentrated on the road conditions.

The wind that had raged during the night had diminished, and even though the skies were gloomy, the temperature registered a decent 15 degrees.

Abbie hadn't seen any of that part of the country. As the miles rolled by she saw prairie land that was different from the ranch. Some of it was flat and worked into crops, and some was rougher grazing, especially when they drove into the breaks of the Cheyenne River—the same river that wound its way to the north and back to the east where they lived.

Wade finally broke the silence when the Black Hills came into view. "I guess we better go to the hospital first and see how Bill is. Maybe we can get some answers."

She nodded but could think of little to say.

"Abbie," his voice was quiet, "thanks for telling the kids."

"I think country kids understand death," she said. "They see it more from the animals." She looked at him and sighed. "I hope we said the right things."

He reached over to take her hand. "I don't know—I don't know where she was in her faith. That's what really bothers me. I should have tried harder to find out those things when we were together." He squeezed her fingers and released them, placing his hand back on the steering wheel.

"Wade, I'm sure you said and did what you could," Abbie said, rubbing his arm. "That's just the way you are."

He glanced over at her and gave a sad smile. "I'm different around you than I was with Kada. You bring out something in me that wasn't there with her. I...I could lose my temper so quick at the things she did or said. I hated the way she was raising Scilla before we were married." He made a derisive laugh. "Kada used to say I married her so I could give Scilla a decent life. There was probably a little truth in that."

"But I can't think that was a bad thing. Scilla thinks the world of you."

Wade slowed down as they neared the outskirts of Rapid. He seemed to know what exit to take to reach the hospital, and soon they were driving into the parking lot.

He put his arm around Abbie's shoulders as they walked toward the entrance.

"I know you hated to leave the kids, but I really need you today," he told her softly.

She put her arm around his waist and looked up at him. "I love you, Wade." She didn't care that he kissed her in front of several people who were leaving the hospital.

They found four of Bill's band members in the waiting room, looking haggard and in shock. When Wade introduced himself, they shook his hand, and slowly the story came out.

The band had played for a dance in the northern part of the state. Everyone had enjoyed themselves and they passed around a hat to collect enough money so the band would play another hour. Kada had sung her heart out, as usual, and had drunk enough coffee that she was still pretty wired when they put their instruments in the van. Either she or Bill always drove the van while the rest of them followed in a different vehicle. Kada elected to drive because Bill was tired.

They had to go pretty fast to keep up with her, they said. Somewhere along the way the wind came up, and there was moisture in the air that started sticking to the pavement. Visibility was getting poor when they saw her try to pass a truck. They figured she must have hit an icy spot and started skidding. It looked like she slammed into a bridge abutment and as the van began a backward descent down the grade it flipped over on the driver's side, grating over rocks and small boulders until it reached the bottom.

The rest was a nightmare for them, they said. Bill was badly hurt—they were afraid Kada was even more so. Because they were miles away from anywhere, it took a couple of hours for the ambulance to transport Bill and Kada to a hospital. Kada never regained consciousness.

Abbie clutched Wade's arm as he looked down. He expelled a pent-up sigh and seemed to be at a loss for words.

"How is Bill?" Abbie asked.

"We were able to talk to him about an hour ago, but he's pretty doped up," one of the band members said. "The nurse said she would come and get us when he came around again."

Abbie looked at their bedraggled, heartsick, and drained demeanors and wondered what she could do to help.

"Have you had anything to eat?" she asked.

They looked at her stupefied and shook their heads. "Just coffee," one of them said.

"Why don't you go eat someplace, and Wade and I will wait here to see Bill."

Wade roused himself. "Here," he said, and pushed a fifty-dollar bill in the hand of the band member standing closest to him. "You guys need a break. We'll stay here."

A blond ponytailed member handed Abbie a blood-smeared purse. "You might want to keep this," he said, and walked off. The others thanked Wade and slowly followed.

Within a half hour, Wade and Abbie were summoned into Bill's room.

Even though Bill was pale and hurting, he said he had things he wanted to tell Wade. He knew Kada had died, he said, his voice breaking. Did Wade know she wanted to be cremated?

"I didn't know that," Wade answered. "If that's what she wanted, that's what we'll do."

"She told me that about a week ago," Bill replied weakly. "She had… other things she talked about. I… I'll tell you later."

"Sure, we'll be back," Wade told him. "I've been thinking on the way up here—I don't have a clue where the service should be held. What are your thoughts?"

"There's a church in Spearfish—she went there once or twice." He thought for a while before he came up with the name. Then he gave a ragged sigh, and Abbie wondered if they should let him rest.

"Bill," Wade said with a catch in his voice, "I want to thank you for being Kada's friend. She thought a lot of you."

The older man nodded and was unable to say any more. Abbie patted the only part of his arm that wasn't connected to something, and said they would let him rest and come back later. He nodded again.

Action was an invigorating force for Wade, Abbie decided. Over an hour later he had used his cell phone from the hospital lobby to make most of the arrangements and was planning a trek back to see Bill.

She stopped him. "Wade, let's take a break ourselves. There's a nice café that I noticed down the road. It's calling to me."

Wade frowned at her. "What's it saying?"

She smiled and took his arm. "It's saying it has unlimited coffee and great food."

The day of the service dawned bright and cold. The mercury had been below zero when Wade left the house to start chores.

Once again the Barrowses were watching the kids. Scilla, when given the choice, wanted to stay with Marilyn.

Early morning saw Abbie and Wade heading west again, and unlike the last time they traveled, Wade was talkative. In the days following Kada's death he had the unfortunate opportunity of visiting with her mother over the phone. She was belligerent and argumentative, and she informed Wade right away that there wasn't any room in the family cemetery plot for another body.

When he mentioned cremation, she informed him it was a heathen practice, and she wouldn't pay a penny of the cost. She was, however, quite sure she was entitled to any money Kada had in the bank. When Wade reminded her that maybe the money should go to Kada's three children, she hung up.

The next time she called, she had contacted a lawyer. She said ugly things, and this time Wade hung up.

Besides attending the service, Wade hoped to clear out Kada's apartment while they were in Spearfish. If they could do all of that in one day, they wouldn't have to make another trip, he said.

As the miles slipped away Wade and Abbie discussed the happenings of the days since Kada's death. There were so many loose ends to tie up that they'd hardly had time to have their morning coffee together. The details of the funeral had slipped into place. The blond ponytailed band member wanted to sing "The Old Rugged Cross" at the funeral. He said Kada had heard him sing that at another funeral and asked him on the spot to sing it at hers. Of course, at the time he'd had no idea it would be so soon.

Wade reiterated his agony of not knowing where she was in her faith. It haunted him, he said.

"If only I had talked more about the important stuff with her and let the other things go," he lamented more than once.

When they arrived at the church, Abbie was pleased to see a good-sized crowd. There were a couple of neighbors she recognized, and Wade's brother and wife had come from North Dakota, but the rest were strangers to them.

Abbie was unwilling to admit she was disappointed in the minister's talk. He delivered some obscure poetry, read the obituary, and talked about Kada's dream of being a songwriter.

When it came time for the song, Abbie found herself unconsciously wringing her hands, wondering how a man who played in a band called the Wild Boys and wore his hair in a ponytail would interpret the old hymn.

When he played a few chords, his deep voice began the familiar words.

"On a hill far away stood an old rugged cross, the emblem of suffering and shame."

Abbie felt tears prick her eyes at the simple beauty of the song and the sincere rendition of it.

"And I love that old cross, where the dearest and best for a world of lost sinners was slain."

She didn't realize she had taken Wade's hand.

"So I'll cherish the old rugged cross till my trophies at last I lay down. I will cling to the old rugged cross and exchange it some day for a crown."

He played an interlude, and then began the second verse. She was surprised he had it memorized.

"Oh the old rugged cross, so despised by the world, has a wondrous attraction for me; for the dear Lamb of God left His glory above to bear it to dark Calvary."

She felt the tears stream down her cheeks and thought that there didn't need to be a sermon. The song said it all.

"In the old rugged cross, stained with blood so divine, a wondrous beauty I see; for 'twas on that old cross Jesus suffered and died to pardon and sanctify me."

When Kada heard those words, did she realize she was a lost sinner who could be forgiven because of Christ's death on the cross? Did she want it sung because of the tender voice of the singer, or did the words have a special meaning for her? If only there was some way to know what had been in her heart.

"To the old rugged cross I will ever be true, its shame and reproach gladly bear; then He'll call me some day to my home far away, where His glory forever I'll share."

To her home far away. That's just about what I told the kids—God called Kada home. Did I ever thank You, Father, for putting the right words in my mouth to tell Kada's children?

Both song and singer had affected Wade as much as they had Abbie. His eyes were moist and he ran his hand over his face. She felt him take a deep breath when the song was over, and she furtively looked around to see if others were as touched as they were.

Indeed, many in the congregation were wiping their eyes.

Abbie thought she would never again hear "The Old Rugged Cross" sung without remembering the compassion and emotion with which this man had sung it. It became a witness as powerful as a sermon.

After the service Abbie made her way to the front of the church. She found the singer putting away his guitar. He seemed lost in thought.

When she complimented him, he smiled briefly.

"I love that song. I sing it whenever I can." He paused and looked away. "I want to tell you and your husband something. I think Kada really believed those words. She had changed these last couple of weeks. We all noticed it. She quit telling dirty jokes; she quit drinking. The

226

last night she sang, she wasn't strutting around the stage like she usually did. Something was happening in her life."

He blinked a few times and added, "I don't understand why she had to die when she was beginning to have so much to live for."

"I don't know, either," Abbie said truthfully. She put her hand on his arm. "But this I do know. I'm grateful that she seemed to have found the Lord before she died."

Wade joined the two of them, shook the singer's hand, and offered his own compliments. Wade was facing the back of the church, and Abbie thought he acted distracted while the singer thanked him. It was when they were getting ready to leave that he asked her if she had taken the Black Hills gold cross necklace that had been beside Kada's picture in the sanctuary.

Abbie was puzzled. "Her necklace? No, Wade. I saw it there, but I didn't take it. Why do you ask?"

"I gave it to her the first Christmas we were married," he said, still looking around. "She wore it almost like a good luck charm, which wasn't what it was intended for. The coroner handed it to me last week, and I put it there this morning. It's gone now."

"Could it have fallen off the table?" Abbie wondered.

"I've looked all around. It isn't there," Wade answered flatly.

"Do you think someone took it?"

He scowled and a dark expression came over his face. "Probably."

Wade's brother and his wife went with them to Kada's apartment. It took very little time for the four of them to clear it out and load her things into the Tahoe. They were somber when they found her Bible. Wade debated between taking it home for the kids or giving it to Bill.

Abbie suggested the four of them eat a quick lunch together, but everyone seemed in a hurry to move on. Wade's brother and wife had a lot of miles to travel to return to Medora and their ranch and wanted to get home before dark. With zero temperatures and a north wind making a wind chill factor of fifteen below zero, they all agreed another time would be better.

One of the band members showed up to collect the assorted music paraphernalia. Suddenly it was just an empty furnished apartment. The person who had eaten, slept, and lived within its walls had disappeared like a vapor.

Now there was only the memory of what once had been.

CHAPTER 26

Visiting Bill

"LET'S STOP AND see how Bill is before we head home," Wade said, pulling off I-90 and heading down the Mt. Rushmore exit. "We probably won't be back here for quite a while. At least I hope we're not."

It was one of the very few things he had said since they left Kada's apartment. Abbie wondered what his thoughts were, but she had discovered when Wade was not in a talkative mood it was useless to force a conversation.

When they entered Bill's hospital room, it was obvious he was feeling better. He told them that some of the band members had visited him after the funeral to tell him the service had been well attended. He seemed to look at Wade with an inquiring look after he made that statement.

"Yeah," Wade answered, and the two men exchanged glances that Abbie couldn't decipher.

Bill adjusted his pillow before continuing. "I don't remember much of what I told you the other day. I guess we talked about the wreck. There were issues in Kada's life—issues with your house, Wade. She told me what happened there."

"If she told up you what actually happened, it's more than what she ever shared with me," Wade said flatly.

"You remember Ace Olson?"

"He was skulking around at the funeral."

Bill nodded. "That's what I heard." He expelled a pent-up breath and looked at the ceiling. "He's not much good—smokes weed all the time. I fired him from being a drummer and back-up singer after I took over the band." He gazed at the two of them with no emotion. "He took it personal, made some goofy threats."

Abbie quickly looked at Wade. He was focused on the older man with his head tilted to one side, giving him his undivided attention.

"I know Ace convinced her that the house needed to mourn a death that had occurred there." Bill shook his head and took a drink of water. "She said she felt her life was threatened by something that happened one night when you were gone and she and Ace were there."

Wade's eyes narrowed and Abbie noticed a muscle twitched along his jaw. "Go on," he said when Bill paused.

"You know, when you travel a lot in the early morning hours, you begin to share a little of your thoughts. I guess it's easier to talk when you can't see each other's face." Bill took another sip of water. "She claims she heard weird sounds in your house. Said she was pushed downstairs and something dang near suffocated her. She really felt the house was trying to kill her."

"Maybe it was this Ace guy that was trying to do her in," Abbie interjected. Goosebumps popped out on her arms.

Bill gave her a slight smile. "Who would know? Maybe. At any rate, Ace convinced her to place the house in mourning with a bunch of dark carpet and curtains. The night they finished that, another weird thing happened, and she felt the whole ranch was possessed by evil spirits."

Wade gave a derisive snort and folded his arms across his chest. "The whole ranch was possessed by evil spirits? That's the most ridiculous thing she ever came up with. What kind of black magic were they playing around with, or were they both messin' around with his funny weed?"

Suddenly Bill looked drained, and when he spoke again his voice sounded tired. "Sometime I'll give you all the details and maybe we can figure out the logical conclusion."

Abbie thought Wade should respond. When he didn't, she gave Bill's shoulder a light pat. "When you're up to more talking, we would like to hear the rest of the story." She glanced at Wade, but he was looking off in space.

"Ah…Bill," she continued, "we've cleared out her apartment, and we have some things in this sack for you. It…it sounded like she had made some changes in her life the last couple of weeks."

Bill nodded and moved as if in discomfort. "I'll tell you about that sometime also."

Abbie decided that must be a hint to leave. She stood up and was relieved to see Wade also rise.

He shook the older man's proffered hand and wished him a speedy recovery. He also thanked him for the information. Abbie thought both men acted as if they knew more than what was being said—they were on a wavelength that was eluding her.

Before they left Rapid City, Wade pulled into the parking lot of the Salvation Army store. At Abbie's questioning look he brusquely said he didn't intend to take Kada's clothes home. He quickly gathered the bags so he could take them into the donation area.

When Wade returned, a young man was with him pushing a cart, and soon most of the other items in the Tahoe had been unloaded and taken away. Abbie stopped him from taking a jewelry box that held Kada's personal mementoes, saying it would mean something to the children some day to have that. For a while she thought he was going to ignore her, but finally he slammed it back down on the seat.

"I suppose you want something to eat," he said, breaking the heavy silence as they started out of town.

"Yes, Mr. Jackson. I was going to suggest we stop somewhere."

"Would the truck stop be suitable for Mrs. Jackson?" There was only a slight trace of good humor in his voice.

"The truck stop will be just fine." She smiled at him.

It was while they were eating their hamburgers that he said softly to her, "I'm mad, Abbie. I don't think I've ever been so blasted mad in my life."

She nodded. "I know you are." She reached over to touch his hand. "You've been upset ever since the funeral. Do you think she was having an affair with this Ace guy?"

"Absolutely. Why else would he be in my house in the middle of the night when I'm not there?" His eyes narrowed and he said through clenched teeth, "I was pretty sure she was sleeping around but I sure as…I sure didn't know it was in my house. That's almost more than I can stomach."

Abbie put down her half-eaten hamburger. "What do you suppose happened those nights that freaked her out?"

He snorted in disgust. "Probably both of them were high on drugs." He paused. "This doesn't set well with me, Abbie. She's chasing around, bringing nutcases onto the place, gets hysterical over some imagined event, and gets herself killed before I can get to the bottom of it."

"On the other hand," Abbie said slowly, "she gave you three beautiful children and was instrumental in bringing us together, and you might say she stepped aside so we could be married."

He finished his hamburger, drank his coffee, and set the cup down with more force than was necessary. "How do I even know Skyler and Sage are mine?"

"Wade, those boys look like you—anyone can see that."

He looked away with doubt on his face. "I wish I knew for sure."

"You could get a blood test."

His face softened and he reached for her hand. "If you're finished eating we should be getting down the road. We've got a long way to go and it isn't getting any better outside."

She wrapped her fingers around his. "Is it better inside now?"

He started sliding out of the booth. "I don't know," he muttered.

CHAPTER 27

The Doubting Mind

*A*ROLLER COASTER—Abbie decided the days and weeks after Kada's death were like being on a roller coaster of emotions. One moment she was incredibly sad that a young life had been snuffed out so quickly, and the next she would feel her spirits soar again that Kada must have found peace in faith. The fact that Kada was trying to improve her life gave testimony to that.

Those feelings would quickly be followed by a haunting question: What happened in their house to infuse such a profound fear that Kada felt her life was endangered?

Indeed, in Abbie's mind the old house's usual creaks and groans had begun to take on a more sinister tone. The secure feeling she used to have within its gracious walls was lessening, and she caught herself hesitating to go downstairs at night unless there was a light on. It was her own imaginings, she scolded herself, and didn't tell Wade her unsubstantiated fears.

Wade's feelings seemed to vacillate between anger and remorse. She noticed him studying the two boys with frowning intensity, and often he would be in his own isolated world that had no room for her. He was edgy with all of them, and even Shy began to follow him at a respectful distance.

February blanketed the ranch and community with snow. The entire month was filled with sunless days and the bleakness seemed to settle over the house until even the kids were subdued.

On the day Clive and Wade decided to go to another bull sale, Abbie breathed a sigh of relief to have some time without Wade's brooding presence. She instantly felt guilty. This all would pass, she was sure, but in the meantime it was a wearing situation.

There were snow flurries in the afternoon. When Torrie called to say she wanted to show Abbie some wedding announcements and could bring Scilla home, Abbie was relieved she didn't have to bundle up the two boys and go out into the cold.

It was good to have something else to think and talk about. She and Torrie admired the different announcements with their fanciful script and enjoyed some girl talk over coffee and cookies.

But once Scilla and the boys became engrossed in a movie, Torrie moved her chair closer to Abbie and asked in a low voice how everything was going after Kada's death.

"Well," Abbie said slowly, not entirely trusting Torrie's newfound friendliness, "there have been some issues that are slowly getting settled."

Torrie's eyes showed understanding. "Clive says Wade is a bear to be around."

Abbie nodded and smiled.

"I have some issues of my own about Kada," Torrie said, leaning back in her chair. "She came bopping up here from Omaha. She was a city girl and thought she could write beautiful music in the country atmosphere, but after Skyler was born, she had enough peace and quiet and wanted back in the limelight."

Abbie decided to broach the subject that had been bothering her. "Torrie, did you know she was afraid of something that had happened in this house?"

Torrie nodded. "Yes. I thought it was very obvious that she was. The fiasco with the carpet and curtains created quite a stir among people. We knew Wade was disgusted, but he was trying to make the best of it."

She looked at Abbie and grinned. "It didn't take long when you came on the scene for the whole shebang to disappear."

"But I wasn't the driving force behind that," Abbie protested. "It was all Wade's idea."

Torrie looked at Abbie thoughtfully. "I chased Wade pretty hard and long after Clive and I broke up." She looked down at her cup. "I figured it would only be a matter of time before Kada would leave, and I was ready to be there."

Abbie fiddled with her napkin and didn't say anything.

"Do you know, Abbie, that Wade talked constantly about the little redheaded Brit in his house?" When Abbie shook her head, Torrie continued. "I don't even think he realized how many stories he told about you, and you can imagine how they affected me."

She drank some coffee and let out a sigh. "But when I saw his face when you were racing down the hill with Jake, I knew he had strong feelings for you. The—the look on his face was of someone who was terrified the one they cared deeply about was going to get hurt. He even said your name several times. I know he didn't realize he was saying it out loud."

"And," she looked at Abbie and smiled ruefully, "we all know how badly I handled that knowledge."

Abbie stood up to refill their coffee cups. "Well, we're probably both glad those days are in the past, Torrie." She placed the filled cups on the table and sat down again. "I'm glad we can be friends. Now, tell me about you and Clive. I think that's a story worth repeating!"

Torrie smiled happily, showing even, white teeth. "We've known each other since we were kids. I don't know if anybody ever told you, but I beat up the redhead that bit him on the lip!"

Abbie laughed long and loud over that. She held up both hands in a surrender gesture. "Trust me, I never kissed him!"

"I know. When I finally really sat down and sorted through all my mixed emotions, the one thing I knew for sure was that I would always love that darned blue-eyed storyteller. The second time he asked me to marry him he made sure I knew it was because he loved me." Torrie looked into space before she added, "It's amazing the crazy things we do when we're running from the truth."

"Which makes me think of Kada again," Abbie said. "I think she ran a marathon away from the truth." She pushed the plate of cookies closer to Torrie. "I would just like to know what happened here."

"I imagine it was something to do with that goofy drummer. Clive always suspected something was going on between Kada and that Ace Olson. Clive said the morning he, Wade, and the kids came back from the fishing trip she looked 'guilty as sin and terrible as warmed-over death,' which sounds like a frightful description." Torrie gave a winsome smile. "Clive generally has very descriptive adjectives."

"Wade said Ace was at the funeral," Abbie offered.

"Really? Wow! I didn't hear about that. Maybe that's what has Wade in a foul mood," she mused. "It would be hard for a man with Wade's pride to think his wife cheated on him with a drummer that everyone suspected of being a druggie, and then having the darn creep sneak into her funeral."

Abbie absently creased and folded her napkin into a tiny little square. The man she loved and married had some issues with his ex-wife that she'd never suspected. She wondered if he even realized the depth of his bitterness over his perception of Kada's behavior.

Several evenings later Wade was in the office while Abbie was finishing up dishes.

"Hey," she heard him call to her, "can you come in here a minute?" He sounded irritated.

"Just who changed my name from Abbie to 'Hey'?" she muttered as she walked into the office.

"What did you say?" He was frowning from behind his desk.

"Nothing. Did you want something?" She didn't realize her voice had been as edgy as his.

"Who keeps sending these e-mails from England with nothing in them?" he asked, pointing to the computer screen.

She gave a half-hearted laugh. "That's Aunt Lena. She's trying to learn all this stuff, and somehow none of her e-mails have anything in them. I guess Tyler is going to go over and help her get it figured out."

He twirled back and forth in his swivel chair without saying anything. When she turned to walk out the French doors, he called her back.

"Abbie, I made an appointment tomorrow for the boys and me to have a blood test."

She looked at him across the room. Neither of them had a hint of a smile.

"I see." She didn't know what else to say.

CHAPTER 28

Pillow Talk

*T*WO THINGS OCCURRED the following week. Wade had the results of the blood test and knew for certain both Sage and Skyler were his sons, and calving season for his heifers began when the first calf was born—dead.

The midnight and four A.M. checks seemed to occur as soon as he closed his eyes for sleep, and with a moan he'd shut off the alarm and slip out of bed. He knew it would be his routine for the next two months. Abbie was already able to sleep through the alarm and would hardly budge when he crawled back into bed.

On this night, under the starry sky, Wade checked the young cows and found them chewing their cuds contentedly. With no sign of deliveries imminent, Wade walked back to the house by himself. Shy had deserted him about the third night, preferring to sleep on the porch.

Before Wade stepped into the house, he stopped and looked up at the galaxies that glorified the night sky. It was a brilliant sight, and it always moved him, even when he was tired, and even, as in recent days, when he was confused, frustrated, and tired.

"When I consider Your heavens, the work of Your fingers, the moon and the stars, which You have set in place, what is man that You are mindful of him, the son of man that You care for him? Psalms chapter eight, verses three and four. Thank you, Mrs. Heck, for making me learn that memory verse in sixth grade," he intoned to the night air. He thought of it every year when he was checking his cattle during the hours of darkness. This time, however, he wasn't in the mood for praise.

I know You care, Lord, but I just can't get the picture out of my mind of Ace Olson sneaking into the church. I know he stole Kada's necklace. Not that it's any big deal, but it burns me up. Her whole affair with him and what they did to the house eats at me until I…until I…I guess I take it out on everyone. I suspected it then, but now I know for sure. I can't forgive either one of them right now. But at least I'm grateful to You that Sage and Skyler are my sons. I had to know that for sure—even though Abbie about passed out when they done the blood test on the boys.

Wade could tell Abbie was about at the end of her patience with him. Several times she had tried to talk to him about his feelings. He knew he was brusque with her. He didn't want to be analyzed, and he didn't want to rationalize Kada's behavior. He knew Abbie was trying to be understanding, but sometimes that alone irritated him. He felt patronized and knew that also was ridiculous.

He sighed and went into the house. It was midnight, and four o'clock would be zipping along in no time. He wished he could let the whole matter go, but it clung to him, and like an old dog with a bone, he kept gnawing on it.

The full moon lit up the bedroom, and as he crawled back in beside Abbie, her hair seemed to reflect moonbeams. He leaned over to see if she might be awake, but if she was, she was keeping her eyes closed.

For a while he stared at her and was unprepared when her eyes flew open. She gave a smothered scream, almost knocking him out with her flailing fists as she sat up.

"What's the matter with you, Abbie?" he yelped, trying to dodge another hit. "Quit hitting me, woman! Good grief!"

"Wade? What were you doing just now?" she demanded.

"I was looking at my lovely bride," he said with a great deal of irritation. "What did you think I was doing?"

"How would I know? I feel this presence and when I open my eyes all I can see is someone hovering over me. Darn you, Wade—you about gave me a heart attack!"

"Just great. I suppose next you'll be redecorating the house because you think something is going to get you." He knew he shouldn't be that sarcastic with her; it was undeserving.

He saw her eyes flash and before he could react she grabbed her pillow and started pummeling him with it. She was on her knees in bed and every chance she could get she hit him again.

"I'm sick and tired of this chip on your shoulder, Wade Jackson! For two months you've been moping around, growling at everyone." Wham, she landed another hit. "Do you think you're the first one to ever be cheated on?" Wham, whack, two more hits.

"Stop it, Abbie, before you get hurt!"

She stood up on their bed and with all her might slammed the pillow against his shoulders.

"Don't you dare compare me with her! That's just about the last straw." She was beginning to run out of breath. "Just get over it, Wade! Get over it!" As she made another swoop at him, she started to fall. She let out a shriek as he caught her and wrestled her into a semblance of submission.

They glared at each other in the moonlit room while they both regained their breath.

"What is this?" Annoyed, he released one of her wrists and pulled at the collar of her moose pajamas.

"Since my husband started sleeping clear over on his side I'm inclined to be cold." Her accent and the snip in her voice dared him to argue with her.

He looked down at her and saw her hair tumbled all around her face, her brown eyes flashing fire, her breath still coming in gasps, and knew the last thing in the world he wanted to do was argue.

The realization suddenly hit him. He could continue to act like a jerk and alienate the woman he loved, or he could take her advice and get over it.

"I'm inclined to kiss you," he finally said and saw the surprise in her eyes. Her free hand started to work its way up to his shoulder. "I was just wondering if you might bite me on the lip if I did."

"I'm slightly tempted." She gave him a tentative smile.

"Abbie, I'm sorry. I'll… get over this. I know you're right. It's gone on long enough."

A man could drown in the beauty of those brown eyes when they looked at him that way. And that man would be a fool to fret about the past while a future with this remarkable woman beckoned. He decided while he was kissing her that she didn't seem even remotely tempted to bite him.

CHAPTER 29

Meet Ace Olson

THE PHONE CALL came late in the morning on an April spring day. When Abbie hung up she was sure she had just agreed to something that was going to make Wade furious.

When he came in at noon, he seemed to take one look at her and know that something was wrong.

"Wade," she said hesitantly as she put Sage in his high chair, "Bill called this morning. He wants to stop in this afternoon."

"He must be feeling quite a bit better than the last time I talked to him," Wade said while helping Skyler onto his booster seat. "I guess that was when he got out of the hospital the first part of March."

"Ah, he's bringing someone with him." When Wade glanced at her she rolled her eyes and shook her head.

"Who?" He scowled as he sat down.

"Let's pray first."

"I pray, Bee. I pray," Skyler asserted. "God bess food. 'men."

With Skyler's prayers, there was only a moment's notice to bow your head. By the time that was done, the prayer was over.

While Wade and Abbie helped the boys get food on their plates, she worried. Wade kept looking at her but seemed to realize she didn't want to say any more in front of the boys.

Skyler was full of excited talk about his upcoming April birthday and the cake Abbie was going to bake him.

"I be three, Daddy! Three! I be older than Scilla!"

Abbie couldn't help but laugh at his arithmetic. "Scilla just turned six, Skyler, so she's still older. But you are ahead of Sage."

Sage nodded even without understanding what the conversation was about.

"Can you hold up one finger, Sage?" Wade asked

Knowing he was at the center of attention, Sage grinned happily and took time from chasing down an elusive green bean to clap enthusiastically. Wade took his little hand and helped him hold up one finger.

"There, Sage says he is one year old. You are two years older than your brother, Skyler. You're a big boy." Wade grinned and tousled Sage's downy hair until it stood on end.

When the boys finally finished eating and scooted into the living room to play, both Abbie and Wade released a pent-up breath.

"So who's Bill bringing that you don't want to tell me about?"

"Well," Abbie began, "when Bill called, he said he was going to Pierre and wanted to stop in. I said sure." She paused and looked at Wade before she continued.

"Then he said that Ace Olson was with him. When I started backpedaling, he said Ace had things he needed to tell you. He felt it was important. Wade, I'm sorry—"

Abbie had run all this together with an anguished look. She stopped abruptly when Wade started shaking his head.

"Absolutely not! That guy is not coming here and that's all there's to it!" To emphasize his point he smacked his open palm on the table.

Abbie sat back in her chair and closed her eyes for a moment. She knew he would react that way. She had prayed all morning for the right words to say.

"Listen to me, sweetheart. Just listen." Abbie leaned forward. "This may be our only chance to find out what happened in this house that was so dreadful to Kada. I want to know. I need to know because my

243

imagination has been conjuring up all sorts of things. I'd like to know the truth."

"Do you think you'll hear the truth from this guy?" Wade asked cynically.

Abbie shrugged. "We won't know until we listen to him."

Wade stood and started muttering while he helped her clear the table. He was still muttering and mumbling as he laid his two sons down for their naps. When he came back downstairs, he leaned against the counter while she finished cleaning up the kitchen.

"I don't like it, Abbie," he said quietly. "But we'll do this for you. Just so you know—I don't like any part of it."

Abbie set down the dishtowel and walked over to him. Leaning into his solid warmth, she hugged him. "I just hope after they leave you can say you didn't like it but you're glad you heard what he had to say."

The minute Ace Olson walked in the door Abbie had the eerie feeling she had seen him before. He was a slender-framed man with brown hair, and he was extremely nervous. Abbie thought if Bill hadn't limped slowly in behind him that he would have bolted and run.

Wade greeted Bill and shook his hand, but he neither said hello to Ace nor offered to shake his hand. It wasn't lost on Ace. He fidgeted from one foot to the other and didn't seem to know where to look.

Abbie led them in and asked if they wanted to sit at the kitchen table, but none of the men acted as if they had heard her. In the awkward silence that followed, she saw Ace reach in his front pocket and bring out a necklace.

"This is, uh, this is Kada's necklace," he said, thrusting it at Wade. "I want to, uh, well, I shouldn't of taken it at the funeral."

"I don't want it." Wade's voice was quiet.

That seemed to throw Ace in a quandary and he didn't know what to do with the gold cross dangling from his hand. He finally walked over to the kitchen table and laid the necklace on a placemat.

Bill eyed the cushioned chairs around the table in the adjoining dining room. "That looks like a comfortable place to sit," he murmured, and with Abbie's nodded agreement, the four of them settled around the table.

Abbie asked about his health, and for several minutes he gave her a rundown of the exercises that were supposed to make his battered leg heal faster.

Finally he turned to Wade. "I very seldom interfere in other people's lives. But Ace has come to me because he's been in a treatment center, and his counselors seem to think he needs to get this matter taken care of before he can move on. I told Kada and I told him—there's a logical explanation to what happened, and if anybody can get to the bottom of it, it's you, Wade."

Abbie looked at Wade—strong and muscular with a quiet confidence—and then she turned to Ace. There was such a contrast in the slighter man's demeanor. She noticed his right leg kept bouncing up and down as if in an uncontrolled rhythm of which he was unaware and his eyes apologetically darted from one of them to the other. He was not at all what she had expected, and there was still that uncanny feeling she had met him before.

Wade seemed to have no intention of making the other man comfortable. Finally Ace cleared his throat.

"I, uh, I first of all want to say that I'm really sorry about what happened to your house." He coughed nervously before he continued. "When I see what it looks like now, and how light it is, it makes what I have to say seem so…" He shrugged his shoulders as if unable to think of the word he wanted to use.

"Why don't you start at the beginning, Ace?" Bill prompted.

"Yeah, well, it's hard to tell another man that his wife was drunk and needed a ride home, but that's how it started that night," Ace said.

Abbie saw Wade clench his jaw muscles. She put her hand on his knee and he covered it with his own, lacing his fingers through hers.

245

Ace fidgeted for a while. He finally took a deep breath and plunged into his story.

"When we got here, it was full moon, and so we didn't need to turn on any lights in the house. We started up those steps." He pointed to the stairway and swallowed a couple of times. "Kada was in front of me and suddenly this groaning seemed to start." He took a shaky breath. "It just kept getting louder and louder. Kada screamed and when she turned she half fell against me, as if something or somebody was pushing her. It was like something was trying to suffocate us. And a sorta demonic laughter started and it got... louder and louder... I can't begin to tell you what it was like." He looked at all of them and it was easy to see whatever he heard still bothered him.

"All the while we were trying to get away from...whatever it was that seemed to be hovering all around us, this insane laughter was going on and on." Ace took a deep breath. "I don't know, truthfully, how we got out. I just remember racing to the car, pulling her with me, and driving away."

"Where did you go from here?" Wade's voice was flat.

Ace had trouble looking at them. "We, uh, we went to a motel. But it wasn't what you think. She was sick, and I passed out. We, uh, were under different influences. Mine was... well, you know what it was and you know what hers was."

Abbie got up to get them all some water to drink. She was discomfited at how grateful Ace was over a simple glass of water and wondered again why he seemed familiar to her.

"Maybe you better go on to the second part and then we can find the answers to what really happened here," Bill suggested.

"Oh, man." Ace covered his face with his hands for a moment and leaned back in his chair. "I started smoking more and more weed, and Kada began to carry that necklace with her wherever she went. She fingered it constantly. Sometimes even when she was singing she would be touching it or holding it. She was really scared about what had happened. She couldn't tell you, Wade, because then she'd had to have said that I was here."

Wade said nothing, but the dark look on his face was a strong indication of how he felt.

"I knew a guy that sorta dabbled in the occult," Ace continued. "He told me there must have been a death in this house and that the house needed to mourn. It sounds so stupid now, but at the time it made sense. Kada had said your uncle died right there." He pointed to the foot of the stairs. "We began to speculate that maybe someone had murdered him."

"No one murdered my uncle—he fell and broke his neck." Wade spat the words out with force.

Ace nodded nervously and continued. "When you and the kids were gone, the three of us came and covered the floors with black carpet the guy had picked up from a motel renovation. The curtains were from the same place. He had fixed some wall coverings, and he said there were black magic incantations on them that would keep evil spirits away."

"You put the occult in my house with my children in here? And Kada let you? What kind of lowlife are you?" Wade shook his hand free from Abbie's and folded both arms across his chest. He glared at Ace with such intensity that Ace seemed to shrink in his chair.

"Wade," Bill said calmly, "let him finish."

"I…I really don't remember much of the rest of that day. I was pretty spaced out." Ace took a large drink of water. "It was warm for the middle of September, and we had the windows open. The guy said we owed him six hundred dollars. After we paid him he said everything would be fine now, and we should light a candle in the evening instead of turning the lights on. Kada had started drinking in the late afternoon, and by the time it was dark, we both were in pretty bad shape."

It was getting harder for Ace to continue, but finally he seemed to pull himself together. He looked at the stairs and his eyes darted nervously from one object to another. When he began talking again he concentrated on a spot above Abbie's head.

"We were sitting here at this table and trying to say every stupid little incantation we could remember. The wind came up and it blew the candle out." Ace looked at Wade helplessly. "Out in the dark a woman started screaming. I suppose she screamed three or four times. Kada was terrified and she began to scream over and over again. I thought we were both going to die."

Abbie felt goosebumps up and down her arm, and she leaned closer to Wade.

Ace swallowed and his adam's apple seemed to bounce in time to the nervous rhythm of his leg. He looked down at the table. "I started to the stairway and must have passed out. The next thing I knew it was morning. The only thing I wanted to do was get out of here. I wanted Kada to go with me, but I was too scared of everything to take her."

He looked drained and leaned back in the chair as if he wasn't sure it would support him. There was a haunted look on his face. It was coupled with remorse in his eyes and Abbie wondered if he felt guilty that he had left Kada to work out her fear and shame by herself.

In the silence that followed, Bill cleared his throat. "That's pretty much the way Kada told me." He looked at Wade. "She really believed this house was trying to kill her. She went to her grave thinking that. I kept telling her to talk to you about it. I think you have the answers."

A shiver went up Abbie's spine as she contemplated his words. When she looked at Wade he seemed lost in thought. Finally he spoke, and as he did he gave Bill a piercing look.

"How do we know it wasn't demonic forces?"

Abbie gasped in horror. She would not stay in that house another night if Wade thought such a thing.

"Wade," Bill said softly, "play on the level. This poor fool has suffered enough thinking such stupidity." The two men studied each other silently.

Wade sighed and looked away. It it was several seconds before he spoke again. "A woman's scream in the night—I would say that must have been a mountain lion going through. They can sound like that.

We had one last October that just about scared the wits out of both of us."

Bill nodded. "That's what I wondered."

"A mountain lion? Here?" Ace was incredulous. "I thought they were just in the Black Hills."

"They're everywhere. If you hadn't been so—whatever you both were—you would have realized that," Wade said.

"But… it seemed to happen right after the wind blew the candle out. I just don't …" Ace looked at Abbie and then to Bill as if they could help him make Wade realize the coincidence of the timing was out of the ordinary.

"You were both very much under the influence," Bill said. "And it happened almost two years ago—people often forget the exact time of details, you know."

Ace flashed Bill an indignant look. "Some things people don't forget, you know."

"What about the first night they were here—what could that noise have been?" Bill meant to get to the bottom of both stories.

Wade looked at Abbie. "Remember Grandma's story at Thanksgiving about the house laughing?"

"Oh! She said when the wind was from the northeast and both porch doors were open it sounded like the house was laughing." Abbie looked at him puzzled. "But it wasn't a demonic laughter."

Wade looked thoughtful. "When I left that night with the kids, I purposely opened both doors and put stops against them so the breeze could come through," he said. "It was hot that day, and I wanted the house to cool down. The wind came up when we were camping, and I remember Clive commenting how strong it was. I would imagine that without someone to shut the porch doors when it started that it would have kept getting louder and louder." He looked at Ace with a hint of malice on his face. "The timing was most—shall we say—interesting."

Ace was flustered. "That might explain the noise but what about the rest—being pushed and suffocated?"

Wade stood and walked over to the stairway. He looked up and seemed to be pondering a question in his mind. Finally he seemed satisfied and walked back over to the table.

"Before we left, I put two heavy old feather pillows on the railing upstairs. I also put a lightweight down comforter there. I had planned to use them for the kids, but at the last minute I changed my mind and got out two sleeping bags. When the wind came up, it must have blown them downstairs. Once again, the timing was interesting."

Ace looked in disbelief at Wade. "I don't think that was it at all," he finally muttered. He stared at the stairway and shook his head. "I can't think that the wind at that precise moment blew pillows and a blanket down on us…" He left the sentence dangling and threw Wade a dark look. "For all we know, it could have been you."

Wade's eyes narrowed and his words were cold. "If I had been here when the two of you started up the stairs to my bedroom, you can bet that you would have known what hit you. They used to kill men who messed with other men's wives."

Ace jerked his hand and almost tipped over the water glass.

"I think I'll make us some coffee," Abbie said and headed to the kitchen.

There was silence in the dining room while Abbie poured water in the coffeemaker and measured out the coffee grounds. She had just flicked the switch to start it when she heard Bill clear his throat and ask, "What about it, Ace, does that satisfy you?" Abbie momentarily stopped what she was doing and looked through the dining room arch at the three men.

Ace rubbed his forehead and gave a hollow laugh. "I…I suppose it could be as you say. It's just that both Kada and I have been in hell the last couple of years thinking it was something demonic, and she… felt like she was being punished for…" He spread his hands out in a hopeless gesture. "I just don't know what to think."

250

"I would say it's what makes sense," Bill said. "Generally things make sense if you put all the pieces together."

"Why did you steal the necklace?" Wade asked, looking directly at Ace.

"I just wanted something that was hers. It meant so much to her. I shouldn't have taken it from the church."

Wade got up and walked out of the dining room to retrieve the necklace from the kitchen table. Abbie saw him look at it for several seconds. His eyes met hers and he raised his eyebrows in an unspoken question. She nodded and he walked back into the dining room with it dangling from his powerful hand.

Putting it on the table in front of Ace, he said in an offhand tone, "You may as well keep it. I don't want it."

Ace reached out a nervous hand and quickly put it back into his pocket.

When Abbie brought the four cups of coffee into the dining room it seemed to signal a more relaxed atmosphere. The plate of cookies was also appreciated, and as they sat there with the sun streaming through the lace-curtained windows, she noticed Ace was looking all around and shaking his head.

"How is the band going?" Abbie asked Bill.

"Well, the Wild Boys Plus One is no more."

At both Wade and Abbie's shocked look, Bill continued. "After Kada's death, Bob, the guy who sang at the funeral, said he wanted to quit and have more family time. Soon after that the drummer had a job transfer to another state. I wasn't feeling up to doing much of anything, and the other lead guitar player said he was tired of all the traveling. So we've disbanded."

Bill gave a little chuckle and said, "I've even changed my image. I thought you might have noticed."

Abbie smiled at him. "You had your hair cut. I noticed right away." The long braid that he had in the hospital had given way to a short haircut. It made him look younger and less scruffy.

"How do you know it was the pillows and comforter that fell down?" Ace was looking at Wade, seemingly unaware that his question came out of the blue.

"When Clive and I got back, I took the kids upstairs to bed," Wade replied. "The pillows and comforter were at the foot of the stairs. I remember that Clive took them on up and put them in the guest room."

"Have you ever heard the wind make that sound in here?" Ace asked, still sounding skeptical.

"No, I never have. My grandmother has always talked about it, though," Wade answered.

"What happened to your uncle?" Ace continued.

"Uncle Blaine had a fondness for whiskey," Wade said, looking at his coffee cup. "My grandparents never admitted it to themselves or anyone else. He was drunk, and he tripped and fell. End of story."

Ace nodded and looked down as well. "I'm relieved, to tell you the truth. I sure didn't want to come here." For the first time there was a faint smile on his face.

Abbie looked at him sharply. *Where have I seen him before?*

Wade was looking at him intently as well. "I sure hope you never come back. I promised my little daughter that she would never have to go with her biological father until it was her choice. I will keep my promise."

Abbie wasn't following the direction this was going, but Ace seemed to know immediately. He looked down and nodded. "I ain't much of a man, but I know she's better off with you."

"Ace is Scilla's dad." Bill made it sound like a statement, but from the look on his face, Abbie knew he was as surprised as she was.

"What?" Abbie was incredulous. "Say what?" She looked at Wade in complete bewilderment. "How did you know?"

"Just—mannerisms," he said. "Some of the things he does I've seen Scilla do. They've got the same brown hair. And it makes sense now. Kada's actions make more sense now." He twisted slightly in his chair.

"I never asked Kada who Scilla's real father was. It didn't matter to me. But for the life of me, I couldn't figure out why she was attracted to a skinny pot-smoking drummer. If she wanted to have an affair, she could have had her choice of a number of men."

Ace blinked at all of them, and his nervous fingers crumbled his cookie slightly onto the table.

Wade looked at Ace again. "It just hit me when you smiled—Scilla's smile. And then it all fell into place. Kada's attraction to you had its roots in the fact that you are Scilla's dad."

Abbie ran her fingers through her hair. Now she knew why Ace looked so familiar—but it wasn't him, it was Scilla's resemblance to him.

It's going to take a week to sort through all of this, she thought.

She looked at the abject young man sitting at the table with downcast eyes. "You mean you and Kada…but why didn't you two get married? If you cared about each other, why didn't you get married?" she asked.

For the first time there was a flash of spirit in Ace Olson's demeanor. "Do you know Kada's mother?" he retorted, giving Abbie a defiant look. "We were two young stupid kids. When she got pregnant, her mother tore Kada apart. She called her every name in the book, and she said if we got married she would make sure we would live to regret it. Kada's dad told us it would be better for Kada to live with them until after the baby was born. He said a lot of things about that woman that scared both of us. She's the wickedest person I've ever been around. I left the country for a while and when I came back and started in the band again, Kada was married to you." He gave Wade a hard look. "I understand you have your own problems with the old rip."

Wade rocked back in his chair and gave Ace a studied gaze. "She's trying to bring a lawsuit against me. She and her lawyer have sent a pile of rotten letters here."

"Is her lawyer still that Hertly guy?" Ace asked.

Wade nodded.

"Get yourself a good lawyer and go after them," Ace said. "He thinks he's a bigshot until the big boys go after him and cut him down to size." Ace looked at Bill and there was bitterness in his voice. "If I knew then what I know now, things might have been different."

"Well," Bill said slowly, "we make our choices in life and we have to live with them. You made a good choice to come here and talk to Wade. Now you know what I was trying to tell both you and Kada. There was a logical explanation for what happened those nights."

Bill took a drink of coffee and his dull eyes never left Ace's face. "Another good choice you made right now is to say you'll stay out of that little girl's life and let Wade and Abbie raise her."

When Ace nodded his head, Bill turned to Abbie. "Kada was glad you and Wade were married. She felt like she should come back here and try again, but when she heard you were married, it was a huge relief to her. She told me you were a better mother to the kids than she ever could hope to be."

Abbie didn't know why tears suddenly blurred her vision. She couldn't say anything.

"Wade, she really wasn't a tramp," Bill continued. "Ace was the only one she… uh, well, he was the only one she was unfaithful with. She drank too much, swore too much, and told too many terrible jokes, but she truly was trying to clean up her act before she died." Bill looked off into space before he continued. "She had a pretty wretched childhood with a very domineering mother. We compared notes on that once. We talked a lot these past weeks about religion. Somehow she found something that gave her a certain amount of satisfaction."

Wade quit rocking his chair and set it down on all four legs. "You led her to faith—which is more than I ever done for her."

Bill shook his head. "I didn't lead her to anything. I don't believe in any of that nonsense. She found what she was looking for herself—"

"She found it in the Bible, Bill," Ace interjected. "I know that because she called me at the treatment center and told me some verses to look up."

A silence descended on the four of them. Abbie was trying to absorb Bill calling faith nonsense. She had never met someone who thought that and it bothered her immediately.

"Ah, Bill." She fidgeted with her napkin. "What are you doing with Kada's Bible?"

For a while she wondered if he was going to answer her. Finally he gave her a slow smile, and for a brief second there was almost a twinkle in his eye. "I'm reading it, Abbie. At least there's some good history applications there."

Bill pushed back his chair and thanked her for the coffee and cookies. Ace followed suit, and within minutes they were standing by the door getting ready to leave.

Bill grasped Wade's arm with both his hands, shaking his head. "Ace, you're lucky it was pillows and a blanket that attacked you," he said, glancing at him. "By the feel of this guy's arm, you would have been mincemeat if it had been him."

To Abbie's amazement, Wade grinned like a schoolboy and lightly cuffed the older man's shoulder. "Thanks for coming, Bill. I guess we've cleared up a lot of things this afternoon." He nodded in Ace's direction. "My wife told me she hoped I'd be able to say that when you left." He put his arm around Abbie's shoulders and gave a gentle squeeze.

"We wish you well with your counseling, Ace," Abbie said. She felt a sudden pity for him; he looked frail and vulnerable. She wondered where his life and his choices would lead him.

Wade took his arm off her shoulders and quickly headed into the dining room.

"I have something for you, Ace," he said, and Abbie could hear him opening up the china cupboard side door. When he reappeared he had a Living Bible, similar to what Kada had.

"Now you and Bill can both read the Word." He handed it to Ace and opened the door so they could leave.

"Next time you see us, we'll both be preachers," Bill snorted and limped out the door.

Ace followed, but at the top of the porch steps he turned and gave Wade a searching look. "Thanks." He held up the Bible. "Thanks for this and for taking Scilla and raising her like your own." He quickly walked down the steps and got into the car.

Back inside the house Wade checked his watch. "I've gotta run, Abbie. My maternity patients need me." He gave her a light kiss on the top of her head. "Are you going to be able to get Scilla from school?" At her nod he stepped into the mudroom and within seconds had on his overshoes and jacket.

Abbie had followed him down the hall. Before he reached for his hat he turned to look at her.

"Abbie? How come you're not saying anything?" he asked.

"I'm… I'm trying to get all this sorted out in my mind. I wish we had some time to talk before the boys wake up and Scilla gets home."

He smiled at her ruefully. "I know, Miss Brit. Lots of questions for you. If there's no problem with the heifers I'll come back in—" He was interrupted by an angry cry from upstairs. "Uh-oh. Skyler must have woken up on the wrong side of the bed." He slapped on his hat and opened the door. "Tonight, Abbie, after our world has settled down, you and I will get cozy on the couch and hash things over."

CHAPTER 30

Northwest Wind

*I*T SEEMED LIKE the afternoon dragged on forever. As much as Abbie tried to keep her mind on the kids and their usual routine, her thoughts were flying in all directions. She had to force herself to listen to Scilla's account of her day at school, and more than once she realized she was scrutinizing the little brown-haired girl for resemblances to her real father.

Scilla had Kada's gray-green eyes, but her features were the finer outlines of her father. She had Ace's quick mannerisms, such as rocking back and forth on her feet, and something Abbie had never noticed before—the quick bursts of speech that had characterized Ace's conversation that afternoon.

To make matters worse, supper was delayed when Wade discovered a listless baby calf with its little ears down, requiring a quick trip into the house to find the right vaccine to doctor it. He'd had a series of challenges all afternoon, he told her, and he would be back in for supper as soon as he could.

Finally, three bathed and pajama-clad kids were tucked into bed, prayers were said, and Abbie and Wade were downstairs by the fireplace. Strangely enough, Abbie thought, neither of them were in the mood to

257

be cozy on the sofa. Wade had slumped into his comfortable recliner on one side of the fireplace, and she had found the rocker on the other side.

The wind had begun its lonesome lament shortly after dusk, and occasionally the windows rattled when a stronger gust fled over the prairie. There was no laughter in the sound of it, Abbie decided—only a lonesomeness that settled over the house and weighed heavily on the two of them as they sat in silence.

"What are you thinking, Abbie?" Wade finally asked.

"I'm trying to remember what I wanted to ask you all afternoon, but I believe the wind has blown all my thoughts away," she said, rocking slowly.

He let out a pent-up breath. "Wind and South Dakota are synonymous." He gave her a tired smile. "I'll tell you what I think. I should be furious at Kada and Ace. I want to be, but they're both so blasted pathetic. Somehow, I'm just too tired right now to waste energy trying to figure the whole thing out."

The fire crackled as a downdraft stirred up the logs, and little sparks exploded in the firebox. Abbie watched them fizzle out before she spoke.

"I guess the fact of the matter is that they were high on booze and pot, with plans of committing adultery right here in your house and somehow, whether by chance or design, they had the fear of death put in them. They dabbled in the occult and somehow, whether by chance or design, in your house, they again had a terrifying experience." Abbie felt goosebumps on her arms. "I can see why Kada had the conclusion that this house hated her. I can almost feel sorry for her that she was so scared, but what I can't understand is why she didn't confess the whole matter to you rather than live in fear for—what—almost two years?"

"She probably would have left quicker but Sage came along. You know the story about all that." There was a tired flatness in his voice. "I... I suppose she..." he stopped and stared into the fire. When he spoke again his voice was subdued.

"I should have been different with her. I always felt superior to her—morally, intellectually. I more or less married her so Scilla would have a home." Once again he gave a deep sigh. "If you could have seen that poor little kid, Abbie, it would have broken your heart. Just a little tiny tot, being dragged all around to dances and falling asleep wherever there was a spot for her. Thin … scared. I was in Ft. Pierre after a sale, and Clive and I went to the bar. It was loud and smoky, and this little tiny girl was holding on to her mother's leg while she sang." He shook his head in remembrance.

"Kada came up to us during a break and introduced herself, and somehow I ended up holding Scilla when it was time for Kada to start singing again. It seemed so wrong that this little kid had to be in the middle of all that noise, so I went outside and found a bench to sit on. For the rest of the evening I held her. Different ones would come out and visit for a while, and some woman brought Scilla's blanket so I could wrap her up. She snuggled down into my arms and slept. I guess she just sorta stole my heart that evening."

He looked at Abbie for a few seconds before his gaze went back to the fire. "We just drifted into a relationship. She'd bring Scilla out here when she sang in the band. I guess she just drifted into my bed and I didn't… I guess I sure didn't say no." Once again he looked at Abbie. "You're, uh, you are probably thinking, and rightly so, that I had no room to hold her to one standard and myself to a different one." He waited for her to answer, and once again a blast of wind blew a downdraft into the fireplace.

Abbie's thoughts were as scattered as the log embers as she studied her husband's face. It was her mother's quiet voice that took control and began to shape her response.

"My mother always told me that it was the woman's responsibility to see that a relationship was respectable," she said. "I grew up believing that I was the one who would have to set the boundaries. Whether that's right or wrong, I don't know. I only know that was what my mother taught me."

Humor briefly flashed over Wade's face. "Even when the lady was wearing moose pajamas, one could sense there was a line in the sand." His demeanor became serious again. "When we're young and dumb we do stupid things, Abbie. I knew better. I even knew we were wrong for each other, but in the back of my mind I kept thinking about what would happen to Scilla if I didn't marry her mother. So I did it. I didn't pray about it, I just did it. It wasn't until after Skyler was born and Kada wanted to go back to the band that I finally admitted all my sins to God. In fact, I almost ruined a good horse before it dawned on me Kada wasn't the only one who'd done something wrong." He shook his head ruefully. "It's so easy to see the splinter in someone else's eye and not realize there's a beam in our own little peepers."

"I know. I know." Abbie stopped rocking and looked down at her hands. "This afternoon, when Ace was telling about the wallpaper and carpet, I could hardly believe they were so gullible. At least we realized we were young and dumb and tried to do better. They just never seemed to get the picture they were piling one pack of troubles onto another pack."

Another gust of wind caused the budded trees to sway in the darkness while drops of rain spattered onto the windows. Abbie gave a slight shiver as she burrowed deeper into the rocking chair cushion.

"Is the wind from the right direction to laugh at us tonight?" she asked.

Wade slowly got up from his chair and walked over to her. "No, little Abbie, it's coming from the northwest and it's a cold spring wind." He pulled her to her feet. "This wind is telling us to end this day and head to bed. There's nothing like snuggling under the covers with the woman you love and a good northwest wind whistling around the house." His arms were around her and he pulled her close to him. "I'll make a quick run to the barn to check the heifers and be back before you know it."

Abbie wrapped her arms around his waist and enjoyed his warmth against her. She agreed with him; it was time to end the day. Tomorrow would have its own set of challenges, but this day was ending and the answers from the questions of the previous days signaled the beginning of peace of mind. In fact, snuggling with Wade under the covers sounded like bliss.

"Will you hurry, Mr. Jackson?"

He gave her a tender kiss before he replied, "I'll hurry, Mrs. Jackson."

CHAPTER 31

Tulip Time

Tell Scilla the scilla are blooming and if that Tyler would ever get over here and take a picture, I could send it to her so she could see what it looks like.

—LT

ABBIE SMILED WHEN she read the terse e-mail. Aunt Lena was finally getting the hang of the Internet. Her notes were always short and to the point. Her first note to Abbie in February had been quite tart.

A great disappointment to all of us. He doesn't begin to compare to Randall.

—LT

Abbie was immediately annoyed and dashed off a pretty tart note herself.

If it wasn't for you and Randall, I would never have met him in the first place.

—AJ

It was a couple of weeks before Lena answered.

How were we to know you'd go and marry your boss?

—LT

As smart as the two of you are, you should have figured it out.

—AJ

Once again there was a length of time before the next message came.

You know, of course, that Randall is a tightwad. However, a British tightwad is still better than that cowboy.

—LT

Abbie sighed when she read that one. *Lord, this could go on forever. What would You have me say?*

I love my cowboy and he gave me a beautiful diamond ring.

—AJ

Abbie thought surely that would put a stop to the bickering. She was wrong. The next day Lena sent another e-mail.

Bragging is rude.

—LT

As soon as that came, Abbie fired back.

So is criticism.

—AJ

Immediately there was a reply.

That's why we get along. We're both rude.

—LT

Abbie couldn't help laughing out loud when she read that remark. She never realized Aunt Lena thought they got along!

On the heels of that announcement came the conciliatory remark about the flowers. Abbie quickly e-mailed Aunt Lena that they would be waiting for pictures of the scilla. Then she decided to shut down the computer and enjoy some outside time.

The tulips she had planted in the fall had sprouted up with determination, and the last days of April were filled with their blossoming beauty of reds, pinks, and yellows. The little flags that resembled miniature irises and had been in the yard for years were also blooming. The prairie was gradually changing from brown to green, and the change was invigorating.

Abbie put Sage on the greening grass and watched him waddle away, followed by the tabby cat. Scilla had decided the day before that the cat's name should be "Wannabe" because, she explained, "He wants to be a housecat." The name made sense to Abbie, but Skyler said no. It took a lot of effort to find out that he didn't like it because he couldn't pronounce it. Just "Be" wouldn't work, because he still called Abbie "Bee." Finally Scilla told him to call it "Wan." That seemed to satisfy everyone.

As fast as the flowers grew, the weeds were growing with even greater speed. Abbie settled down to some serious weeding and was soon absorbed in her task. Sage and Wannabe were parading back and forth in front of her, and whenever Sage lost his balance and sat down, the patient tabby rubbed against him until he got back up again.

"This is quite a picture." Abbie glanced up to see Wade standing next to the porch with Skyler by his side. "You three seem to be enjoying this nice spring morning."

"Absolutely," Abbie responded. "The kid and the cat have made at least ten rounds while I've been weeding." She sat back on her haunches and asked, "What's new out in the pasture?"

"Lots of little calves runnin' around their mommas. I caked the cows for the last time. I opened the gate into the next pasture so hopefully they'll head out into fresh grass, and this afternoon I'll finish moving them all out." He eased himself down on the porch step. "I'm thinking of branding in about three weeks. Your folks will be here then, and that's generally my time slot."

Skyler found some little trucks and busied himself in the sandpile. His motor began to sputter as he made roads, and his ego soared when Sage went over to watch in awe.

Abbie stood and joined Wade on the porch steps. He put his hand on her knee and gave it a gentle squeeze.

"I was wondering, Mrs. Jackson, if there wasn't something you might want to tell me," he said softly.

Abbie knew when she looked at him that she had fake innocence written all over her face. "Something to tell you?" She giggled self-consciously.

He raised both eyebrows and grinned at her. "You've been acting a little giddy for the past couple of days."

"Well, yes. I wanted to wait until I was positive. But I'm pretty sure right now." She beamed at him. "The old barn cat is going to have kittens!" She roared with laughter at the dismayed expression on his face.

For several seconds he watched her mirth, but finally he got up and walked into the house, shaking his head and muttering about nannies and their weird sense of humor.

Abbie quickly followed him, still chuckling, and watched as he poured two cups of coffee. When he handed her one, she set it down on the counter. She stepped close to him and wrapped her arms around his waist to give him a hug.

"Wade, I probably won't be drinking so much coffee from now on." She tilted her head back to look at him. "Our baby doesn't seem to like it as much as his mother does."

He put both hands around her face and slowly kissed her. "I thought so. A December baby?"

265

She nodded and gave a long sigh. "Not the best time with weather and the holiday season, but I'm pretty excited about it. How about you?"

"Hey, we're in the baby business already—we may as well have our kids grow up with my kids." He smiled at her as she traced the fine lines around his eyes. "We need to get those adoption papers going so these three are yours as well as mine."

Abbie nodded and glanced out the window. She was startled when she saw an empty sandbox and quickly moved out of Wade's arms to have a better look out the window. He turned to look also and made a fast exit out the door.

"They can't have gotten very far. They were just here a minute ago," he said over his shoulder as she came scurrying after him.

Abbie saw an empty yard when she hurried outside. She groaned and dashed to the east of the house, and Wade headed toward the barn. She heard him calling both boys' names, and then to her immense relief she suddenly heard Skyler's voice answering with a "Here, Daddy!"

Her relief was short lived. When she quickly followed the sound of his voice, she saw Wade standing by the old wind charger tower looking up with grimness etched on his features. Skyler was climbing the metal ladder and had already passed the first level. Sage was on the ground clapping his little fat hands together as if each step up the ladder was a huge triumph.

"Skyler, you've gone high enough. It's time to come down now." Wade's voice was calm.

Abbie felt her heart start to pound. If he fell it would be about a twelve-foot drop. She could imagine all sorts of broken little body parts.

"I go clear high!" Skyler called.

"No, Skyler. You stay right where you are and Daddy will come after you. Don't go any higher," Wade said, moving to the ladder.

Skyler climbed another step. "Sage wants me to."

"No, he doesn't, Skyler," Abbie said quickly. "Sage says you have gone far enough."

266

Wade was already several steps up the ladder and within moments reached Skyler's perch. "OK, you can let go now, and I'll carry you down," he said from behind Skyler.

Skyler gripped the metal rung. "No, Daddy."

Wade's voice was beginning to have an edge to it. "Yes, Skyler. Let go so I can get us down from here."

"I scared."

"No need to be scared. I have a hold on you and you won't fall." Wade had one arm wrapped around the metal ladder and one arm around Skyler's waist.

Skyler's little hands held tight to the ladder and his lips began to tremble. He looked as if he would rather cling to the ladder than let his dad carry him down. Abbie cleared her throat and tried to think of what would appeal to his three-year-old mind.

"Pretend you're a monkey, Skyler," she said, and quickly added, "when you let go of the ladder you can swing right around and hang on to the big ape's neck."

"Thanks a lot, Abbie," Wade said, and scowled down at her.

"Make a monkey noise like this," Abbie added, ignoring Wade's look. She began to jump up and down and raised her lips to show her teeth. "EEEE EEEE EEE!"

"You funny, Bee!" Skyler laughed. With a little more coaching he finally turned around and yelled his monkey sound right into his dad's ear. All the way down the ladder he and Abbie made their sounds at each other until he was safely on the ground.

Abbie breathed a quick prayer of gratitude and noticed Wade had beads of sweat on his face. When he had both boys' attention he began a long and detailed explanation of why they weren't ever to crawl up on the wind charger ladder again.

Skyler nodded solemnly, and Sage followed his example and nodded also. Taking each little boy's hand in her own, Abbie led the little procession back to the house and, after adding some cautionary words of her own, settled them down in the sand box once more.

Wade slumped down on the porch steps. "You know I'm terrified of heights," he muttered when she sat down beside him.

Her eyes widened and she clasped her hand to her mouth. "I didn't know that! I could have gone after him—I don't mind high places at all."

"Probably because of all that monkey business," he groused, shaking his head at her.

She hugged his arm. "You were wonderfully brave, Mr. Ape Man. I'm impressed."

He shook his arm away from her hold and quickly put it around her shoulders, pulling her close to him. "What would you have done if I'd died laughing at your monkey business, Miss Abigail? Do you have any idea of what you looked like with your lips all puckered up and jumping up and down?" He hugged her. "If I hadn't been so scared myself I would have died laughing."

"Please don't tell Clive," she begged. "The neighborhood will think you married a fruitcake!"

"The neighborhood knows I'm one lucky monkey," he said, puckering up his lips and planting a slobbery kiss on her freckled nose.

That afternoon, while Wade was riding through the pasture getting the rest of the cows and calves out, Abbie set out two cups. Torrie was stopping in after school and had stated with no small amount of anxiety that she needed to talk to Abbie over coffee. She had said it wasn't anything connected to Scilla and school, which caused Abbie's mind to conjure all sorts of scenarios.

The boys had gotten up from their afternoon naps and were impatiently waiting for Scilla to come home. She generally colored a picture for each of them, and they had a bulletin board in their room overflowing with colored treasures.

When Torrie pulled into the yard, Scilla raced out of the car and up the steps with her usual enthusiasm, and all three kids congregated on the porch to assess the new pictures.

"Hey, Torrie," Abbie said, walking over to the car.

"Hey." Torrie's voice sounded bleak as she slowly got out of the outfit.

"A rough day at school?" Abbie asked.

Torrie shook her head. "I've got a major problem, Abbie, and it's been a long day. Any coffee at your house?"

Abbie grinned at her as they started up the steps to the porch. "Coffee or tea, whichever is your pleasure, and some cookies."

Once inside, Torrie slumped into a kitchen chair and stared morosely at the coffee Abbie placed in front of her. "I just found out my friend from college can't be the maid of honor. Something about her dad having surgery and her needing to be there." Torrie took a cookie and broke it in half.

Abbie set her cup of herbal tea on the table and hoped Torrie didn't notice she wasn't drinking coffee. "That's a bummer. You already have the dresses, don't you? Can you find somebody to replace her who could wear that size dress?"

Torrie raised her eyes and studied Abbie carefully. "Yes, I will have to replace her. Yes, I have the dress. And yes, I know of someone who is that size." She stopped abruptly and drank some coffee. "Abbie," she said after a pause, "all my life I've wanted this big, perfect wedding. I wanted lots of attendants, lots of flower girls, and lots of little ring bearers." She shook her head with a great sigh of weariness.

"The four kindergarten and first-grade girls are going to be flower girls—of course you already knew that from Scilla—and the four second- and third-grade little guys will be ring bearers, and I have shopped until I'm ready to drop to get everything ready by the middle of June."

Abbie nodded. She knew Torrie and Clive had made countless trips to different stores to get wedding paraphernalia.

"I thought I would take care of the wedding, and Clive could take care of where we would live and get a trailer or something for our home. I should have known better." She grabbed a napkin and blew her nose into it. Abbie noticed her eyes were filmy and there was a slight tremor on her lips.

Torrie looked out the window before she continued. "It's the countdown now. And as far as I know, he hasn't even looked at any place for us to live—I keep asking him, and he keeps stalling." She blinked a couple of times and looked back at Abbie. "Just tell me why the heck I love that blue-eyed lazy bum anyway!"

"Well," Abbie said slowly, and reached over to give Torrie's hand a quick squeeze, "I suppose it's because you know he has a heart of gold, and he's cute and cuddly and—"

Torrie eyes flashed. "How do you know he's cuddly?"

Abbie burst out laughing. "He looks cuddly, Torrie, but I sure as the world have no idea if he actually is! Remember, I'm a redhead, and he steers clear away from the likes of me."

Torrie gave her a sheepish smile and shook her head. "I don't know, Abbie. Sometimes I wish we would have just had a small ceremony and been done with it—except I know that I would have always regretted it."

"It'll be beautiful. Things have a way of working out," Abbie tried to assure her.

Torrie took another drink of coffee and sat back in her chair. "I suppose we'll live with one of our folks until he finally gets something figured out. I don't like it at all, but trying to push Clive into doing something he's not ready to do is like pushing a log chain."

Pushing a log chain. It was an expression Abbie had never heard before, and she was silent as she contemplated the utter futility of such an endeavor. It was a good thing Torrie knew Clive's weaknesses before she married him. And what were Torrie's weak points? Whatever they were, Clive knew them and loved her in spite of them. It was amazing how opposites attract, Abbie reflected as the silence in the kitchen seemed to deepen, although it always seemed to her that she and Wade were more alike than opposite.

"Earth to Abbie," she heard Torrie say with a hint of humor resonating in her voice.

"Here. I'm here," Abbie said with a chuckle. "I was just thinking of how you and Clive are different in a lot of ways, but on the basic issues you're both on the same page. Like religion and politics."

Torrie smiled at that remark. "I know—Christians and conservatives—but I tell you, Abbie, there are times when I just wish he had more ambition, even if he is cuddly and can dance up a storm and tell the most fascinating stories and has a heart of gold." She held out her cup as Abbie brought over the carafe to refill.

"How come no coffee for you?" Torrie asked.

"I must be homesick for England and tea."

"Well, I didn't come here to complain about my beloved." Torrie spooned a bit of sugar into her coffee. "What I need is a favor from you, Abbie. Wade is Clive's best man, and since my friend can't be the maid of honor, I was wondering if you would be my matron of honor."

Abbie knew she looked horrified at the suggestion. "Oh, boy. Oh, boy. Torrie, I just am not a real good choice. I get all nervous in front of people—I mean I get really nervous! I would probably do something dumb like stand on your veil. And besides," she paused as a wonderful thought zipped through her mind, "I need to be with the boys." She thought that was a perfect excuse.

Torrie looked at her with speculating eyes. "You're not refusing because I had this thing for Wade, are you? Because you surely know by now that I really always was Clive's girl." She gave an embarrassed laugh. "I think I scared Wade half to death."

"No, but Torrie, I really do need to be with the boys, and I'll bet you know lots of friends who could take her place."

"But no one who could wear that dress," Torrie all but wailed. "Listen, Abbie, I've already arranged for childcare people—the boys will be fine with them. Please?"

Abbie heard Wade's booted steps in the hallway. As he walked into the kitchen he grinned at both young women.

"Any coffee left for me?" He quickly reached for a cup and soon had joined them at the table. "Did I interrupt something?" he asked innocently as he picked up a couple of cookies.

Torrie poured out her tale of woe while Abbie went to check on the children. When she returned Wade winked at her, and she reacted, as always, with an increased pulse rate and flushed pleasure.

"I think if I'm best man, Abbie should sure be best woman," he said with arched eyebrows and a pleased smile on his face.

Torrie nodded furiously. "Absolutely! That's absolutely right and I don't know why Clive and I didn't think of it in the first place."

"But the wedding is six weeks from now," Abbie said, looking pointedly at Wade. Had the man forgotten that not only was she nervous in front of people, but also that her waistline would be expanding?

"That's long enough to get your hair fixed and your nails done," he said flippantly, giving her arm a light pat. "You won't even have too much time to stew over being a public figure."

She opened her mouth and closed it without saying a word. Torrie looked at her puzzled.

"You aren't the star of the show, Abbie. People won't be watching you," she offered helpfully.

Abbie gave a distressed sigh. "What if the dress is too little?"

"Oh, no problem there. I'll bring it down tomorrow and you can try it on—I know it'll be plenty big on you." Torrie eyed her hopefully. "It would really mean a lot to both of us, Abbie, and as Wade said, he's the best man and it would be cute for you to be best woman—I mean, matron of honor."

"I could be patron of honor, if that would help any," Wade offered grandly.

"Wade, have you thought of the children?" Abbie asked him and watched in fascination as his eyebrows moved up and down, a classic example of Shy or Randall, she wasn't sure which.

"But I already told you that I have childcare lined up and the boys will be fine," Torrie interposed.

"The children will be fine, Abbie, and the dress will be fine, and you will be fine, and you may as well say yes because you're overruled and outnumbered." Wade rested his hand on her shoulder and gave a gentle squeeze.

Abbie thought it was distinctly unfair of him to look at her with dark eyes that radiated love and concern, along with a touch of mischievousness. She supposed she should feel honored that Torrie even wanted her. But all she really felt, she moaned inwardly, was cowardly fear of being in front of people.

"I just hope the blasted dress isn't yellow," she mumbled into her tea cup.

CHAPTER 32

Torrie and Clive

THE SCHOOL WEEK was finished the afternoon Torrie drove down the gravel road to meet Clive. He had called her at school only minutes before dismissal time and told her to meet him at the Barrowses' mailbox. He'd hung up immediately after she said she would.

As she pulled up to his battered blue pickup, he opened the door. The words Abbie had said about him being cute and cuddly flashed through her mind.

"Hello, gorgeous." He smiled at her through her open car window. "Do you mind picking up a poor, lonesome cowboy?"

"It all depends on where he wants to go. If I'm supposed to haul you to the card room, you can forget it."

"Well, I actually had a different spot in mind," he answered, his blue eyes twinkling at her as he sauntered around to get into the passenger side. Once he was in the car he leaned over to kiss her and ran his hands through her long, dark hair. "You really are gorgeous, Torrie," he sighed. "Almost too much for a bashful fellow like me."

"Uh-huh. The only time you're bashful is when you're around redheads. Which reminds me, I never told you what happened when I took the dress to Abbie."

"That was the same day the sheriff came?"

"You must have been talking to Wade." She shook her head. "I don't think I've ever seen him so mad."

"Yeah, I called him that evening and he was about to blow a fuse. I think he was more worried that Abbie was upset than anything."

Torrie put her car in reverse. "Where are we going? We better talk while I'm driving—I have a million things to do."

She frowned when Clive directed her to a little-used road directly across from the Barrowses' mailbox. "We should have taken your pickup on this road—I don't even know if the culverts are still in place."

"They're OK. Trust me."

For a mile Torrie drove at a slow pace over the rutted road that headed directly north. When she crested a small hill and saw the abandoned buildings of the old McGee place, she began to have an inkling of what Clive had in mind.

"I've been thinking about this place for a long time, Torrie." His eyes were imploring her to agree with him. While she drove down the hill, over the wooden bridge, and then the short distance to the McGee turnoff, he explained why he thought it would be a good spot for them.

"It's in between our folks' places, only three miles from school, has electricity already, and there's good water here. The county said they'd gravel the road, and I found a double-wide that we could move out here." He paused. "I just need to see what you think of it. I know there'll be a lot of work getting it cleaned up, but I think the location is what we need. When we move the new house in, it'll look pretty good, don't you think?"

Torrie stopped the car in front of a gray stucco house. It had a forlorn demeanor with its boarded windows and sagging front door.

The two trees beside it looked more dead than alive, and what used to be a fence drooped in several places. The barn was to the east of the house, and from what she could see, there appeared to be several missing boards along its side, plus missing tin on the roof.

She got out of the car and stood with her hands on her shapely hips. "How long ago did your folks buy this place?"

Clive had also gotten out of the car. "About ten years ago. The McGees only had three quarters, you know, but it hooked right onto the place. I thought we could make the old house into a garage and put the double-wide over there. Tear out the fence, fix up the corrals and barn—like I said, I don't think it would be too bad a place."

Torrie looked toward the west and saw a pleasant view with a little creek winding northward. The hill toward the north would help keep the winter winds at bay, and the road that continued northward would be a quick cut-across route to the school. She looked east and saw prairie and yucca plants and thought of how this was close to both parents and yet separate, so she and Clive would have privacy.

"Where did you find a double-wide?" She hadn't realized he had even been looking.

Once again he smiled at her and slowly walked over to where she was standing. "The Hagens are getting a modular home and want their double-wide out of there. It won't be far to move, and as soon as we get a foundation, we could get it over here. That is, if you like the house and you like this place."

"At this point in time I like anything, you big sap," she said, gently punching his arm. "I just figured we'd have to live with our parents because I didn't know you were even looking at anything."

He put his arms around her. "I always hoped we could live here, but the past couple of years I gave up on that dream." He looked away before he added, "I just figured you had your sights set on a different ranch, with a big house."

Torrie rested her head on his shoulder. "I want you, Clive, not a ranch, not a house. Just gabby old you. I don't know why but I've loved you forever." She hugged his waist and said, "This will work just fine. Do you think you can get it all ready before our wedding?"

"I don't know. I'll get at putting a foundation in right away, but all the brandings and cattle work and farming are coming up." He shrugged. "You know how it is."

Torrie knew. Clive was always behind on his work. He liked to watch the clouds and listen to the bird songs. He took time to pick plum blossoms and knew every wildflower that grew on the prairies. He could identify birds by their call, knew the best fishing spots, and was current on all political issues, but sometimes he forgot to put gas in his pickup or change the oil. She knew it, and she loved him anyway. She also knew he wouldn't get things ready before their wedding, but at least there was a plan.

They spent an hour touring the old place. She hadn't realized he had been hauling away junk for the past couple of years, even when he thought she would never marry him. When they got back into the car they had made several decisions, and both were excited about what they envisioned for the future.

"I'll get back to wedding plans now," Torrie said as they drove away. "The dress will work for Abbie." She mentally visualized red-haired Abbie in the green dress, and then her thoughts abruptly popped to a different subject.

"What do you suppose will happen with the lawsuit Kada's mother is slapping on them?"

"Wade said he had a law firm in Pierre to represent him. He called them and they were going over the case. He said the firm had heard of Hertly, the lawyer for the old warhorse. They didn't seem to like him very much." Clive shook his head. "I can't believe she wants to take him to court for Kada's money. Kada never had much of anything—Wade took care of all the funeral expenses, the van was totaled, and the money she made as a waitress went into the apartment and living expenses. Somehow her mother has the idea that she had made quite a bit of money singing in the band. She must not realize that it was divided among at least five different people. I guess the band leader, Bill, got a subpoena and called Wade to tell him he'd help pay the lawyer fee to back both Hertly and Kada's mother into a corner."

Clive gave a short laugh. "Bill Rissix said any decent mother would want her only grandchildren to have the money put away in trust, but that woman seems to think she's entitled to everything Kada had. I've heard of women like her, but I hope to God I never see one. No wonder Kada had so many hang-ups—it must have been a nightmare growing up with that kind of mother."

Torrie nodded. "You and I wouldn't have a clue about such things. Our moms are both pretty special. I have to remember to get the corsages for them and boutonnieres for the dads and all the groomsmen…maybe corsages for the rest of the wedding party…" Torrie was lost in thought and wished she could write down some of her ideas before she forgot them.

"Torrie, my love," Clive laid his hand on her knee, "you've driven past the mailbox. Are you taking me to your house?"

CHAPTER 33

That Still, Small Voice

WADE NUDGED THE black horse into a trot as he started down the ridge toward the barn. Lippy, who liked to snatch mouthfuls of green grass as he walked along, gave a disgusted snort. The horse acted even more disgusted at the German shepherd panting alongside him. If Wade didn't keep him in check, he would nip at Shy, unlike the tolerant Jake.

Late again tonight, Wade mused as he pulled down his hat against the forever blowing wind. The last several nights he'd been late, thanks to his former mother-in-law and her surly attorney. He had spent hours on the phone with his newly acquired lawyer going over the impending lawsuit. Every time he hung up the phone he cursed the woman for the extra time and money he had to spend to fight her greed.

Wade had been worried that Abbie would be overly distraught when the sheriff brought out the subpoena papers. He should have known she was made of stiff-backed English fortitude. After the first shock, she brought out the phone book and began poring over the yellow pages, determined to find the best law firm to represent him.

He suspected it was a calculated ploy to wait until he was the busiest to spring the news he was being taken to court. With Abbie's parents coming in a couple of weeks, farming, brandings, and his own cattle to watch, he didn't have a minute to waste.

A grim smile hovered around Wade's mouth. He enjoyed his animals' antics, and it annoyed him that one greedy old woman was keeping him so busy he hardly had time to notice. Abbie told him not to let the thing "steal his joy." Good advice but hard to put into practice, he'd told her. She had wrapped her arms around his waist and hugged him after she said that. For a brief second it had crossed his mind that he was too busy to smooch. That thought was followed by a mental slap in the face. Life should never be so busy that he couldn't take time to hold and enjoy this woman who was carrying his child.

He gave Lippy another nudge with his spurs. Abbie would be in for a lot of work with three busy kids and one new baby. But if she was bothered by that fact, she never acknowledged it to him. She was looking forward to her parents coming the middle of May. His folks and his brother and family were coming for the branding and to meet the Miller family. It would be a full house, and already Abbie was working overtime cleaning every spot in sight plus trying to get the yard shaped up.

The only good thing about the impending lawsuit was that it kept Abbie from thinking about being Torrie's matron of honor. He was surprised she seemed so uptight about such a simple matter. He had asked her what in her mind would be the worst-case scenario, and she'd shaken her finger in his face and said one word: "fainting." He was puzzled until she explained that her dress might be so tight in her "condition" that she'd faint. He had scoffed at that nonsense.

The sun was slowly sinking beyond the western hills when he swung down from the saddle in front of the barn. Instantly two bouncing little bodies careened out the sliding door and both Skyler and Scilla were talking to him at once.

"We shut the chickens up! We were waiting for you and there's oats in Lippy's pan! Mom gave Sage his bath already!" He understood the gist of their excited conversation and slowly led Lippy into the barn to unsaddle him.

"Sounds like you two have been busy." He smiled at them while he put the stirrup over the saddle seat to uncinch his saddle.

"We help!" Skyler was adamant as he tried to hold Lippy's reins.

"Maybe you better stand back in the saddle room, Skyler, before Lippy accidentally steps on your foot," Wade admonished gently as he pulled the saddle off.

"Then you'd limp like this!" Scilla informed him as she hobbled into the small room where the tack was kept. Skyler followed her with a greatly exaggerated limp, and Wade almost stumbled over both of them as he put his saddle on its rack.

He shook his head and laughed softly. He wondered if they had "helped" Abbie all afternoon in the same manner. She usually had worlds of patience with the kids, but the last couple of days he had noticed a sharpness in her voice that usually wasn't there. He knew she was feeling the pressure of too many things to do and too little time to get it all done.

Later that evening, after the kids had been tucked into bed, Wade read the letter his lawyer had drafted to Hertly and Kada's mother. Unlike the veiled threats and belligerence of Hertly's letters, this had an impersonal professionalism. It clearly outlined Wade's actions and Kada's mother's actions in regard to the payment of Kada's expenses. It dealt in proven facts, and made Hertly and his client look like simpletons. Wade reread it with great satisfaction, and when Abbie came into the den he was e-mailing his lawyer his approval to have it sent to Hertly's office.

"It was well written," Abbie commented as he clicked the send button.

"Very well written, Mrs. Jackson. You did a bang-up job of finding a good lawyer." He grinned at her and started shutting down the computer for the evening.

"It's nice he got right on it," she said as she settled into a wicker rocker she had discovered in a basement corner and had decided would be perfect in Wade's office.

He nodded and swung his chair around to face her. "So," he said, folding his arms across his chest and stretching his legs out before him, "is this letter the reason you seem pretty chipper tonight?"

Her brown eyes twinkled at him. "It's partly the reason."

"What's the rest of the reason?"

"I prayed."

He raised his eyebrows at her. "I thought you always prayed."

She gave him a high-wattage smile before she answered. "I always pray, but sometimes I don't listen to what God is trying to tell me. Today I listened for a change."

"And what did you hear?"

"I heard a voice, surprisingly sounding like yours, Wade, and it said, 'Abbie, the house doesn't have to be spotless, the yard doesn't have to be perfect, the branding dinner doesn't have to be the outstanding meal of the year, and your parents and Wade's parents will be delighted to help you rather than have you wait on them hand and foot.'"

"How about that—God and I are on the same page," Wade said dryly.

She gave a soft giggle. "I decided since God and you were saying the same thing, I needed to stop worrying about all the crazy stuff I thought I should be doing and just get the basics done."

"You had quite an enlightening afternoon."

Once again she smiled at him. "I did. I was all worked up in a dither when you left after talking to the lawyer after dinner. It seemed like everything was piling up and I hardly knew which pile of work to start on first. So I went outside and sat on the porch step and said, 'OK, I've rattled on about all my problems, Lord, and now I'm going to be quiet and listen to what You want me to do about them.'"

"Yeah," he nodded. "I do a lot of rattling myself. Rattling and ranting." He gave her a lazy grin. "We've had a lot to work out the few months we've been married. I wonder if we'll ever have some quiet days when we can just enjoy the kids and each other and the ranch."

She studied him thoughtfully before she answered. "I have this feeling that we'll have to fit those moments into our busy days."

Once again he nodded and there was silence between them as the wind whistled around the windows and whipped the trees into dancing forms.

"Abbie," he said softly, "I'm going to take *this* moment and tell you how much I appreciate your prayers and your willingness to listen for answers." He reached over and squeezed both of her knees. "When the lady of the house has peace, it's a blessed home."

She ran her slender fingers over his large hands and her brown eyes gazed at him with a depth of feeling that made his heart start to beat faster.

"When the gentleman of the house takes time to say those kind words, it makes this lady very happy." She stood and leaned over to hug him around the neck. "And since we are now both happy with this day, maybe we better hustle on up to bed before the phone rings or something else happens to make us unhappy."

Abbie's words were barely out of her mouth before the phone's shrill tone echoed throughout the den. She straightened, looked at the caller ID, and shook her head. "It's Clive. I'll see you later." She blew Wade a kiss and hustled herself right out the door.

"I'll be right up," he called after her. He knew Clive could ramble on forever, but he had no intention of letting the lady of the house sleep in the middle of the bed all by herself.

CHAPTER 34

Rope 'Em, Throw, and Brand 'Em

*T*HE LIGHT BREEZE in the early morning dawn softly drifted over the riders as they made their way toward the pasture containing Wade's cattle. There were twenty-one on horseback, not counting the excited kids who tried to contain themselves by walking their horses sedately with the adults.

Wade looked over at his dad and wondered what the older man's thoughts were at being back on the home ranch for branding day. For Wade it was, as always, the time to enjoy the camaraderie with his friends and neighbors while getting an important job done.

The community was almost halfway through branding season. They took turns, based on when their calves were born. Wade's turn was in the middle. As much as he looked forward to getting the job done at his place, he was always relieved when he could go to someone else's branding and not have all the responsibility of overseeing the work.

"Want me to shut this gate, Wade?" David McGovern had opened the barbed wire gate for all the riders to go through. They would be rounding up the cattle and pushing them to the other end of the pasture, but Wade liked his gates closed in case of some unforeseen scenario.

He nodded and reined in Jake to wait for David to close the gate and remount.

The riders separated into several groups as they covered the pasture, and soon yips and yelps were heard as they gathered the cows and calves into one bunch and headed for the branding corrals.

Those who had driven pickups were already at the corrals, and Wade knew his grandfather would be testing the wind to see where to put the branding fire. At 83, Art Jackson had become the chief fire designator, and he took his job seriously. He also brought out rolls and doughnuts, which made him popular with everyone.

Wade breathed a sigh of relief when all the cows and calves were in the corral and the gate was closed.

"Making a wing with those panels sure makes it a lot easier to pen 'em," his dad commented. Wade nodded. He had started doing that several years earlier and it saved a lot of hard riding as the cattle funneled through the gate into the pen.

He noted with satisfaction that Vince and Clive were sorting cows away from calves. Without being told, the crew found the place where they needed to be to make the sorting easier and faster, and within a short time the mother cows were on the outside of the corral and the calves to be branded were on the inside.

It was a loud, noisy symphony that rose into the morning air. Every mother cow was bellowing for her baby, and every calf was calling for momma.

Wade's brother, Wyatt, was digging the fire pit, and several other young men were helping. Before long the wood was in place and with the help of a propane torch, a hot blazing fire was crackling and heating the branding irons.

"Here's your coffee," Art said, handing Wade a steaming foam cup as the crew congregated by the pickup with all the goodies. "By golly, Clive, you haven't had a doughnut yet. Whatcha waiting for?"

"I was being a perfect gentleman and gave Abbie's dad one first," Clive retorted, licking some frosting off his fingers.

"Hey, I knew you must be Abbie's dad," one of the neighbors commented, walking over to shake Ben Miller's hand. "We sure have enjoyed having her in the community."

"Well, I tried to raise her right." Ben grinned as he was being introduced to several people. "She was my right-hand gal when she was growing up, and she helped me a lot in the vet practice."

"I didn't know that," Torrie said, returning Ben's handshake. "She never mentioned she helped."

"My grandson has kept her so busy with taking care of him and the kids she probably forgot," Art said with a good-humored nudge in Wade's ribs. "Marilyn, did you get a doughnut?"

"Oh, yes, no one keeps tasty goodies away from this little fat lady." Marilyn grinned, and poured herself another cup of coffee.

The ropers who were going to begin dragging calves to the branding fire were tightening their cinches and getting down their ropes. Soon everyone was assigned a job, and the assembly line of wrestlers was waiting for the first calf to be roped.

"Scilla, are you ready with your marking chalk?" Ben asked the bouncing brown-haired girl beside him.

"Yup! And when I get bigger I'll vaccinate just like you, Ben!"

"I have no doubt about that," he answered and gave her brown ponytail a gentle pull.

Within minutes there were several calves on the ground to be vaccinated as prevention against Black Leg and other diseases. Ben gave the shot and Scilla marked the calf so someone else wouldn't revaccinate it. The identifying brand belonging to Wade was burned onto the calf's hide, and if the calf was a heifer, the wrestlers let it up to head to the far corner of the pen. If it was a bull calf, it was castrated and made into a steer and then it was released.

The crew worked with clockwork precision. As the sun rose higher, the dust, fire, and noise were witnesses to the teamwork and bantering among the crew. Wade noticed it took very little time for Ben to be accepted as one of the bunch. He was a hard worker, and he and Scilla joined in the good humor as the morning progressed.

"Yuck! You should have watched where you sat!" Scilla informed one of the young wrestlers who inadvertently landed on a fresh cowpie.

"You should have watched where you stepped," he retorted with a grin, and to Scilla's great dismay she looked down to see her black boots were a distinct shade of green.

"Look, Dad!" she hollered to Wade as he came around with the branding iron. "See?" she pointed to her boots.

"See?" He pointed to his own boot covered with dust and manure. "It happens to all of us," he told her with a laugh.

During the second break the crew was more interested in the coolers packed with ice and cold drinks. The day was warming up and with the heat from the fires, the ones who branded were especially glad to have a cool respite.

Wade found Torrie visiting with some other gals and asked her if she'd like to help rope the next bunch of calves.

"Only if Clive ropes too," she said, a taunting smile on her face. "We have a continual bet going, you know. We try to outdo each other."

"What's that?" Clive asked innocently, leading his horse as he came from behind her.

Wade shook his head at them. "You two rope this time. Do you think Marilyn wants to get in this family feud too?"

"Nope." Clive shook his head. "Mom says she ain't gonna wrestle, and she ain't gonna rope. In fact, right now she's over there visiting with your new mother-in-law." He pointed to the pickup where his, Abbie's, and Wade's mothers were sitting.

After he lined up a couple of more ropers, Wade walked over to say hello to the three ladies. Lois gave him a smile that reminded him of Abbie.

"This is quite a procedure!" Her accent was delightfully British. "I'm so glad we could be here to see it. Your mother and Marilyn have been explaining the finer points to me. Perfectly delightful!"

287

"Yeah, it's quite a deal," he agreed. "When Mom was here at the ranch she never got to see our branding because she was too busy cooking." He grinned at his mother, who nodded her head in confirmation.

"Abbie and your grandmother are watching the beans bubble now," his mother said. "Skyler is in the back end of the pickup, but Sage stayed home to sample some of Abbie's desserts."

"Daddy! I here!" Skyler was trying to climb out of the pickup box.

"I see you're here." Wade picked him up and wanted to laugh at Skyler's attempt to be like everyone else. He had wrapped a bright yellow bandanna handkerchief around his small neck and slapped one of Wade's old hats over his head. It was way too big for him, and he had to keep pushing it up so it wouldn't flop over his eyes.

"I'll put Skyler in Granddad's pickup. He can keep an eye on him," Wade told the ladies as he started walking back to the fire and action.

"I rope!" Skyler shouted to one of the neighbors.

"Sure you will—but first you need a lariat," he was informed.

"It wouldn't hurt to have a horse, either," someone else added.

Wade deposited his son in Art's pickup. "Now you stay put. I don't want you out of this pickup box until I tell you to get down," he warned sternly.

"I think he means both of us, Skyler," Art said with a wink at the little boy. "Old men and little boys better stick together and stay out of the road."

Once again the rhythm of the branding started. By the end of the next hour the pace was slower, the crew was quieter, and the sun seemed quite a bit warmer. The only one still enthusiastic was Skyler. He cheered with great gusto whenever Clive or Torrie drug in another calf, and he regularly called out advice to Scilla.

Finally, there were only about a half-dozen calves left to rope. They were the ones who had constantly avoided getting caught and were eyeing the ropers with a canniness born of desperation. Torrie swung a beautiful loop but came up empty. Once again she built a loop, and this time when she swung, she caught one hind leg of a large calf. She swore a little as she made a quick dally. Her rope was too high on the calf's leg.

The calf bellowed and kicked, and as Torrie drug it to the fire, several wrestlers zeroed in to throw it on its side. The calf began a frenzied kicking, and before anyone could stop it, the calf made a wild half circle with the rope and rider as its pivot point. Torrie, trying to keep the rope tight, almost collided with Clive, who had roped another calf and was bringing it to other wrestlers.

One of the wrestlers grabbed the rope only to have his feet knocked out from underneath him as the calf changed directions and swung in the opposite way—directly over the fire. The propane tank and irons flew in complete disarray. Wade dodged back in the nick of time and, dropping his irons back into the fire, raced over several downed wrestlers and managed to grab the rope. Giving it a jerk, he made the excited calf stumble. Quickly, helping hands pulled the tail to offset the calf's balance, and within seconds the battle between men and little beast was waning. When the dust settled, there were several scraped and raw places on some of the men, but even that little fighter was thrown and branded.

Ben had grabbed Scilla with his free hand when the ruckus started, and in two strides deposited her in the pickup box beside Skyler. For once, the ever-talking Scilla was speechless. Skyler looked at her with concern.

"OK, Scilla?" he asked.

"I dropped my chalk," she finally muttered, but she made no move to try to find it.

The whole episode made a great story, and it was greatly embellished by the time everyone came in to feast on the noon meal. Clive especially enjoyed reciting all the details, and he seemed to know exactly where everyone was and what everyone did. He spoke of Ben picking up Scilla with one hand and holding his vaccinating gun in the other hand while he raced over to the safety of the pickup. He described Wade's face as the calf flew over the fire and knocked the propane tank on its side.

He repeated the swear word Torrie used when she caught the calf and realized the rope was high on the hind leg. He repeated the swear word the wrestler said when he was knocked down. He recalled in perfect detail his actions when Torrie and her horse nearly ran into him. He was sure he had prevented a worse scene by his quick actions.

No one was quite sure what he meant by that, and most of them couldn't have cared less. They were a hungry lot, and the food was more important than Clive's ramblings.

"That must be the guy Lena keeps calling 'Clipe,'" Lois murmured to Ben as they stood together beside Wade to watch the men with spurs and chinks take heaping platefuls of food out to the picnic tables set up under the cottonwood tree.

Ben chuckled. "He's a friendly chap, and he thinks the world of the woman he's talking about. See—she's the one he's going over to sit by."

"She's quite lovely. From what I could tell, she's also quite a roper." Lois bent down to scratch Shy's ears.

"You gals and the kids must have slipped out right after all the excitement," Wade said, looking around to find his bride.

"We thought Abbie might need some help, so Marilyn told her husband to lead her horse back here. She and the kids came back with us." Lois gave Shy one last pat before she straightened up and gave her son-in-law a bemused smile. "Abbie seemed to have it all under control, and she and your grandmother were having quite a visit."

"You know, Wade, Abbie has changed," Ben said. "She has matured so much since she left England. She acts like a young woman who is at peace with the world and herself."

The young woman they were discussing walked out of the kitchen onto the busy porch and they could see her searching the crowd. When she spotted them she gave a big smile and quickly walked down the steps toward them.

"Well, what did you guys think of the branding?" she asked her parents.

"Rather a good show!" Ben answered enthusiastically.

Wade couldn't help it. He reached over and tousled the red curls and was rewarded with one of her high-wattage smiles and fluttering eyelashes. He put his arm around her and drew her close. Even though his shirt smelled like branding smoke, she seemed delighted.

"How is the cook doing?" he grinned down at her.

"The cook thinks all the family should come back next year to help! I don't know what I would have done without everyone."

"Ah, yup. That might be a good plan," Ben said and added, "what do you think, Lois—could we leave those twins again next year and head this direction?"

Wade thought Lois gave Abbie a probing glance. "I would imagine that would be a good idea," she answered thoughtfully. Turning to Ben she smiled and said, "And, good sir, it might also be a good idea to grab some food before it's all gone!"

Ben took her arm and winked at Wade. "We can leave these two here to flirt with each other until they decide they're hungry as well as in love."

"Have I told you that I like your folks?" Wade wondered as he and Abbie watched them walk away.

"Ah, yup," Abbie said, imitating her dad. "And did I mention I like your family as well?"

Wade gave her a hug before he released her. "I got that impression, Mrs. Jackson."

CHAPTER 35

Marie's Story

"WHEW!" ABBIE SANK into a dining room chair that afternoon. "I think it's time this kitchen crew took a well-deserved break."

Her mother-in-law yawned and nodded in agreement. "We fed over fifty people, I'm sure. It was fun seeing the old neighborhood again. Wayne and I had good times here." She hesitated at the dining room arch. "Anybody for coffee?"

"Or pie?" Lois wondered as she eyed the pie plates lining the kitchen counter.

"Both. I want both coffee and pie," Marie Jackson stated emphatically. "I enjoyed the Swiss steak and scalloped potatoes at noon, and now I'm ready for dessert!"

Abbie was glad the big pots and pans had been cleaned and put away. She had tried to keep everything washed up as she prepared the food, and amazingly, by the time the last hungry soul had left, the amount of cleanup was minimal.

Lois brought a tray of filled coffee cups into the dining room while Karen, Abbie's sister-in-law, took orders for pie.

Abbie herself was trying to will enough energy into her tired body to at least get some forks around. She was facing a dilemma. With all the family around to visit with, the uppermost thought on her mind was a wonderful, long nap. How she envied Grandpa Art snoozing on the east porch on one of the wicker rockers. For that matter, her dad was nodding away on the glider. Lucky beasts.

She was slightly embarrassed when Marie swiftly set forks and napkins around. An eighty-year-old woman shouldn't have more energy than a person her age—even if she was two and a half months pregnant. *I wonder if I should tell them now that Wade and I are expecting a baby?* She blinked her eyes sleepily.

The others were discussing recipes and branding menus. Abbie listened quietly and hoped no one noticed she wasn't drinking her coffee.

She realized her mother was looking at her thoughtfully.

"Abbie, when is Torrie's wedding?" Lois asked her.

"Three weeks from now. Why?"

"Hmmm. Oh, I just wondered," Lois said, taking a drink of coffee and looking pointedly at Abbie's full cup.

Abbie sighed. There were some things that one couldn't hide for very long, and a baby in the womb was one of them.

She grinned lazily at her mother. "Are you wondering if I'll fit into my dress?"

Lois raised a well-defined eyebrow at her. "The thought had entered my mind."

Marie was clearly puzzled, but both Shelly and Karen exchanged knowing glances.

"I have an announcement to make." Abbie put energy into her voice. "I may as well tell all of you at once. Wade and I are expecting a baby in December."

Only Marie was surprised. The others informed Abbie that they were quite suspicious, especially since they had all noted she had quit drinking coffee. A round of enthusiastic congratulations was extended.

"I'm happy for you and Wade," Shelly said, "but you are going to be one busy gal with a six-year-old, a three-year-old, a toddler, and a baby. I wish Wayne and I could help out more."

"Quite right," Lois added quickly. "Ben and I are even farther away."

Abbie looked at both of them and smiled. "You know, taking care of kids doesn't worry me half as much as this blasted wedding coming up." She shook her head. "What if I fall asleep during the 'I do' part?"

"Even worse," Karen added helpfully, "what if you faint because your dress is too tight? That actually happened to a pregnant friend of mine!"

Abbie rolled her eyes and shuddered.

"Well," Marie said calmly, "I doubt any of that will happen."

Abbie wasn't so sure. She had mental visions of slowly sinking to the floor in an untidy heap with a large crowd of witnesses watching her descent. Torrie would be furious.

"You'll be fine, Abbie." Her mother smiled reassuringly at her. "Remember how worried you were about Clair and Tyler's wedding? Everything went quite smoothly at that. I wouldn't worry about it a bit if I were you."

"You sound like Wade," Abbie said, a little crossly. "He's always telling me, 'It's just a wedding.'"

"Speaking of Wade, where is he?" Lois wondered as she glanced out the dining room windows.

"The Jackson men took all the Jackson kids and went back out to the corrals to make sure the branding fire was out. They were afraid the wind might come up and get something started," Karen informed her.

"Oh!" Abbie sat up straighter. "That reminds me of something I wanted to ask you, Grandma."

Marie set down her cup and gave Abbie a questioning look.

"Kada and this guy Ace had such a weird experience in this house. They thought it was haunted because of a sound that was like demonic laughter." Abbie had everyone's attention.

"Wade decided it was because of the wind blowing through the two porch doors, like you had mentioned at Thanksgiving. I wanted to tell you about that because he gave you a hard time about the northeast wind."

"Demonic laughter?" Shelly said, looking at the open porch door. "Marie, you always said it chuckled. That's quite a stretch from saying it sounded like a haunted house." She shivered slightly and gave a nervous glance at the stairway.

Marie nodded her head slowly and put her napkin beside her cup. "There was a time, when Art's mother was still alive, that I was...," she looked at Abbie and paused, "well, I would just have to say that I was frightened by the suddenness and loudness of that sound."

Abbie was startled by the seriousness of Marie's voice.

Marie glanced at all of them before she continued. "We were sitting right here at this table and suddenly a northeast wind hit the house. That isn't uncommon out here." She smiled at Lois.

"But what was uncommon was the noise that began immediately and, like poor Kada thought, it really did sound like demonic laughter." Marie fiddled with her fork slightly before she said any more. "This crazy-sounding laughter just kept getting louder and louder and even Art's mother was startled. It seemed to fill the house instantly, and I was truthfully petrified with fear."

Marie paused again. There was complete silence as the rest of the women waited to hear more. When Karen accidentally bumped her fork and it clattered to the table, they all jumped.

Marie joined their nervous laughter before she continued. "Art's mother got up to shut the east porch door, and the wind was strong enough that she had a little trouble getting it latched. As soon as the door was shut, the sound was gone." Marie was once again looking at Abbie. "I can still see her as she turned around and looked at me, sitting like a zombie here at the table. She put her hands on her hips and told me it was just the laughter in the wind."

"I would have been outta here if I ever heard that," Shelly said, and to suit her actions to her words, she rose and went to the kitchen.

Marie watched her departing back and smiled reassuringly at Abbie. "That was the only time I ever heard that sound. Most of the time, the laughter in the wind is merely a delightful chuckle coming into the house when both porch doors are open and the wind is from the northeast."

Shelly was back with the coffee carafe and refilled their empty cups. She noted Abbie's still-full cup and passed her by. "Crazy sounds that fill the house would give me the creeps." She patted her mother-in-law's shoulder and added, "You did well to stay here after all that. I wouldn't have—not for a minute."

Marie gave her an understanding smile. "But I've always loved this house, Shelly. Even with all its quirks and laughter. It's a gentle and gracious house."

Abbie nodded. She felt the same way. She looked around the dining room with the afternoon sun pouring through the south windows and felt the usual satisfaction. The breeze outside was quietly rustling the cottonwood leaves and through the open windows bird songs were floating in with sweet clarity.

Today the ranch had been filled with family and helping friends. There had been good-natured fun and teasing, and now a contented quietness seemed to blanket the prairie hills.

She doubted Kada would have ever understood the almost overwhelming peace of mind Abbie was feeling at this moment. She glanced around the table at the other women visiting with one another, then at her dad and Wade's grandfather still snoozing on the east porch, and her happiness almost brought tears to her eyes.

Abbie glanced at Grandmother Marie and saw the older woman give her an almost imperceptible nod. Abbie returned the gesture with a discerning smile. She knew without words that she and Marie Jackson shared a mutual sentiment regarding the house, the prairie, and the people surrounding them.

CHAPTER 36

Scilla and Seeds

THE DAY AFTER Abbie's parents left was a cool and cloudy spring day. Abbie sat disconsolately beside the iris bed and glared at the grass and weeds that seemed to have sprung up overnight throughout her whole yard. She hated to admit there was a huge void in her world after she watched the plane taking Ben and Lois back to England become a mere speck in the cloudless May sky. She hadn't realized how much she missed England and her parents until the pleasant hours they spent together the past two weeks seemed to dissipate like a vapor, and now the much-anticipated visit was over.

She pulled on her garden gloves and started yanking out the wild lettuce by the roots. "Blasted stuff," she grumbled, tossing it in the cart.

Scilla had also donned some gloves and was having a go at tracing down a long, creeping jenny plant. "Eureka!" she hollered, pulling the vine out with a small piece of root attached. "I'll throw this monstrous tare into the whinnying cart."

Abbie glanced at her with a trace of annoyance. Ever since her parents had given Scilla some children's DVDs with parables from the Bible, she had dramatically tackled every problem with her own version of the stories.

297

"I think you mean 'winnowing,' Scilla," she corrected her.

Scilla shrugged and started on another creeping jenny plant. "These dumb irises are letting the worries of the world take over," she informed Abbie. "That's what the Bible says. Creeps and thorny lettuce turn up and they choke 'em up."

Abbie yanked out another wild lettuce and gave it a toss. The fine stickers on it glistened in the sun. "I see," she said, trying to figure out which parable Scilla was muddling.

"And then there's the poor little marigold seed that you dropped on the road and the monstrous hawk swooped down and ate it." Scilla flattened several irises in her zeal to get to the bottom of the creeping jenny weed. "You know, of course, what that means." Scilla scowled at Abbie in her best Aunt Lena imitation.

"Oh, sure," Abbie muttered as she pulled on some contrary brome grass.

"That means," Scilla jumped out of the flowerbed with a bedraggled little vine clutched in one hand, "that all the stupid jerks that have a hard heart and won't listen to God will have the devil come flying in." She flapped her arms like a huge bird, grabbed an imaginary seed, and pretended to fly over the cart. "He'll take the seed of God's Word and gobble it up so the jerks can't have it." She landed in the cart with a thud. "Maybe not a hawk. A vulture. Oh, I don't know, some kind of ugly bird." She crawled out of the cart with bits of creeping jenny sticking to her hair.

Abbie sat back on her haunches and looked at Scilla with enlightenment. "You must be talking about the parable of the seeds," she mused. "Seeds and soil." She tossed more weeds into the cart. "So what about the seeds that fell on stony places, the ground where there is just a little dirt over some rocks?"

Scilla gazed at her two brothers playing trucks in the sandbox and seemed to momentarily lose track of her sermon. Suddenly she whirled around to Abbie and hopped on one foot. "They're the ones who are all excited about God and get all goofy and when trouble comes they wilt because they're shallow-like."

"Bravo, Scilla!" Abbie clapped her hands. "What about the seeds that are sown in good soil?"

"A no-brainer, Mom. They're the people who love God, see, and they have lots of flowers…or fruit. One of the two. And those irises better shape up or they'll find them own selves in the whinnying cart." Scilla tore over to the two boys peacefully playing in the sandbox. Abbie figured it would just be a matter of time before there was a sibling conflict.

She was right. In just a few minutes Skyler was making tracks toward her, overflowing with wounded dignity. She sighed and almost wished for school to still be in session.

"Me no weed! Scilla say that to me!" His big brown eyes were flooded with tears. He turned to his sister in a fury. "I yank you out, Scilla!" He was crying even harder as he turned back to Abbie. "She say that to me!"

"Scilla, come over here," Abbie said. She gave Skyler a hug while Scilla raced toward her full throttle. "What exactly did you say to him?" she asked the breathless girl.

"I just said he was a weed in God's garden and I was going to yank him out before he choked out the good flowers." It was plain to see that Scilla thought she was doing the Lord's work.

"You weed! I no weed!" Skyler roared at her and would have attacked his bouncing sister if Abbie hadn't had a tight hold on him.

Abbie pursed her lips. "Skyler, quit crying and listen to me. Scilla, stand still and you listen to me, young lady."

There was silence and stillness as both kids paused.

"Scilla, Skyler is not a weed," she began. "He is a tender little flower that needs loving care, just as you are. You both are in good soil, and your hearts are ready to hear God's Word. OK? You must not ever think you have the right to yank someone out of God's garden. He'll do the pulling Himself. You just water and take care of the flowers and let God handle the weeds."

Abbie took a deep breath and gave Skyler another hug. "Now you can go back and play with Sage. Scilla didn't mean—"

"What if God thinks I'm a weed?" Scilla shrieked, gazing fearfully up to the sky.

Abbie released Skyler and tried to head him back to the sandpile but he stopped in front of Scilla, looking at her with soulful dark eyes.

"You no weed, Scilla," he said.

Abbie was about to praise him for being so kind when he added, "You just dumb."

Much later, after she had convinced Scilla that God knew she was His child in the garden of life—and not a dumb one at that—Abbie looked up the parable of the seeds. She found it in Matthew thirteen and read it over in her study Bible several times. "When anyone hears the word of the kingdom, and does not understand it, then the wicked one comes and snatches away what was sown in his heart. This is he who received seed by the wayside."

Abbie shut her Bible and let the words sink into her mind. Bill Rissix's face seemed to flash in front of her. Even though it had been over a month since his and Ace's visit, his disbelief in God still bothered her.

What if Satan did take away the seeds of God's Word from Bill's life? What if Bill's heart was so hardened that he refused to let God's love settle in and grow? He wasn't a wicked man; on the contrary, he seemed like someone who wanted to do the right thing. Yet what would happen to a man like him whose heart toward God seemed to be "by the wayside"?

Bill was on her mind the rest of the morning and stayed there for several days afterward. He was a strange man. There was more to him than one would suppose. For some reason, he seemed to have a soft spot in his heart for Ace. And who needed that extra counsel and friendship more than Ace Olson?

In fact, when Abbie thought of Ace, she shook her head in puzzlement. He had been arrested several times for possession of marijuana. The last time he came before the judge, he was sent to a treatment center for thirty days. Now he was on supervised probation, and where or what he would do in the future was anybody's guess.

Because she had been thinking so much of both Bill and Ace, it came as no surprise when the phone rang one morning and Bill's nasal voice was speaking in her ear. *Divine intervention—You must have put Bill in my mind for some reason, Lord.*

He was driving through, he said, and wondered if he could stop after lunch to see her and Wade. He was alone this time, he added, and he had something to give Kada's kids.

Abbie's heart sank when she heard that. He must mean he was returning her Bible, she reasoned. He must have decided he had read enough.

Her heart plunged clear down to her toes when she watched Bill limp up the porch steps. His hair was back to a braid and he was holding Kada's Bible, just as she feared. She and Wade exchanged dismayed glances before they opened the kitchen door to greet him.

"The country looks a little greener than when I was here before," he said in way of greeting. "Hello, Abbie, you're looking good. Been keeping this rascal in line?"

He shook Wade's proffered hand and his glance throughout the kitchen took in the three kids as they hovered in different stages of bashfulness behind their dad.

"How about something to drink?" Wade offered, pulling back a kitchen chair so Bill could sit down.

"Sounds good," Bill answered, slowly settling himself onto the chair. "So these are the three rug rats, I presume," he added, looking around at the kids. Sage was toddling over to Abbie as fast as his little legs would take him.

When she picked him up, he burrowed his head into her collarbone, and Skyler was almost as bashful, coming close to her side. Abbie took a chair across from Bill, and soon Wade had iced tea poured for the three of them. Scilla helped, and for some reason she took a seat close to their visitor. She seemed in awe of a braid on a man and was scrutinizing Bill with a scowl that gave Abbie an uneasy apprehension.

After small talk about his returning health, Bill turned toward Scilla. "And how are you, young lady?"

"Quite well, thank you," Scilla answered primly, with a decided bit of Abbie's accent in her voice. It sounded so unlike her that once again Abbie and Wade exchanged glances.

Bill's dull eyes took on a momentary glint, and he gave a slight smile. "When I was in the hospital a while back, your Dad gave me this," he said, tapping the Bible with his index finger. "I thought it was time I brought it back." He slid it slightly toward Scilla.

Scilla slid it back to him. "I don't read so good yet. Maybe you should keep it."

Bill's mouth twitched slightly and he tilted his head back to view Scilla through half-closed eyes.

"Uh," Wade's voice sounded uncertain, "you can keep it if you want to, Bill. You really didn't have to bring it back."

Bill gave a slight chuckle and took a drink of tea. "So how is our court case coming, Wade? Any more news?" It was a definite change of subject, and Abbie didn't know if she was relieved or disappointed.

"Good news for a change. Hertly seems to be eager to drop the whole matter, which aggravates the war horse," Wade gave a slight nod toward the kids as an indication he didn't want to mention Kada's mother in front of them.

Bill smiled in understanding. "I'd enjoy taking 'em to the cleaners—I don't appreciate the time I had to spend looking up the band's finances."

Abbie nodded. "We understood by the time our lawyer went through your information, it was quite evident no large amount of money was made."

"Nope, it's just the joy of putting songs together. Bands seldom make a huge profit—it's more about liking what you do than about money." Bill leaned back in his chair and gave Abbie an absent look. "I thought I would quit the whole business, but lately I've… well, I guess I miss it."

"Are you thinking of putting together another band?" Wade asked.

"Maybe. I just don't know yet. Guess I was waiting to see how this court thing played out."

"I believe it's going to be dropped," Wade said. "She can't prove there was any money I absconded with, and Hertly has had the wind knocked out of his sails. I would guess the next move is ours—deciding if we want to drop it or have our day in court just to prove 'em wrong." Wade looked at Bill with a searching gaze. "Abbie and I would like to drop the whole mess and not spend any more money or time—or thought—on the matter."

Abbie nodded in agreement and shifted Sage's drowsy weight to a more comfortable position. He had his little fingers entwined in her hair. When she moved him, his hand slid down to her neck.

"I'll put him down for his nap," Wade offered. "You may as well come too, Skyler," he added as he reached toward Abbie to gather Sage into his arms. "I'll be right back," he directed at Bill, and made a quick exit carrying one sleepy boy while the other followed behind him with his dark eyes still riveted on their visitor.

"Can I get you some more tea?" Abbie asked but Bill shook his head and twirled the half empty glass around with his long, thin fingers.

"It's interesting that you called, Bill. We've been thinking about you," Abbie said slowly.

Scilla leaned forward with heightened interest. "'Cause of the hard road, you know, of course," she informed Bill.

He looked down at Scilla and then returned Abbie's look with a slight frown. "'Hard road'?"

Before Abbie could answer, Scilla interjected with amazing force for a six-year-old girl. "The road where the seed falls and Satan swoops it away. Abbie thinks your heart is a hard road."

Abbie groaned inwardly. She had said as much to Wade when she thought there were no little listening ears to hear. She should have remembered Scilla's lurking habits.

She felt her face heating up; Bill's was noncommittal.

Abbie shook her head at Scilla, willing her to stop talking. "Uh, yes. Well, we were having a conversation about… about different heart attitudes concerning the Word of God." She paused, knowing her face was bright red. It was embarrassing to admit she thought Bill's heart was unreceptive.

Scilla looked at her impatiently. "See, I know this story," she informed Bill. "God plants seeds of good news in our hearts. Hard ground means hard hearts, rocky ground means shallow hearts, weedy ground means worldly hearts, but," she paused dramatically while looking at Bill with Kada eyes, "good ground means good hearts."

Once again Bill gave Scilla a speculating look and with a shake of his head looked back at Abbie. "Is she gonna be a preacher when she grows up?"

"It would be a noble calling." Abbie smiled slightly and felt thwarted that a little girl had given a better testimony than she had.

"It's right in here," Scilla tapped Kada's Bible. "Abbie looked it up." She pushed the Bible toward Abbie. "I don't read so good. Where's it at?"

Bill gave a dismissive gesture. "It don't matter where it's at. I'll take your word for it, young lady." He seemed to reflect a while before continuing. "But I do want the kids to have Kada's Bible. She underlined a lot of things in there. They should know what her thoughts were the last weeks of her life. Maybe it doesn't matter to 'em now, but it will later on in life."

"Yes, you're right—that's a good idea." Abbie hesitated before adding, "We'd like to give you one to replace it unless, of course, you already have one."

Bill looked as if he would like to refuse her offer, but suddenly he shrugged as if to say the matter wasn't important but to please them he would take it.

Scilla seemed to take that as a cue to leave, and she almost collided with Wade as he came through the archway.

"I have this feeling she always has big business somewhere," Bill said mildly, watching her scurry away.

"Have you seen Ace lately?" Wade asked quietly as he returned to his chair.

"Yeah," Bill said disgustedly. "He's in love with a nurse right at the moment."

"Is he still on probation?" Abbie wondered.

"Yeah, just for a little longer, though. Right now he's trying to get a job," Bill responded. "We've talked a bit about getting a band together. I'm supposed to meet him up at Pierre this afternoon to look at some sound equipment that's on sale."

Suddenly Scilla burst into the room with a small New Testament from the Gideons. "This is just what you need," she told Bill confidently. "It's small enough so you can put it in your pocket and read it any time you want." She boldly reached over and put it in his front shirt pocket. "That story is in there—sort of at the beginning, I think. And if you know what's good for you, you won't let Satan swoop it away." She industriously buttoned the little Bible into the pocket.

Bill tilted his head back and chuckled good-humoredly at her directness. "I suppose if I don't read it you'll call down hell's fire on me," he said with only a slight trace of sarcasm.

The sunset that evening tinged the sky with hues of flaming orange, and Abbie, sitting on the new glider her parents had gifted her before leaving, mulled over the afternoon conversation.

305

"Wouldn't it be awful," she asked Wade as he sat beside her, "to see all this beauty and not have a clue who to thank for it?"

He put his arm around her shoulders and gave her a light hug. "Wouldn't it be awful to not have someone to share this with?"

She glanced at him with sparks of happiness inside. "I think I love you, Wade."

"That's good, Abbie. Especially since we're going to have a baby together."

She laughed lightly and snuggled closer to him. After a short silence, she sighed. "I wonder if Bill will ever come back. I couldn't read his expression this afternoon."

Wade slightly tightened his arm around her. "He thought a lot of Kada, so he might want to come back and see her kids."

They watched the sky change from shades of orange to softer hues of amber before Abbie spoke again. "I would imagine Scilla made more impact on him than a hundred sermons."

"Yeah." He gave a soft chuckle. "She really has taken hold of the seeds and soil story."

"I know." Abbie watched the amber colors fade into a soft glow behind the green hills and felt quiet contentment. "She's quite a little girl. I hope she always has this passion for Christ."

Wade kissed the top of her head. "Unfortunately, she'll probably find out we can't cultivate the whole world into fertile ground."

The twilight was deepening before Abbie spoke of another matter heavy on her heart. "Wade, do you think Torrie would understand if I had someone else take my place at her wedding?"

"No, darling," Wade answered. "She would hold a grudge against you forever, and she'd probably beat you up—like she did the other little redheaded gal."

CHAPTER 37

Mellowing Ground

BILL GRUMBLED A lot on the way to Pierre. It galled him that his stated "no faith" seemed to galvanize every do-gooder in the country to convert him—even little kids, for Pete's sake. He started to unbutton his shirt pocket to throw out the little green Bible, but he had to put both hands back on the wheel while he passed a semi.

He was not convertible to religion. People might as well get used to that. A long time ago—several wars ago—he had become convinced faith was a weak crutch he didn't need or want.

It didn't take long to find a parking place on the capitol grounds. He had told Ace he'd meet him at the Veterans Memorial, and he slowly limped over to a bench that overlooked the pond.

He didn't know why he had chosen this spot. Bill was tired of wars and symbols of wars. He felt his whole lifetime had been a battle. So much death. Kada had almost been the last straw. He couldn't seem to get over his grief of losing her and then the band. If he had been a drinking man he would have drowned his sorrows in booze. If he had been a praying man he might have found peace of mind in God. Bill Rissix knew he was neither.

"Hey, Bill," Ace was hurrying down the sidewalk toward him. As usual, his pace was quick and his movements seemed in syncopated time.

"How's it going, drummer boy?" Bill wondered at himself for being even a little glad to see Ace.

The younger man seemed to throw himself onto the bench beside Bill. "Not bad! I finally was able to get a driver's license. Now Mandy doesn't need to drive me everywhere."

"Oh, yeah, Mandy—your little love bug." Bill shrugged his shoulders disinterestedly.

Ace's foot was tapping a staccato on the cement sidewalk. He looked quickly at Bill and then his eyes darted to the war memorials.

"Uh, Bill, about the band starting up again… I guess you better count me out."

"Why?"

"Well… well, I sort of have a chance to start a different life. Mandy and me are planning on getting married, and her dad says he could use some help with his carpentry work. They live down in Missouri." Ace watched Bill with anxious eyes and finally rubbed both hands across his knees. "I might not get another second chance like this, Bill. I know you think she's not much of a looker, but—" the younger man looked at him imploringly.

"If you got a chance at some happiness, you better grab it, kid." Bill knew his tone was pretty flat.

"I sure hate dragging you all the way from Spearfish on a wild goose chase. This sorta just happened this morning about Mandy's dad. We've made a lot of decisions today." Ace jumped up from the park bench and started pacing back and forth in front of Bill.

"When we sorta got things thought through, I wanted to call to stop you but I couldn't reach you on your cell phone." Ace began fumbling in his pocket. "Here's some money for gas."

Bill waved the money away and watched Ace as he slammed back down on the park bench as if puppet strings had been cut. "Did you look at the sound equipment?" he asked. Even if Ace wasn't going to stick around, it wouldn't be a wasted trip if he could buy a system for a reasonable price.

"Well, uh, no. I just thought I'd wait until you were here and we'd look at it together." Ace fumbled in his pocket again and pulled out a piece of paper with an address on it. He silently handed it to Bill and broke into another burst of words. "Uh, I probably won't even bother to look at it now, because, uh, well, Mandy and me are gonna go see a preacher yet this afternoon. See, the deal is, her dad is really needing help right now and we just thought... well, Mandy wants to do things right and get married."

"Ace the carpenter." Bill mustered up a smile when he looked at the younger man. "You better walk the straight and narrow way, fella, and getting married is the first step. I think your lady love is waiting by her little car over there," he said, pointing to a chubby young woman anxiously standing on the sidewalk next to a Nissan. His nasal voice had a hint of sarcasm in it.

Ace looked over in the direction Bill indicated and waved. "Well, I'll tell you something. She is my lady love, but there'll always be a little piece of my heart that belongs to Kada." He shook his head. "We just weren't good for each other. I... I don't know why I've got a second chance and she never did."

Bill grunted. "Who knows when or why the dog shakes and the fleas fall off."

Ace looked at him puzzled. "Huh? No, don't try to explain that to me." He quickly reached over to shake Bill's hand. "I guess this is good-bye. Thanks for all you've done for me. I really do appreciate it, especially getting things figured out about those times at that dang house."

He pumped Bill's hand some more and suddenly released it. "I hope something works out for you, Bill." He again jumped up from the park bench and stood for a brief second with concern on his face, and then turned and rapidly walked over to the waiting young woman.

She seemed extraordinarily happy to see Ace; Bill could hear their excited voices and watched her give Ace a long hug before they both got into the Nissan.

For quite a long time Bill sat there, a lonely figure in his jeans and white shirt. He scarcely noticed the yellow lab that padded close to the bench where he was sitting. The dog lay down close to his feet and gazed at him with its amber eyes. It wasn't until Bill heard the tapping of a cane that he came out of his reverie.

An older man with sightless eyes and a pleasant smile on his face was almost upon them. The dog immediately gave a low whine and slowly stood, nuzzling the man's pant leg and waiting patiently.

"I thought you would be here, Buffy," the man said kindly, and unerringly found Buffy's soft ears to give them a gentle scratch.

"Your seeing eye dog?" Bill asked gruffly. He would have preferred not to say anything but he thought the blind guy should know he was sitting there.

Immediately the man's head turned to the sound, and he smiled in Bill's direction. "Buffy is—was—my friend's dog. He passed away last week. The two of them spent a lot of time sitting here."

"Oh." Bill said nothing more. He was in no mood for idle conversation.

"Do you mind if I share your bench? My wife is coming along pretty soon, and I told her we'd be here."

"I'm sitting on your right-hand side," Bill answered, and was rewarded with another smile as the man carefully found the empty spot and sat. The dog lay on the pavement between them. She occasionally looked at her blind benefactor and wagged her tail slowly.

After a short silence the man held out his hand in Bill's direction. "My name is Lynn. I work here at the capitol, and this is one of my favorite spots."

Bill shook the proffered hand, noting there were calluses on the surprisingly strong fingers. He sighed before he answered. "They call me Bill."

"Perhaps I could impose upon you, Bill, to be my eyes for a second. Is there a rather fat goose sitting over there by the Governor's Memorial?"

With a quick glance in the direction the man had indicated, Bill shook his head. He realized his mistake immediately and rather loudly said, "No."

Lynn laughed softly. "Praise the Lord. Henrietta has taken an acute dislike to both me and Buffy and doesn't mind letting us know about it."

"You can praise the Lord if you want to. I never found a time when I thought it was necessary." The words were out of Bill's mouth before he even realized it.

Lynn tilted his head to one side and his smile became even wider. "I detect a tone of... uh, slight bitterness. Have you and the Lord had an argument?"

Bill gave a disgruntled snort. "I don't argue with nonexistent entities."

Once again the sightless man tilted his head. An interested expression flitted across his face. "I don't often have the opportunity to visit with someone who has no god. Tell me why you think that, if you don't mind sharing with a stranger."

Bill knew his next words were going to be rude. He really didn't care. He had fought all the battles he was going to fight for one day.

"I do mind. I don't care to share anything with anybody. I'm an atheist and let's just leave it at that." He paused before adding in a softer tone of voice. "I'm sorry, sir. I've already had a little girl preach me a sermon, and I just don't care to hear another one."

The dog was upset by Bill's outburst and immediately got to her feet. She put her head on Lynn's lap and whined quietly. Lynn patted her head tenderly and soothed her with "It's OK, Buffy, you can lie back down." She refused, standing between the two men with her head on the blind man's lap.

Lynn continued to pet her while a smile hovered around his lips. "A little girl preached you a sermon? She must be a special young lady who thinks a great deal of you. Most kids couldn't care less what adults have for faith."

Bill frowned. Scilla was just a typical kid to him. She was Kada's kid, and she deserved to have Kada's Bible. That was all there was to that, and he didn't need this guy telling him that Scilla was anything more than a skinny little girl with an overactive imagination.

"Bill," Lynn said, breaking the silence that had descended upon them, "I often ask people this—do you play guitar?"

Bill glanced at the blind man, and nodded in surprise. Again realizing his mistake, he answered, "Yeah, I play—or rather, I did play—in a band."

"Have you ever tried to play with some strings missing?"

"Well, of course not. There's no way to make decent music unless you have all the strings."

"I see," Lynn said reflectively.

Bill gave him a sharp glance. A blind man saying he could see was as ridiculous as thinking you could play a guitar without all the strings.

As if he could read Bill's mind, Lynn's next words were jolting. "Obviously I can't see, you know. It's just an expression. I'm blind because a drunk driver slammed into my car. I consider myself blessed to be alive. It killed him."

"Generally the drunks live and the innocents die," Bill said bitterly. "I've had that experience. My wife and son were killed and the guy walked away without a scratch."

Lynn tilted his head and was silent for several seconds. When he spoke, his voice was full of compassion. "I'm so sorry, Bill. I'm very sorry. Not just that you obviously have had to deal with a lot of grief, but that you have tried to play your guitar without all the strings."

He tilted his head toward the sound of steps coming at them. "I believe you need the string of faith in God to make the music complete.

It just does not work any other way." He stood slowly as a slender middle-aged woman walked up to them.

"Are you and Buffy ready to walk home?" she asked, her voice as pleasant as Lynn's smile. "Hello," she greeted Bill. "He only needs me to help him cross the streets, but it's good exercise for all of us." She patted Buffy and added merrily, "Even the dog."

Lynn reached in his pocket and held out a business card in Bill's general direction. "If you ever want to play in a band, give me a call. Most of us are handicapped in some way, but we have a lot of fun making music."

Bill took the offered card and mumbled a "thanks."

Lynn paused while his wife and the dog waited patiently. "Bill, it's important to find the string."

"Sure." Bill didn't know what else to say.

The trio walked off, wife and husband visiting softly while the dog walked between them. As they left, Lynn stumbled slightly over a crack in the sidewalk. Bill heard him laugh and say, "I forget that little bugger every time." He couldn't hear the wife's response, but the dog's tail was wagging faster, as if the three of them were enjoying a private joke.

Bill felt alone as he watched people leave from work, calling out to one another, getting in their cars, and going home. Generally, he never thought about being alone. He usually had places to go, things to do. He guessed if he wanted to he could check out the sound equipment, but somehow he had lost all enthusiasm for even looking at it.

He read the card Lynn had given him. *Lynn Decker and family and friends musical group—making a joyful noise unto the Lord.*

Lynn's phone number was listed, as well as an address. Lynn Decker. Dr. Lynn Decker. Bill squinted as the sun's rays reflected in the pond. If he remembered the news stories correctly, Lynn Decker had been a specialized optical surgeon. He was skilled in using instruments in delicate operations that required dexterity and concentration. His blindness had ended that career abruptly.

As it all came back to him, Bill shook his head. He shouldn't have been such a jerk with the guy.

He slowly put the card in the same pocket in which Scilla had placed the Bible. As he was buttoning the flap, an obese goose waddled around the pond and made a beeline for him. She seemed to be slightly cross-eyed, and right now those eyes were riveted on his tennis shoes.

"Listen, you fat, ugly goose. You peck me and no veterinarian in the state will revive you."

She slowed her pace at his admonishment but continued to waddle toward him with her head bobbing. Giving him a defiant and nasal honk, she zeroed in on his orange shoelace and started pulling on it. He jerked his foot back, and she flapped her wings and hissed at him.

"Henrietta, I presume," Bill hissed back at her.

Once again she bobbed her head and tugged at his shoelace. This time Bill thrust his foot straight ahead of him.

"Go ahead," he dared her. "Try to take my shoelace and see how far you get."

Henrietta tugged, flapped her wings, hissed, and all but sat on Bill to get his shoestring. She was a determined goose, and while he watched her, the first genuine smile of amusement he had had for a long time crept over his face.

Finally he wearied of her antics. Pushing her head away, he quickly unlaced his shoe and tossed the goose-pecked shoelace on the grass next to the bench.

She paraded back and forth in front of him before she went over to grab her treasure. With a loud honk, she waddled victoriously back to the pond with a bright orange shoelace dangling from her bill.

"Stupid goose," he said aloud, but the smile was still on his face. He looked at his laceless shoe and thought it ironic that a goose had made off with his prized orange shoestring and a blind man had accused him of trying to play guitar with a string missing.

"I'm going home," he announced to no one. He abruptly stood and started heading toward his truck. He had to bunch up his toes to keep the flopping tennis shoe on, and all humor had left his face by the time he reached his vehicle.

It was a long drive from Pierre to Spearfish—193 miles to be exact—and to Bill's weary mind and body, it seemed like every mile lasted forever, which gave him way too much time to think.

Ever since Roz and their son had been killed, he had shut the door on memories. When the news came of their deaths while he was deployed overseas, a chaplain had tried to talk to him about heaven. He had shouted obscenities at the man. Odd, the look on the chaplain's face was similar to the blind man's face today when he overreacted.

Bill blew out a pent-up breath of air. Even opening that memory door just a crack made his gut hurt. He wanted to slam it shut again, but like Pandora's box, once the memories started to flow they couldn't be contained. Mile after mile his mind raced from the agonies of his childhood to the ecstasy of his marriage, and back again to the unbearable agony of losing the only ray of sunshine he had ever known.

By the time he pulled into his driveway, Bill was exhausted. His shoulders sagged as he let himself into his orderly home. He wished he could keep his thoughts in the same sterile environment his house was. Before he crashed from fatigue, he went into the stark guest room. As long as he was torturing himself with memories, he figured he may as well unlock and open the cedar chest where he had stored Roz's and his son's mementos.

Every item he pulled out twisted the knife in his heart a little more. The memories—the joys they had experienced, the sorrows they had shared together—all washed over him. When he was practically bent over with the pain of grief, he shook both fists in the air. One fist clenched his son's much-loved teddy bear while the other held Roz's first attempt at a knitted afghan.

"You took everything away from me. Everything!" he railed. "I was fighting a war and You were supposed to watch over them. You let some scumball kill the only reason I had to come back home. You've never been there for me!"

He sank onto the bed and buried his face in the afghan. Bill wept bitter tears—the first time he had allowed himself to cry since he was a tiny boy on the reservation.

He woke slowly in the gray dawn. His head hammered, his sore leg throbbed, and when he slowly sat up his reflection in the mirror made him gasp. When had he started looking like the old men he had grown up abhorring?

Bill's hair straggled down over his face, his gray whiskers made his face look ashen, and his eyes were dead—like those old men without hope. He might as well have boozed it up every day of his life. He wouldn't have looked any worse than he did right then.

That blind man's eyes probably had more life than mine, he acknowledged to himself. What that man lacked in vision he made up for with his smile and lively manner.

He would take one step at a time. He would shower and shave, have breakfast and some good black coffee. He knew life would return to its usual pattern. That's the way life worked. Routines. Schedules. Emptiness.

And he would put the memories back in the cedar box and lock it up again. No matter what a blind guy and a little girl said, there was no God.

Days later, however, that child's faith, the blind man's concern, and a fat goose's obsession with an orange shoelace were still lingering in Bill's mind. He would hear Scilla's little voice piping up to warn him about hell at the oddest moments, and he could almost realize the logic of the missing guitar string. When he thought of Henrietta, a smile would flit over his grim features.

He also could not put away the memories of his past. They haunted him as he went about his life, and as each memory burned itself into his heart, he found his emotions to be embarrassingly tender.

Bill could not remember a time when he had been so unsure about things. Finally, in a burst of determination to get at least some of his life under control, he had his hair cut short. He bought new shoelaces—black this time.

And after long and careful consideration, he made a phone call.

"This is Lynn," the cheerful voice on the other end of the line answered.

"This is Bill."

There was a short pause before he heard, "Bill from the park bench?"

"Bill from the park bench."

"Good to hear from you! Are you going to join our band?"

"I… only if you'll help me find a missing guitar string."

CHAPTER 38

We Do

WAITING FOR THE bride's procession, Wade viewed his sweating friend with very little sympathy.

Any darn fool that would let his bride talk him into a mammoth outdoor wedding in South Dakota deserved to be nervous, even if it is June, and even if they did spray for flies and mosquitoes.

Clive wasn't prepared for the fact that his lovely Torrie would make him and his groomsmen dress up in tuxedoes, complete with shoes instead of boots, of all stupid things. When he broke the news to Wade, he was in more of a tizzy than Wade had ever seen the usually unflappable storyteller. For a short while the groomsmen had thought of mutiny, but when they had realized Torrie meant business when she said it would either be her way or no way, they had rallied around the disconcerted groom and decided to grin and bear it.

The huge tent looked as wilted in the unexpected June heat as Clive did. Torrie had insisted a tent would be cooler than the smaller church sanctuary. Wrong!

Wade narrowed his eyes as he surveyed the flower-festooned entryway. It seemed like the groom and the four groomsmen had been standing in front of the crowd—waiting—for hours.

Finally the music began for the flower girls. Scilla walked forward with her three little friends and grinned delightedly at her dad. Heat didn't bother kids, Wade realized. He just hoped it wouldn't bother the matron of honor.

After the four little ring bearers came soberly toward the front, the first of the four bridesmaids came in. Wade absently wondered if Torrie had picked the first three so there wouldn't be any competition for good looks.

She had goofed when it came to Abbie, he decided when he saw her enter. With those expressive brown eyes and gentle smile, she was absolutely the most beautiful creature who had ever come down a wedding aisle, he decided. Wade winked at her when she took her place, and the smile she gave him almost made him forget where he was.

Amazing how one petite little English redhead can make my heart race even after several months of marriage.

He was still looking at Abbie when the wedding march began. Even though everyone else was turned toward the entry for a first glimpse of Torrie, his eyes lingered on his own bride. She must have felt his gaze because she gave him a quick glance and raised one arched eyebrow.

Reluctantly he turned his head to watch Torrie float down the aisle, a vision of loveliness, to be sure. He thought it rather odd that Torrie was obsessed with every detail of her wedding and so disinterested in the house that had hurriedly been set on its foundation a week earlier.

He knew Clive was disappointed she had never stopped in to see the house he got for her. However, by the look on Clive's face now, it was plain to see that he was as besotted with his soon-to-be wife as always.

As the ceremony progressed, Wade found himself worrying more and more about the effect the heat would have on Abbie. He wished he hadn't insisted she take the other woman's place. He frowned and scrutinized her face again—did she seem a little pale?

Oh, man, now that long, drawn-out song while Torrie and Clive light the candles.

Clive was sweating beyond measure.

Wade would never forgive himself if Abbie passed out. A woman in her condition had no business standing in that heat for so long. The soft voice of reason tried to convince him that she wasn't in any danger, but he was sure the six freckles on her nose were standing out in stark comparison to her white face.

If she would ever look at him, he'd motion for her to sit down. He fretted and fidgeted while the song and the candle lighting seemed to take forever.

Wade gave a sigh of relief when the minister began the vows. Once again he looked at Abbie and was sure she was beginning to weave. She turned to him and motioned slightly with her hands. He was ready to dash to her side when Clive whispered to him.

"Wade, we need the rings!"

He grinned at her foolishly and fished in his pocket for the two wedding bands.

Finally, Clive and Torrie were pronounced Mr. and Mrs. Barrows, and Wade wondered if any newly married couple ever took so long to wander to the finish line. Before it was proper, he walked the short distance to where Abbie was standing and put his arm under her elbow.

"How are you doing?" he murmured in her ear.

"Fine—how are you doing?"

"I'm OK, but I'm not the one who's pregnant."

Her soft laughter drifted up to him. "Is that why you've been staring at me all during the ceremony?"

"Mrs. Jackson, I was sure you were going to faint in all this heat."

Her eyes were full of merriment as she took his arm. "I'm really quite all right, Mr. Jackson, but it's our turn to waltz out of here. If you would please take your foot off the hem of my dress, I believe we could proceed."

It was against all wedding protocol, but the best man suddenly and unreservedly kissed the best woman.

The wedding supper was well underway by the time pictures were taken. Wade insisted Abbie stand in the shade of the elm trees that graced the churchyard. She shook her head at him, but when he ushered her into the cooler air under the spreading branches, she gave him a grateful smile.

"You're being rather ridiculous, Wade," she scolded lightly and promptly sat on a folding chair.

"I know. You have that effect on me." He grinned at her. "Have I mentioned that I'm glad we didn't have all this hullabaloo for our wedding?"

"I think this is about the fourth or fifth time you've said that in the past hour."

"Good grief, the pictures are taking longer than the ceremony. I wonder how much longer those little girls are going to be able to stand there?"

"They're all agog over their pretty teacher getting married—remember, heat doesn't bother kids." Abbie looked at the church with a worried expression. "I wonder how the boys are doing in the church basement with their babysitters."

"Want me to go check?"

"Well, I suppose about the time you leave you'll be needed for another picture."

The photographer was finally finished, and all the relatives and friends whose cameras had been clicking like castanets also moved away. Wade wondered if Clive was as relieved as he was to have that tiresome ordeal over with. He decided his friend was in a daze with all the attention and posing.

The guests had been allowed to eat during the picture session, and now the wedding party was supposed to go to the head table to be served. While Abbie waited in the shade, Wade made a quick dash to the church to see about the boys.

The boys' young caretakers had already gotten plates of food for them, and it only took a glance to see all was well in that department.

He headed back to Abbie under the shade tree so they could get the next part over with. He was beginning to understand why she had dreaded this day so much. For some reason his head was beginning to ache—probably because he was so worried about the heat effect on Abbie.

Where in the deuce is she? His mind quickly conjured up all sorts of scenarios, each one worse than the other, until he finally was sure she had felt faint and went someplace to lie down. *But who would know where that would be?* He was ready to go back to the church to see if she was stretched out on a pew when he heard her light laughter and saw her with the wedding party under the tent.

The cooler evening air was slowly creeping over the assembly. Flushed faces were beginning to take on a more normal shade, laughter was increasing, and the wilted wedding party seemed to find new life. The caterers were bringing in overflowing plates of roast beef and potato salad, along with side dishes of watermelon and other fruit.

Torrie's seating arrangement had Abbie sitting beside her, and Wade beside Clive. For a brief moment he wanted to thwart the finely tuned, orchestrated event and sit by his best woman, but courtesy ruled, and he reluctantly sat beside Clive.

"It's gonna take Torrie a couple of years of teaching school to pay for this," Wade grumbled to his friend.

"Yeah, but this is what she's always wanted. We've heard her talk about her wedding since we were kids." Clive looked as contented as a mama cow.

With a disgruntled shake of his head, Wade decided if Clive had a cud he'd be chewing it. *What's more,* he thought, *Torrie most likely would have a ring through his nose and he would follow her every whim.*

Disgusting.

I wonder if Abbie has any aspirin.

He had forgotten about the toasts until Abbie pushed back her chair and came over to quietly remind him. Torrie wanted it all to be heard, so a cordless mike was suddenly handed to him, and a great shushing went forth throughout the tent.

322

Panic hit him full force. He couldn't bring to mind a single thing he should say. No wonder Abbie had taken the time to jot down a few notes for herself. He had teased her about that a couple of days earlier and had told her she was being silly. He figured he could just stand up and talk about his friends without even preparing for it. After all, he told her, it's just a wedding. She had ignored him and continued on with her notes.

He gave her an imploring look before he stood. Abbie winked at him and gave him a thumbs-up signal. "It's just a wedding," he heard her say softly.

Once he was standing, Wade realized just how many people were scattered throughout the large tent. Hundreds of eyes were looking at him. Torrie and Clive would be incensed beyond measure if he botched up this moment.

This fool needs help again, Lord. I can't believe I didn't prepare for this.

When the tent full of people was completely quiet, Wade threw another glance at Abbie. There was almost a malicious glint of humor in those brown eyes.

Leave it to that redhead to think this is funny.

A thought clicked into his mind and he took a deep breath.

"You may not know this," he addressed the crowd, "but years ago, when Clive and Torrie and I were all attending school just down the road, a little girl had a huge crush on Clive. Torrie teased him about her without mercy, but Clive, being the good-natured kid he was, and still is, just shrugged it off and enjoyed the extra attention."

Wade patted his friend's shoulder. A little ripple of mirth went through the crowd.

"One day the little girl announced at recess that she was going to kiss him. That threw the whole school in an uproar, and we all gathered around to witness this momentous occasion."

Out of the corner of his eye he saw Torrie look at him in puzzlement. Clive had a bemused grin on his face.

"I don't really remember how it all happened, but suddenly, without warning, the little girl bit Clive on the lip. I don't know, maybe he puckered up too much and she didn't like it, but whatever, he yelped like a wounded puppy, and to add insult to injury, the little gal slapped him on the face."

Wade couldn't help laughing at the recollection. The audience broke into loud chuckling and it was hard to tell whether it was from the story or from Wade's own amusement.

When he regained his composure, Wade continued. "Well, after school that day, the little girl left for home with her dad. She had some scratches on her face, dirt in her hair, dust on her shirt, and a smear of mud that went from one cheek, across her nose, and over to the other cheek. And Torrie here, well she went home with the biggest black eye I've ever seen."

The crowd roared with laughter and Torrie glared at him. He could feel it even though he didn't turn around to look at her.

"Now here's the rest of the story, and it's why I'm telling this in the first place. You see, Torrie wouldn't allow anybody to make sport of her friend without consequences. She might tease Clive, and for sure he teased her right back, but when push came to shove, she was on his side. Just as Clive has always been, and always will be, on her side."

Wade turned to both Clive and Torrie and gave them a somber smile. His voice lost the amusement and became serious as he finished.

"Torrie is going to stand by her man. Always. She has been Clive's confidante and best friend since they were kids, and Clive has considered her his sweetheart ever since the day she beat up that little gal."

He reached for his champagne glass and held it in the air. "To Clive and Torrie and a long and lasting love. And, to a long and lasting friendship between the Barrowses and the Jacksons."

It was when the best man was dancing with the bride that Torrie finally mentioned his toast.

"You didn't have a clue what you were going to say, did you?" she accused him as they began to dance. He missed a beat and took a couple of awkward steps to get back into time.

"I'm truly repentant, Torrie. I actually never gave it a thought until I was standing in front of everyone. I just thought I could breeze through something but my mind went blank until I saw Abbie's red hair."

"I thought so." She was silent as they took a few more steps to the music. "You darn clown. I was so choked up by what you said I thought my mascara would run." She gave him a slight hug while they danced. "I owe a lot to the redheads. One made me realize that Clive was my best friend, and the other prevented me from making a huge mistake."

"How is that?" Wade wanted to know.

"If Abbie hadn't come into the picture and turned your head, I might have still been chasing you. And that would have been a huge mistake, Wade. You said so yourself."

Wade glanced over to where Abbie and Clive were dancing. They were laughing while Clive dipped her and two-stepped to the music. Abbie's eyes were full of mischievous sparks and her hair reflected the tent's dim lights.

He looked down at the beautiful woman with whom he was dancing. They had been friends and almost lovers. She was in many ways an admirable young lady. But Abbie was his soulmate, his port in the storm. He needed her probably more than she would ever know.

"Torrie, my friend," he said softly, "Abbie is the sunshine in my life. Has she told you we're expecting a baby in December?"

Torrie stopped in the middle of the floor. "So that's why you've been keeping such a close eye on her! Good grief, everyone's talking about how you won't let her out of your sight. You big goof! Do you think she's going to melt down because she's pregnant?"

He grinned at her as they resumed the last few steps of the song before it ended. "I think I have one heck of a headache because I've been worried about her all afternoon. We're going home after I dance with her, Torrie. We'll go home, put three little kids to bed, and then we'll sit out on the porch swing while she tells me all about the great time she had today."

CHAPTER 39

And What If...

ABBIE YAWNED AS Wade herded her and the children into the house. It was almost eleven P.M.—she didn't know where the time had disappeared to at the wedding. She and Wade had started to leave earlier, but this one and that one wanted to visit. Before she knew it, the time had fled and three bedraggled but happy kids were pulling at her arms, leading her toward the car.

Sage and Skyler were asleep several minutes after they started down the road, but Scilla was chattering all the way home about her part in the ceremony.

Even as Abbie helped her undress and get ready for bed, Scilla eyes danced and she whisked from one thought to another. But finally, even Scilla wound down, and when she was ready for prayers, her eyes began to droop.

"I better remember Bill," she muttered as she dropped to her knees beside her bed. "Dear Lord Jesus, speak to that Bill in a loud voice so he hears You. We both know he's going to be swooped up by that buzzard if he doesn't start listening. I'm too tired to pray anymore, God. Amen."

Abbie suppressed a smile. Scilla's prayers were a study in little-girl innocence and Aunt Lena directness. Without any suggestion from

Wade or her, Scilla prayed for Bill every night. She had different ways of bringing him up before the Lord, and Abbie often added her own "amen" to Scilla's request for the unbelieving Bill. She thought if he knew how often he was being brought before the Lord he would smirk and shrug his shoulders.

Wade already had the boys into their pajamas and into bed. He was so good about that, she thought, as she walked tiredly into their bedroom. All of a sudden she was exhausted. The day she had been dreading since she found out she was to be the matron of honor was past. However, she had to admit she had enjoyed it far more than she thought she would.

"Well, Mrs. Life-of-the-Party Jackson, turn around and I'll unzip your dress," Wade said. He already had his tux jacket and tie off. Abbie wondered bemusedly if she would always have a racing heart when she saw her husband with his dark hair slightly mussed and shirt untucked.

"Did you have fun, Wade?" she asked, turning her back obediently to him.

He kissed the back of her neck before he answered. "Actually, no."

She frowned as he fiddled with the tiny hook, then gave a sigh of relief as the zipper smoothly released her from the snug confinement of her dress.

"Our child probably thought she was in a girdle all night," he muttered, noting the red marks on her thickening waist.

Abbie looked at the two of them reflected in the dresser mirror before she spoke. He was dark and solidly built in contrast to her fairness and lighter frame. She thought he was the most handsome man at the wedding. She wanted to tell him that.

"Wade, I love you," she said instead, and saw his slow smile reflected in the mirror. She turned into his arms and enjoyed the strength of him as he hugged her. "I also thought there wasn't a man there tonight who could hold a candle to you."

"That's good. I would hate to think of you running off with some dude and leaving me alone with three kids."

She grinned at him and ran her fingers over the little curl of hair that always tumbled over his forehead. "But what I want to know is why you fussed around and gave yourself a headache." She looked at him seriously. "It isn't like you, Wade—I was the one who was supposed to be all uptight about this. You've been telling me for weeks to calm down."

He kissed her before he replied. "It's all your fault, woman. All these things you fretted about I was afraid would happen." He grinned lazily at her. "Besides, the best woman looked so delightful I had trouble keeping my mind on what I was doing."

She could have stayed in his arms indefinitely while they bantered back and forth, but a tired yawn escaped her, and she reluctantly stepped back and started getting ready for bed.

It was after the lights were out and they had ceased talking and were drifting into sleep, that she heard Wade laughing.

"What's funny?" she asked sleepily, not really caring.

"Huh?"

She heard him laugh again.

"I said, what's so funny?"

"What's funny?"

He laughed even louder.

"Wade! Stop that! You're giving me the creeps!"

He jerked himself into a sitting position, and laughter seemed to fill the room. "What the—" she heard him say as he flung himself out of bed.

By now Abbie was wide awake. She could see in the moonlight that he was standing beside their bed, and for some unknown reason a jolt of fear went through her.

"Wade?" Her voice was tremulous.

"That must be the wind!" he said softly as another peal of laughter burst out.

"W—wind?" Her heart was thumping.

"Grandma's 'laughter in the wind,' Abbie. Both doors are open downstairs—I opened up the house so the breeze could come in. That must be what it is. I've never heard it before." He said the last part over his shoulder as he hurried out of the room.

She could hear him go down the stairs, and then she heard a door shut. Within minutes he was back upstairs and in their room again.

"Abbie? Are you OK?" he asked as he settled under the sheet.

She seemed frozen in a half reclining position. A memory was tugging at her mind—elusive, just beyond her reach.

"I think—" she didn't move for fear the memory would leave altogether. "I think I've heard that before."

"When?"

"I can't remember!"

He reached over to pull her beside him. "Like last week, maybe?"

"No, no, long before that." She snuggled into his side and felt her heart beat return to normal.

They lay quietly together, and it was as she relaxed and began drifting back to sleep that she remembered.

"I know!" Her eyes flew open and she felt his arm tighten around her. "It was the first week I was here. The Sunday after we had painted everything. I was sleeping on the couch downstairs, and I dreamed you were laughing at the way I'd painted! It was so real that when I woke up I almost expected you to be standing there."

"I think I'm jealous," Wade said quietly. "I've lived here practically all my life and never heard the wind laugh. You're here one week and the house is so delighted with you it tells you right away."

They lay in silence for a while before Abbie spoke again. "Wade, I'm thinking of Kada."

"I know."

"I'm wondering what our lives would have been like if she had heard this like we just did."

"I know."

She said softly, "I might still be in England."

"No."

She thought he was going to say more but after several moments of silence she asked, "No? What do you mean?"

"I mean," his voice was beginning to sound sleepy, "I mean—no. On this June evening, on the prairies of Dakota, with a northeast wind blowing"—he paused and yawned "—and the house laughing, you, Abigail Miller Jackson, were destined by a Power greater than our knowledge to be right here beside me. Amen and go to sleep."

Her shoulders shook with silent laughter while she rolled onto her side and wrapped her arm around him. She could hear the wind blow harder as it whistled across the prairie, and she wondered if would bring in a rain before morning. Slowly Abbie relaxed again, comforted by Wade's steady breathing and the warmth of their bed.

And what if, she thought dreamily, God was in the wind, sweeping across the earth as the clouds became the dust of His feet? And what if He used the night as a blanket to cover His children as they slept? And what if He found delight in their joy of Him—would it be possible they would hear His laughter…in the wind?

Also from Joyce Wheeler:

My Lady

Jolene O'Neil grew up on the family ranch with the goal of becoming a lady rancher and continuing with the lifestyle she loves.

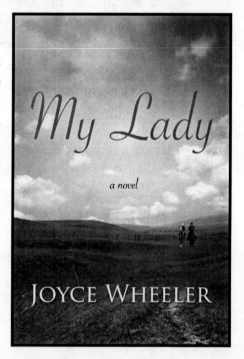

Her plans and her life change when she falls in love with and marries John, an Air Force pilot. His career continuously moves them far from the Nebraska prairie. When her young husband is killed, her hopes and dreams must change again, and she becomes intrigued with the charms of handsome and urbane Dexter DeLange.

The night Jolene flees from Dexter, she begins to answer the unwanted questions. Did Dexter really murder her beloved John, and is she going to be his next victim? Will the Master Weaver, who has woven her life with such care, abandon her now? And what is she to do about Chauncey Sullivan, the delightful cowboy who has come into her life and refuses to leave?

My Lady is a fast-moving and sometimes humorous novel that mixes hardworking ranch life with glamorous modeling, romance with fear, crusty relatives with charming friends, and life's difficult moments with the beauty of God's love.

CPSIA information can be obtained at www.ICGtesting.com

233598LV00001B/9/P